THE
REVOLUTIONISTS

a novel by

BIFF PRICE

SEVENHORNS
PUBLISHING

A Division of SevenHorns, LLC.
PO Box 269
Randolph MA 02368
www.sevenhornspublishing.com   www.biffprice.com

This book is a work of fiction. Incidents, names, characters, and places are products of the author's imagination and used fictitiously. Resemblances to actual locales or events or persons living or dead is entirely coincidental.

Designed by SevenHorns Design

Manufactured in the United States of America

Library of Congress Control Number: 2014933565
ISBN-13: 978-0-9838-4279-8 (hc)
ISBN-13: 978-0-9838-4275-0 (ebook)

*Dedicated to the people of the real
"Clear Haven," Pennsylvania, who have been
clinging to their God and guns since the 1700's,
and to the beautiful great-great-great-great granddaughter
of one of its founders, who is still dancing with me to this day.*

The Revolutionists

CHAPTER 1

The vision in the scope took his breath away. Michael opened his right eye farther and counted the antler tips. Twelve? No… there were fourteen! It had to be the one the Old Man spotted two years ago. The Old Man said he'd been at the base of Cobb's Mountain at twilight. As the sun was sinking behind the crest, he'd looked up and seen the outline of a huge deer standing high above him. He'd tried to count the antlers, but the sun's glare had made it impossible.

Michael took aim at a spot just behind the beast's shoulder, softly drew in his breath, and held it. He was using the fork of a young oak as a bench rest, and he held the rifle steady. It was one of the Old Man's favorites, a .222 Remington. The weapon would have been inadequate for the task in anyone else's hands, but Michael Stonebreaker was up to the job. The rifle had great muzzle velocity, and there was no doubt in his mind—the prize was his. He squeezed the trigger. The rifle fired, and the bullet ran true to where he'd aimed.

It struck a large oak to the right of the deer sending the great animal disappearing into the deep woods. He knew he would never see it again. It had been an omen, probably from the Old Man himself. Last May when the Old Man lay dying in the hospital, he'd said, "I don't want to kill them anymore, Michael. I just want to look at them. My killing days are over."

A tear squeezed from his right eye and ran down his cheek at the memory. His younger brother Henry crouched several hundred yards away on his right flank. He would tell Henry that something had distracted him and he'd missed his chance. Henry would pretend to believe him. They wouldn't talk about it. They didn't have to. Each of them carried the Old Man in his heart. The Old Man lived on in his grandsons. His spirit was near them, shadowing every trek through the Pennsylvania woods.

The Old Man, James Michael Stonebreaker, had served in a tank battalion in World War II. After the Germans obliterated four heavily armored vehicles in front of his, a shell blew his tank to hell, leaving him and one other survivor. He'd spent a lot of time in Walter Reed before finally returning home, where he took a job running a dragline in the hills of Clear Haven, Pennsylvania. He carried his wounds with him, and his ever-gracious government provided him with the glorious sum of fifty dollars a month for his trouble.

His son's war was fought in the jungles of Vietnam. Later, father and son both worked as dragline operators, the only work that was available in the strip-mining town. Agent Orange and cancer took his son three years before they took the Old Man.

Michael Ogden Stonebreaker, senior himself fathered two sons. His elder son Michael's war had been the Gulf War under Bush, '41. Michael had been an Army first lieutenant when he helped chase Saddam out of Kuwait. He was now a major serving in Intelligence at the Pentagon. Second son, Henry had served in the Marines and finished his tour before 9/11. Stonebreaker men were strong and purposeful, men who loved their country.

At six feet tall and a hundred-ninety solid pounds, Michael was smaller than his baby brother. Though Henry was six years younger, he topped out at six-three, two-twenty.

"How big was it?"

The voice startled Michael and he whipped around. As big as he was, Henry could move through the woods like a spirit, a skill which served him well as a hunter. "You scared the hell out of me!"

"Sorry, Mike. So, what did you shoot at...and why'd you miss it?"

"Who said I missed?"

"The bullet hit a tree."

"You heard that? You're spooky, man."

Henry smiled his lazy, slow smile. "Me spooky, you spooky, we all spooky! What was it?"

"The monster—"

"The one the Old Man talked about? How many?"

"Fourteen points. I counted them."

"Fourteen? It must be big as a barn! How'd you miss it?"

"A fly on the scope—"

"Yeah, it's twenty degrees out here and the flies are everywhere."

"Honest, it was a fly."

Snow flurries started falling at that moment, and the wind picked up. The cold fall winds in the central Pennsylvania hills cut through a man no matter how well he dressed against it.

Michael shivered. "Let's get out of here. Mom will have the food on the table and be getting madder by the minute."

They turned and began their trek back to the pickup. Henry was a step behind Michael. He studied his brother as they made their way through the brush.

The Old Man had been quiet in the woods. He taught his grandsons to move catlike through the brush, but Michael was truly the spookiest of all the Stonebreakers who had ever walked these hills. Henry was taller and heavier than his older brother, but he'd always felt Michael possessed a steely resolve that made the difference in their sizes irrelevant. In Henry's estimation, Michael was the steadiest man he'd ever met. He was also the scariest.

One Saturday morning when Henry was eight and Michael fourteen, Michael had taken Henry for a swimming lesson at the YMCA in Clear Haven. When the lesson was over, the two boys were heading toward the lobby of the building, and an older kid named Bob Martin approached them.

Bob Martin was a bully. He'd left school a year or so before at seventeen to work as a mechanic. Nearly six feet tall and well over two hundred pounds, he towered over the two younger boys. He'd grabbed Michael by the front of his shirt with a beefy right hand and slammed him against a wall. "What the hell you lookin' at, boy?"

Henry stood there, readying a cry for help, when an incredible thing happened. Michael stepped into the bigger boy's body, and grabbed him by the front of his shirt and his crotch. He then lifted him over his head, and threw him like a sack of potatoes across the lobby. Martin slammed to the floor on his back, the force of the impact knocking the air from his lungs. The whole building went silent, and everyone in the lobby stood staring in amazement at what Michael Stonebreaker had done.

At least twenty children, teens, and adults had seen the thin, wiry boy pick up the bully and throw him across the room. Harold Roberts, the Y director, was one of them. He hurried across the room and knelt beside Martin.

"Ehhhhhhhhhhhhhhnnnn..." There was a noise coming from Martin that reminded Henry of the pitiful bleating of a sheep. Henry and some of the other kids had started to laugh when Michael whipped around and grabbed him by the shoulders. There was a look on Michael's face that frightened Henry so badly he almost wet his pants. Through clenched teeth Michael hissed, "Never laugh at someone when they're down! Do you understand me?"

Henry didn't know what to do, so he grabbed his brother by the waist and hugged him fiercely, tears spilling onto his cheeks. "I'm sorry, Mike... I didn't mean..."

The scary far away look left Michael's eyes, and he hugged his little brother to him. "Sorry, Henry, it's okay. You'll be all right. It's over. We'll be getting on home."

Mr. Reynolds had loosened Martin's belt buckle helped him sit up. The bully was fighting to get air, and he was having a hard time of it. Gradually, he got one breath, and then a second. His terrified face said that he was afraid of dying in front of everyone right there on the floor at the YMCA. No one was laughing now.

Michael had a gentle hand on Henry's shoulder, and the two boys stood and watched while Mr. Roberts comforted the bully and helped him to control his breathing. After five long minutes, he helped Martin to his feet, but Martin was shaky and moved stiffly. The fall left an ugly bruised on his back and neck.

Mr. Roberts was taller and more athletic than the bully, and he reached out to steady him. "Martin, you've got to see a doctor. Let me take you—"

Martin brushed away his hand. "I'm getting the hell out of here… goin' home. Gonna get away from that freak. Keep him away from me." Hurt and embarrassed, Martin stumbled by Michael and Henry. Henry never forgot the look of fear in his eyes. The bully lumbered through the front door and out onto the sidewalk.

Mr. Roberts turned to Michael and looked him in the face. A slight smile played at the corners of his mouth, but it was clear he wasn't about to give in to it. He ran a hand through his sandy brown crew cut. "Best you take your brother home, Michael. Say hi to your dad for me. Tell him I'll give him a call."

"Yes, sir, Mr. Roberts. I'll tell him."

Michael picked up Henry's gym bag, took Henry by the hand, and led him to the front door. Henry felt everyone's eyes on them as they left the building, but he remained quiet.

In a town of six thousand people, everyone knew everyone else. The confrontation between big Bob Martin and skinny Michael Stonebreaker took a matter of hours to become the stuff of small-town legend. It was not the sort of thing Michael wanted talked about, and when schoolmates and friends tried to bring it up he asked them not to speak of it. Some kids thought this was odd, but if they went on talking about what he did to Bob Martin, Michael simply walked away.

Small-town rumor mills have a life cycle of their own, and eventually the incident at the Y was mostly forgotten.

Henry never forgot.

More and more Henry realized Michael was different from most of the older boys he knew. While his brother had a sense of humor, enjoyed playing sports of all kinds, and had an extraordinary natural physical strength, Michael did not play organized school sports; he didn't even try out for the teams. He preferred books and spending time with the Old Man and their father to chasing girls. His grades ranked him near the top of his class.

A few boys Michael's age thought he might be afraid to go out for school sports, until they played against him in pick up games of football and baseball during summer vacations. They soon discovered they couldn't keep up with him, and no one could best him when play got rough. Still, Michael preferred quiet and reading to standing on the street and bragging with his friends.

As a junior in high school he surprised everyone by trying out for football, but no one was surprised that he made the team easily. Henry asked why he'd done it, and Michael, in his usual cryptic fashion, said, "You'll know soon enough, Henry." That year Clear Haven High boasted a winning season, and Michael made substantial contributions on the field. The town newspaper and the local radio station were eloquent in their praise of the running back, Mike Stonebreaker. He set new school records in touchdowns and yards rushed.

In the spring of the same school year Michael made the track team and broke more records. He ranked best in the pole vault and high jump, and was Clear Haven's second fastest man on the high hurdles.

The second incident that made Michael Stonebreaker the stuff of legend took place during track practice when shot putter Albert Ogden injured his shoulder. A meet with arch rival Johnstown High was scheduled for two days later, and Coach Snyder was ready to write off the event. Ogden, the strongest member of the team at six-four and two hundred twenty-five pounds, was one of the biggest kids at school. He'd also played center on the football team. A senior, Ogden easily over shot most of the competition. Dan Davis, the second best shot putter on the Clear Haven team, was at least five feet behind him on every try. It was hopeless.

Coach Snyder stood looking at Ogden. The big teen towered

over him by four inches, agony stamped across his face. Snyder sent him to the locker room, telling him to see the school nurse and then get checked by his family doctor. Snyder turned around to discover Michael Stonebreaker standing in front of him.

"Yes, Stonebreaker...what is it?"

"I'd like to help, Coach."

"Help what? Ogden may be out for the rest of the year, and Davis cannot possibly beat Reynolds in the meet. We'll just have to scratch this event."

"Let me try it."

"The shot? Are you kidding me?" His arms went up in the air. "Look, Michael, I know you're a good athlete, but what do you weigh? I bet you don't top a hundred and sixty pounds soaking wet. Can you even pick up that ball?" The coach brought one hand to rest on Michael's shoulder. "Don't get me wrong, son. I'm not down on your desire and your heart. I know you've got tons of both, but that ball is heavy! I doubt you can throw it thirty feet."

Michael didn't say anything. He just smiled, bent down, picked up the shot put and walked to the practice circle. He set it to his neck as if he'd always known how to do it, and began his spin. Once, twice, three times, and he released the ball with a mighty shove. It arched through the air and thudded to the ground...five feet farther than Ogden had ever thrown it.

Stunned silence blanketed the practice field, and then Charlie Sanders, a heavyset kid who served as equipment manager, blurted, "Holy shit!" Sanders cringed and his face turned bright red. No one in his right mind ever used profanity within earshot of Coach Harold Snyder. He would not tolerate it from anyone, and the Good Lord help the student who forgot.

For a million years no one coughed, or laughed, or made a sound. Then, miraculously, Snyder reached out to put a big hand on Sanders' shoulder and said, "My sentiments exactly, Charlie."

The coach looked at Michael for a long moment. "Okay, we'll see how you do Saturday against Reynolds. He's huge...a giant." He eyed the young man who stood smiling before him. "Where'd you come from, Michael…Mars?" Then, he opened his mouth in a wide grin and laughed out loud. The tension was broken. Another Michael Stonebreaker legend was born.

Fans packed the bleachers at Clear Haven's home field. As it turned out, Reynolds was a giant. They watched in awe as the big kid picked up the metal ball in a hand so huge it looked like a catcher's mitt. On his first attempt he put the shot ten feet farther than Albert Ogden had ever done. When the crowd saw Ogden dressed in street clothes with his arm in a sling they groaned aloud. They groaned even louder when Davis put the shot fifteen feet behind the giant's first try.

The second man on the Johnstown team, Eric Dryden, was an African-American kid whose sinewy muscles rippled in the morning sunlight. He was four inches shorter than Reynolds, but with his broad shoulders he looked like Adonis, ready to carry the world. Dryden's first attempt beat the giant's by six inches. The hometown crowd was silenced by the cheers of Johnstown fans who'd traveled the sixty miles to support their team.

When Michael Stonebreaker stepped forward and stripped off his windbreaker for his first try, Clear Haven fans resumed groaning. Michael was muscular and athletic, and the home crowd had witnessed his exploits on the football team. They admired him for his winning ways on the track team as well, but he was scrawny compared to the behemoths competing in the shot put.

A few Johnstown fans laughed out loud, and others joined in. Clear Haven fans began to get angry, yelling at them to shut up. After a minute or two, Coach Snyder turned to face the stands and held up his right hand, his palm facing the crowd. People noticed, and the yelling died down. The home crowd wouldn't dare disrespect the man. Johnstown fans too, got quiet. In the ensuing silence, a breeze blew as Michael knelt to pick up the shot, then cradled it to his neck. A moment later it was sailing through the air, passing all the other attempts by five feet before smacking into the earth with a solid thump.

The crowd went insane. They clapped their hands, stomped their feet, yelled, whistled, and cheered. No one believed what they just witnessed. On the sideline, Coach Snyder leaned over and gently boxed Charlie Sander's left ear. He whispered, "Charlie, keep it clean from now on. Understood?"

"Yes, sir, Coach!" Charlie was grinning from ear-to-ear, and Coach Snyder grinned back at him.

Michael's parents, grandparents, and Henry stood on their feet in the stands, cheering him on. Henry kept yelling, "He's my brother!" but no one heard him over the roar of the crowd.

Reynolds had not tried too hard on his first attempt because Clear Haven's best man, Ogden, was hurt and not competing. When his own teammate beat him, and then the skinny kid beat them both, he was furious. Clear Haven fans were quiet, while Johnstown fans chanted, "Reynolds! Reynolds!" His next throw thudded out in front by another five feet. It looked like Johnstown would take the event.

Out of sheer frustration, on his turn Dan Davis made the best throw he'd ever managed in his life. Clear Haven fans were again on their feet and shouting. The heavy ball had gone six inches beyond Reynold's second throw.

Dryden's muscles bunched as he hoisted the iron ball to his neck, whirled and released. With incredible hang time, his throw beat the Davis mark by another two feet.

The crowd held its breath. Michael had taken his position in the throwing circle and picked up the shot. He spun and released, sending the ball arcing through the air to beat Dryden's mark by three feet. The fans went wild.

Many moments in his life were frozen in his memory, but Henry Stonebreaker would carry this one forever in his heart. His big brother Michael was like a god in his mind, and the roar of the crowd around him intensified his belief.

The Johnstown behemoth's third attempt fell short, and Dan Davis did his best, but failed to match his second throw. The event would be won or lost by Johnstown's Dryden or Clear Haven's Stonebreaker. The two boys eyed each other on the field.

Fans on both sides were chanting the names of their favorites and getting louder and louder when Michael stepped forward and extended his hand to his opponent. Surprised, Dryden hesitated, and then firmly grasped Michael's hand in his own.

Michael told Henry that he'd felt pure strength in Eric's grip. Years later Eric Dryden shared with both of them that the experience of shaking Michael's hand was amazing. He said it was like grabbing hold of a hand made of stone. "There was no give in it."

A hush fell over the stadium as the boys shook hands, and then the crowd erupted in approval of their sudden display of good sportsmanship.

Eric Dryden stepped into the throwing circle and took his position. He raised the ball to his shoulder, whirled three times and threw. He shouted with the effort as the shot put flew through the air. Finally, it hit the ground with a mighty thump and lay there. Johnstown fans were on their feet yelling and screaming. The measurement was taken. The throw had exceeded the state high school record by seven inches. The crowd went crazy whistling, yelling Eric's name, and patting each other on the back. Clear Haven fans were as excited as the Johnstown fans. They knew they were eyewitnesses to history being made.

Michael returned to the throwing circle. The crowd noise subsided. Henry's eyes grew wide, and fear filled his stomach as he looked at his brother. What if he couldn't do it? What if he couldn't throw farther than the other guy? Compared to Dryden, Michael looked like a skinny kid. Henry said a silent prayer. He felt the Old Man's hand on his shoulder and looked up. His grandfather's gaze was steady. It said, "It will be all right." Henry breathed a sigh.

Michael reached down and picked up the shot. He took his position, set the ball to his neck, whirled and released. The ball flew through the air and seemed to hang forever. It descended, then slammed into the earth. Officials huddled around the shot and measured again. The crowd watched as a second measurement was taken, and then a third.

A referee wrote something on a slip of paper and another man took it up to the public address booth. The announcer turned on the microphone, and his voice boomed out over the crowd.

"Michael Stonebreaker has broken the Pennsylvania state high school record."

The crowd roared its approval, and the stadium erupted in absolute bedlam. Fans whistled, cheered, laughed, cried, and congratulated each other.

"However," the announcer's voice broke in on the celebrations, "Dryden has won the shot by one and a half inches. Johnstown wins!"

A great moan went up from the Clear Haven side, but it quickly gave way to a renewed roar of celebration. Fans poured out of the bleachers and onto the field, surrounding Michael and Eric in a sea of well-wishers. The two stood together, shaking hand after outstretched hand.

A reporter from WECU sports radio got a microphone between their faces. "With new records set at both Johnstown and Clear Haven, how does it feel to make history, boys?" The Clarion photographer took pictures, while a roving reporter shorthanded their answers on a notepad.

No one wanted to leave the field. Finally, Coach Snyder blew his whistle, and the announcer urged people to return to their seats. The track meet had to resume; there were other events on the schedule.

Eric Dryden looked Michael in the eye and reached out to shake his hand. "You're something else, Stonebreaker!"

"It's Michael to my friends."

"You've got a friend if you want one."

"Then we're friends, Eric." The two shook hands and made plans to stay in touch.

"Oh, I'll be in touch, all right," Eric said, nodding. "Did you throw as hard as you could on that last shot?"

Michael looked at the other boy. "I always do my best, Eric."

"That's not what I asked you."

"You only won by an inch—"

"And a half!"

"Okay, an inch and a half…but I would have beat you on my next throw."

Eric looked at Michael, a big grin spreading over his face. "I believe you would beat me…and then I would beat you…and then—"

"And so on until we'd hold all the records in the world," Michael said, grinning back at him. They shook hands and headed for their respective teams.

Henry was devastated. Michael had lost. It wasn't possible for his big brother to lose at anything, but he had done just that. Henry hung his head, chin resting on his chest. The loss threatened to topple Michael's godlike status in Henry's mind. His grandfather's big hand rested on his shoulder. Henry felt tears start in his eyes, and heaved a sob as he buried his face in the Old Man's chest.

"It's okay, Henry. Michael will always be a winner. He picked up the shot put two days ago, and today he set a record and even came within a couple inches of beating Johnstown's guy." His rough hand tousled Henry's hair. "If the shot put were really Michael's event, one he practiced every day, why no one would even get close to him. You do understand that, don't you?"

Henry stifled another sob, hiccupped, and looked wide-eyed at his grandfather. "You really mean that, Pop Pop?"

"You'd better believe it, Henry. Nobody beats Michael when he gets determined. It's as though he goes to another place when he gets like that. I've only seen him do it a few times, but when he gets a certain look on his face you can tell his mind's made up. There's nothing and no one who can stop him." His grandfather smiled.

"Yeah, he's something when he gets like that isn't he?" Henry said. He smiled back at his grandfather, his faith in his big brother stronger than ever.

The track meet went on, but that day on the field a friendship was born...one that would change the world.

CHAPTER 2

A year later Henry was sitting in his second floor bedroom when he heard yelling downstairs. He ran from his room, and plunged down the steps, racing toward the sound. When Henry reached the kitchen, Michael was practically jumping up and down with excitement. Their father was beaming from ear-to-ear, and their mother was crying and smiling at the same time.

"What's going on? What happened?" Henry yelled.

Michael bent down, picked Henry up and whirled around and around. "I'm in, Henry! I'm in! It's all I've wanted! I'm going to West Point! West Point! I'm going to be a cadet at West Point!"

Henry, at age eleven, wasn't too sure what West Point was, but he was excited for his brother. "Where is it? What is it?" He looked down from atop Michael's outstretched arms.

Michael gently dropped Henry to his feet. "It's West Point…the US Army's military academy at West Point, New York. The greatest generals in American history have gone there, and I've been accepted! One day I'll be an officer in the United States Army!"

Henry understood, and though he was proud of his brother, he felt sad, too. Michael would be leaving home. His big brother wouldn't be around to confide in anymore. He would miss him like crazy.

"Will you write me and call me, Michael?"

Tears were welling up in Michael's eyes, and suddenly Henry knew Michael was going to miss him a lot, too.

"You know I'll write you, and I'll call you as often as I can. I know it will be really busy at school. They expect a lot from you, but I have a good friend there. I'll get to see him, as well."

"Who do you mean?"

"Eric goes there. He started last year."

Now, Henry understood. Eric Dryden and Michael had become close since the track meet where they'd met. Eric even visited with them a few times. On one visit Eric wore his uniform, and Henry asked him about it.

"Why do you have to wear a uniform in school?"

"It's a military academy. The cadets have to wear them. It's part of the tradition. When I graduate I'll be an officer, and when I'm on duty I'll always be dressed in a uniform," Eric explained.

Michael's voice broke into his thoughts. "Pop Pop wore a uniform in the Army, and Dad wore a uniform in the Marines."

"Yeah, soldiers wear uniforms," Henry said. He grinned at Michael. "Someday I'll wear a uniform!"

"What kind do you want to wear?"

"I want to be a Marine, like Dad."

"Great, Henry! The Marines are really tough guys!" His dad tousled his hair.

"How 'bout the Army? Are they tough, too?"

"They're all tough…the Marines, the Navy, the Army, the Air Force and the Coast Guard," Michael said. "They're all trained to do different things."

"I'm gonna miss you, Michael."

"We've got the whole summer, Henry. We'll see each other every day."

"Yeah, but you'll leave and I'll still be here."

"I'll be home for the holidays and other times, too."

Even at eleven Henry knew not having Michael at home would be a big adjustment for their family. He knew that his brother loved him, but it had been hard to think of him leaving. Mom and Dad would still be around. The Old Man and Grandmother lived just a few blocks away. Clear Haven wasn't that big. He could ride his bike from one end of town to the other in a few minutes, and he had his friends in the neighborhood. All of this would help while Michael was at school, but Henry would still miss sitting on the front porch swing telling Michael about his day. He would miss hanging out in his brother's room, talking about the things that were important to him.

Looking back on it now, Henry knew what he'd missed most of all was the quiet certainty and assurance that Michael brought to his life. Michael had always been there to tell him things, to help guide him as he grew, and to back him up when things got confused or scary. Michael was a steady rock in a storm. Henry trusted him as much as he trusted his Dad and the Old Man. He had been glad he still had both of them. He'd gotten through it.

Michael never treated him like a pain, the way other older brothers did. He always made sure Henry felt protected, and knew that his opinion mattered. Henry knew he meant more to Michael than any school.

Henry once overheard a conversation between his parents in which his Mom called Michael an old soul. He wasn't sure exactly what that meant, but he knew Michael was stronger and wiser than any other boys his age.

****

Michael remembered wishing for a younger brother from the time he himself was a little boy. When Henry was born he had been grateful. From then on he had always took time to be with Henry. He attended all his school events to cheer him on. They shared an unbreakable bond.

West Point had been his goal from the time he was twelve years old. One afternoon he saw a cadet on the street in Clear Haven. The uniform had so impressed him that he'd gone to the Clear Haven library to find out all he could about West Point. The more he read about all the famous men who trained and studied there, the more determined he became to join their ranks. Certain he would be among America's best when he stepped onto the campus, he understood that he would have to compete at a level far beyond anything he ever faced in his life. His emotions seesawed between confidence and nervousness. Now, years later he knew that had been a normal reaction.

One thing he had known even then; discipline would be the key to getting in to West Point, and the pathway to success in life for him. He was nothing if not disciplined. He avoided trouble growing up, even as others gravitated toward it. An excellent student from the time he had entered elementary school, he'd become even more focused in junior high. He hadn't applied himself to anything else, but his interest in West Point triggered his pursuit of high school sports.

Cadets were student athletes. He would become one as well. He'd tried out for football, and took advantage of an opportunity to join the track team. He'd worked hard and set records. If others gave a hundred percent, he gave a hundred and twenty-five. He made a point of exceeding expectations.

The payoff had come. He was going to West Point. His dream had come true.

CHAPTER 3

West Point was everything Michael expected and more. He did well and finished near the top of his class. The Gulf War came and went. He married the special girl from Clear Haven with whom he had always been in love, but had avoided for one simple reason—she overwhelmed him. His love for Joan Godin was the one thing he kept secret from everyone since the time he first saw her in high school.

Joan grew up in Clear Haven, and her large family had been around since the town was founded. They both attended Clear Haven Middle School, but it wasn't until high school that he'd looked up from his textbooks to see the girl of his dreams. He was a junior and she was a sophomore. She intrigued him. She would get a look on her face that made him want to grab her and kiss her. He was so attracted to her that he knew if he gave in to his feelings he would lose his motivation for other important things.

He had gone off to West Point, and a year later she'd entered a local college and was studying to be an elementary school teacher. In his second year at West Point, he went home for Christmas break and wore his uniform to a party at the home of a friend. Joan was there, and when they saw each other the barriers came down. Michael was smitten by her, but he'd hidden his feelings well. She, too, had thought about him in high school, but when he'd left for West Point she'd assumed he wasn't interested in her at all. That night they talked until two o'clock in the morning, and when he drove her home he'd hoped she wouldn't get in trouble with her parents. She hadn't.

Long distance relationships are hard, and it was no different for him and Joan. Their infrequent contact proved difficult, but they managed to get through it. After she graduated they were married at West Point's Cadet Chapel, surrounded by friends and family.

When duty called Michael answered, and though she was frightened while he served in the Gulf War, Joan maintained their home and was grateful when he returned safe and sound. As daughters Angela, and then Louise arrived and changes in duty came she adjusted well to life as an officer's wife. She raised their two girls while managing to land and hold teaching positions, despite their frequent moves.

There were hard years, but since he began work at the Pentagon life seemed more tranquil and secure. They both hoped things would stay that way for a long time. He smiled. Through the years his wife Joan remained the love of his life. They'd settled their young family not far from the Washington Beltway, where his classified duties as an Army intelligence officer were enough to occupy his days.

Then the events of 9/11 changed life in America in ways that few understood. Happy Days were long gone—as a television series and as a way of life. The reality of a New World Order was spreading like a cancer all over the country. He was assigned to a high level unit whose focus was international terrorism and protecting the American people from such attacks. A good and loyal soldier, and a man who loved his nation, he watched the evolution of that protection with growing alarm.

The government appeared to be out of control. Big Brother was no longer merely something people read about in a book. Bloated federal spending, massive regulations, an army of IRS agents, and cameras everywhere all but assured the permanence of its invasive overreach. Under its auspices, Homeland Security was busily organizing a police state in which freedoms were being cast aside for the sake of so-called security for the population. Increasingly, people were willing to sacrifice their privacy for that protection, and as if on cue, the NSA was apparently monitoring the emails and phone calls of countless Americans. He understood such efforts were necessary to a degree, especially at airports and the like, but he did not like seeing people's rights trampled on by nameless, faceless bureaucrats.

A soldier in mind, body, and spirit, he didn't care much for politics. Gazing out of his office windows, he wondered where all the change was leading. He was certain the "Day of the Progressives" had arrived. They had taken control and intended to keep it. What loomed on the horizon was frightening to those with an inkling of what was coming. The inmates were finally running the asylum.

Stationed near small towns across the country between the uptight, out-of-sight Northeast and the elitist Left Coast, Michael saw people doing their best to maintain a sense of patriotism, decency, and fair play. He could also see the handwriting on the wall—hell was coming to them in ways they had not foreseen. An obscene level of federal spending was mortgaging the futures of their great-great-great grandchildren. An unwanted national health care system that would bankrupt the middle class was voted into law, despite the majority of Americans wanting no parts of it. Nationalization of the auto industry, financial institutions, and bailing out businesses deemed "too big to fail" were prime examples of how Progressives wrested control through so-called czars and overburdening regulations. The president also had a penchant for bypassing the normal legislative process, implementing his agenda by executive order.

In the name of charity, social justice, and perverted democracy the same liberals on steroids, as he termed them, were intent on toppling the American Republic and remaking it into a world of their choosing. Soon success and entrepreneurship would be hamstrung by unwarranted confiscatory taxation without representation, and illegal immigrants and the so-called poor would have their votes bought by the Progressives for generations to come.

Michael shifted his gaze from the windows to his desk, where Joan and his daughters smiled at him from a favorite photo. He was a very happy man. He enjoyed his work, and his family completed the American Dream for him—he lived a happy, productive life with a loving family. Despite the smiling faces of his wife and daughters staring back at him, he couldn't help but feel a storm was brewing.

Congress saw itself as an entitled ruling class, with members guilty of such hubris that their greed bordered on the unbelievable. Coupled with the unprecedented arrogance displayed in the White House the government had created an adversarial relationship with the majority of Americans. The people were mad as hell and seeking a way back to the America they believed in, one that their fathers and grandfathers fought and died to preserve. His own father and grandfather were among them. He didn't need to watch Fox News to know that years of wars in Iraq and Afghanistan and their cost in American lives and treasure weren't the only things on the minds of good Americans. An internal war was brewing in the coffee shops, living rooms and over the back fences of people everywhere. Their quiet resolve would end in a correction at the ballot box, or in a correction of another sort too painful to think about.

He let his eyes fall on a photograph of his best friend, Eric Dryden. Their friendship developed over the years since that fateful day at the high school track meet. Now they golfed as often as possible. Joan and Eric's wife Yvette had grown fond of each other, and vacations to the beach with Erin and Erica were a favorite for Angela and Louise. The Stonebreakers and the Drydens both had their share of photos of four little girls in floppy beach hats and big sunglasses from years gone by.

Eric also served at the Pentagon, and he and Michael were on several short lists for top spots in the military hierarchy. Their intelligence, service, and dedication to duty marked them as the best the Army produced. They'd lived up to their West Point credentials and earned the respect of their peers and senior officers. Eric was a black ops specialist; they steered clear of political discussions; their conversations and friendship focused on family matters, golf, and life

in general—things far removed from the work they did for a living.
All of that was about to change.

CHAPTER   4

Henry steered the Ford F-150 into the driveway. Twilight was settling in as they walked into their boyhood home. The delightful odors of Thanksgiving dinner engulfed them at the door. Michael smiled at the sight of his daughters Angela and Louise playing Scrabble in the living room with Henry's son Dylan. The cousins sprawled out on the floor around the game much the same way he, Henry, and the Old Man had years before.

A chorus of "Hi's" trailed them down the hallway and into the kitchen. The elder Mrs. Stonebreaker stood at the counter by the sink mashing potatoes, while Joan took fresh rolls out of the oven. Henry's wife Susan gathered dishes and prepared to take them to the dining room for setting the table. Memories of countless Thanksgiving dinners flooded his mind. The only thing missing from this one was the Old Man. His absence made Michael's heart ache.

"Where have you been? Did you want to miss dinner?" Mrs. Stonebreaker asked without turning her head.

"Sorry, Mom. We just lost track of time," Henry said. "And Michael missed the big one."

"I didn't miss him," Michael said. "There was a speck on my

scope."

"You said it was a fly," Henry reminded him.

"We don't have flies in November," Mrs. Stonebreaker said, turning to look at them. "Go get your hunting clothes off and wash up. You've got five minutes. Everything is ready!"

Evelyn Stonebreaker wore her sixty-eight years of age well. She always treated her sons as grown men, except during the holidays. They might as well have been grade school children when she was on a mission to get the family settled around the holiday meal. There was no mistaking the tone of her voice, and they knew better than to take issue with her.

Michael and Henry headed for the garage to get cleaned up for dinner. A small porch light shone above the door at the rear of the house. They descended the well-worn steps from the porch in silence, and crossed the backyard on a walkway that led to the wooden building, which doubled as a garage and a storage area. They entered the large heated room. Their father walled off a section on one side of the building to create the space when they were boys. He built a closet for hunting gear and installed a large lockable gun safe for rifles, shotguns and ammunition, along with a second closet for fishing gear.

Michael's eyes rested on the octagonal card table where two generations of Stonebreakers and their friends enjoyed countless poker games in times past.

"How about playing some poker later?" Henry asked. Michael looked up, and Henry nodded toward the table.

"We haven't played in years," Michael said. "I'm not sure I remember how."

"Joan and Susan would rather play pinochle. A game of poker will give us a couple of hours alone. After we clean up from dinner, there's something I want to talk to you about."

"Why couldn't you talk to me when we were hunting?" Michael asked. They stripped off coats and gear.

"We don't talk in the woods—Old Man's Rule," Henry said.

"He's not here anymore, Henry. That's why I missed the monster today. In the hospital, right before the end, he told me he just wanted to look at them. I couldn't kill it. It was as big as an elk, but I just didn't want to bring it down. Let it live another day." He paused. "I wish he was still here."

Both men were silent for a moment, busying themselves with soap, water, and towels at the huge farmhouse sink.

"What I have to talk to you about is important, and I can't discuss it with anyone else in the family," Henry said.

Michael, quickly concerned, asked, "Is everything all right? Is your job okay?"

The question was valid. Coal was king in Clear Haven when they were boys. Thanks to the greenies, as Henry called them, the town had fallen on hard times. Coal wasn't politically correct, despite being the most plentiful fuel in America.

"Work's fine. The eco-wackos haven't plowed us under yet."

Michael smiled at another of Henry's colorful descriptions. He knew his brother wasn't against wind or solar. As an educated, yet practical man Henry believed America needed to use all its fuel resources, to gain independence from foreign oil suppliers who wanted to destroy the US.

Michael had to agree.

"Even though the technology gets better and better for making clean use of nature's burnable rock, the greenies still want no part of it."

Henry didn't have the roaming gene, as he called it, and so he had been content to return to Clear Haven after serving in the Marine Corps. He worked as a heavy equipment mechanic for a major dealer on the highway west of town. Work had been steady, but the economy was in dreadful shape, and Michael feared his brother would be laid off.

"We'll discuss it later," Henry said. "We'd better get inside before Mom comes out here with the belt."

Michael laughed. On the one and only time the belt had been pulled out for them, they had been firing at tin cans in the backyard. "Remember we shot out Mrs. Potter's garage window with that old BB gun?"

"Yeah." Henry smiled. "Mom insisted Dad get the belt out, even though it was a ricochet that hit the window." Their dad herded them into the garage where their mother couldn't see, showed them the belt, and then proceeded to whip an old saddle strapped on a sawhorse.

They had the presence of mind to yell, "Ow, ow, ow!" as the belt was administered. After a convincing number of licks, their father had sworn them to silence.

The three of them returned to the house to find their mother in tears. She hugged the boys and made them promise never to do anything like that again. They promised her, but neither boy ever revealed the truth of what their father had done.

Michael and Henry went back inside, and the Stonebreakers enjoyed their Thanksgiving meal. Michael had to admit, it was a joy to be under the same roof again. He treasured this time of the year, and even now was looking forward to repeating the family fellowship in a few weeks again at Christmas time. Preparing the holiday meal with Joan and Susan, playing games with the grandkids, and just the sound of family voices in the old house brought joy to his mother's face and lifted her spirits since Dad had been gone. Through tears, he and Henry made an ironclad commitment to their father as he lay dying; they would always take care of their mother. As long as she lived, that would never change.

After the meal, Michael and Henry chased everyone from the kitchen and did the dishes. When they finished, they announced that they were going to play poker. Mild protests ensued, but in the end the women relented. The women agreed that the brothers spent so little time together during the year, it would be good for them to enjoy each others' company for a while. They promised to limit their play to just an hour or so, and then rejoin the family to watch a movie in the living room. It would be *The Wizard of Oz,* another family tradition.

Out at the card table, Henry dealt a round of five-card draw, deuces wild. "So, Michael, how are things in Washington these days?"

"You know I can't talk about my work. The bad guys are still out there. We're still trying to find them. Life goes on."

"I'm not talking about Afghanistan or Iraq. I'm talking about here at home...the economy and all this other crap that's on the news every day. What do you think about it?" Henry asked.

Michael shifted in his chair, trying to get more comfortable. "I've never understood how grown men could play poker for endless hours on these hard wooden chairs with no cushions." Their father insisted that a hard seat made for a sharper focus when it came to cards.

"Truthfully, Henry, I don't know much about it." Michael returned to Henry's question. "Just what I see on TV or read in the paper. You probably know a lot more than I do."

"I'd like you to take a ride with me tomorrow. I want you to meet some people. The girls will be off Black Friday shopping with Mom, and the kids will be over at Aunt Grace's for a few hours. It'll give us a chance to be together for a while. I really miss seeing you."

The first part of what Henry said had not gone unnoticed. "A ride to where? Who are we meeting?"

"I can't tell you that. You'll know when we meet them."

"Why are you being so mysterious?"

"Do you trust me, Michael?"

"Trust you? Of course, I trust you with my life! You're my brother. But what's this all about?"

"You'll know soon enough," Henry said.

"So, my younger brother is being cryptic with me?"

"Hey, you were the one who was always so mysterious when we were growing up. A little payback never hurts now and then," Henry said.

"Okay, sure. Let's play cards."

The game began.

CHAPTER 5

By ten o'clock the following morning the sun was shining, the children were visiting second cousins at their Aunt Grace's house, and Mrs. Stonebreaker, Joan, and Susan were off to the mall. Henry and Michael drove steadily west in Henry's pickup.

The Pennsylvania hills along Route 80 showed great stretches where the leaves had fallen for another winter. The autumn colors were mostly gone this late in the year, and the dark mountains contrasted starkly against the whiteness of the clouds overhead. Snow was forecast for later in the day, but the morning was clear and bright. Michael sat, content to be riding in the truck next to his brother, listening to a country singer's lament on the radio.

After a few miles he asked, "So, where did you say we're going?"

"I didn't say."

"Why can't you tell me?"

"It's for your own protection."

"Now, wait a minute. I'm a major in the US Army. It's my job to help protect you. What's this all about?" Michael said, annoyance creeping into his voice.

"I asked you last night if you trusted me. I'm a Marine. Do you trust me, Michael?"

"Of course I do, dammit! Henry, but why—"

"Then cool your jets, brother. We're almost to where we get off this road. After that, you'll have the answer to your question."

Michael stared ahead. He expected that they would be getting off at the next exit, but Henry surprised him by turning off Route 80 onto what appeared to be a private access road. Normally such a road would have been restricted to Pennsylvania State Police or other official use.

Henry carefully drove up a steep grade and stopped in front of a locked, heavy, chain-link gate. He got out of the truck and unlocked the gate. Once he'd driven through, he got out and re-locked the gate behind them.

When he got back in the truck Michael was staring at him, but Henry looked straight ahead. They drove up a rise where the hidden road leveled out, then Henry made a right turn and drove through a thick stand of trees. Clear of the trees, he continued along a dirt track that led deeper into the woods.

After about three miles the road opened out in front of a tall chain link fence with razor wire running along its top. A guard in a small wooden building stepped out as they approached. Henry waved, and after a moment the guard waved back.

The guard activated a switch, and the gates swung inward. Henry drove through the gate and stopped.

The guard approached the driver's side window. "Good morning, Mr. Jones."

Henry responded, "Good morning to you, Mr. Smith."

"May I know the name of your passenger, Mr. Jones?"

"Yes, this is Mr. Brown. We'll be visiting the Manor."

The guard handed Henry a blindfold.

Henry turned to Michael. "I'm going to need you to wear this, or we can't go any further. Trust me."

Michael suspected Henry was up to some sort of elaborate joke. "You can't be serious." Henry's face looked solemn, but Michael still figured he knew his younger brother well enough to know that some big scheme was probably being played out here. He was sure a huge laugh was waiting at the end. He decided to play along.

"Okay, I'll wear it. But don't expect me to find this as funny as you do."

He hadn't seen the look on Henry's face before. "It's a matter of national security. No one is playing a joke here."

Michael instantly sobered at Henry's reply. "Let's go," he said. He put the blindfold on. They got moving, and Michael sensed they had driven for several miles before the pickup finally stopped.

"Don't remove the blindfold, Michael. Keep it in place. I'll help you get out of the truck."

Michael sat still. He heard Henry get out of the truck, walk around it, and open the door. Henry gently grasped his right arm and talked him down over the running board to the ground. Michael heard someone else approaching.

Henry and the unknown person guided him over a long hard-surfaced walk to a set of steps, and then up the steps to what must have been a porch. He was guided through a door and into a building, where they led him down a hallway. They stopped in front of what Michael assumed was an elevator. He heard the sound of a button being pushed and soft bells pinging somewhere above them. The doors opened, and they stepped into the car.

When the doors closed, Michael said, "You can remove the blindfold."

Michael took off the blindfold and was momentarily blinded by the light. His eyes adjusted, and he could see Henry standing on his right. A young man dressed in military fatigues with very short hair, a wrestler's build, and a square jaw stood on his left. Henry introduced them. "Mr. Brown, meet Mr. Black."

The powerfully built young man pivoted and snapped a salute. "I'm please to meet you, sir!"

Michael saluted in return. "My pleasure, Mr. Black."

The elevator stopped and the three men walked down a wide hallway toward a massive steel door at the end. Henry placed his hand over a palm reader to the right of the door, then set his chin on a rest in front of a retinal scanner. He stepped away, and the young soldier did the same.

A metallic sounding voice came from a speaker above the reader. "Identify visitor."

"Mr. Brown." Henry answered.

"I will scan. Step forward please."

Michael stepped forward. He placed his hand on the reader and subjected his eye to the retinal scanner.

"Identified," the voice said. "Proceed."

The great door opened onto a large area outside a tunnel carved into the rock. The roof was dimly visible above them, lit by powerful sodium lamps that lined the tunnel far into the distance. The underground passage appeared to extend far longer than Michael imagined was possible into the solid rock of the Pennsylvania mountains.

An eight-passenger tram waited for them at the entrance to the tunnel. It was driven by another muscular young man dressed in the same garb as Mr. Black. They boarded the electric tram and drove into the mouth of the tunnel. The vehicle moved silently along, its tires gliding along on the hard smooth surface of the tunnel floor. Michael could see the tram's instrument panel from where he sat in the rear of the car. His training as an intelligence officer kicked in, and he noted that they drove along at about ten miles per hour, for a little under three miles.

Two more men dressed in military garb were stationed at another steel doorway. Michael, Henry, and Mr. Black disembarked from the tram. The same procedure with a palm reader and a retinal scanner was followed, after which the door opened and they stepped into a long corridor. A second doorway at its end was flanked by a third set of scanners, which gained them access to a room paneled in dark, rich mahogany. The security reminded Michael of a high level military installation.

At least forty people sat waiting for them around a long conference table in the center of the room. All of them stood up when the three men entered the room. The men and women were dressed in both military uniforms and civilian clothes.

The wall at the far end of the room was filled with flat screen monitors that appeared to Michael to be filled with notes and diagrams. From where he stood he could not tell exactly what was on the screens. A high backed chair faced away from the table, toward the monitors. The chair slowly turned, and the man sitting in it stood up. He smartly saluted Michael.

It was Eric Dryden.

CHAPTER 6

Michael wavered on his feet, and Henry quickly reached out a hand to steady him. "Eric? What is this? What are you doing here? Who are these people?"

"My name is Mr. Gray, and you are Mr. Brown," Eric responded. "Such protocol is necessary. We keep things formal here." He was not smiling. He motioned toward three chairs at the end of the table. "I've asked that you be brought here because I believe that you are the best person for the task that lies ahead of us. Please be seated."

Michael, Henry, Mr. Black, and the others standing around the table sat down.

Eric introduced each of the people present. "Meet Mr. Orange, Miss Yellow, Mr. Green, Mrs. Pink, Mr. Red, Miss Purple, Mr. …"

Eric indicated people by these names, and as he named them, one-by-one they tilted their heads toward Michael in acknowledgment.

"To provide a measure of security and for identification purposes," Eric continued, "those who work inside this complex carry the name of a color. Those who work outside, such as Mr. Jones," he said, indicating Henry, "carry simple one-syllable names.

"As to why I am here, I am a facilitator. We do not have titles of rank or importance here. Our purpose is singular. We prepare for the inevitable. We prepare for the conflict that is coming. We are here to protect the American people."

"Protect them from what?" Michael asked from the opposite end of the table.

"Mr. Brown, I asked Mr. Jones to bring you here today to meet our colleagues, to begin to understand what we are facing and embrace the resulting challenges." He paused. "And, we hope that you will agree to accept the greatest commission you will ever be offered. I know of no finer, more capable man than you. You have the strength, character, and sense of purpose that is necessary to lead in this time of national crisis."

"I truly appreciate your confidence, Eri—" Michael caught himself, "Uh, Mr. Gray, is it?"

Eric nodded.

"Mr. Gray. Thank you for the compliments. Before I can begin to consider any kind of commission, which you obviously intend to offer, I'd like to know exactly to what national crisis are you referring?"

"And I am happy to oblige, Mr. Brown," Eric continued. "Our nation is being destroyed. It is decaying from within. It is being brought to its knees by those who would first compromise our principles, undermine them, and then reduce our population to utter dependency. It is the goal of those who occupy the White House, Congress, and far too many of the State houses to subvert our people and to control every aspect of our lives from cradle to grave. If you call it socialism you're on the right path. If you name it Progressivism, you have hit the mark." The men and women around the table nodded in agreement.

"Our internal enemy has been working toward this goal for over one hundred years," Eric continued. "They hate America and Americans. They are the prophets and the architects of a New World Order, one that creates a World State in which morals are corrupted, principles are compromised, law is only for the subjugated, and Judaism and Christianity are eradicated from the earth.

"Every aspect of conservative culture is under attack every day. The media spouts the talking points of Progressive ideologues and idiots, and champions their cause. It's worth noting that they are one and the same. These people are the very embodiment of evil. They have mortgaged the futures of generations of children to come, and they would sell their very souls if it were possible."

"I agree," Michael held up a hand, "liberals have hijacked American culture, but surely, if they ever moved to physically attack American citizens to advance their utopian agenda, the US military would act to stop them."

"It is their fervent wish to do away with our military so that our nation is unprotected, and under the current administration they've succeeded in hollowing out our ranks to pre-World War I levels. As a member of the American military you are hated more than civilians. They are considered dolts and dullards, but they see you as their ultimate enemy. They despise you and everything for which you and I stand. Moreover, they're confident that getting rid of military men like you will pave the way for them to take over this country once and for all.

"We have known each other for many years. I know everything there is to know about you. You are as much a brother to me as the man sitting next to you; it couldn't be more so if we had the same parents."

Henry nodded at Eric's words.

"But there is a war coming," Eric went on. "We have not had a war of brother-against-brother on this soil since 1865. Sadly, war on American soil may be imminent, and inevitable. This ideological conflict will not end at the ballot box, as some hope. The Progressives manipulate the media through misdirection and manufactured crises contrived for the sole purpose of controlling the masses.

"Allowing them to continue unchecked will lead to more fear mongering, and eventually bloodshed. Those who bury their heads in the sand hoping the crisis will go away will have their heads cut off in the end. We do not intend to lose our heads to ignorance."

"What is it you are asking of me? I serve this country in the capacity afforded me at this point. If I could do more to preserve conservative values in this country, I would." Michael leaned forward as he spoke.

Eric nodded in agreement. "As a soldier you took an oath to

defend this country, and this country is nothing more or less than the people you serve. I'm asking you to serve your God, your nation, and your people. I'm asking you to join what amounts to a second American Revolution."

Michael sat in stunned silence. *What kind of nightmare have I wandered into? I must be home in bed dreaming. God, let it be so.*

The silence went on for a long time. Finally, Michael found his voice. "Mr. Gray, I don't know how to respond to you and the others here. I never imagined that anything like your organization existed. At this moment, frankly, I don't know what to believe. I—"

Eric interrupted him. "That is to be expected. You'll need time to comprehend and then embrace the truth. What little you've seen in this complex is merely a fraction of what exists. There are places like this across the nation. You know me well enough to know I speak the truth.

"Of course we do not expect you to accept the commission, or the circumstances by which it will come about, until you understand the purpose and goals of The Movement, and The Revolution 2.0. Due to the nature of what we are discussing, we will not communicate with you openly. During the Christmas holiday you are invited to come here again and stay overnight. Mr. Jones has been given the task of working out the details so that your family will not be concerned about your absence during that time.

"When we meet again outside this place we will not discuss any aspect of this meeting. It never happened." Eric stood. Everyone at the stood, and Michael did so as well. Eric saluted him from the opposite end of the table. Michael saluted in return.

Henry and Mr. Black led Michael back through the door they entered, and the three of them returned to the elevator.

Michael was asked to place the blindfold over his eyes, and he did so. He was led back to the pickup. Henry retraced the route back to the gate where Michael gave the blindfold back to the guard at the booth.

The brothers did not speak on the return trip home. Michael found himself studying Henry as they drove along. He thought he knew everything there was to know about Henry Louis Stonebreaker. He wondered if he would ever be able to have another lighthearted conversation with his brother the rest of their lives. He doubted it.

CHAPTER 7

Driving to the Pentagon Monday morning, Michael thought about the words of Colonel Eric Dryden, or Mr. Gray, as he called himself. He replayed the scene in the secret room over and over in his mind. As an intelligence officer he was trained to remember things down to the smallest detail, and to notice what might not be obvious to others. Traffic was heavy and the trip was slower than usual, so he spent the time putting those skills to use to recall his observations from the meeting.

An equal number of uniformed and civilian personnel sat at the table. One man, about three-quarters of the way down on his left wore a general's stars. A Navy captain occupied a seat on his right. He recognized several people in the room, including a well-known television anchor and a financial expert he'd seen on a national cable channel.

Three doors flanked the room besides the one he'd been brought in through. State-of-the-art tech filled the room. A bank of large flat-screen monitors covered an entire wall. Recessed lighting dotted the gleaming white ceiling.

He was amazed at the overall size of the place, and at the monetary investment it represented. Eric said the compound existed for years, perhaps decades. *What did it all mean? Who had the money and the influence to gather such a group of people together?* He wondered how many levels there were to this shadow organization, and who led it. *Eric?* He'd called himself a facilitator, and said there were other compounds like the one in Pennsylvania scattered across America. It was obvious that The Movement had been active for some time before the present administration came to power, but *how long had they been around?*

Since he honored Henry's request to wear the blindfold, he wasn't even sure where the compound was. After all, when your brother asks you to do something, and he's a man of excellent character, you do it. But now, Henry had become something of an enigma in his mind. *How long was he with The Movement? Had his brother sought them out, or was he enlisted by them?* His mind reeled with questions.

Michael braked hard as a teenager cut into the lane in front of him.

They chose Henry to get to him. *They were dreaming*, he thought. What they intended would require more effort, money, and power than even they could imagine. Ousting the liberal ideologues would take nothing less than a bloody revolution.

Scenes from the Gulf War filled his mind. Bodies lying in the desert, blasted buildings, bomb craters...the hell of human conflict... he pushed away the images.

At the entrance to the Pentagon parking area he turned in and drove to his assigned space, once again contemplating the implications of becoming further involved with The Movement.

Walking into the building, he considered that taking the meeting meant his life would be turned upside down. He needed to find out what The Movement was up to. *Did these people represent the truth, or were they just as clever as the liberals at pushing their own lies?* He trusted Henry and Eric, but *what had they gotten themselves into?* He swore an oath of loyalty to his country. Whatever happened, he would not violate that promise. He stepped inside his office and closed the door.

****

Eric Dryden arrived at his section hours before Michael came to work. He spent the early hours in quiet contemplation. He thought about Michael's introduction to the group in the boardroom. Its members were as diverse as the areas of society they represented. Representatives from the military, science, business, the media, academia—experts in all sorts of disciplines came at his request to take their first look at Michael Stonebreaker.

Everything was riding on what happened in the next few months. He was certain Michael was the right man for the job. He believed he had met someone truly extraordinary when he'd grasped that stone-hard hand on the field at the track meet all those years ago. Now he knew why.

He let his mind wander over the events that led to the founding of The Movement. During the Eisenhower administration, certain individuals recognized the need for a planned strategy to combat growing liberal Progressivism in the United States. A group of four men and one woman met secretly on the pretext of attending a gathering of the country's rich and powerful at The Hay-Adams in Washington, DC. Their discussion that October morning resulted in a pact to join forces and to enlist others in support of a return to the Constitutional values that produced The Great American Experiment.

The five secretly used their power, wealth, and, most importantly, their obscurity to recruit like-minded proponents to their cause. Every member, from then until now, pledged their secret loyalty. Miraculously, those vows had been kept; The Movement grew powerful, yet remained secret as the years slipped by.

The original group was expanded to sixteen, and the nation was divided into sixteen quadrants under their leadership. They began secretly enlisting new members and raising money. In the late 50's and early 60's while people were building bomb shelters in their backyards in case of nuclear war, excavations were begun for building the underground sites that would serve as meeting places, central weapon stockpiles, and planning centers in each of the quadrants. Members accessed private capital sufficient for completing the massive infrastructure which now served as The Movement's network of hidden compounds.

Eric pushed his chair back from his desk and walked over to the stately handcrafted wood-art sideboard his wife Yvette bought him as a gift to celebrate achieving the rank of colonel. A wedding photo and several of her and their twin girls adorned the wall. He poured himself a cup of coffee from the service and touched the corner of a framed baby picture of Erin and Erica before returning to his desk and his thoughts.

Above all, members of The Movement exercised patience to match that of the Progressives, who seized opportunities to implement their warped ideology in the early 1900s. Their true desire for total control over Americans' economic and social affairs was camouflaged in programs to eliminate corruption, waste, and injustice in state and local government, the media, industry, and other areas of society. In the years since, they extended the use of so-called experts and government intervention to manipulate and tax everything from currency to cow farts.

The Movement understood the underlying motives of the Progressives, and vowed to thwart the fulfillment of their oppressive agenda on American soil. The idea of TR2.0 began to take shape. If it ever became necessary to preserve the God-given rights to life, liberty, and the pursuit of happiness, the plan would be executed to ensure those rights would remain at the heart of American society. Progressives would not be permitted to outlaw the American Dream, or to replace market-driven free enterprise and capitalism with the stagnating stranglehold of socialism and communism.

The light of dawn shone through the windows of Eric's office, interrupting his contemplation. Snow had fallen during the night. He stood up and looked at the clean white scene stretched pure and unmarred across the parking lot. He vaguely wished the circumstances of his own life were as pristine. Long ago he resigned himself to the fact that a man who'd seen the worst man could do to his fellow man, and accepted the responsibility for exacting retribution didn't have that luxury. Some parts of his memory would never be clean.

He stretched, absently flexing taut shoulder muscles. He sighed. The weight of the mission was like a physical thing resting solidly on his back. It was a burden he was glad to bear, along with so many others committed to The Movement. Among them, Michael Stonebreaker was the man. He was right for the job. Of that, Eric had no doubt. Michael's steadfast resolve and military service to his country and its people echoed the sentiments of The Movement's founders. His unblemished character and commitment to his family were a rare combination nowadays.

But, the task would be a daunting one. How would he convince his friend of the urgent need to act soon to save the country? Things were heating to a boiling point. The Movement would not stand by in silence much longer. The Progressives' campaign to strip citizens of their individual rights in exchange for national security was becoming more aggressive every day. They'd become masters of using crises to justify massive power grabs to implement their hellish plans. On that front, The Movement had been caught napping. Thankfully, the planning and the mechanisms that evolved over the past fifty years into the current iteration of TR2.0 were capable of adjusting and responding quickly.

The Progressives were smug, self-righteous, and overconfident. Their arrogance toward the American people made victory seem to them inevitable. Eric let a small smile form on his lips. They underestimated the passion and sheer determination of a vast, silent majority in America. And they'd underestimated the power of truth. The Movement was prepared. The time had come to act.

Eric picked up and read the first field report of the day. An issue in an area of Pakistan was of particular concern. He dealt with it.

CHAPTER 8

Henry Stonebreaker wished with all his heart that he could talk openly with his brother about what he'd gotten him into. His own association with The Movement began with a seemingly innocent phone call a year before on a November evening shortly after 8:00. Usually his wife Susan would answer, but since she was at the church with a women's group planning a church supper, and his son was at the library doing expanded research for a paper, he'd picked up the phone.

"Hello."

"Hello, is that you, Henry?"

"Yes, who is it?"

"Eric Dryden."

"Hey friend, it's great to talk to you. It's been a long, long time. How are Yvette and the girls? My gosh, it's been years!"

"The family's fine, kids are growing like weeds. How about Susan? And Dylan must be about Erin and Erica's age, right?"

"Everybody's great. Dylan's in high school. Susan's good, though we both feel like the years are flying by. Glad to hear things are well with you all. Seems like a call out of the blue from you means more than catching up on family. What can I do for you?"

"Actually, I'm passing through town. I'm calling from the Clear Haven Diner. I have a meeting near Pittsburgh tomorrow morning and I thought of you when I stopped here to grab a bite. Is there any chance of you coming by and seeing me? I won't keep you long."

Looking back, Henry thought the invitation a bit unusual. Eric was Michael's great friend, but he liked and admired the man a whole lot, so he'd accepted. "Sure, but I don't have too long. Susan is out for a while, and my son's at the library. I can give you half an hour."

"Great! I'll see you here."

They met over coffee and made small talk for a few minutes, catching up on family news and whatnot. Any hesitation Henry felt about the odd nature of their meeting flew out of the window they started talking. Eric exuded the same confident, affable nature Henry remembered. He sensed that in many ways Eric was sizing him up as well. Seemingly satisfied with his assessment, Eric motioned for the check and said the reason for his visit was something he wanted to give Henry out in his car. When they reached the parking lot behind the diner Eric opened the front passenger-side door of a nondescript black sedan, took a small envelope from the glove box, and handed it to Henry.

"What's this?"

"It's a key. It opens a gate."

"What gate?"

"You turn right onto an access road fifteen miles west of Clear Haven off of Route 80 at mile marker 93. Go up a steep grade. The gate's at the top of the rise."

"Why are you giving it to me?"

Ignoring his question, Eric went on. "Open the gate, drive through, and lock it behind you. Follow the road as it leads you. Don't stop until you come to a second gate where a guard will be posted. He'll take it from there."

"Why should I do this?"

"National security."

"I left the Marines, Eric. What's this all about?"

"You know what I do for a living, Henry?"

"Michael says your job is classified."

"He's right. I can't talk about it."

"So, why give me this key?"

"You are Henry Stonebreaker, are you not?" Henry could still remember the set of Eric's jaw and his eyes, narrowed in the lamplight.

"Yes, but—"

Eric hardly waited for Henry's reply. "You're the brother of the best friend I have in this world. That makes you a very special man. I cannot tell you what you're going to find beyond that gate, but I know you well enough to know that I can trust you with my life."

"Thanks for the vote of confidence, Eric, but I still don't understand why I should do this. Convince me."

Eric sighed. "It involves your brother—"

"What? What about Michael? Is he okay?"

"He's fine, but I can't tell you yet how it involves him. I can only say this, call in sick in two days, take the key and go through the gate. You'll find all your answers there. I've got to get on the road. It's been great seeing you. I'll see you again…soon."

Henry pocketed the envelope. They shook hands and said goodbye.

✳✳✳✳✳✳✳

As Henry drove home he thought about the key in his pocket. *What lay beyond the gate? How was Michael involved, and what did all this have to do with national security?* He intended to find out.

When Henry drove through the gate and locked it behind him two days later, he was still wondering what this could possibly be all about. Two armed special forces soldiers were waiting at the second gate. He underwent the same blindfold routine that he would subject Michael to on his first visit to the compound. What was revealed to him in the hidden mountain retreat over the six months that followed convinced him beyond any doubt. He had become part of a plan that must move forward if there was any hope of saving the country. America was in deep trouble. It was time to repair the damage, and do whatever was necessary to get the nation back on track.

****

The Christmas holidays arrived. Michael and Joan brought their girls home to Clear Haven to spend time with their grandmother. Henry arranged a two-day trip for him and Michael to get together at a hunting camp with some old buddies from town. Joan and Susan weren't totally happy about the trip. "But, boys will be boys," they'd agreed, laughing.

When Henry and Michael arrived at the second gate after threading the back road off Route 80, Michael was again required to wear the blindfold. As they bumped along what Michael was certain was an unpaved dirt road, he asked, "When do I get to take this thing off this time?"

"I had to wear it for three months before they let me go without one. It has to do with commitment—"

"On their part?"

"No, on yours."

Henry's response silenced him.

When they arrived at the secret board room and the door opened there was only one person present. Eric Dryden sat at the end of the huge table at the opposite end of the room, flanked by a second door. He stood and saluted Michael. The brothers approached him and sat down. The flat screen monitors behind Eric were blank, and the only sound was the soft hiss of the air handlers that kept the room at a comfortable seventy-two degrees. Michael quickly took in the room's details and then focused his attention on Eric Dryden like a laser. It was time to find out what this was all about.

Eric smiled. "Henry, Michael, welcome."

Henry returned his smile. "Good to see you, Eric."

Michael remained silent.

"So, my friend, aren't you going to say hello?"

"In the past month I've discovered that my brother and my best friend are knee deep in preparing to take action against the nation that I serve in uniform, and that I plan to serve until I retire from the United States Army. How do you think I feel at this moment?" Michael wasn't smiling.

Eric's smile vanished. "We've been friends forever, Michael. Nothing has changed in that regard. I'm your friend now, and I'll be your friend in the future."

"I would hope so, Eric. But what in God's name is this all about? Locked gates where no one expects them to be, blindfolds, a secret mansion, tunnels and blast doors with palm and retinal readers, and people gathered around a table that looks like the one in the White House situation room."

"We used it as a model for ours."

"Dammit, Eric, this isn't funny!"

"I'm not joking. You have questions. I have answers, or at least some that I can share at this time. Ask me."

"Why me? Why you and Henry? What is this place?"

"Would you like some coffee?" Eric motioned for Michael to sit. This is going to take some time to explain."

Henry said, "I'll get the coffee, Eric." He headed for a door at the opposite end of the room, behind where Eric was sitting when they entered.

When the door closed behind him, Eric spoke. "Why you? Why Henry and me? Before I tell you why let me tell you a story. It's complicated, and I won't be telling you the names of the people involved, but it's a story of patriotism, faith in God, the terror of totalitarianism, and an unshakable belief in what the founders of this nation established back in 1776."

Michael sat down, and Eric continued.

"In the early 1950s in Washington, DC, five people gathered in a hotel room. While this next fact is related to their characters, it's not the most important point: three were Christians and two were Jews. They were wealthy people who wielded great power and influence, but they were virtually unknown to the general public. They preferred to live quietly, exerting their power and influence effectively from behind social, industrial, and political scenes. Each possessed what would be considered sizable wealth for that time." Eric shifted in his chair, leaning forward to look steadily into Michael's eyes.

"These five individuals came together not by chance, but deliberately. They watched the growth of Progressive ideology in America, saw government toy with a number of ill-advised relationships via Congress and the Roosevelt Administration, and raged against the culmination of true evil in Hitler's camps. Traveling in some of the same rarefied circles of influence, they discovered they shared the same values and eventually decided to meet to explore ideas for wielding their power and wealth to halt the country's downward spiral into a liberal utopia."

Michael asked, "So they formed a political lobby? A patriotic think-tank? What?"

"In a sense, both of those, and much more. They were determined to see America remain strong and hold fast to the values and freedoms that made her great. They used their considerable means to form the genesis of what we now call The Movement." He sat back in his chair and made a sweeping gesture with his hand. "Construction of this, their first facility, began during the postwar period when people were building bomb shelters in their backyards because of the nuclear threat from the old Soviet Union."

"How big is this place, and what are these secret locations for?"

"Compounds like this one dot the country. Larger states like Alaska, Texas, California and Montana have more than one such facility, while smaller states may have only one or none at all. We're in the largest of the compounds, and it is positioned to serve the Pennsylvania, New Jersey, Delaware and New York areas. It also serves as a hub where facilitators from all over the nation gather when face-to-face meetings are required and information technology is thought to be too risky to use.

"Our mission is straightforward: to preserve America. To that end, the originators of The Movement and each successive member has followed in the footsteps of the original founders of this great nation. We have pledged our lives, our fortunes and our sacred honor to preserve this nation under God, with liberty and justice for all."

"A noble cause, for sure," Michael nodded, "but why all the secrecy? Why not rally the like-minded publicly to garner support for your cause from the people?"

"Over many decades of deadly determination and seemingly unending patience, progressive spies and ideologues have been able to infiltrate American military, corporations, educational institutions, and even Congress itself, but The Movement has never been compromised. We are the most secret organization in the United States because we have to be. In order to break free of the overwhelming control of Progressives in this country we must rely on the only weapon at our disposal that remains out of their reach." Eric paused, and Michael waited, half expecting that he would not reveal their secret weapon.

"It is simply the element of surprise. As I said, The Movement has never been compromised. This is not said out of conceit; it is said with a deadly determination equal to that of our enemy. We allow no one in this organization that has not first been properly vetted down to the level of their DNA. If someone inside our organization attempted to turn on us, that person, his family, and all of his contacts would simply disappear."

Michael's right hand shot forward to grip the edge of the table so hard his fingertips turned bloodless white. "You mean you have them killed?"

"No," Eric said calmly. "As I said, they disappear. I will not explain what that means at this time. Suffice it to say, they are gone. They will not appear again. Any damage they might have attempted would be eradicated immediately. At the appropriate moment you'll be told what that solution is, and how it's carried out. I believe you'll be satisfied with what you're told."

Michael relaxed his grip on the table and waited for Eric to continue.

"As far as the size and scope of our installations, I cannot tell you now."

"What about weapons? What do you have?"

"Everything the military has is available to us."

"Eric, how is that possible?"

"Michael, you're in military intelligence. Who did you see at this table when you first came here?"

"I saw at least two officers; one was a General…"

"Exactly. We have the necessary resources to do whatever is required."

"Including the possibility of waging war against Americans?" Michael asked quietly. "We answer to the Commander in Chief of the United States. We obey orders. Hell, you obey orders just like I do, Colonel Dryden! When we are commanded how will you answer?"

A long silence lay between the two men. Finally, Eric spoke. "The Progressives have taken control of many of our institutions. They are governing through regulations and marginalizing the power to legislate. They use powerful members of Congress as whipping boys and girls to do their bidding. The press, for the most part, is in their pocket. They will say and do anything to destroy American conservatism. Worst of all, they totally control the White House—"

"But they can be voted out in the next election!" Michael exclaimed. "Let the peaceful process of the American election system work—"

"They will not be stopped at the ballot box. Not now. Not ever."

"You mean the people in this with you are willing to sacrifice American lives in battle to—"

"Yes, that's what I mean. Yes, that is what this is all about if it becomes necessary. Yes, yes, yes, Michael! This is not a game we are engaged in. Our fight is for the continued existence of this country we love and serve.

"I am a colonel in the US Army. We both graduated from West Point. We served in the Gulf War, we serve in other capacities now, and our foremost oath is to the people of this nation. I will never compromise my oath. Never!" Eric pounded a clenched fist hard on the table. "But I will not allow this country to become a socialist-communist utopia in which the federal government dictates every aspect of the lives of my family, my children, and grandchildren. I will die on the steps of the White House itself to ensure that freedom continues for all Americans."

Michael held up a hand, nodding his head. "On these

things we're in total agreement, Eric. But short of a coup, how will members of The Movement rallying in secret—no matter how wealthy or powerful—halt the slide? Americans have too willingly traded freedoms for security for too long. Though misguided in their approach, progressive liberals tout leveling the playing field, making everyone pay their fair share, saving the planet, and the rest as the chief motives behind their political agenda."

"Progressives, Michael, are the most evil people who have ever existed on the face of this earth. Though we call them by other names, Hitler, Stalin and Mao were progressives. Far too many in Congress are progressives. The White House is saturated with Progressives. These ideologues have sought, and continue to seek control of everything. This country could be totally energy independent within a decade or less, but they won't allow it. They play footsie with wackos in Iran, Venezuela, North Korea, and elsewhere, thinking rhetoric alone can placate bastards who want to rule the world for their own perverted reasons. They want your children and grandchildren to know nothing but their so-called benevolence from the cradle-to-the-grave, just as long as they serve as good little members of the Collective."

"Do you really believe they can be forced, militarily or otherwise, to give up that kind of control?"

"Give up? Michael, they'll never give up. They must be removed. They must go away. They must leave America to real Americans who believe in freedom, free enterprise, entrepreneurship, church, synagogue and mosque."

Michael raised a speculative eyebrow.

"Yes, I said mosque!" Eric continued. "Michael, we have religious tolerance and freedom here. Muslims are welcome here, but so are Jews, Hindus, Christians and members of every other faith, along with those who don't even believe in God. We have freedom of religion, not freedom from it!"

"It's worth noting," Michael pointed out, "that it wasn't a gang of Methodists, Baptists or Episcopalians who ran those airplanes into the Twin Towers, the Pentagon, and that Pennsylvania field on 9/11. It was radical Islamic fundamentalists. However, I agree, Muslims are free to worship here as long as they leave everyone else the hell alone!"

"Amen, brother! But that's another issue for another time. Our bigger problem is the Progressives. That's why Henry brought you here. We'd like you to join us. We have a job to do, and we have a job for you when the dust settles and the battle is over."

"I'm yet to be convinced that you're on the right track," Michael said, holding up his hand. "What's the job?"

"President of the United States!" The silence in the room went on for a long time.

CHAPTER 9

As Special Assistant to the President of the United States, Robert Hoopes had access. In Washington, access was everything. It opened doors, got responses, greased the rails of progress, smoothed ruffled feathers, helped to reassure patrons, and put stars in the eyes of interns.

According to the tabloids, Hoopes was hot. A bachelor and a Harvard man of considerable wealth, he also played a mean game of tennis, and his blond good looks were enough to make female reporters gush and ubiquitous interns swoon.

The problem with Robert Hoopes was that it was all a sham. He was an elitist and a progressive to the core. He hated Jews and Christians alike, and he, himself did not believe in any god. He was addicted to sexual conquest and overly fond of expensive Scotch.

Hoopes also detested the military to the point of physically avoiding contact with uniformed personnel on duty in the White House. He would walk on the opposite side of a corridor, or turn around in hallways if someone in uniform was walking towards him. He would duck into offices that weren't his until the offending party passed by, and then re-enter the hallway and continue on his way.

His strange behavior did not go unnoticed, but as administrations changed from one to another over the years, old hands accepted psychological aberrations in the denizens who came to work there every four to eight years. Hoopes was mild compared to some of the eccentrics who graced the presidential mansion.

He was uncomfortable around military people for two reasons. First, he knew instinctively that he lacked the capacity to be one of them. He was all show and no substance. He was not brave in any sense, although he possessed a strong sense of self-preservation and would have done his best to defend himself in a fight. He studied Taekwondo in high school and college, but he had done so primarily to impress a couple of girls he dated back then.

The second reason for his aversion was that his older brother Steven was an Air Force captain. He hated Steven more than anyone else in the world. The amazing thing was that Steven was oblivious to the enmity his younger brother felt for him. Their father, The Honorable Judge Randall A. Hoopes favored his eldest son in all things and on all levels while they were growing up. Since their father always made Steven the center of attention, Robert was an afterthought in any family gathering. Over the years he'd built up a mountain of misplaced resentment and hatred toward Steven.

Now, Hoopes was in his glory. He positioned himself carefully to come to the White House with this administration. He had access. He had power. He could make things happen. He could have all the women he wanted. There wasn't much not to like, except the one problem with having such a position; he was actually required to work. He hated working, but he loved the rush of ordering others to do his bidding. In a perfect world he would have been able to sit in his office all day playing video games on his computer, go out for drinks at the end of the day, and end the evening in the arms of yet another intern. Unfortunately his job demanded he work long hard hours to stay ahead of the next scandal and on the right side of the next political power broker.

Now, the biggest problem on his desk was the damned senator

from Illinois, who wasn't playing fair. He expected too much for his vote on the next stimulus package. The idiot didn't understand that the real intention of the bill was to further bankrupt the US, not bolster any possibility of economic recovery. The goal was to drive America over the edge and secure absolute power for generations to come through bailouts, handouts, draw downs, and any other means tool that could be used to whittle away at the average citizen's resolve to live outside of government control.

A small smile played around his lips. What a devious and delightful scheme, he mused. The bankrupting of the nation would come through the hated health care bill, stimulus package upon stimulus package, nationalizing the finance, banking and auto industries. He nearly laughed out loud at the thought of sticking a liberal finger in the collective eye of Americans everywhere.

The assholes who weren't smart enough to go to college, who got their hands dirty every day, who worked for a living, were a joke. He traced the letters of the shiny brass name plate on his desk that spelled out *Robert Hoopes,* and cast a prideful glance at the title, *Special Assistant to the President* on his fine White House stationery. Yes, the masses of laboring Americans would answer someday to him and to the others in ways they couldn't even imagine.

To Hoopes, average Americans were nothing but serfs. He wished he could have been a knight, or maybe even a duke or an earl in the days of Feudal Europe. He would have ridden down the masses with his men and horses. A fleeting thought of the senator jerked him from his fantasy. The man was a problem.

The phone on his desk binged softly and he picked it up.

His secretary Helen's voice floated over the line. "There's a Mr. Clark on the phone for you. He says you'll know what it's about. Do you want to take the call?"

"Yes, yes. I'll take it."

"Greetings, Mr. Hoopes," a voice said.

"Get to the point." Hoopes ordered, disgusted by the caller's overly familiar tone.

The voice changed, instantly sounding rigid and unfriendly.

"The subject thought that he would not get caught in, shall we say, a compromised position. He was wrong. He was home on a campaign trip last week, and while his wife went off to see her mother, the subject visited a particular motel that evening. We have pictures."

"Are they good pictures?" Hoopes leaned forward in his chair.

"I believe you'll find them stimulating," the voice said.

"Thank you. Someone will pick them up at your location within the hour. The courier will have an envelope for you. Goodbye."

Hoopes was nearly giddy with excitement. The senator from Illinois would no longer be a problem. The good senator was about to be stimulated on behalf of the stimulus. He laughed inwardly at his pun. It was going to be a glorious afternoon and evening. He smiled and picked up the phone. His president was waiting for good news. It was his task to make him happy.

CHAPTER   10

"President! You've got to be kidding. There are millions of people far more qualified for that job than I will ever be." Michael said.

"You are wrong in that assumption." Eric said. "The problem we have is that there are moral cretins all around us who run for office at local, state and national levels. They want the office because they want power over others. We no longer need people who want to run for office. Those days are gone forever. We are precisely where we are because Progressives have entered the ranks, positioned themselves, and won the highest offices in the land."

The two men faced each other across the table in the brightly lit room. Henry returned with coffee. A tray with cups, sugar, and spoons sat untouched between Michael and Eric.

"Michael," Eric continued, "we need people, men and women, who represent the very best we have among us. I know your soul, my friend. I trust you with my life. I trust the lives of my wife and children with you. I trust you with the lives of Americans everywhere." He raised a hand to silence Michael's attempt at protest. "You are the most extraordinary man I've ever met in my life. I know everything about you that one man can know about another. Henry thinks you're the—the word he uses is *spookiest*—man who has ever walked on this earth."

"He's my brother. He's biased."

"Perhaps, but what he means is that you move forward with total purpose. You don't waste your efforts. You think through things, plan carefully, allow for all contingencies, and execute flawlessly. You rarely change course because you spend so much time evaluating where you need to go that when you do commit the outcome is almost certain. Your work at the Pentagon is the stuff of legends."

"How would you know about my work?" Michael demanded.

"Your work makes my work possible. My section could not function without your work."

"What do you do, Eric?"

"If I tell you I have to kill you." He smiled and sat back in his chair, clearly enjoying the chance to lighten the interaction.

"At this point I'd like to see you try." Michael said, smiling as well. "You've put a hell of a lot on my plate. I still don't know why you would even suggest that I play such a role, that is, if you can convince me it's necessary."

Eric's face was again serious. "The models have been run in our super computers. Your name ranked among our top five choices. We don't leave things to chance here. We can't afford to make mistakes. We'll only have one chance to do this right because if we screw it up it will be the end of our nation. Look, this is the first of many conversations." He shrugged. "There are no decisions to be made today. The changes we have to make will be made, but I cannot tell you what the time frame is because your participation will have to be set before we go too much further."

"If I'm in the top five, why don't you pick one of the other people? It sounds like the others are qualified," Michael said.

"You don't understand. Yes, there are five in the final group. You might find it interesting that when this search began there were almost 35,000 people in the first pool. The search went on for eighteen months. People fell by the wayside as we entered more and more qualifying criteria into the database. We were searching for as close to perfect as we could find. Computers are amazing machines when you put the right data in."

Eric nodded, and went on. "Yes, you're in the top five. In fact, you're the number one choice of the five. You outdistanced your closest competitor by over a thousand basis points in our model. We'll never choose second best, not when it comes to our country. We arrived at our choice a little over a year ago. It took a year to get Henry inside and convinced of our reality. Henry was the key to bringing you here. I could have done it myself, but blood is normally thicker than water."

"Did you brainwash Henry?"

"He's your brother, Michael. What do you think?"

"No, I don't think anyone could do that. Henry pretends, at times, to not be that swift mentally. It's all an act. He likes small town USA, and he never wanted to get a college degree. He's good with his hands, strong as an ox, loyal beyond fault, faithful to his family and friends, and a Marine. He believes in Semper Fi. He's every bit as bright as I will ever hope to be. Had he been motivated to go to a service academy, any of them, he would have finished at the top. One thing you'd better never do is underestimate the abilities and intelligence of Henry Stonebreaker."

"I'll remember that."

"So, where are we, Eric? Where do we go from here?"

"If I can inject another bit of humor into this, the fat lady has yet to sing. We'll know when she's ready to mount the stage, and that is the moment when it all comes together. We will move swiftly. It will be with such force and resolution that there will be little time for our enemy to react. What comes after is what will be problematic."

"Why?"

"When you take the bennies away from people, and the checks and free hand-outs aren't flowing, you can expect resistance. Major cities and urban areas could become war zones, albeit, briefly. Right wing militias, would-be Nazi's, skinheads, and other wackos may decide to attack police, and take over towns and other areas in the process. Universities and colleges could become centers for riots and civil unrest stirred up by activists who always hang around academia eager to foment revolution. Many of them are at the front of the classroom spouting Marxist-Leninist doctrine daily."

He reached for the coffee cup nearest him. "People are going to have to work in order to eat. It will be a new experience for some. When it's over the states rule themselves again. The federal government, as we know it, will be reduced to funding the military and protecting the nation and its borders. That's all, and that's enough."

Michael took a sip of hot strong coffee from his own cup. "What about the congress? Surely you don't think you can get that bunch to agree with your plan?"

"While we were searching for you, we also looked for the right people to serve in congress. I mentioned the 35,000 earlier. We've identified them, as well. Five hundred and thirty-five new people will be ready when called upon. There will be term limits: six years in the Senate, four years in the House. No repeats. No empire-building. No more earmarks. No more lobbying."

"And the president?" Michael asked.

"As the president you'll stand for election for the second term–and it will be two terms of four years. The Supreme Court term is reduced to one term of eight years. A life time career is out of the question. A Supreme Court justice should not be able to be in power longer than a two-term president."

"What about all the federal government programs and departments? You'll be putting millions of people out of work."

"Not immediately. They will have time to make transitions. There will be incentives for companies to take over what the government is now funding. It is the ruling class who will go away, not the workers. Yes, they'll have to adapt, but a plan will be in place to help them keep their lives going. We have no desire to hurt people. We have every intention to help them."

"It sounds like an impossible job." Michael said.

"Preparation for this began decades ago. The plans are updated every six months to allow for new technology and new modeling. There is never a day we are not planning. The people deserve the best when the madness goes away. We're prepared to supply it."

Henry came back into the room at that moment with a fresh pot of steaming coffee.

"The man of the hour," Michael said.

"You would be wrong, my brother," Henry said.

"Why?"

"That would be you, Mr. President." Henry smiled his slow, lazy smile.

Michael couldn't help it. He laughed. The other two joined him.

A thousand feet above where they sat, snow fell steadily in the woods.

CHAPTER 11

He looked like an American. Medium brown hair, regular facial features, brown eyes, and average height and build made him completely unremarkable. His demeanor would cause people to look through him as he passed on the street.

His passport said that his name was Norman Blesco, that he was born May 14, 1974, and that his home address was in New Brunswick, New Jersey.

He worked for the telephone company as a line and equipment repairman. He was single, and he told people that his parents were retired and living in Florida. He had no siblings and no close friends. He did not drink or smoke, and saw no reason to go to bars. His home was a modest eighty-year-old, two-story, clapboard structure on a nondescript street several blocks from the Rutgers University campus. There was no yard in front, and a postage-stamp-sized patch of dirt at the back of the house bordered an alleyway. The one-car garage at the rear of the property contained an eight-year-old Toyota Corolla.

His real name was not pronounceable in English. His mother was an American who dreamed of liberating oppressed peoples as a global freedom-fighter. She traveled to Jordan intending to help with the Palestinian resistance against Israel. Instead of freeing the masses she got pregnant. Two months before he was born, Norman's father blew himself up trying to wire a bomb into a vest. His mother left her infant son with his father's family in hopes of finding a Socialist utopia in the crumbling Soviet Union.

The child was raised as a Muslim, but he was treated harshly because his father was dead and his mother was an American. Angry and confused, he sought people on the street who would treat him better. He came to the attention of a man who took him in, showed him kindness, and began to instruct him in the real law. His anger was given a focus, and as a youth he was sent to a private camp where he received specialized training. His superiors were very excited about his progress, and plans were being made for him that would make use of his particularly nondescript American looking features.

He was placed with a group of young men who all grew up in America. They spoke English in the American fashion, and he too, learned how to speak like an American, how to act like an American, and how to be an American. He was a quick study. In a few months no one would ever guess that he was not a native born American.

He was to be a sleeper. Arrangements were made for him to travel to America and land in New York. He was taken under the wing of an Imam in New York City, where he remained for three years. During the day he worked for the local telephone company in his Manhattan neighborhood, and he studied the law at night. All the while preparations were made.

At the end of three years he was moved out of the city to Bayonne, New Jersey, and a year after that to the house in New Brunswick. He'd lived in New Brunswick for one year when the events of 9/11 took place. He was overwhelmed by what happened. He was so keyed up that his boss, thinking that Norman was distraught because of the news, sent him home for the rest of the day. It was not grief and horror, but joy and envy that filled Norman's heart. The thought that his brothers accomplished such a thing in New York and Washington filled him with pride. They died so nobly and accomplished so much.

He envied them.

He even dreamed that he was on one of the planes. At impact he saw the smiling faces of his comrades around him. His joy was so heady he felt like dancing.

Aside from the intoxicating excitement of the dream in private, Norman controlled his emotions outwardly. His day was coming. The money, time, and effort invested in training him were significant. He would act in concert with other sleepers who were already in place. He did not work for the telephone company by accident.

Citations showed that he was an outstanding employee. He knew systems, equipment, and was skilled at repairing the most difficult problems. He also knew how to destroy in ways that were not easily reparable. Norman Blesco was dangerous in ways no one imagined, and he would be a sword in the hand of Allah when the time came.

CHAPTER 12

Michael opened his eyes after a fitful night's sleep. He was still groggy, despite a night spent in a well appointed hotel suite inside The Movement's headquarters. He still wasn't used to the idea that they were so far inside a mountain, and presumably, underground.

He and Henry arrived yesterday, and after they'd entered the house and cleared several security check points with palm and retina scanners, a guard led them down a hallway and through a set of wooden double doors. The doors opened on a wider, more brightly lit corridor, and a second set of doors which stood closed at the opposite end of the passage. These were made of steel and led to a cavernous hangar that seemed to Michael to be a sort of transport hub. They boarded a tram which carried them deep into the mountain and underground through a tunnel. Blasted from the rock, its walls stretched ahead of them on either side and above their heads.

Eventually the tunnel widened and branched off to the left. The tram driver followed the branch for some time until they reached an opening in the rock. Once through the opening, Michael was stunned at what he saw. The road they were on ran along a high ledge. The tunnel's ceiling rose high above them, and on their right and below he saw what could only be described as a bustling city. He studied it as they descended a gentle slope that led down into its streets.

He couldn't help thinking the cost to build this place must have been astronomical. This was no fly-by-night militia group hiding in the Montana hills. He looked back and saw a massive blast door being lowered into the opening the tram had come through. These people are serious, he thought. He began to wonder just how much they were capable of. The thought unsettled him.

At the bottom of the incline they drove into the city on a broad avenue that was four lanes across, and Michael noticed that the side streets were equally wide. The city planners even thought to counter the claustrophobic effect of being in a cavern. The tallest buildings looked to him to be about six stories high, but the view overhead was the true marvel. Some genius created a visually stunning replica of open blue sky with white puffy clouds floating above. The sight nearly took Michael's breath away. The incredible display of technology ratcheted his regard for The Movement's technological capabilities up another notch. These people seemed to have enough money and creativity to do whatever they wanted.

The tram traveled farther into the underground city where people walked along sidewalks looking in shop windows and dined at cafe tables outside restaurants. Great care and attention had been given to every detail, including the need for living plants. Landscaped trees stood along the sidewalks and colorful flowers spilled out from planter boxes beneath street lights.

Michael turned in his seat to find Henry smiling at him. "Incredible isn't it?"

"Yes, it is." Michael nodded. "I've never seen anything like this in my life. Henry, people could live here all the time."

"Some do. There are people here who haven't been to the surface in years. They prefer it here. I must admit I find that a bit strange," he shrugged, "but to each his own. We're quite a ways down," he went on, "so day and night are simulated to allow plants to grow, and for people to move between here and the world above without suffering any adverse effects." Parks with gardens and gazebos dotted their route, rising up between street with rows of buildings made of wood, glass, and stone.

"Where are we going?"

"Right now, we're heading for the hotel. Get some rest tonight. In the morning we'll visit the Truman Administration Building. It's that huge silvery hexagon in the center of the city. Reminds me a little of Epcot at Disney World," Henry said.

"Truman? You mean Harry Truman? Did he know about this place?"

"Yes, he did. So did Ike. The last president who knew about it was Jack Kennedy. Of course, it didn't look like this back then. Everything you see here has been constructed since 1982. Most of it was built in the 90's."

"How much money did all of this cost?" Michael asked.

"Vast amounts of money. Since the 1950s the founders and those who followed have wisely pursued investments that have grown in value. The harvest of money began in 1982 and has continued to this day for maintenance and upgrades. You're looking at billions of dollars."

"I can believe it."

"This is only part of it," Henry said. "Beyond this central cavern there are thousands of acres of underground storage areas, military complexes, and weapons caches. Hangars with airplanes and helicopters, state-of-the-art medical facilities, and libraries have been built to accommodate the city's needs. There are enough general supplies, food and water stores to last a couple hundred years."

The look on Michael's face made Henry laugh out loud. "Gotcha, bro! Yes, sir, I gotcha!" He slapped his knee. "How's that for something impressive? Here you thought your baby brother could never surprise you, but I think I just did! So, what do you think of that, Major Stonebreaker?"

Michael was speechless. "Thousands of acres?"

"At more than a thousand feet below ground. The exact distance is classified." Henry smiled. "Everything here is perfectly controlled, and only those in The Movement know about it," Henry added, still smiling.

"But, the light?...The power?...How do they...?"

"A nuclear reactor, among other things. Listen, Michael, I know this is all new to you. I felt the same way you did when I first saw it. The word is overwhelmed! These folks are for real. As Eric said, this isn't a game. This is the real deal."

"But, Henry, why is there so much here? What are they planning for? What do they think is going to happen?"

"I don't have those answers, but I am a member of this community. I'm committed to it. The Movement is on the move, and I'm with it all the way to the end. When you're ready, you'll be given the answers you need."

The tram came to a halt outside the canopied entrance of a beautiful glass and stone fronted building.

"We're here. We'll have dinner in the hotel restaurant, and then I suggest you get a good night's sleep for tomorrow." Henry stepped from the tram and held the door open for Michael. "If you think what you've seen so far is impressive, just wait."

That was last night. Compared to what he'd already seen, Michael wondered how The Movement could possibly have anything more impressive in store.

CHAPTER   13

The esteemed Senator from Illinois was steamed. He was as mad as hell, but there was nothing he could do about it. His conversation with the President's assistant over lunch earlier that day left him with more than heartburn.

He loathed Robert Hoopes. He would have liked nothing better than to have taken a two-by-four to the man's head and splattered his brains all over the restaurant's floor. *Bet people would have lost their lunch at that one.* He was forced to sit there and take it from an S. O. B. who amounted to little more than human scum in a thousand-dollar suit.

Hoopes had been friendly enough at the beginning of the lunch. "I fully understand why you want more in exchange for your vote, but times are tough," he said. "The damn right-wing cable channel is carving us a new one every day, and we can't risk loading the new stimulus bill up with any more earmarks."

The Senator tried to play hardball. He insisted on a public works earmark that would have lined the pockets of everyone he knew along Lake Michigan. "I absolutely must have the public works project, or I cannot, in good conscience, vote in favor of the bill."

That's when it got ugly. Hoopes removed a 9x12 envelope from his briefcase and slid it across the table. He smiled at the Senator. "We really need your vote. In fact, we have to have it. What's in the envelope is for your eyes only. Look at the material carefully. We have copies of everything—to protect everyone involved."

When the Senator saw the first photograph he practically choked on his breadstick. His face grew bright red. The vein in his right temple started throbbing.

He looked across the table at the smiling face and wanted to stand up and smash his fist into it. He took a deep breath, pushed the photos back into the envelope, and slid it back across the table.

"You know, there was a time not many years ago when I would have taken you outside and beaten the living hell out of you, Mr. Hoopes. I work out every day—I still could. You were never in the military. I know. I've looked into you, as well. I was a Marine. However, this is a public place and we need to keep things pleasant so as not to make the six o'clock news." The senator took a sip of water from a crystal water goblet and let the icy liquid calm him. He sighed and continued, "People like you crawl out from under rocks and slither into this town with every administration. You're just another in a long line of spineless creatures who think you have what it takes to run a country. Well, you can go back and tell your boss that I will vote for the bill against my better judgment." He leaned forward, his voice low and steady.

"Now, a word of caution. Beware of old dogs, Mr. Hoopes. Beware of crossing men who have been in this game for as long as I have. Watch your back. You never know what's coming your way!" He wiped a corner of his mouth with a white lined napkin. "Of one thing I can assure you. It will be swift, and certain. Good day to you, young sir."

With those words, the senator gathered what was left of his dignity and rose from the table. He left the check for young Mr. Hoopes to pay.

The status of the senator and the Special Assistant to the President allowed for a private table at the restaurant. Robert Hoopes sat alone for a long time after the senator departed. He imagined he would feel a sense of triumph when he revealed the photographs. He engineered the moment and executed it in his mind a hundred times before they met. Instead, he was a little unsettled. It never entered his mind that the S. O. B. would threaten him in return. The man was big, beefy, and too well fed in his estimation. But, he was who he was. Four terms in the Senate no doubt bred confidence. He wondered if the man was capable of carrying out his threat. He mistakenly assumed that members of the House and Senate would be putty in his hands, easily manipulated by someone with his power and influence. In this case, he won the vote, but at what cost?

Soul-searching was not his strong suit. He was ill-equipped to ponder anything that made him uncomfortable for very long.

A dark-haired waiter appeared in the doorway of the private room. "I'll have the check," Hoopes said, looking with disdain. The waiter returned to place the check on the table. With barely a glance at Hoopes he turned and left the room.

Instead of using his credit card, Hoopes put cash on the table. He did not include a tip. He left the room in a rush and escaped to the parking lot where his driver was waiting for him. During the drive back to his office he allowed his mind to drift to more pleasant things. He was going to fire his secretary and replace her with someone who was more attractive. He savored the thought.

✶✶✶✶✶✶

The Senator returned to his office, told his secretary to hold his calls for the next half hour, closed and locked his door and sat behind his desk. He could not remember the last time he'd been so angry. He was beyond rage. Almost from the outset of his long and distinguished career, he practiced a motto he learned from a colleague in the Senate. Don't get mad—get even. He'd even had it engraved on brass and mounted on a polished piece of mahogany that sat on the credenza behind his desk. He swung his chair around and stared at the words for a moment.

In twenty-three years in this office he'd seen them come and go. His own reputation was that of a fixer who could get things done. He chaired two important committees and served as vice-chair on two others. No one messed with him. His friends and enemies lived on both sides of the political aisle, but no one ever dared treat him with such disrespect as young Mr. Hoopes had done.

The contents of the envelope flashed across his mind. He loved his wife Mary, and his dalliances with the other love in his life should not have been committed to film. In times past merely hinting of knowledge of his extra-marital activities would have sufficed to secure his cooperation. These people in the White House represented a new breed of ruthlessness. They would stop at nothing to get what they wanted.

How would he get even?

He sat quietly looking out the window. Ten minutes slipped by. He made a decision. He unlocked a bottom drawer in his desk, and removed a small cardboard box from it. At one time the box held business cards. He opened it, and a small white envelope lay inside. He lifted the envelope and removed the single sheet of folded paper it contained. The paper was yellowed with age. He unfolded it and read a neatly printed telephone number.

He fished a disposable cell phone from another of his desk drawers. *One can never be too careful,* he thought. He dialed the number.

"Yes?"

"It's lovely on the Potomac.

The answer came back, "It is also lovely on the Gulf."

"I have a problem."

"Problems can be solved in many ways," the voice said.

The senator explained about young Mr. Hoopes. "I need to know everything about him. If he cheated in school, if he ever got a girl pregnant, everything he has ever done wrong…a complete dossier." He hesitated.

"And?"

"I lost my head and warned him to look over his shoulder. I should have remained silent. So, give it a year to eighteen months. When the dossier is ready, send it to me via secure courier." He drummed lightly on his desk with his fingers.

"Once I've seen the dossier I will call you to set things in motion. It must be brutal, painful, terrifying, and he should disappear."

"Does any individual warrant such anger?"

"You've done more for much less."

"We are even, then. I return service for service rendered. I thank you for your kindness in the past."

The Senator responded. "You are most gracious. I thank you in return. The Potomac is lovely in all seasons."

"So is the Gulf. Goodbye."

The senator helped the person on the other end of the phone out of a jam nearly twenty years ago. It had been a difficult and costly exercise, but it had been done to the man's complete satisfaction. He'd seen the truth of what the man needed, and he was uniquely positioned to help him. It was handled with discretion. No one would ever know he'd sold his soul to buy the favor.

Now, his would be returned. He smiled. *Robert Hoopes,* he thought, *inescapable ruin will come upon you when you least expect it. Revenge is sweet.*

The telephone on his desk sounded a musical note. Time to get back to work.

CHAPTER   14

They entered the polished metal and glass structure, which proved to be as spectacular inside as it was from the street. An enormous American flag dominated the lobby, hanging a full six stories from the open ceiling above. Behind it a bank of scenic glass elevators rose and fell soundlessly between floors. A curved wall of one-way glass occupied a full quarter of the circular building, extending from the second floor to the roof. Henry led Michael past the flag to one of the elevators. The transparent car afforded an exquisite view of the colors of the flag reflected in the smooth glass wall.

When they reached the second level, Michael followed Henry off the elevator and to the right along the curve of the building. They followed a path of gleaming white tile and walls lined with framed images from American history. Sets of polished steel six-panel doors were spaced evenly along the hall, behind which Michael assumed were offices. A quarter of the way around the building Henry stopped outside one of them.

"Michael, as I said, there is more to see and learn. However, what is about to happen now is extraordinary for other reasons. When we walk through this doorway everything in your life will change forever. I'm not saying this to frighten you. Frankly, I know there's not too much that would." He smiled. "I asked you to wear your full-dress uniform today for a reason. Eric and I have talked about this moment for months, and we could think of no better way to handle this point in the learning process."

"I have one thing to say before we go through this door..." Henry reached out with his right hand, but then gave his brother a quick hug instead. He stepped back. "I love you, Michael," he said, his voice full of emotion. "You're my brother now and forever, but after today I'm going to have to share you with the world."

Tears spring to Michael's eyes as Henry spoke. He took a deep breath. "Whatever this is, I'm glad you're here with me, Henry. Let's do this together."

Henry opened the door to a wide well-lit hallway that ended in a second door. Henry opened it, letting them into a space at the right of a massive stage bordered by a waist-high glass barrier. The stage opened onto the lobby at the center of the building. From where they stood, Michael could see a dozen people sitting center-stage behind a long rectangular table. Eric, wearing his full-dress uniform, commanded a podium in front of the table. To his left, the six-story American flag hung in the open lobby. He smiled. Michael and Henry stepped onto the stage, and Michael was overwhelmed by what he saw.

Across the lobby, the darkened glass panels had been retracted to reveal tiers of seats rising from the second story to the sixth. The building seemed to have magically transformed into an enormous amphitheater. Every seat in every tier was occupied; the air was electrified with anticipation.

Eric addressed the waiting audience. "Ladies and gentlemen, it is with the greatest pleasure that I present to you the next President of the United States, Mr. Brown."

The crowd surged to its feet, roaring its approval. Michael was stunned. He felt the reassuring pressure of Henry's strong hand on his shoulder. Great cheers, whistles, and shouts went on and on, sending Michael's mind reeling. This was the last thing he'd ever expected to happen in his life. He liked his job. He loved his family and his country. He served them faithfully. He believed utterly and with total conviction in God. Nothing prepared him for this moment. He stood, overwhelmed by the ovation.

As the crowd began to quiet, Eric raised his right hand and then lowered it over his heart. "Please, join me everyone." Everyone fixed their eyes on the American flag, and Eric led them in reciting the oath.

"I pledge allegiance to the Flag of the United States of America, and to the republic for which it stands, one Nation, under God, indivisible, with liberty and justice for all."

At the conclusion of the pledge, Eric introduced the three gentlemen who would address the assembly next. "It is my great privilege to invite three highly esteemed members of the clergy to usher in this momentous occasion with words to stir our hearts, reminding us of our history and our God." The three men crossed the stage opposite Michael and Henry and approached the podium. "Please welcome Bishop Anthony Rosario, Rabbi Abram Goldman, and Reverend Hugh Gibson," Eric said.

The audience erupted in thunderous applause. When the ovation died down, Rabbi Goldman read from the Declaration of Independence, emphasizing every human being's God-given rights, government based on the consent of the governed, and the responsibility of legitimate government to secure those rights. He concluded his remarks with a prayer that the new government would be committed to this purpose. Bishop Rosario next quoted from Thomas Jefferson's letter to the Danbury Baptist Association of Connecticut and his words from the Virginia Statute of Religious Freedom on the matter of separation of church and state at the federal level. Bishop Rosario also concluded his remarks with a prayer for piety and the peaceful co-existence of religion in the nation. Last, Reverend Gibson read part of George Washington's farewell address, encouraging national unity and commitment to the existence of the United States as a sovereign and independent nation. He too, ended with a prayer, asking God to right the course of the nation for the benefit of mankind.

A standing ovation ensued as the three men shook hands and left the stage. Eric returned to the podium.

Colonel Eric Dryden stood shoulder to shoulder with Michael Stonebreaker at roughly six-foot-four. His movie-star good looks and gleaming smile dazzled people, but his honest warmth and charm made everyone feel welcome. Ambition and a fine mind earned him West Point credentials and a respected career in the Army.

He spoke at length about their search for a new leader, the criteria that were used, and about how the final choice came down to five people. Then, with genuine affection, he turned to Michael and placed his left hand on his shoulder.

"Michael Stonebreaker is an extraordinary man, something I learned the very first time we met." Eric relayed how he'd first met and competed against Michael at a high school track meet. "Michael's uncompromising character and strength are only two of the reasons he is the first choice candidate to emerge from our extensive selection process.

"I had no idea that the friend of my youth, as impressive as he was to me and everyone present on that day, would be chosen for such a time and circumstance as we face in this country right now. The founders of this nation were men of vision who pledged their lives, reputations, and all they owned to fulfill the dream of a free land—one where all men would be acknowledged as equal, and equally endowed by Almighty God with the right to life, liberty, and the pursuit of happiness. Slavery soiled that dream, and the Civil War nearly destroyed it, but, by the grace of God, The Great American Experiment survived and went on to become a beacon of light and freedom in the world.

"That dream is being threatened again, by people who are determined to pull down our institutions, obliterate our principles and values, and enslave us and our children in a progressive-socialist dystopia in which they rule every aspect of our lives. Today, the reality is, if the Progressives are allowed to pursue their agenda unchecked, we all face the ultimate form of slavery.

"If you'll allow me to digress for just a moment, my grandfather fought in World War I, and my father is a veteran of the war in Viet Nam. Both men fought with a singular objective in mind—to win. Have you ever wondered why, after decades of the government fighting the war on poverty, African-Americans are still largely at the bottom of the economic barrel? Yet nearly every black liberal declaring the United States of America a racist country does so from a platform of free speech guaranteed by the First Amendment and wealth secured in a color-blind free market economy. They've benefited from access to educational opportunities our ancestors dreamed of, and often fought and died to secure, hoping their descendants would prove that ultimately, The Great American Experiment was a success for all people, without regard to race, religion, or creed. And so, more than two hundred years after the founding of this great country, we've come to the need for a second revolution." The crowd was instantly on its feet, applauding and shouting approval.

"We cannot allow our collective dream of freedom to die at the hands of Progressives whose goal is to control not just our bodies, as in times past, but our very thoughts. We must win this new battle for freedom. We have come full circle. We must fully and finally establish these United States of America, founded upon Godly principles, as the last best hope of this world.

"Ladies and gentlemen, fellow Americans all, I'm proud to present to you the man we have chosen to lead us in The Revolution 2.0...a man who I dearly pray will accept the challenge to serve as our next President, Mr. Brown."

The crowd stood on its feet. Applause and a roar of enthusiasm greeted Michael as he stepped to the podium. Like sentinels, Henry and Eric stood on either side behind him.

In contrast to Eric's handsomeness, Michael was what women would call a "nice looking man." He wasn't flashy, but there was a steadiness in him that was calming to those around him. It was what happened when he opened his mouth and spoke that set him apart from others.

The Old Man, his grandfather, had been a man of few words. He, too, was someone others looked up to for his quiet observations and intelligent approach to solving problems. Michael was like him, introspective, extremely intelligent and fair-minded. He took pains to be considerate of the opinions and feelings of others.

At the podium, he took a deep breath and smiled. "We've got to stop meeting like this…" Laughter rose up from the crowd. "We won't get anything done if all we do is have meetings. I do not know how to tell you this except to say it. Honesty is what we need. I am a career officer in the United States Army. I work at the Pentagon. My life is an open book. As thorough as you folks apparently are, I'm sure you realize that anything you want to know about me can be readily found out.

"I'm generally not much for small talk, and I would rather be at home with my family than out at a party. The Pittsburgh Steelers and the Pirates are my teams. I enjoy hunting, fishing, and sports in general; but I do realize that as president I might have to spend a little less time on those things." At this, the audience's wave of laughter morphed into a standing ovation. "I've kept my political opinions to myself all my life. I believe in God, and attend church regularly. By today's standards I'm sure I'd be considered quite dull—but I judge myself by a higher standard."

"Do I have thoughts and opinions on all sorts of things, like you all must have? Yes. Does that make me an expert? No. A man I worked with years ago used to say, 'An "ex" is a has-been, and a "spert" is a drip under pressure.'" Laughter rippled around the room.

"To say that I am stunned that this place and you exist is to put it mildly. I'm still trying to grasp what all this means. What it appears to mean is that in The Revolution 2.0, you have created a plan to return this country to the principles and values upon which it was founded, but with the benefit of the clear vision afforded by historical hindsight." The audience erupted in applause.

"However, being the suspicious type—one cannot work in intelligence and ignore the often devious motivations behind much of human behavior—I am not prone to make decisions without due deliberation. I do not act on assumptions without irrefutable proof.

"That said, you must also know that I am not a big talker. I'd rather be doing than speaking. Both of us, you and I, deserve the best we can give to each other. In fairness to you, I'm willing to take the time to learn why all of you find this necessary." He gestured, encompassing the room with an outstretched arm. "I'm convinced of your sincerity, and this place is certainly a testament to an incredible commitment of money, time, planning and dedication on your part and that of the members who've gone before you.

"I cannot, for the life of me, understand why I was chosen to lead The Revolution 2.0. I know at least fifty other people who would, in my opinion, be better qualified to do it. However, should we come to the place where I agree to accept the responsibility of serving as president, you have my word that I will serve our nation with all that I have to give, so help me God." He nodded to the audience and stepped away from the podium.

The crowd was on its feet whistling, cheering and applauding. Michael had spoken his mind. He would listen, learn, and then decide. As far as he was concerned, The Movement could not reasonably ask for more.

Little did he know, by his reluctance to assume the mantle of power, Michael embodied the spirit of the man who led the first American Revolution. Now more than ever, the members of The Movement were convinced; Michael Stonebreaker was the man to lead the nation back into the light.

CHAPTER 15

The knock on his door came at a few minutes past 11:00. The insistent tapping startled him, and he reached for the remote to turn down the late night news. His stomach knotted. *Who would visit his home at such an hour?*

Norman Blesco got up from the sofa in his sparsely furnished living room, and crept to the front door. He turned on the porch light and, peered through the glass. The knot of fear in his stomach grew tighter. Very near his window, he saw the distorted shape of a man standing outside.

"Yes, who is it?

"The ship has sailed." The response came in heavily accented English.

Norman recalled the training he received years before.

"I wish you safe passage," he said.

"Praise to Allah," the man responded.

"Yes, praise him, my brother."

Norman slid back the deadbolt and opened the door. A man in a tan windbreaker, red scarf, dark trousers, and a dark knit cap quickly stepped into the room. Norman closed the door behind him. The man removed his cap. He appeared to Norman to be in his twenties, with thick dark hair and eyebrows.

Norman reached out in the American fashion and shook the man's hand.

"Norman Blesco."

"I am Ishmael," the man said in response. He did not smile.

"No last name?" Norman asked.

"Last names are unnecessary. Time grows short. The hammer of Allah is about to fall. I've come to provide you with what is required."

Norman felt both excitement and fear at the man's words. "When will it be?"

Ishmael handed him a thick manila envelope. "Everything is in there. Read it. There are copies of each page. Read all of it. Memorize everything. Burn the originals. Clip the copies together. Place them back in the envelope. Do you have the computer?"

"Yes, I purchased the laptop six months ago, as instructed."

"Here is a key to a locker in New York. Take the envelope to the address you find inside. You'll find lockers there. When you open the locker there will be a set of DVD's in an envelope for your computer. Leave the envelope in the locker. We'll retrieve it. Do you understand?"

"Yes," Norman said. "When should I go to New York?"

"Saturday." The man replaced his cap and moved toward the door. "I must leave now. We'll not see each other again. May Allah bless you my brother."

"May he guide your steps," Norman said in return.

Ishmael left as quickly as he had arrived.

Norman glanced at his watch. It was 11:15 p.m. He went back to his sofa, turned off the TV, and opened the envelope.

He read through the entire contents of the package three times. Along with detailed instructions, the envelope contained tickets for two one-way flights dated three weeks apart, a stack of twenty-dollar bills totaling $5,000 in cash, and a complete set of communication schematics for the target. He also found an architectural blueprint with four different escape routes traced in red.

The scope of the plan nearly overwhelmed him. The attack

would dwarf those on 9/11. He was certain all the training and the years of waiting had been worth it. Only one only thing disappointed him. He was not being asked to give his life in the mission. He assumed that meant their were plans for him in the future. Nevertheless, it was the will of Allah. He said a special prayer of thanks.

He would enjoy every minute of the part he would play in killing tens of thousands of the infidels! He was going to Disney World. *Soon to become the unhappiest place on earth.* He relished the thought.

CHAPTER 16

As the audience of thousands filed out of the theater, Eric introduced Michael to the people sitting at the table on stage behind him. One of them was the general who greeted him in the board room on his first visit. According to their code of anonymity, he was identified simply as General Cobalt. Michael figured the name was fitting, given the color of the man's Air Force uniform. They chatted for a moment, and General Cobalt told him that he would see him later that day.

Until then, Henry and Eric were to escort Michael on a whirlwind tour of as much of the facility as possible. The day would end around four, so the brothers could keep their promise to be at their mother's for dinner by five.

The Truman building, with its six-story American flag and state-of-the-art amphitheater, was primarily a meeting facility. They visited planning centers, medical facilities, and storage warehouses. Michael recalled the plasma screens in the board room as they toured a massive technology center, where input from cameras all over the country was monitored twenty-four hours a day.

They traveled by tram, barely stopping for a boxed lunch between visits to one of the training centers and a residential area a few blocks off the broad street that ran through the center of the compound. Michael was amazed at its size, and potential capabilities.

After lunch they headed to the airport for a one o'clock meeting with General Cobalt. To Michael, the airport seemed to house everything needed to wage an aerial war. Pilots and maintenance crew busied about a collection of fighter jets, helicopters, and other aircraft. They toured construction and repair facilities, along with a control center outfitted with radar and stealth tracking technology. The fact that the airport was underground was not lost on Michael. "How does all this get to the surface for flying?" Michael asked the general.

"Good question. We can get any of these aircraft to the surface in less than three minutes using a portable lift system. If you look closely, you'll see tracks integrated into the hangars, allowing us to position each of the aircraft for transport and lift." He pointed out a section of track. "Once on the surface, we've camouflaged a significant stretch of runway with computer generated images of trees and foliage. We can clear the CGI instantly to allow anything from helicopters to fighter jets to take off."

When they'd completed the tour, they thanked General Cobalt and headed back to The Truman Building.

By three o'clock Eric, Henry, and Michael were back in the board room debriefing over coffee. Michael made a mental note that if he and Henry left at four they would be in Clear Haven in time to make their wives and mother happy.

"So, what do you think now, Michael?" Eric asked.

"Are the other facilities around the country as big as the one here?"

"No, this is the largest. There's a good reason for it. Fully a third of the nation's people live here in the Northeast. Well over half a million people live in Washington, DC, alone. When all of this is activated we'll be moving as fast as we can."

"How many Progressives will be killed in the process?"

Eric was not caught off guard by Michael's bluntness. "The

decision to shed blood is not one we plan to make, except when absolutely necessary."

"Come on Eric! If you really believe that, why do you have an Air Force here, not to mention the combat ready equipment I saw today?" He leaned forward. "How can there be a peaceful overthrow of the US Government? What The Movement is contemplating is not possible."

"Peace in this world comes at a price, Michael. It has been paid in full by the men and women who have served this nation since its creation, and by the families, friends and neighbors who buried them! You've served in war times. You know this stuff as well as I do. Peace isn't something you wake up with each day and assume you're owed, or guaranteed to receive it from some benevolent government."

Michael regarded Eric steadily. "My main concern is the loss of life, civilian as well as those who wear the uniforms. How will you avoid hurting and killing people?"

Eric sighed. "Michael, the military mission was defined long before we came along. It's been established that the military's purpose is to kill people and break things. We're not a troop of Boy Scouts, trained just to help old ladies cross the street. And I mean no disrespect to the 'Scouts.'" Eric waved a hand in the air.

"We have the finest trained military and the best equipment in the world. Yes, when we set this plan in motion, we face the possibility of civilian casualties. There may be rioting in major urban areas that will need to be put down. We're prepared, and we've planned with the expectation that such events will be minimal."

"The political powers that be will not just go quietly into the night," Michael challenged. "How do you plan to deal with their inevitable resistance? Especially if violence ensues?"

"Granted," Eric nodded, agreeing. "The Progressives are another matter. When you commit to take this position you'll see the full operational plan. You'll understand then why this will work. It will be seamless. Everything will go forward at once, including quelling resistance from any quarter. Nothing will be left to chance."

"Eric, you and I know what FUBAR means. Henry's a Marine;

he gets it, too. Things get screwed up. Communication breaks down. Equipment malfunctions. Someone forgets to hit the right key on the keyboard, or gets confused in the field. A million things can go wrong. Murphy's Law never stops working. How can you avoid *coulda-woulda-shoulda* syndrome?"

"You're perfect for the position. One of the reasons you've been chosen for this task is precisely because of what you are doing now, Michael."

"What's that?"

"You question everything, analyze it to make sure it is as flawless as humanly possible, and then execute. You're careful to a fault, and you always consider those who serve under you and alongside you. You're the best leader I ever saw in combat. With the right people around you—and believe me when I say we have the right people— you'll make a wonderful president."

Michael knew Eric well. He knew when he was pulling his leg, and he knew when he was being straight with him. He read the sincerity in the man's eyes, and from what he'd seen this day he knew The Movement was for real.

Regardless of his friend's sincerity, he still needed to know more. Politics wasn't a subject he thought much about. In his line of work, he was far more concerned about what motivated people to strap bombs to themselves and walk into markets, schools, and houses of worship, or fly airplanes into buildings.

He took along breath. "How soon do you need my decision?"

Eric responded without hesitation. "We need it now."

"Can you give me more time?"

"Not much. We need your commitment as soon as possible. You've no idea how much more there is to learn. The preparation you'll be going through is beyond anything you've ever tackled before. It makes West Point look like a cake walk."

"Fair enough. You'll have my decision in two weeks time. I'll call Henry and he can pass my decision through to you."

"How will we understand what you've decided? The information must be coded in some way."

Michael thought for a moment. "If I have decided to accept, the message will be this, 'You only won by an inch and a half. It's my turn.' If I decide to turn you down it will be, 'Keep the record.'"

Eric laughed. "Are you still upset over that? Listen, I was a senior, and you were a junior who'd never heaved a shot put in your life. The odds were stacked against you, man." He looked thoughtful. "The following year you beat my record."

"You know, we never got to match up again." Michael raised an eyebrow.

"Yeah, well you'd probably beat the pants off me now. I've seen your workout. There's no way I'm going to ever pick up a shot put again."

Michael laughed before returning to the question at hand. "Should I decide to join you, there will be conditions on my acceptance."

Eric groaned. "What kind of conditions?"

"Don't worry. They'll be things you and The Movement can live with. I promise you that. It's just that if I accept, I'm going to need certain things."

"Like what?"

"I'll tell you when I decide. Now, we've got to get out of here. There is someone who scares me more than you do."

"Really? Who's that?"

"My mother. We don't dare be late for dinner."

CHAPTER   17

Michael and Joan couldn't decide which crisis posed a greater threat to the US. Was it successive wackos in the Middle East with access to a nuclear reactor, North Korea's maniacal saber rattling, or the bearded-wonders emerging from caves in Afghanistan to mercilessly conduct their jihad? Or was it the politically driven sleight of hand that transformed global warming into climate change due to the lack thereof, or the impoverished billions of the world who were being disenfranchised by dictators, despots, and religious zealots?

"In truth, the Progressives inside America have been pulling it down piece-by-piece, brick-by-brick, and regulation-by-regulation," Micheal continued their conversation. "Our government has become a bunch of elitists. They don't even try to hide their elation over implementing an agenda that has the country going to hell in a handbasket."

Joan nodded. "It's sad to see so many people unemployed and without prospects. But I've read that we're not even getting a true picture of how serious things are. The media, the message, the market, and the masses are ruled by powerful people with a misguided agenda."

"I think you're right on that score, honey. And they would, by-God, have their way with all of it—or rather, by-nothing, because they sure don't believe in God, benevolent or otherwise."

Their day in the sun had been a long time coming. It began in the dim days of the early years of the twentieth century, spread its ideas to Europe and the likes of Marx & Lenin, Joe Stalin, Mao, and ended in the hellish torture and untimely deaths of a hundred million people.

"If the road to hell is paved with good intentions, Pennsylvania Avenue must be ten thousand miles thick," Michael joked, only half kidding.

"Progressives do love to talk about ideas like compassion and charity, helping the poor and minorities, and rescuing the hopeless and illegal immigrants. But that seems to be as far as their good intentions go." Joan swung her legs up onto the couch. "Yep. But they soon get to their real idea of a good time—robbing the rich, the middle-class, and even the poor and then doling out monies with strings attached to those they deem worthy." Michael sat down on the couch next to his wife. "Or anyone owed a payback. Progressives love and worship big government and wielding power over others."

"Michael, where do you think that kind of mindset comes from? I can't for the life of me understand why some people live to control other people's lives!"

"It seems crazy, doesn't it? Maybe most politicians are narcissistic at the core. And Progressives really believe they're superior to everyone else; they cannot abide the average American."

"Well, it sure doesn't stop them for pandering for votes, thank you kindly! *And* taxing everyone near to death!"

"But they will not permit opposition if they can snuff it out. They will not listen to other points of view. What's supposed to be fair and balanced debate turns into shouting and name calling whenever they're confronted with too many facts."

"In many ways they sound more like some second-graders—whining, screaming, and crying, demanding to be heard. I can't stand it when people resort to yelling over each other and refusing to allow anyone who disagrees with them to have a say."

"They seem to operate with the attitude that opponents must be silenced."

Michael and Joan both enjoyed the subject of history, and their conversation turned to discussing the intent of the country's founding documents penned by its forefathers.

In preparing for the role he'd been asked to assume by The Movement, Michael made an exhaustive study of American history. He read traditional and alternative points of view regarding events that shaped the nation. Michael was a voracious reader as a young man, and Joan, too enjoyed reading immensely. They enjoyed sharing ideas gleaned from their pursuits, including how the truth of history was being revised to fit a particular political agenda. Joan worried particularly about the growing instances of misdirection and tap dancing around the truth done by the federal government through the decades.

"A friend of my father's served in Panama during the Vietnam War as a communication specialist," Michael said at one point in their conversation. "Right before he was to go on leave to New York, news of a very nasty battle in Vietnam came through on the military's internal channels. Upwards of fifteen hundred Americans had been killed. The man clearly heard the report in Panama, but by the time he'd got on a plane and landed in New York the American news media was reporting that just five hundred Americans died in the battle."

"Wow!" Joan was incredulous. "I guess lying to the public is nothing new!"

Through his intense study and conversations with his wife, Michael began to see why Eric and Henry joined The Movement. The case they made for being part of such an incredible organization only made more sense as his research went on, but it was ultimately his wife's insight that convinced him of his obligation to join them.

"You know, honey," she said, "I think it's the Progressives who pose the greatest threat to the nation, not only because they hate capitalism and love socialism, but primarily because they are already here." Her eyes were wide and solemn. "They're already inside America doing their dirty work."

Michael nodded. "Indeed, the republic of Rome collapsed from within; if left unchecked, the Progressive movement's agenda could cause the American republic to do the same."

Michael reached his decision. It was time to share his initial dealings with The Movement and their offer with his greatest friend in the world.

Joan Stonebreaker was beautiful in every conceivable way. She was a loving mother to their children, and a fantastic homemaker and cook. Their home was a testimony to her impeccable design skills. She earned a reputation as an excellent, no-nonsense school teacher who was committed to her students' success. Joan was adored by children and adults alike, and yet she was the most grounded and giving person Michael knew. He trusted his wife's judgment completely.

"Hey, why don't we go for a drive?"

"I think I'd like that!" She smiled and stood up, heading for the hall closet. "I'll grab a sweater."

✱✱✱✱✱✱✱

The weather was unusually warm for January. He drove into the city and made his way through the traffic to the Mall. He parked the car and they walked hand-in-hand to the Lincoln Memorial. The statue of the great leader was one of their favorite spots to visit in the nation's capital.

Michael wasted no words. He could not tell Joan about The Movement since he was sworn to silence for the time being; but he told her about his research, and about the unsettling conclusions he'd drawn. "A great change is coming in our nation, sweetheart, and frankly, it's a frightening one."

They sat in silence for a few moments, then Michael asked, "Joanie, what do you think he would have said about all this?" He indicated Lincoln seated above them on his great marble chair.

"Michael, his whole world was torn apart, his nation was in a shambles. He probably spent as much time on his knees as he did standing." She paused, slipping her hand into his. "I think he would have drawn the same conclusions you have. I'm sure that whatever we're facing as a country can be overcome, but only if our people agree on what they need to do."

"Getting people together to agree on anything these days is nearly impossible." Michael's voice hinted at frustration.

"Maybe I teach second graders, but they have more sense at times than the people who work in that building over there." She nodded toward the Capitol. "But you didn't bring me here just to keep talking about the state of the Union." She smiled. "There is something bothering you. I know you can't talk about your work, and I really don't need to know about it because I know you're helping to protect all of us." She sighed. "But something has really gotten to you lately."

"How can you tell?"

"I read you like a book. The girls have been complaining about how distracted you are when they talk to you. And Grover's a mutt, but even he deserves better; it's not like you at all to neglect him."

Grover joined their family five years ago as a pup. Michael always joked that he and the dog needed to stick together as the only males in the house. Grover's funny bark sounded just like that of his fuzzy blue namesake from Sesame Street. Thinking about it, Michael felt bad that he'd been ignoring the people dearest to him and his canine buddy.

"I'm sorry, I've been caught up doing a lot of research lately." He paused, then dove right in. "I've been asked to take a new position."

"You're being promoted?"

"You could put it that way."

"This is wonderful news! When does this happen?"

"It won't be for a while…a few months, perhaps longer."

"But you seem so down about it. Michael, what's wrong?"

"I'll have to leave the military."

Joan's eyes widened and she started to speak twice before finally finding words. "You can't be serious!"

"I'm as serious as Aunt Sally."

Joan laughed. Her Aunt Sally had absolutely no sense of humor.

They were sure she was the only person on the planet born without a funny bone.

Michael sighed. "I'm not sure how I feel about it. It would be a big step for me. I was in for the whole tour. If I accept this job, I'll have to take off the uniform and wear a suit."

"You'll be just as handsome in a suit as you are in your uniform."

"Ah, you say that to all the guys."

"No, just to you. When do you have to decide?"

"Saturday."

"This weekend? Michael, why did you keep this from me? One of the most important decisions in your life and you're telling me three days before you have to decide? That's not fair!"

"Wait, please…don't get mad at me. The offer was made just ten days ago. I was given two weeks to decide, and I needed to do a ton of research to get my head around the idea first."

"Well, have you decided?"

"I couldn't make a decision like this without you. Honestly, I wasn't sure how to even bring it up, but our conversation today seems to have put us in a perfect place for me to tell you as much as I can. Hopefully it will be enough for us to decide together." He held her hand in both of his. "I've made it clear that if I do accept the position, I have some conditions that will have to be met."

"What are they?"

"I can't tell you yet. It's all very hush-hush. It involves national security."

"Can we stay in this area? Do I have to quit my job? Can you tell me that much?"

"The answers are yes, and no."

"Oh, you're impossible!"

"Yes, we'll stay in this area, and no, I don't think you'll have to quit your job."

"What do you mean? That's so indefinite… How can I be certain of anything with answers like that?"

"Dear Joan, I can tell you that one of my conditions is that if you can stay in your job then I'm in. If not, I'm out. That's the only decision I'd make on this before talking with you."

She threw her arms around him and kissed him. "You're so mysterious, Mr. Intelligence! Will you never give me a straight answer to anything?"

Michael looked into her face, and his heart skipped a beat, just like the first time he'd seen her in class all those years ago. "Sweetheart, as soon as it is humanly possible you will be told everything there is to know about this. I promise you." He kissed the tip of her nose. "Now, let's go to Cherry Blossom Drive and park."

"It's January, the blossoms are months away, and I'd rather be home in our nice warm house."

"That can be arranged. Have I ever told you that I love you?"

"Yes, when you want something."

"That's how guys are, sweetheart."

"Guys are often overrated."

"Is it because we're not as smart as women?"

"You're in Intelligence. You figure it out."

✶✶✶✶✶✶

Michael and Joan continued talking the rest of the afternoon and well into the night. He shared as much as he could about whether or not he would accept what Joan began referring to as his mysterious new position.

The following day at lunch time Michael called Henry. They chatted about the family, the weather, and when they could get together again. Then Michael said, "Tell our old friend that he only won by an inch and a half. It's my turn."

There was a soft intake of breath on the other end of the phone.

"You're going to take a walk in the park Michael?"

"Remind him of my conditions. He'll accept them. It's time to get on with the program. Henry, I miss you, brother. Tell Susan, Dylan, and Mom that I send my love."

"See you soon, Michael."

"Hey, before you hang up, I want you to know that you and

Eric are right on all counts. I apologize if I came off as too judgmental."

"Apology accepted. No harm done," Henry said.

"Besides, I'm tired of wearing the blindfold."

Henry laughed. The blindfold was indeed about to come off.

CHAPTER 18

The president's trip to Louisiana would consist of a public meeting in New Orleans and another secret meeting which it was Robert Hoopes' job to arrange. His boss would attend this second meeting unbeknownst to the press. No one understood better than Hoopes that some gatherings were best done in secret. That was his department. As the Special Assistant, it was his job to arrange such clandestine meetings between POTUS and special people. Every one of the attendees of this particular gathering was in charge of a specific aspect of the Progressive takeover of America.

Hoopes chose Bocage Mansion outside New Orleans for the meeting. The plantation was a wedding gift to fourteen-year-old Fanny Bringier of the prominent Bringier family. As with each of their children, the Bringiers gifted Fanny a full fledged plantation on the occasion of her marriage to French refugee Christophe Colomb. Colomb claimed to be a descendant of famed explorer Christopher Columbus. Preferring to indulge in the arts to running a plantation, Colomb left such work completely in the hands of his young wife. Hoopes loved the rich history of the mansion as a backdrop for gathering the country's elite and powerful.

More recently Bocage Plantation served as a filming location for an Academy Award-winning movie about the life of Solomon Northup, a free black man who was kidnapped from his home in New York and sold into slavery in the South. Hoopes smiled, ticking off liberal talking points and enjoying the smug satisfaction of having chosen a location that touched on nearly every one of them. The men would love the atmosphere of elitist power and prestige the luxurious mansion afforded, while the women would champion Fanny Bringier as a pioneering example of women's industrial and intellectual fortitude. The guilt of the "white man's burden" they bore would be assuaged by the fact that ultimately Solomon Northup escaped the bonds of slavery and returned to the freedom-loving North. Check, check, and check. He would make sure everyone knew the history of the place so they could appreciate his genius.

Hoopes secured the entire mansion under the pretext of hosting a private showing for the POTUS and a classified guest list. It took the better part of an hour to park all the black limousines and to usher the guests through the Secret Service checkpoint. While that was being accomplished, Hoopes moved about the double parlor on the main floor, welcoming invitees to the elegant reception which would precede the meeting in earnest. He discreetly tuned his ears to catch snatches of conversations between the world's most powerful Progressive elite. He'd happened upon many bits of information that proved useful to his boss at such meetings in the past. Experience assured him that would also be the case here.

Two male senators and a woman Hoopes recognized as a lobbyist from the health insurance industry had settled in with drinks under the Waterford crystal chandelier. "The healthcare bill is a marvel, even if those who lack vision think it was shoved down the public's throat. They only think they didn't want it," Hoopes overheard one of the senators saying.

The lobbyist nodded. "It's monstrously complex, and it's turning into a virtual nightmare to implement fully, but the genius bit is that the IRS will take on the role of an American Gestapo to enforce it."

"That's true, but it sounds so extreme. Of course some aspects of the bill may sound harsh, but they will be enforced with the public's best interest in mind," the second senator said, then took a sip from his glass. "Millions who've never been able to afford healthcare will get it, and eventually the system will be free of high cost, high frequency users."

"True, we can't afford to care for everybody." This came from the lobbyist.

The first senator nodded in agreement. "Policies are in place to make tough decisions. How much sense does it make to keep spending money on consumers who've outlived their ability to make useful contributions to society, or who will die anyway, no matter how much treatment they receive?"

Hoopes caught the eye of one of the senators; he nodded a greeting before moving past the trio. He held his own thoughts about the healthcare bill. The financial strain on employers would be enormous. It was a bureaucrat's dream of a bill, but he wondered if it so tied up everything in knots that the American people would come to rue the day the bill was signed into law.

"The country is broke thanks to the collapse of the real estate and financial industries." Hoopes overheard a prominent financier declaring to a Keynesian economist from a highly regarded think tank.

"You sound like Nikita Krushchev pounding his shoe at the United Nations," said the economist. "Hitler and Hirohito couldn't do it. The Soviet Union couldn't do it. 9/11 and terrorism couldn't do it, but today the wealth of this country is being redistributed from within. Bankrupting America and redistributing the wealth it stole through colonialist overreach are one and the same. It's absolutely brilliant."

Hoopes smiled politely and continued moving through the crowd. A conversation between a Harvard professor and a tech industry billionaire briefly held his attention.

"Of course he'll remain in office for a third, maybe even a fourth term. Why not? FDR, the greatest Progressive to run this country was voted in four times."

"That was before term limits."

"We've learned to never waste a crisis, my friend. Well into the president's second term, and definitely before it's finished, what's to say a national crisis that would eradicate term limits won't take place?"

Hoopes plucked a champagne flute from a passing tray and made his way toward two women and a man who was obviously trying to impress them into something more than an ideological meeting of the minds.

"You're rubbing elbows with the true players of the Progressive effort in America, and it's a good thing," the man said. He touched the elbow of a stunning brunette with almond eyes in a flawlessly tailored business suit. "We've waited over a hundred years for this moment, but now that we have the power we have to move quickly." He lightly tapped the shoulder of an equally attractive redhead. "Coordinating our efforts more solidly is key, and we've got to establish a time line."

"I agree," Hoopes inserted himself into the conversation, "this is an impressive and unprecedented gathering of the best and the brightest Progressive minds—"

"That's right! We're the generation we've been waiting for," the man said. Hoopes vaguely recognized him as a social media whiz kid who'd built a multi-billion dollar internet concern. "But between the loudmouth *fuzz ball* on the radio railing against our efforts every day, and the king of that noxious cable TV channel with his no spin zone—they take issue with everything we do."

"And what's with the guy throwing the football? And the screamer in the underground bunker?" The redhead flashed Hoopes a dazzling smile. "Whatever! They all need to be silenced."

"The blonde with the files is kinda cute, but that kind of vocal opposition can no longer be tolerated." The whiz kid went back to working on the brunette.

"I thought that was being handled with the Fairness Doctrine..." Hoopes heard her say. He was momentarily distracted as the redhead stepped close and slipped a card into the pocket of his suit jacket. He returned her steady gaze long enough to convey his interest before excusing himself to continue welcoming the other guests.

Snippets of various conversations drifted in and out of his ears.

"The threat of the Tea Party movement has largely been neutralized. They've been vilified, condemned, marginalized and in some cases even driven out of areas they infested. Oh, for the power to just round them up and have all of them euthanized!"

People spoke freely here. These were Progressives whose deepest convictions had only been expressed in the shadows where they would remain hidden, at least for the time being.

Hoopes noticed the attorney general addressing a former head of state and a supreme court justice. "We know our enemies, and we'll deal with them. None of them know who the real movers and shakers are—"

"But that wunderkind with the damn red phone is working to expose us all. Old George would have had him shot on camera if he could get away with it," the head of state interrupted.

"Hell, we own the mainstream press and television. The talking heads spew more liberal bias than half the people here," the attorney general said. "If they weren't spouting our talking points I'd be nauseated from the stink."

The supreme court justice raised his glass. "Here's to their never-ending river of effluvium, breathed out over the airwaves upon the population daily." They doubled over with laughter, and clicked their wine glasses in a toast.

At precisely six o-clock the group was herded upstairs to dine in the exquisite Napoleon dining room where each place was set with fine china, silver flatware, and crystal goblets. Saucer-sized lush magnolia blossoms in antique Parisian vases filled the dining room with a lemony-sweet scent. After a decadent meal of Trout Ponchartrain, seared scallop-stuffed mirliton, dirty rice, and grilled vegetables, hot spiced coffee laced with brandy and bananas Foster flamed at table were served for dessert. Hoopes then rose to introduce the man of the hour.

"Ladies and gentlemen, we come to the point for which you have been called to this meeting. We have the privilege to serve this country under the leadership of a man of unparalleled intellect, who has achieved unprecedented success in the forwarding of our ideological agenda. He has restored America to a place of benevolent partnership with the world, largely through his charm, grace...and inimitable swagger." The audience laughed appreciatively and began to applaud, even as Hoopes made the introduction. "Esteemed friends, I give you the President of the United States."

The president stood, and for several minutes graciously received the applause and shouts of adulation. He smiled, nodding and pointing in acknowledgment to several especially favored luminaries in the room. He raised his hand for silence, and as the crowd reluctantly quieted down, he began his remarks.

"Friends, we're gathered here at a moment of great import in our country. Unfortunately, far too many Americans are too naive to understand what's really happening in our nation and in the world. They want to cling to old values and principles that have outlived their usefulness for modern times. The Constitution, as valuable as it has been, is a living document that has become antiquated in it's principles. We're not conquering the wild west anymore, so you can't just let everyone have guns! Look at the levels of crime and gun violence on the streets and in the schools. Plain and simple, people no longer need some of these rules, instead, they need to be ruled. Our education system has improved significantly under my administration to the extent that children are often times better off under the care of the state to help them grow best in body, mind and spirit. The population and the world needs to be protected from the effects of climate change, and the United States needs to lead on that front and others. When the history books and archives are rewritten to reflect the truth, the world will know that we were right.

"The decision has been made. In the face of an unprecedented crisis on American soil I fully intend to take executive action to suspend the process of electing a new president for as long as it takes to secure the safety and security of our citizenship. Considering the current state of upheaval in the world I anticipate that such action may become necessary within a year, at most two. As I near the end of my second term in office, world events all but demand that the hand of leadership of these United States remain steady and consistent. It is with this in mind that I will continue to pursue a strategy of non-engagement and coalition building. I will not put American boots on the ground anywhere in the world to intervene in conflicts where sovereign nations need to fight their own battles. If that means our enemies are emboldened to strike on our shores, so be it! We will take them on and win!"

His audience erupted in thunderous applause. "Now, our opposition, with its high handed, melodramatic rhetoric would call our undertaking the greatest misdirection and mass manipulation of public opinion in the history of the world. They'd say we're planning to deceive Americans in ways no one's ever dreamed of. But in the aftermath of the crisis we will emerge as the solution to rebuilding America. In the nation that has made advertising and propaganda into an art form, no expense will be spared to assure ordinary citizens that our government is the benevolent and bountiful provider that they will so desperately need.

"Ladies and gentlemen, the path we have chosen to ensure that the United States of America pays its fair share among the nations of this world, and that power and leadership remains in the hands of the best and brightest during these turbulent times is...well, it's pure genius."

✳✳✳✳✳✳✳

Hoopes was tired when he returned to his room late that night. A crisis was coming that would make 9/11 look like a Sunday-go-to-meetin' picnic. The perpetrators themselves were being manipulated by Progressive power brokers at the highest levels. They were being duped into serving as the catalyst that would put the whole of the United States on lockdown under martial law. He considered himself something of a master manipulator, but the commander in chief's charismatic oratorical skills were the stuff of legend.

The president was flown back to Washington after dinner, but Hoopes remained behind. There were other things to which he needed to attend. He would fly back by small private jet the next morning and give the president a full report.

God, he loved power! He smirked at his reflection in the ornately framed gold leafed mirror of his luxuriously appointed room in the Bocage. Food and drink flowed freely during the reception and dinner, but the heady intoxication of power only whetted his appetite, leaving him famished for something more. He fished the redhead's card from his pocket and decided to take the hour drive into New Orleans to Bourbon Street. He planned to enjoy some jazz and the company of the woman for the night.

He left the mansion, slid into the driver's seat of his black SUV and headed for the Quarter. He didn't notice the man who was following him. The master manipulator failed to look over his own shoulder.

CHAPTER 19

Norman Blesco was distracted all day at work. His boss, Joe Rumfolo, was worried about him. Norman was always a straight arrow, always showed up on time, did whatever he was asked to do, and worked weekends and holidays when necessary. He never complained. He wasn't the most fun guy on the crew, but he was a hard worker and could be counted on to do his job well. Norman never smiled, and Joe figured he just wasn't the emotional type. Other employees invited him to backyard barbecues in the summers and other gatherings during the year to celebrate birthdays, anniversaries, etc., but Norman always made an excuse not to attend. He didn't fraternize outside of work.

One day Joe's secretary, Helen Orbison, got him laughing about Norman so hard that he almost wet his pants. She said that Norman was probably a serial killer who ate his victims, and that he probably had a fully stocked refrigerator at home. The idea was so ludicrous that Joe couldn't get the image out of his mind: quiet, reserved Norman Blesco, who never even raised his voice—a serial killer. Joe almost fell off his chair when Helen said she meant cereal killer, and that Norman secretly bought extra boxes of Wheaties and

Corn Flakes for his stash and then beat them at night with a baseball bat. Joe laughed so hard tears streamed down his face.

But this day, Norman seemed visibly annoyed over something.

"You okay, Norm? Something bothering you?" Joe was genuinely concerned, the guy didn't seem to have a friend in the world. "Is there something I can help you with?"

"No, Mr. Rumfolo. Everything is fine."

Joe liked Norman, not only because he was a hard worker, but also because he was always polite. He was the only one on the whole crew who called him "Mr. Rumfolo."

"You really seem agitated today. If you need some time off, take it. You haven't taken a vacation since you started here. A man needs a break every now and then. Seriously, Norm, why don't you take a vacation? Go away. Go down to Florida and see your folks. You haven't seen them in years, right?"

"Mr. Rumfolo, I will take a trip this year. I am going to take some vacation time. I'll give you plenty of advance notice so you can get someone to cover for me."

"Norm, you could give me an hour's notice and it wouldn't bother me. What are you up to at this point? You must have at least five weeks vacation! You need some rest and relaxation, man! It's good for you."

"Don't worry. I will take a vacation. I'm just feeling a little tired today because I was up late last night watching a serial on TV."

At this remark Joe lost it. He started laughing so hard that his face got red and he couldn't catch his breath.

Norman stared at him. He thought the man was strange. Why was what he said so funny? He walked away and went back to work.

When Joe Rumfolo finally got control of himself he called Helen into the office. "Guess what, Helen. You were right." He told her about his exchange with Norman.

While Joe and Helen shared their joke at his expense, Norman made a point of appearing to be hard at work at his desk. The truth was, his thoughts were on the monumental task that lay ahead. He'd spent most of his life preparing for an assignment to come. His dreams were of something spectacular, but what he was being called to do was unprecedented; he felt inadequate.

The destruction that he and others would bring to America would be where thousands of stupid Americans and their infidel children went to play and have fun. He did not understand the American penchant for make-believe and fantasy. Animals that could talk! Cartoons that depicted life among moving images on a screen! The thought of their foolish indulgences turned his stomach. Allah's warriors would punish them so severely that their memories of 9/11 would pale in comparison.

Years of planning and thought went into the plan. The Great Satan would wail in anguish over the havoc he and his brethren would wreak. They would strike a harsh blow; not even he had imagined such a bold and brash thing! He shivered in anticipation of the hell he would bring to these people. His mentors chose rightly. He would be brave and true. He would not fail, not even if it cost him his life.

Had Joe and Helen known what was in Norman's mind at that moment they would have run screaming into the street. No serial killer who ever lived would be able to match the carnage he would inflict on America. His hatred boiled within him. He was ready.

CHAPTER 20

February and March slipped away. April began. Then Easter was upon them, and the Stonebreaker clan from Washington made its way to the mountains of central Pennsylvania, ostensibly to visit with family and do some fishing.

In reality, Henry had planned another visit to The Movement. Michael would present his list of conditions to Eric. If they were acceptable he would return from the visit minus the blindfold. Although he accepted the offer, the conditions would either make or break the relationship. They knew that Michael would never violate their confidence or tell anyone about the group's existence. That was a given. However, if they could not meet his demands, The Movement would have to choose someone else.

When they sat down Eric wasted no time. "What are your conditions?"

"Protection for our families."

"Done. When the change begins families of The Movement will be taken to safe havens all over the country. That includes their extended families and close friends."

"You have the space and capacity to do this?"

"It's not a problem."

"Joan gets to keep her job."

"I can't promise that. It will be a very unsettled time. She would have to be protected while at work."

"If she can't keep her job, I can't take the job." Michael said.

"That's not being fair, Michael."

"Yes, it is. Life as we know it is going to be stood on its head. Her work is as important to her as mine is to me. If she can keep her position the purpose of her life goes on."

"But it's going to be ugly in our country for a time. We'll be doing our best to make the transition a smooth one, but the media will be out of its mind, there will be fear and anxiety everywhere, and the biggest problem of all will be people wondering what happened to the people who were in charge? Where have they gone? The questions will be flying everywhere. We have a plan for all of it, and Joan's job will be the least of our worries."

Eric sighed. "Michael, I'm married. I understand she has needs. You know I love your family and I get your concerns about how they'll make it through the transition, but right now I cannot promise anything as far as Joan keeping her current job."

"Okay, then she comes inside soon and you explain everything to her. While you're at it, bring Susan and my mother in, as well. Tell them what's going to happen. Henry and I will have enough on our hands. We don't need wives who are unhappy and afraid. Yvette should be brought into this, too. We need agreement in our households about how to support each other." Michael said.

Eric looked at Michael with wonder in his eyes. "You're a military man, Michael—to the core—but ever the peace maker."

"Oh, and as to Henry," he turned to his brother, "what role do you play in all this? What do you want to do in this new world order?"

"Fix draglines and 'dozers." Henry said.

"Well, brother, I'll have other plans for you in my administration, so you won't be staying in Clear Haven. Sorry, but I'll need you beside me."

"Doing what?" The concern on Henry's face was real. "What am I qualified to do in government? Nothing that I can think of! Michael, I'd be as useless to you as a fishing pole without a line."

"No, you have value beyond anything you've ever imagined. You'll be First Friend to this President. You'll watch my back, keep me straight, humble, and be a prayer warrior when I need one. And I'll need one every day!"

"Are there other conditions?" Eric asked.

"I name my vice president."

"The thinking is that one of the other top five candidates would be the VP." Eric said.

"That's not acceptable. In this case it's my way or the highway."

"Who's your choice?"

"I'm looking at him!"

"Me?" Eric exclaimed. "Why me?"

"For the same reason The Movement is doing what it's doing. You said you're choosing people who do not want to run for office, let alone high office, but who have the best qualifications to lead this country in the right direction. That's you, my friend. You're the guy who's getting me into this, and you're the guy who's going to be standing next to me. If anything happens to me I know you'll take care of business. I know you'll defend this country and our people. I know your soul. I want you. I trust you."

"What if the leadership rejects the idea?" Eric asked, giving in to the set look of Michael's jaw and the determination in his eyes.

"They won't…not if they want me. That's it. It's not a long list, but these conditions must be met or I don't walk the walk."

Eric rubbed his chin as he spoke. "Protection we can supply. Getting our wives in here is a whole new wrinkle. We try to think of everything, and they all have to know eventually, but we believe we're months away from having to act. It might even be a couple of years before things get to the point where we step in."

"I understand, Eric, but we've got to have our wives and children on board so we don't go crazy trying to carry this every day without those closest to us knowing what's going on. It's bad enough we can't share with our families what we do for a living, but this is different. This is life-changing for them!

"I will not take this job if you're not by my side. I can't do this without Henry and you being with me every day. I need your strengths, your insights, and, most of all, your love and prayers. This will be the most challenging and scary thing we've ever faced! We're going to try to restore America to what it once was. It has taken decades to fall to this level. How long will it take to put it right? I sure don't know, but I've got to have the two best men I know in my corner." Michael looked at them.

"We're in your corner, Michael." Henry said.

"You know we are." Eric said.

"Then, let's do something right now that the three of us have never done before together." Michael said.

"What's that?" Eric asked softly.

"Let's pray." Michael slid off his chair onto his knees and bowed his head. Eric and Henry hesitated for a moment, and then joined him.

"Lord," Michael said. "This is the biggest thing we'll ever face and we can't do it alone. Please be with us now and all the days to come. Keep us straight and true. Lead us to right thinking and good decisions. Protect our families, our colleagues, and all the people in this country—those we agree with and those who want to harm us—and guide us daily. Amen."

Henry and Eric echoed his "Amen."

Michael stood. "Please inform the leadership of my conditions at once."

"Consider it done." Eric said. "Now, let's go into the city. I believe they'll ultimately agree with what you've requested, though it will take some selling up front. I can contact all the decision makers from the Truman building communication center within the hour. If they agree we can begin work today. There is so much you need to know that it's going to take many weeks to bring you up to speed."

They left the room and boarded the tram.

A phrase from their favorite family film drifted through Henry's mind. *Follow the yellow brick road.*

Michael was about to become the man behind the curtain. Henry didn't know whether he should be relieved or worried about what was coming.

CHAPTER 21

Pierce Armstrong appreciated what he considered genius, even in its most heinous forms. Adolph Hitler, Joseph Stalin and China's Chairman Mao were among his heroes. Despite their cruelty, he appreciated that they achieved many of their goals.

Currently, he was enamored with Fidel Castro, who stood up to imperialist America all these years without backing down. He admired Hugo Chavez for his tenacity in the face of American aggression. He absolutely adored the current US president and his administration, and he was totally in love with the decline of the country under their watch. After all, it was his plan that was being executed. It was his dream that was being fulfilled.

Armstrong wore his sixty-three years well. Although his hair was gray, he stood erect, lifted weights, and walked vigorously every morning. He drank very little alcohol, nor did he use tobacco or drugs. There was nothing in his life to distract him from his work, since his third wife walked out on him a decade ago and he had no children.

He was invisible to the cable network who attacked the administration on a daily basis. The last place anyone would look for him would be in America's Heartland in a tiny community thirty miles from Lincoln, Nebraska. He laughed to himself. A heartworm in the heart of America, he was quietly devouring its patriotic principles of freedom and replacing them with Progressivism, amorality and division.

Pierce had been taught by his father, whom his grandfather taught before him, that fame and notoriety were counterproductive for stripping away the personal rights of the masses. To that end, his pamphlets, essays and books were published under many pseudonyms. A student of history, he made a point of cultivating the ear of those in positions of influence through whom he could anonymously impose his will. The current president spent many hours in his living room and an equal number of hours at the picnic table under the huge oak tree in his front yard before he'd gone to Washington. Well-known modern Progressives had taken meals in his expansive dining room. Anyone allowed to make his privileged acquaintance underwent an extreme vetting process before being informed of his existence. His work was published under so many respected names that when people invited into his inner circle discovered him to be the sole author, they fawned on him as if he were some sort of god. He was a living legend in progressive circles. He read, thought deeply, and distilled the absolute best in liberal thinking from the last hundred years. He was, indisputably, a genius.

Pierce Armstrong was the living architect of the modern American progressive movement, and few but the powerful elite knew that he even existed. It was a delicious thought. That made him hungry. Pierce's one great vice was food, and plenty of it. Fortunately for him he inherited a sizable estate from his late father. He could buy all the good food he wanted, and he was a superb cook. He had never done a day of physical work in his life, choosing instead to earn a living writing and selling his ideas on paper. His metabolism was such that he didn't gain weight, thankfully, so he could indulge his passion for eating all day long and still burn the calories.

Pierce Armstrong believed in One World Government. That's how he thought of the concept: in Capital Letters. He recognized decades earlier that government must be infiltrated, and that capitalism must be replaced with socialism. Socialism, itself, was only a way station on the way to his personal idea of Utopia: a world totally controlled by an intellectual elite who would dictate the lives of the working class from cradle-to-grave.

The elites were destined to run the whole world, not just America. He'd met with his counterparts in other nations over the years and they all agreed that a united world under the control of their kind was greatly to be desired. He had not met his intellectual match during his travels, but he found common ground in Europe's social democracies, as well as in the totalitarian dictatorships. There were elites on every continent who were what he called "Big Picture People."

His people now had control. It was his genius that led to the idea of bankrupting America and bringing it to its knees from within. While 9/11 served as a wake-up call to the conservatives, he planned a far worse crisis that would allow the present administration to declare martial law. They would fill the streets with troops, and begin to *protect Americans for their own good.* The idea was so delicious; he enjoyed another bite of apple cake.

He thought up a singular system of national identity/debit cards to track people's whereabouts and control their financial transactions. Eliminating the need for paper and coin money would allow government to dictate every aspect of American life. It was his idea to place cameras all over the American landscape in the name of national security. It was also originally his brilliant idea for the IRS to enforce the national health care bill when it was fully implemented.

Pierce gloated over what was happening. His appetite called for a large glass of milk. He went to his refrigerator, removed a carton and poured himself a much-deserved glass of the sweet, white liquid. His late mother loved milk…before his father murdered her. She shared her passion with her only son before she died. He thought of how perfect that moment was when they laughed and drank milk together in their kitchen…right before he shot her.

After all, true revolution called for bloodied hands—figuratively, of course. The thought of touching anyone's blood sickened him. He would, however bring about a revolution of the privileged elite in the world. His desires were simple. He sought orderliness, the necessary time to think, reserved, of course, only for true progressives, and a world where the peasants worked and kept their mouths shut.

And of course his utopia would be perfect without religious fools and minorities. Armstrong hated the very idea of God. He also hated the people Liberals claimed to love and protect every day in order to push their agenda—the minorities. Minorities, in his profound opinion, should be gassed. But for now, they served a purpose and he tolerated them. The federal government designated Lincoln, Nebraska a "refugee-friendly city" in the 1970s, and *the brown flood* ensued. Many minorities hailed from North Omaha, including one high profile candidate for president. Nonetheless, when his people took final control he would rid the planet of such creatures.

His home was hidden away several miles from the nearby community. He hated going to town, but the need for groceries demanded that he do so at least once, sometimes twice a week. A man must eat, and he didn't trust his servants to shop for his produce. It was too bad that biology required sustenance through food, but fresh food was so delicious! *He simply must enjoy another piece of apple cake.* He inhaled the intoxicating aroma and filled his mouth with the sweet goodness, even as dreams of his own grandeur filled his mind.

He imagined statues of himself erected in public squares all over the country. His reputation would, no doubt, exceed that of George Washington. He would be long gone, of course, but he would posthumously receive the recognition he so richly deserved. He thought of the movie Forrest Gump. How he loved that movie! He sat enthralled in the darkness as Tom Hanks, in the character of Gump met George Wallace, Jack Kennedy, and other historical figures. Hollywood had outdone itself. Such technology was wonderful, magical, and incredible. It would allow the Progressives to one day open all the archives to remake every bit of film and re-write history for themselves. Hitler could have only dreamed of having such a propaganda tool. The idea made him hungry. He enjoyed more cake.

CHAPTER 22

The leaders of The Movement agreed to Michael's conditions, and he agreed to begin working immediately. Many months were required to prepare him to become the leader of the free world.

Michael firmly believed the trouble with running for political office in the United States was that too often elections turned out to be popularity contests. The process simply seated career politicians who were totally inadequate for the job of governing. Unfortunately government incompetence appeared to be a problem worldwide. It seemed nations just did the best they could with whoever was available, even if the results were increasingly disastrous.

Michael decided he would be the best prepared man to walk into the Oval Office since George H. W. Bush. He admired the man, but took careful note of what he thought to be Bush's one political flaw. Despite being highly trained in different arenas before serving as President, Mr. Bush appeared to be out of touch with the common man, a huge mistake when it came to gathering votes. And his infamous *Read my lips...no new taxes!* declaration sealed his fate in his bid for a second term.

Michael reasoned he would be the best-trained man to ever serve in the job, without the popularity contest, and with his finger on the pulse of the average American. Citizens wanted control of their own lives. They wanted to be free of the nanny state government that sought to control their thoughts, what they ate, their education, what kind of healthcare they could have—the list got longer everyday. He would not make off-the-cuff campaign speech promises, but he would be like Bush '41 in his commitment to be thoroughly prepared intellectually to take office. There were people with decades of experience mentoring him in subjects a newly elected president typically learned on-the-job, only after being sworn in.

High-ranking military personnel took him though his paces on the entire history and service of the military to the nation since the Marine Corps came into existence in 1775. He learned about the inner workings of the Pentagon at the top levels, weapons systems in place, in development, and on the drawing board, and troop strength and deployment around the world. Although he was an Intelligence officer, he needed to broaden his knowledge exponentially to take on the responsibility of being the commander in chief.

Everyone he'd seen on his first visit to the compound who'd sat at the conference table also interacted with him in his training. Media people taught him about media, advertising, promotion, marketing and propaganda. Economists taught him about markets and the economy, bankers taught him about finance, jurists talked about the law and its applications, and constitutional experts explained the implications of the United States operating as a true republic, with power wielded by the people and their representatives. There were many discussions about how government should function on behalf of the citizenry.

Captains of industry mentored him on business, profit and loss, entrepreneurship, capital, risk, and business development. Keenly intelligent, Michael grasped things quickly, but he also understood why a president needed a cabinet to do the job. It was not a one-man show. No human being was bright enough to lead the Free World without the support and insight of an army of true experts in various disciplines.

Months of training began to take a toll on his family. Joan

wondered at the long nights of study he put in and if she would ever have time with her husband again. She knew he had yet to take this new job, and that he was studying to prepare for the position. He was away during most of his summer leave. He kept promising to clue her in, but that time had not come, and she was beginning to resent whatever it was he'd got himself into.

Their daughter Angela was beginning her junior year at Georgetown, and Louise was a senior in high school. The girls missed their dad being around on weekends for day trips to the beach and to the many historical sites around DC. Each summer they spent a family week on Maryland's Eastern Shore, but this year Michael missed all but the last two days with them. He vowed to make it up to them.

The mid-term elections of the administration's first term came and went. The Progressives lost control of the House, but hung on to the Senate, albeit by a slim margin. One insane bill after another sailed through the House and on to the Senate during the lame duck session. The national debt was growing by billions of dollars a day.

The Movement made ready for when they would launch TR2.0 and halt the decline. The right to personal privacy and private property, small government, and strong protected borders were the pillars on which they would begin restoring the country to right-thinking and fiscal responsibility. The era of tax and spend government was coming to an end. Everyone in the organization was eager to do away with the police state America was becoming.

Michael rehearsed key elements of the plan to cement them in his mind. When The Movement took power, the IRS would be gone. A flat tax across the board would free up personal income, and free people to spend more of their hard earned money in ways of their own choosing. History showed that even charitable giving rose when people brought home more of their wages than they turned over to the government. The elimination of many money-grabbing government fiats would bolster the economy more than propping up debt with costly and ineffective stimulus packages.

It would be an ambitious undertaking, but a massive empowerment of Americans was in the wings. Mechanisms were in place to prepare people, young and old alike, for a world in which America could compete with China, India, and developing countries for manufacturing and production jobs. Colleges and universities would be retooled academically to make education useful, applicable, and above all, profitable for those who succeeded in their course work. Curriculum would need to be ahead of the curve worldwide, and there were people ready to see that it happened.

Though millions would be thrown out of work under such a massive downsizing of the Federal Government, Michael could see how these folks would find work in the expanded private sector under The Movement's plan. Untold billions of dollars would flow back into the states, whose bloated bureaucracies would also be substantially scaled back. The fairytale of never-ending-spending would be halted at both the federal and state levels.

There would also be real change at every level of American society. Credit cards would disappear altogether. Never again would Americans be able to borrow against the future to live in the present. Michael wasn't foolish enough to believe all of this would happen overnight. The banking industry would have as part of its mission to remedy crushing consumer debt slowly but effectively. Saving money would be the order of the day, in stark contrast to the now pervasive attitude of reckless spending modeled by the Congress. A paradigm shift from freewheeling spending to saving balanced with spending to revitalize the American economy would eventually take root and prevail. It would require years of steady implementation, but it would be done.

Michael mentally steeled himself against the overwhelming opposition he knew would arise against bringing Social Security to an end over the next generation. The program would be replaced with savings and investment plans in which individuals would exercise control over their own retirement money. The ultimate intent being that personal responsibility and economic opportunity would encourage people to save and invest to produce the money to live on in retirement.

Free market principles would also govern the health care

system, subjecting the ungodly costs and out-of-control charges for medical services to the laws of supply and demand. Michael could see no reason for an aspirin to cost two cents at Walgreen's but $40 in a hospital, or for an eye-exam to cost $90 at Lens Crafters, but $600.00 through Medicare. Real change was coming, but not at the expense of the American taxpayer.

The Movement's strategy included establishing American energy independence. A Manhattan Project sized effort was already mapped out to implement offshore drilling, build nuclear power plants, develop wind and solar farms, and utilize natural gas and coal at levels presently undreamed of in the United States. The nation would control it's own energy supply within a decade. It was going to happen. America would stop buying oil from those who shipped both oil and terrorists to her shores.

He retrieved one of several manuals detailing The Movement's plan for wresting control of the nation from the Progressives and restoring its Constitutional values. He flipped through several pages and continued reviewing the information, intent on committing it to memory.

The entire American educational system was about to receive a wake-up call. The days of bloated bureaucracy were over. Local property taxes would no longer be used to fund public schools. Instead, education would be overseen by the states, shaped by the people and approved or disapproved at the ballot box. Facilities would be built through private sector competition. Michael agreed, education didn't require a palace. It required proper space and reasonably adequate teaching-centered resources that could be secured cost effectively.

He flipped through more pages, skimming the now familiar tenets of TR2.0. The federal government's primary task would be to maintain a strong military, and protect the citizens of the United States. We would continue to maintain a military presence in some far away lands as necessary in such a dangerous world, but with key differences in strategy. America's leaders would no longer tolerate those who spoke out of both sides of their mouths. False promises and frivolous concessions designed purely to buy time for undermining the processes of establishing and maintaining peace would no longer be accepted as good faith negotiations.

Michael particularly liked the idea of honest and forthright relations with other countries, and returning America to a position of strength in the world. The US military would cease to be used as nation builders, and like children who can't play well together, nations unable to leave other nations alone would be dealt with swiftly and decisively. Loud-mouthed dictators and religious freaks could yell and scream all they wanted. Their days would be numbered if they threatened other people. He also agreed that Israel should be protected. Period.

The Movement crafted a comprehensive plan to restore America to greatness on every level. It would require far more than one term, and Michael would not see the task completed even if he stood for re-election and was voted into a second four years. It was more than enough to think about. The more he read through TR2.0, the more he came to appreciate how vast it was, and how much thought and genuine concern had gone into its creation. The people who developed its various components were people of great intelligence and compassion. The human element was evident everywhere within its pages.

The old physician's rule of *First, do no harm!* rang true in every part of the work. He understood why those five people came together in the early 1950s, the danger to the nation that drove them forward, and the dedication of all who followed them in preparing for this time. He was awed by their accomplishment. Their love for America was carved into the very rock of the underground fortress in the mountains of Pennsylvania, quietly waiting for the moment when the time was right and the hour was at hand. These days his thoughts turned frequently to the monumental task that lay ahead. The time was fast approaching. He felt it in his bones. Instinct warned him to prepare. Instinct always served him well on the playing field…and the battlefield.

CHAPTER 23

Despite around-the-clock access to the leader of the free world, Special Assistant to the President of the United States, Robert Hoopes knew nothing of the president's dealings with the man in Nebraska.

In all of America there were less than thirty Progressives who knew of him, and fewer than fifteen actually spent time with him. The man's well-guarded life was such that it was literally harder to get an audience with him than it was to meet the Pope in Rome or drop by the White House for a chat about politics with the president.

As the architect of the modern progressive movement in America, the writer of hundreds of pamphlets, essays, and books under a myriad of fictitious names, the man hidden in the heartland believed he was safe from any enemy.

The third year of the president's second term ended. The election year was in full swing, and the Progressives needed a win in November. Their man must be returned to the Oval Office if they were to take complete control of every aspect of American life.

On a Wednesday evening early in January Hoopes was called in to see the president. There was another man in the room that he did not know. The president did not bother to introduce him, and Hoopes knew well enough not to complain. Instead he took in as many details about the man as he could without staring. Tall, perhaps six-foot-three, he looked solid, as though he spent a lot of time in the gym. He had dark gray hair, and looked to be about fifty. His long angular face framed deep dimples in his cheeks. His eyes were dark, almost black. Hoopes thought he resembled a stereotypical lead bad guy in a Hollywood movie, minus the handlebar mustache. The man didn't speak while Hoopes was in the room; he sat quietly on the sofa, openly eyeing Hoopes in return.

The president explained that he wanted Hoopes on a private jet the next morning.

He would be flying to Omaha, Nebraska, and a car and driver would be there to take him to an undisclosed location to meet with someone. He was not told what the meeting would be about, nor was he instructed to say anything to the other party when they met.

Hoopes was dismissed, and he left the room immediately.

Hoopes' title was "Special Assistant" because there wasn't anything else he could be called. "Assistant for Dirty Tricks" would not have been acceptable. "Assistant for Extortion, Bribery and Conspiracy" would have been equally unacceptable. He kept his mouth shut, did what he was told, and always did his best to exceed what was asked of him. He was rewarded handsomely with a government-paid salary, and even more handsomely with a regular supply of "undisclosed" funds that arrived magically in his bank account from he knew-not-where. This type of "cloak-and-dagger" mission was par for the course, and the perks for handling these things for the president made constantly getting his hands dirty completely worthwhile.

Hoopes left the White House and went home. It would be an early flight, so he grabbed a TV dinner. He hated pre-packaged food but there was no choice. He ate in front of the television, smirking at the irony of his food selection. He flipped through the news stations, taking in the reports absently and noting the parroting of liberal talking points consistent from network to network. He stopped and listened more intently when he reached the one network that notoriously refused to toe the line. He made some mental notes and clicked the set off. He dropped what was left of his meal into the trash and headed for his bedroom.

Sighing heavily, Hoopes laid out his clothes for the following morning. It was going to be a very long day. He would be returning to Washington tomorrow night. He could try sleeping on the plane, but he was a nervous flyer so he seldom rested while in the air.

He dialed the service that provided his wake-up calls and went to bed. He lay in the darkened room wondering just who was important enough for the President of the United States to send his Special Assistant to call on him like some sort of lap dog? Maybe he was wrong? Maybe it was a she instead of a he? He fell asleep.

The phone rang at 4:30 am. "Damn!" he said, stumbling out of bed and heading for the shower. His ride picked him up at 5:15, and he was in the air forty-five minutes later. There was, fortunately, little turbulence and the flight made good time. When they landed in Omaha they taxied to a large hangar near the edge of the field away from the bustle of the huge passenger jets. Just outside the hangar a black Lincoln was waiting with its motor running.

Hoopes got in back and discovered a manila envelope lying on the seat with the words: *Open, Read, Follow Instructions* written on it. He opened the envelope. A single sheet of white paper and a blindfold were inside. On the paper he read:

> *"At the appropriate moment the driver will instruct you to put on the blindfold. You will wear it until you reach your final destination. DO NOT ATTEMPT TO SHIFT THE BLINDFOLD! IF YOU FAIL TO OBEY, THERE WILL BE SEVERE CONSEQUENCES!"*

What the heck was this all about? Who was the person he was going to see? The whole thing reminded him of the opening scenes from all those Mission: Impossible movies. Except he had no choice but to accept this mission.

"How long is this trip?" Hoopes asked the driver, a man in his middle forties with graying hair and a bland, nondescript face. The man did not answer him. Hoopes grunted. It figures, he thought. He settled into the seat, positioning his briefcase on his left so that he could access it, and snapped into his seatbelt. At the click of the buckle the driver put the car in gear and drove off towards a tall chain link fence where a gate stood open. Once through the gate they took a ramp onto a highway and sped along the road.

Robert Hoopes did not have the best sense of direction, but he could tell from the position of the morning sun that they were heading south. There was nothing more to read in the envelope, so he stared out the window at the landscape. He wondered why anyone would want to live in flyover country. It was boring. Being in Washington where the ultimate action was made all the difference in the world, and being steps away from the most powerful man in the world was all he wanted at this stage of his life.

An hour slipped by and the scenery became even more rural. "Please put on the blindfold," the driver said after driving the whole trip in silence.

"How much further do we have to go?" Hoopes asked. The driver didn't answer.

Hoopes felt like saying something nasty to him, but he bit his tongue and refused to give in to the sarcasm he employed with others beneath his pay grade. He dutifully covered his eyes with the black strip of cloth and tied it behind his head.

Another hour may have slipped by, or they may have been driving less time than that—he couldn't tell. He felt the car swing off the highway and onto a side road. The sound of the tires was different, but he had no idea what the road's surface was made from. He resisted the temptation to peek. Many more minutes passed before the driver took another turn and stopped. Hoopes assumed they were in a driveway.

"Do not remove the blindfold." The driver's gruff voice grated against Hoopes' ears like sandpaper. "Someone will be here in a moment to take you to your destination."

Hoopes felt tense. *Why all this cloak and dagger crap? Who was he meeting? What was the big deal?* He'd conducted secret meetings on the president's behalf that required many levels of security, but none of them involved him blindfolded and waiting to be picked up in what had to be the middle of nowhere.

He wanted to kick himself for jumping as the car door opened, but a soft voice with a slight lisp said, "Mr. Hoopes, I'm going to take your arm and help you exit from the car. Mind your head. When we're through the front door I'll tell you when you can remove the blindfold. My, it's a lovely day, don't you think?"

A very large hand took his right arm and he was led away from the car, up a small flight of steps, and through a door. He reached up to take off the blindfold but was stopped cold as the hand squeezed his upper arm in a vice-like grip.

"Do NOT remove the blindfold until I tell you to! Understood?" The soft voice took on a menacing undertone.

Hoopes winced at the pain in his arm. "Yes. Sorry. It's uncomfortable—"

Whoever was with him closed a door behind him. The voice said, "All right, you may remove it."

When Robert Hoopes removed the blindfold he was amazed at the creature standing before him. The man was huge, towering perhaps six-foot-eight or more, massive in girth, and dressed in a butler's uniform. He was as bald as a billiard ball, with eyebrows that were so blond they appeared to be white. His round face was equally white. He looked for all the world like the Pillsbury Doughboy, and Robert almost choked as the thought fleetingly crossed his mind.

There was nothing of the Doughboy's sweetness in this man. Hoopes was certain he detected the glint of pure evil in the man's cerulean blue eyes. Hoopes was sure the man could kill him as easily as he would swat a fly. His voice was a bit shaky. "Are you the man I'm to see?"

The creature smiled at him with teeth that were perfectly white and even. "Oh my, no, of course not. We'll go into the living room. Your host will be along presently." He gestured for Hoopes to follow. "Follow me."

They left the grand foyer where they had been standing, and Hoopes had little time to look at his surroundings as he followed the giant down a hallway to a massive living room. A huge fieldstone fireplace dominated the wall opposite the entrance to the room. Hoopes looked out a bank of windows that ran the length of one wall to his right. He saw trees, grass and out buildings, but little else that would help him identify where he was.

He turned to say something to the hellish butler, but he had disappeared. He stood alone in the room, uncertain whether he should sit or simply stand there waiting. The furniture in the room was covered in rich maroon leather. About ten feet from the fireplace twin sofas faced each other with a beautifully worked oak coffee table between them. The room was richly furnished with more oak tables, antique lamps, and sumptuous area rugs over an oak hardwood floor. The room spoke volumes about the tastes and wealth of the home's occupant. It was opulent and stylish, and as beautiful and as comfortable as a room in a Martha Stewart magazine.

There were no pictures on the wall and Hoopes found that to be curious.

"Good morning, Mr. Hoopes." A pleasant voice said. "Would you care for some breakfast? I was just about to sit down and enjoy mine."

Hoopes turned toward the voice. It's owner stood before him wearing a comfortable looking lightweight white cashmere sweater over a dark blue shirt, dark blue slacks, and expensive loafers. He appeared to be about sixty, fit, and his brown eyes stared steadily back at him. Hoopes felt overdressed in his Armani suit.

He reached out to shake the man's hand, but stopped short as his host said what seemed to Hoopes a most curious thing. "I don't shake hands, Mr. Hoopes. It is not my custom." Ignoring Hoopes' proffered hand, the man started toward a doorway while motioning for him to follow. The doorway, it turned out, led to the most incredible kitchen that Hoopes had ever seen.

If the living room was very large, the only word to describe the kitchen was vast. To his left another bank of windows looked out on a lovely garden where a fountain sprayed water into the morning air. Two huge islands topped with polished granite occupied the center of the kitchen. They each contained sinks, stove tops, and utensil holders lined up in perfect order. It's owner obviously spared no expense in creating a virtual chef's paradise. To his right, the long wall was filled with ornately carved and gleaming polished wood cabinetry. Huge built-in Sub-Zero refrigerators stood like twin sentinels on the wall opposite two built-in industrial sized microwaves, and a door that must have opened on a huge pantry. Along the windows, a massive antique salvaged door had been re-purposed into a gorgeous table. Hoopes calculated that there was room to seat at least twenty people, but oddly, only two chairs were set to the table, one at each end.

Every inch of the room was immaculate. One of the islands boasted an overhanging counter flanked by six leather backed stools arranged in perfect order. When Hoopes thought about it later he was sure that someone must have taken a ruler and aligned the chairs precisely so there would be no variance in the distances that separated the chairs from the counter or each other.

His host led him to the chair at the end of this row and indicated that he should sit down.

"Sir," Hoopes ventured, "you know my name. May I inquire as to yours?"

Instead of answering his question the man said, "How wonderful. You speak with good diction. Good breeding shows. I understand your father is a judge."

The remark caught Hoopes by surprise. He hated his father more than he hated his older brother. He stumbled in his response. "Uh, well, yes sir. I grew up in Rhode Island. I attended—"

"In Newport...is that correct?"

"Yes, sir. I don't want to appear impolite, but I have no idea who you are."

"Mr. Hoopes, that isn't necessary. Your time here will be brief. I'll be giving you something to deliver to the president. Now, how do you like your eggs?"

His host prepared a meal of eggs-over-easy with a side of sausage and wheat toast for Hoopes, and scrambled eggs, rye toast, and bacon for himself. Hoopes watched as the man displayed great dexterity in the kitchen, and he became aware of light classical music playing softly through speakers hidden somewhere in the room.

When the meal was ready the man carried it on a tray to the long table by the window. He placed his food at the near end of the table in front of the single chair set there. He then took his guest's plate to the opposite end of the table and set it down in front of the other chair. He indicated that Hoopes should take his place at the table.

Hoopes slid off the stool and started towards the table when he saw that his host was frowning at him. He turned around and did his best to reposition the bar chair he'd been sitting on. When he turned back his host was smiling at him.

Once they'd both taken their places at the table Hoopes began to think it was the most bizarre meal he'd ever shared with anyone in his life. Most people would have sat next to a guest, but his host sat at least twenty feet away from him. Hoopes noticed that the silverware was perfectly aligned with his plate. He watched as the man unfolded his napkin and positioned it perfectly on his lap. Hoopes followed suit.

The man did not speak during the meal. He ate with great gusto and seemed almost enraptured with each mouthful and the sensation of taste. Hoopes acquired a habit of gulping down his food when he was young, so he could leave the dinner table to get away from his parents and brother as quickly as possible. He half feared that if he ate in his normal fashion, the butler would burst into the room and he would be on the menu the next day.

He found himself thinking that he'd stepped into an episode of *The Twilight Zone* re-runs he'd watched on television as a kid. The whole thing was just too weird. He paced himself so that he finished his meal when his host was done.

"Coffee or tea, Mr. Hoopes?"

"Coffee would be wonderful, sir."

"Cream and sugar?"

"Yes, please."

"Ah, courtesy is such a wonderful thing in a young man."

His host brought coffee to the table. Hoopes drank his coffee while the man sipped tea. When they were finished his host stood up. He started to take his plates from the table when the man said, "Don't touch them!"

"Sir?"

"Don't even think about picking those up!" This statement was said with such anger that Hoopes almost dropped his dish and silverware on the table.

"I'm sorry, I—"

"My servant will take care of the dishes. There are those who lead and those who serve. Our duties are well defined. The classes should not mix. Ever!"

"I wasn't trying to offend you. I assumed that, I mean, I didn't know—"

"Of course you didn't. How could you?" His host's tone of voice was less strident. "You've learned a valuable lesson today, Mr. Hoopes. People of our station do not do the work of those who were bred to serve us. Their tasks are defined, just as our job is to lead them, protect them, see that they have their basic needs, and thin the herd when necessary. Do you understand?"

Hoopes understood, including the part about thinning the herd.

"I'm sorry, sir. It won't happen again."

"Well, it certainly won't happen here. It's time you were on your way. Please convey my pleasure and approval to the president for the fine job he's doing. Thank him for sending a courteous young patrician as his courier. It has been a joy meeting you. Now, I have work to do, so I must say goodbye. Someone will let you out. You must wear the blindfold for part of the way. It is necessary. One can't be too careful. You'll find the package on a table next to the front door. Have a good trip."

That was it. The man turned and left the room. Hoopes stood in the kitchen for a moment pondering the man's words. Whatever this place was, whoever this man was, the audacity of him sending his approval to the president was over the top. *How arrogant,* he thought.

Hoopes left the kitchen and went to the living room. The blindfold was lying on top of the package. He picked up the package, put on the blindfold and waited by the door, feeling like a fool.

A moment later a hand slipped under his arm, and a woman's voice said, "I'll lead you through the door to the car. Mind your step and your head please."

A few moments later he was in the car and on his way back to Omaha. It seemed like a long time, but finally the driver told him he could remove the blindfold. He stared out over fields of wheat as they drove. It had been an exhausting day. He probably wouldn't get home until ten tonight.

CHAPTER 24

The infamous Pennsylvania groundhog had seen his shadow, but winter in Clear Haven seemed to last six months of the year whether the rodent's prognostication was for an early spring or not.

February turned to March and the Easter season arrived. Michael and Joan traveled to Pennsylvania for the holiday without their daughters. Angela decided to visit Boston for the holiday with her college roommate, and Louise's job with a mall department store meant she needed to stay at home. Short-staffed for the holiday, store management asked her to fill in for a woman who was off having a baby.

Susan and Henry arrived without Dylan. He was participating in a bike race in Altoona, and would not be home until late in the evening.

Minus the kids, dinner was a quiet affair. After the dishes were cleared Henry suggested they all go for a drive. They piled into Henry's SUV and headed off in what the women assumed was no particular direction.

As Henry pulled onto Route 80 heading westbound Susan

asked, "Henry, where are you going? Is there a purpose to this trip?"

"The answer is yes. You'll know where soon enough."

They reached the access road and Henry pulled off the highway and started up the hill. "Have you lost your mind?" The elder Mrs. Stonebreaker's voice crackled with alarm. "We can't be on this road. It's official access only. What if a State Trooper sees us? We'll be in big trouble, Henry!"

Michael said, "Don't worry, Mom. It's all right. We have a surprise for all of you. Enjoy the ride."

"You're in on this, too, Michael?"

"Yes, Mom, I am. Today is the day when everything changes. This is the day when the three of you learn all about my new job, and Henry's, too."

"I didn't know you were getting a new job."

"I haven't been able to talk about it with anyone except Joan, but today you all learn what's going on."

"Why so mysterious?" Susan asked.

"It's the best kept secret in America." After that cryptic remark the five of them rode in silence until they reached the guarded gate, where Colonel Eric Dryden was waiting for them. He was smiling broadly. An enormous Hummer was parked off to the side just beyond the gate. When Henry drove through the gate he pulled his SUV in front of the Hummer and parked. They all got out and Eric greeted them.

"If you'll get into my ride we can all travel together." Eric said. A Special Forces operative in camo sat behind the wheel of the Hummer with the motor running.

The women were not asked to put on blindfolds because Michael insisted that it was unnecessary. Things were changing rapidly, and it was time to move forward full speed in preparation for what lay ahead. The families would know all about The Movement from this day forward. Michael wanted the blindfolds off literally.

The Pennsylvania mountain scenery was still bleak from the ravages of a harsh, cold winter. Ice and snow did not give up easily to an arriving spring that was still a couple weeks off on the calendar.

The road wound through the hills, and at one point they passed through massive blast doors in a hillside and drove at least a quarter mile before they exited on the other side of the hill. It was the first of many such doors through which they would pass this day. As they approached a second hill with similar doors the women began wondering aloud what they implied.

"It's all a precaution." Eric said. "When we get where we are going you'll understand why they're necessary."

They finally arrived at what The Movement referred to as The Manor. It resembled a large hunting camp. A wide porch ran the length of the front of the building, which was constructed of massive logs. Eric led the women through the front door and down the hallway, with Michael and Henry following behind. When they halted in front of what looked like a blank wall, the women were mystified.

Joan asked, "Eric, is this a joke? Are you having fun with us?"

Eric smiled at her and held his right hand up in front of the wall. A hidden sensor responded, the wall slid back to reveal huge elevator doors. Eric placed his palm on a reader, and put his right eye in front of a retinal scanner. "The president and his party have arrived," he said.

The doors opened and they stepped into the elevator. One thousand feet below ground they finally stopped and the doors opened. Eric turned to the group. "Joan, Susan, and Mrs. Stonebreaker, what you're about to see and experience began a long time ago. It has been kept secret for reasons that you'll learn very soon. Michael, Henry, and I are part of something that may, at first seem unimaginable to you. I assure you that everything you see is real, and the people you'll meet and talk to today are wholeheartedly committed to restoring the United States of America to greatness."

Eric led them through a blast door to a waiting tram, and they took the long tunnel to the area just outside the conference room. The little party exited the tram and Eric led them to a set of double doors. He opened them and ushered the group into the room. Nearly all the seats at the long table were occupied.

"Ladies and gentlemen," Eric announced, "The president, and

his party." Everyone at the table stood, and the room broke out in light applause. Eric led the party to seats left open for them, and when they were seated he walked to the far end of the table.

"In the early days of the Eisenhower administration a group of people came together in a hotel in Washington, DC. At that meeting…" Eric told the story of The Movement's founding and its history up to the present. When he finished others at the table were called on to describe the roles they played within its ranks. An hour passed, then two.

Finally, Eric raised his hand and everyone became silent. "It's time for the family to see what we have here. There will be a reception at the Truman Building at seventeen-hundred hours. The ladies will have a chance to talk with all of you one-on-one at that time. Now, if you'll excuse us…"

Eric led the five of them through the door into the tunnel where another tram waited for them. As they rode through the tunnel and out onto the ledge road, the women cried out in amazement at the view of the underground city.

For the next two hours they were given an extensive tour of the underground complex. There were new revelations around every corner. The more they saw and wondered aloud at the vastness of the place, the more they exchanged looks with the husbands who'd kept it a secret from them.

"Well, gang, it's time we head back for the reception." With that, the tour ended and they began the return trip to the main building. After several moments, Joan was the first to speak, but she was certain the other women were thinking the same thing.

"Michael, I understand to a degree why you didn't tell me about all of this, but don't you think I deserved to know?" Her voice was tinged with anger. "When you said you were offered a new job I never imagined it was to overthrow the US government! Are you out of your mind?"

Eric started to respond when Joan snapped at him, "Let Michael speak for himself! I deserve an answer!"

Michael did not smile at Joan, and for a moment he wondered

if he'd done the right thing in insisting that she be brought here. "You know politics is not a topic lightly discussed in our home. We're a military family. I depend on the US government for my job, my pay, and my professional life. I have the greatest respect for the office of the commander in chief and the White House. But unfortunately, our government has betrayed all of us." He let the words sink in.

"I was initially brought into this kicking and screaming, because I was not comfortable with the premise of this plan. But, given time to research and study what is happening in America, the conclusions are irrefutable. The elitists in power are taking over. They are building a Progressive utopia in which they'll tell us where we can and cannot go, what we can and cannot eat, what sort of vehicle we will be permitted to drive, the kind of house we'll be allowed to live in, the kind of health care we'll get—and that's not even all they want to control. Our children will be so brainwashed that a generation from now there will be no memory of the wonderful nation the United States of America was founded to be. Before our freedoms are completely obliterated The Movement is ready to take swift, certain, and irrevocable action."

"What exactly are you anticipating?" The elder Mrs. Stonebreaker asked.

"There is a great crisis coming," Eric answered. "The current administration plans to use that crisis to take full and final control of the population. The Movement will not allow that to happen."

Michael nodded. "Our family will be protected. Joan, I insisted that if it were humanly possible in the aftermath that your career will continue, as well."

"It only makes sense for very effort to be made to move forward with as much normalcy as possible," Henry said. "We'll be rebuilding the nation."

"You can't think this will all go off without a hitch!" Susan raised an eyebrow.

Eric spoke softly but with resolve. "There may be a period of unrest. In the space of a night and a day everything will change, but it will be many months before people begin to fully grasp what has occurred. The American people will be able to take comfort in the fact that our institutions and leadership will remain in place."

"What if you'd decided not to take the job—of president—then what, Michael?" She waved her hand in the air. "Does all this just go away?" Joan looked directly in his eyes.

"It was my choice to accept or reject this job. If I turned them down it wouldn't have changed anything. The Movement still must do all that is necessary to take back America."

"You honestly believe this Movement can win?" Joan asked. "Do you know for sure that what you say will be done can, in fact, be done?" Her brow wrinkled in fear and doubt.

Henry answered, and his unexpected response startled Joan into listening.

"The enemies of individual freedom have been building their infrastructure and working their plan for a hundred years, and this organization has been doing the same for nearly sixty of those same years. While the safety and security of the American people has always been paramount in The Movement's plan, the power mad career politicians controlling our country don't care about the people, and the people know it!

"The facility you've seen here is just one of many in nearly every state in this country. The people and resources involved are beyond anything you could ever imagine. When the time comes you'll realize just how much time, talent, and treasure has been invested and why this is going to change our nation for the better.

"Joan, you've got nothing to worry about. Michael doesn't make mistakes. He never has. You know him better than anyone, and we all know him well. You can trust his belief in what The Movement is doing."

"That's all well and good, Henry Stonebreaker, but Joan's not the only one who's upset!" Susan gazed steadily at her husband. "What are we going to do if the government finds out about this? Where will we be able to live if they get word of it?"

"Susan, for reasons I can't go into now, the government is not going to find out about this." He took her hand. "I understand your fear, but honey, more than anything else, it's the future of our children that concerns me. You and I both want them to be truly free in America, without some hideous Big Brother telling them what to do with their lives. I'm asking you to trust Michael, Eric and me to be part of making that a reality."

The elder Mrs. Stonebreaker spoke next, "Are you telling me that my son is going to be the President of the United States? Are you serious? How is that possible?"

"Where will we live?"

"What about the children? What will we tell them?"

Everyone started talking at once and then Michael yelled, "Please, listen for a moment!" They became quiet. "Yes, Mom, I'm going to be president, possibly for one term, two if I'm re-elected. During the transition everyone will be living here for a while. I cannot tell you how exactly this is all going to happen; I can only say that it will."

Eric addressed the ladies. "For obvious reasons, you will be sworn to silence, but I know that is not a problem. We're protecting our kids, our extended families and our friends by that silence. Everyone will be brought here to Clear Haven at the first sign of the crisis; it's part of the zone of protection."

"And your family, Eric? Does Yvette know about this place and The Movement?" Joan's mouth was set in a firm line.

"She's as new to this as you all are." Eric paused. "I get that you all feel upset, and even angry at being kept in the dark about all of this. The secrecy is difficult to explain, except to say that the people we need to unseat are in no way to be trifled with."

"They've gone to the extent of arranging accidents for members of their own party who threatened to expose them," Henry added.

"Yes, and we believe their ruthlessness extends to threatening the families of political opponents in order to get them to withdraw from races, or to keep them from running at all. As a man, and I know Michael and Henry agree with me, we couldn't risk involving you all until it became absolutely necessary."

"And we're trusting God to give you peace and understanding now that you know," Michael said softly, but with firm conviction.

"We need you to stand with us in this."

As Michael was speaking the tram approached the front of the Truman Building and stopped. They exited the car and again made their way into the stunning lobby. They road the scenic elevator to the reception, which was being held in a beautifully decorated room on the fourth floor. A wall of glass opened onto the lobby, giving them a stunning view of the United States flag suspended from the ceiling two stories above.

Michael and Henry introduced their wives to many of the people seated back in the conference room. They asked questions and received as much information as possible under the circumstances.

The ride home was quiet. When Henry pulled into the driveway they filed silently into the house. No one spoke for a long time, each lost in his or her own thoughts.

It was after ten when Dylan arrived, and after filling them in on the bike race Henry, Susan and Dylan said their goodbyes and got in the SUV to head home. Mrs. Stonebreaker also said goodnight and retired to her bedroom.

Joan and Michael sat in the kitchen. They sat quietly in the dark, with only the light from one of Mrs. Stonebreaker's scented candles glowing on the counter. The scent of cinnamon and apples wafted gently through the room.

"Michael, I'm scared. What if this doesn't work out? What will we do? Where will we go? How can the girls have a normal life? Did you think about any of these things when you agreed to this? Did you even think about us?"

Michael stood up, came around the table, got on his knees and hugged Joan to him. She clung to him desperately. "I'm so afraid," she said. He felt her trembling.

"Joanie, I will not make promises I can't keep. I can't say that failure isn't possible, but I can say it's not probable. I would have never agreed to this if I didn't think it was right. At the end of the day my concerns are for you and the girls. I want what's best for you and them…and for me, too. Our country is in deep trouble. If things aren't changed in very short order there will be nothing left to change."

"But how can you change it? How can you beat them? They control everything. They tell everybody what to do—even you! They make the laws, they run the courts, and they have the power to destroy us! How can we fight against anything that powerful?"

"There is a chink in their armor. There's something they haven't thought of in all their deceptive scheming. They're weak in a way they cannot see."

"How is that?"

"You'll know soon enough. For now, I have to ask you to trust me, Joanie. Let's go to bed."

"I'm not sure I'll ever be able to sleep soundly again."

CHAPTER 25

Pierce Armstrong referred to the place where he lived as "The Farm." His grandfather purchased a thousand acres for pennies on the dollar from a farmer who lost everything during the Great Depression. In the years that followed he cultivated the land, and access to The Farm, built on fifteen acres, was hidden from view.

A series of fields, or buffers, were leased to a local farmer. No record of The Farm itself appeared on any deed, map or other official document. In essence, it did not exist.

Armstrong would go into the nearby community once or twice a week to buy fresh produce. When he went out he wore bib overalls, and a fake beard and mustache. He drove an old beat up pick-up that appeared to be on its last legs. The townspeople knew him as Jacob Hornsby. He would often make conversation with Ken Wallace, the manager of the small grocery store, and Tim Harliss, the only barber in town. In his costume most people thought of him as old and he presented himself as eccentric, crotchety, and generally unimportant. They knew he lived somewhere out of town, but they were all vague as to just where that might be, and had no reason to care. "Jacob

Hornsby" was just a local fixture in their minds that popped up on a regular basis and then disappeared. Beyond that, they weren't even curious.

Unless one has stood on the vast Nebraska plains and looked out at the land for seemingly unending miles in every direction it is hard to comprehend what it is like to live there. Rural Nebraska is a haven for anyone who loves solitude. The land is farmed in quarter miles that make up square miles. From the air it is a giant checker board of perfectly straight roads with vast fields that are often irrigated by a central well sunk in the center of a quarter square mile of acres. The well water is pumped through a giant pivot, a tall system of pipes and wheels that can take days to make one pass covering a hundred and sixty acres of ground.

Pierce Armstrong was an obsessive compulsive who insisted everything in his world be perfectly neat and immaculate. He employed precisely six servants to care for the house and grounds. Three women attended the cleaning duties in the main house, two men maintained the out buildings, mowed the grass, did general maintenance duties including plumbing, electrical and carpentry work when required. Ironically, the hellish butler, as Robert Hoopes thought of him, was Armstong's own special assistant and bodyguard. Ollie Larson was known among the staff as the *butler from hell.*

Twelve of the fifteen acres of The Farm appeared to be dense woods. The other three had been left open in the center of the plot, with trees strategically planted so that their canopy concealed the view of the center area from above. The Farm sprawled beneath the cover of the trees, and consisted of the main residence, a barn, a large barracks, and a garage that housed four cars and the old pickup. A separate guest quarters that could sleep up to twenty people stood well apart from the main house, but still out of view.

Within his well hidden compound, the architect of the American Progressive movement was beside himself with anxiety. Someone tried to follow young Mr. Hoopes to The Farm. *This was most disturbing,* he thought, absently straightening a perfectly aligned stool in the row at the kitchen island.

Unbeknownst to Armstrong, the man who loved the Gulf promised the senator that Hoopes would be tailed, and that a complete dossier of his every move would be compiled. A surveillance team tracked him to the airport in Washington, the flight plan of the jet had been flagged, a call was made, and a man was assigned to follow Hoopes from the airport the minute he landed in Omaha.

Armstrong was fully aware that the man was in a room below the barn suffering unspeakable treatment at the hands of his butler.

Two cars cut off the man's nondescript tan Ford Escape where the road turned off the main highway roughly three miles from The Farm. The man had been brought to the barn and shackled in the secret room.

Ollie Larson, the butler from hell, did resemble the Pillsbury Doughboy, but there was no kindness in him. Anyone who tried to poke him in the stomach to evoke that famous chuckle would have his arm ripped off and be beaten to death with it.

 Ollie enjoyed nothing more than inflicting pain on others. At the moment he was using a blowtorch to find out how much his captive knew, and he was frustrated because the man he was slowly roasting could only be described as a Mob goon who could take a lot of treatment, as Ollie thought of it, but was giving very little information in return. The screams reassured Ollie of his level of expertise with the torch. The hidden room was filled with all sorts of things gathered from around the world over many years. A complete set of cruel-looking devices liberated from a Nazi concentration camp filled a metal cabinet from the same camp, and a rack dating back to the Middle Ages occupied a corner of the room. A small, ornately carved, antique cabinet housed an assortment of powerful drugs, syringes and scalpels. Overhead, a beam outfitted with straps, hooks and mean looking nails ran the length of the room; all were designed for the sole purpose of hanging a human being in demented and excruciatingly painful positions. Screams were usually followed by whimpering, and Ollie was not disappointed.

The nice thing, in Ollie's twisted mind, was that when he was done with inflicting pain on someone he got to kill them. He liked that almost as much as causing pain. Ollie considered himself a true craftsman, indeed, an artist in the practice of torture. He read a good deal on the subject thanks to Pierce Armstrong, whose seemingly limitless resources supplied him with new books, treatises and translations of relevant ancient documents.

As a child Ollie enjoyed ripping wings off butterflies, stomping on new born kittens and puppies, and beating full grown dogs and cats with sticks. His father beat him almost every day of his life when he was growing up. Ollie grew big enough to best him in an all-out brawl, and killed the Old Man when he was seventeen.

Ollie was the one outsider among the Armstrong employees. He had been in the man's employ long enough to have known Pierce's late father, but he never met the grandfather.

Young Ollie attracted the attention of Pierce Armstrong a few years later when he got a flat tire on the old pickup on his way back from town. Armstrong had a spare, but since there was no jack in the truck bed, and he did not ever get his hands dirty with common labor, he walked to the one service station in town to see if he could find someone to help him.

Ollie had been sitting on an oil drum drinking a Coke when he heard Armstrong's plea to the station owner and volunteered to help. He and Armstrong walked back to the pickup only to find there was no jack.

To Armstrong's amazement, Ollie picked up the back of the truck, while for the first and last time in his life, Armstrong had gotten his hands dirty with menial labor. He dragged two cement blocks out of the truck bed and positioning them under the axle at Ollie's direction. Fortunately, there was a tire iron in the bed. Ollie changed the tire and a bond was formed. That had been fifteen years ago.

Pierce Armstrong did not like the lower classes, but he saw in Ollie a creature that could be useful to him in a number of ways. The torture room was one of them. Pierce did not touch other people. Ever. As he would say when it came to shaking hands, it was not his "custom." Torture requires touching, and he was so terribly afraid of germs that he could not bring himself to touch another human being.

Ollie became the expert in this area. Ollie had killed his own father, but was freed after a judge ruled the death accidental.

A few years later Pierce talked Ollie into wearing the butler's uniform when he hosted a gathering of leading Progressives for a long weekend. The event ended when a drunken member of the gathering became ill and threw up all over Pierce Armstrong's dining room table to his guests' disgust.

Armstrong ordered Ollie to take the man to one of the guest rooms. He retired to his own suite, where he spent two hours showering the filth from his body. He had his clothing burned.

During the night Ollie escorted the drunk to the special room. Pierce told the remaining members of the party at breakfast the following morning that the drunk left the night before in embarrassment. The man was never seen outside The Farm again.

Ollie kept him alive for the better part of a week before killing him on the ancient rack. No one touched Pierce Armstrong and lived.

The current victim, whose name was Sal, was a contract man. He worked out of Omaha as local muscle when required. He knew nothing about Robert Hoopes, only that he was hired to follow him. That was all. Ollie's experience told him there was no more information to be gleaned from Sal. The whimpering became tedious. *Time to escalate the fun.* Ollie reached for the pliers.

CHAPTER 26

The President of the United States opened the package he'd received from Pierce Armstrong. He sat and read the contents for the better part of an hour. Then he summoned his Special Assistant.

Robert Hoopes sat silently at his desk, waiting for the call. When it came he went to the Oval Office, took the package from the president, and carried it back to his office. Once inside, he closed and locked the door. He then opened the package and began feeding the contents into his shredder. He did not look at what was printed on the twenty-five or so pages. He simply went about the business of destroying it quickly.

He always played a game with himself whenever he did anything like this. His rationale was simple: If he did not read it, he knew nothing about it, and if he knew nothing about it he could not be questioned about it, and if he could not be questioned about it, it never existed in the first place.

✳✳✳✳✳✳✳

Miles away in the country's heartland, Pierce Armstrong carved into an exquisite filet mignon wrapped in a perfectly crisp slice of premium bacon. The rare meat melted like butter on his tongue as he contemplated the straw that would break the proverbial camel's back and make his dreams of controlling the wealthiest nation in the world come true. Special Assistant to the President, Robert Hoopes might not know the document he was shredding was brilliant, but the man who wrote it did. Every detail of Pierce Armstrong's plan was brilliant.

At heart, his strategy was deceptively simple. He would drive the country to its knees with a catastrophic event of such magnitude that the president would have no choice but to implement martial law. The president would seize control of the nation, and the transition to a dictatorship would be almost natural. As the architect and brains behind the ideology currently controlling the White House, he would continue to play the role of puppet master to the leader of the free world. He laughed out loud at the thought.

But how exactly did one go about orchestrating a catastrophe that would bring a nation the size of America under martial law? He contemplated various approaches throughout the '80s and into the '90s, when the universe seemed to open up and drop elements of the solution in his lap. Terrorism was nothing new to the Middle East, but it was beginning to take root in the Western world, specifically in the United States, right under the people's noses. The Weather Underground's World Trade Center bombing, the Columbine massacre, the DC sniper attacks, the Underwear Bomber, the shootings at Fort Hood and Virginia Tech, the Boston Marathon bombing... he lost track of the incidents. The admitted targeting and murder of Americans in the name of jihad by a gunman who openly confessed that his motivation was retaliation for the United States' actions in the Middle East signaled a perfect catalyst for his plan. He turned his attention to a steaming heap of freshly roasted asparagus spears and red potatoes in a spicy garlic sauce.

And so it had come to him. He proposed radicalizing an

organization whose sole ideological objective was destroying the United States. The group would never know that the US government and its agents were aware of its existence, let alone funding and orchestrating their operation. They would simply carry out what they believed was their plan, ignorant of who they were working for. Of course, the death and destruction they would cause was a necessary evil, one that would be the catalyst for a breakdown of civil authority that would warrant instituting martial law across the nation. Under the control of the president the military would rule, with it's laws superseding civil laws. The so called Constitutional rights of the population would be wiped out with one fell swoop.

Previous administrations had done their best to protect the public with the Patriot Act, Homeland Security, and increased surveillance through the NSA and other less well known entities. However, if a massive enough terrorist act took place again on American soil, the current administration could impose martial law on a temporary basis under the pretext of finding and eliminating all threats to the public's safety. Deciding how long that would take would be up to the president alone. Morphing a temporary situation into a permanent one would require finesse, but it could be accomplished as long as ongoing threats loomed on the horizon. Martial law could become the law of the land. He took a generous sip of a robust red Bordeaux blend he'd been given by the French ambassador. He puckered his mouth around the earthy notes of blackcurrant and tobacco.

Eventually, the people could even be restricted from gathering under the threat of being labeled a potential terrorist threat. Personal and media communication could be censored or shut down completely if its content was deemed a threat to the common good. Dissenting viewpoints could be silenced in the interest of protecting the nation. Disarming the population through gun control laws was a stroke of genius borrowed from Hitler's Nazi regime. Most of the people would be defenseless against the onslaught of government control. Forcing citizens to register their guns would make it easy to take out any pockets of armed resistance that were bound to flare up.

Ultimately, his objective was mind control, which was only

possible through the control of information. The damn cable network and talk radio must be silenced. Reimplementation and selective application of the Fairness Doctrine would take care of that. The attack would take place before the next election, and the president would be the darling of the media once again for showing strong leadership in the face of such an unprecedented crisis. Instituting martial law to protect Americans would make heroes of the president and the reigning politicians, no matter which political party they belonged to. He helped himself to a huge piece of chocolate cake smothered in a bittersweet chocolate ganache and a cup of steaming mocha java coffee made with his prized Yemen Mocha Mattari beans.

He was initially struck by the phenomena when in the midst of the 9/11 crisis, President George Bush's most vociferous political enemies embraced him openly before the cameras during his initial address to the nation. He came to the conclusion that nothing creates more love, trust, and cooperation across the political aisle faster than a good national crisis. A key strategist among the Progressive elite had listened well at his dining room table and run with the concept.

Of course, he considered his work brilliant in theory, but in practice it would be nothing less than spectacular! The players were in place and gearing up. Thousands of innocent people were going to die, but that could not be helped. The fact that so many of them would be children was even more egregious, but this would add fuel to the fire of public opinion in favor of imposing martial law. The only viable option for preventing more monstrous acts of terror from being perpetrated on American soil would be to place the entire country on lockdown.

Finding unwitting conspirators who were true enemies of the United States had not been a problem. They were plenty of radicalized zealots who were eager to serve as dupes to carry out the heinous act. Afterward, when they were caught and endlessly paraded across American television screens the people would be entirely focused on hanging the terrorists in the streets if they could get their hands on them. The American people would hardly complain that their own precious freedoms were being stripped away in the name of national security, and that they were becoming little more than a cash cow for the government to milk at will. Under martial law the president was the government, and of course, he controlled the president.

His plan was ingenious. He ate another slice of cake.

******

The president knew he never wanted Pierce Armstrong as an enemy. The man was merciless. He was evil in a way that made the garden variety demons inside the Beltway pale in comparison. Armstrong was the most twisted character he'd ever encountered.

The deal would go down in October. The president sighed and ran a hand through his hair. Public sentiment turned against his leadership in the past couple of years, but his response to a massive terror attack could turn it back again. It didn't matter one way or the other. He would implement martial law ostensibly to protect the public and as a show of strength. The real reason for doing so would be to justify issuing an executive order to halt the presidential election, allowing him and his cabinet to remain in power.

The radical group incited to carry out the attack acted without knowing that their mission was engineered and funded through the misdirection of US funds and resources. Strategically placed operatives funneled monies to the terrorists to help them plan, design, and ultimately execute a horrific slaughter for the purpose of establishing him as the last president of the United States.

He was sure that if hell itself had a face, it would be Pierce Armstrong's.

He picked up the phone and dialed. *It was time to put the final phase of the evil genius's plan in motion.*

CHAPTER 27

Norman Blesco was praying. He was so deeply entrenched in his role as an American that he did not pray openly in public, but he was that much more devoted to prayer in the privacy of his home. His heart sang as he prayed. His would be one of the hands that would hurt the Great Satan more grievously than ever before. Its destruction had been long in the planning. The day was fast approaching.

The sleepers had been in place for years, waiting to blow the world apart. He prayed that thousands of infidels would die, and that thousands more would be injured. He prayed that the slaughter would take as many of their children as possible. He prayed for their pain to be excruciating, and their torment unending.

He envisioned himself walking through the street covered with gore and blood, singing a song of praise, arms held high. He held the head of an infidel clutched by the hair in his right hand, and his knife in the other hand. The blood lust was on him. He was a warrior in the battle for truth. He and his brothers would not be defeated. They would take the world for Allah and remove every infidel from the earth.

Americans were predictable. The anniversary of 9/11

was coming and they always prepared for the possibility that his brotherhood would attack again on that day. His brothers learned to be unpredictable. Their plan was simple: do the most harm in the most beloved of all American places where they came to indulge themselves and their children—Disney World.

His brother sleepers had been in place in the resort for years. Some were Disney cast members, on staff within the complex. One was a man who delivered food to the four theme parks. Another built and maintained the equipment for operating the rides, primarily at night when the parks were empty and the infidels slept in their decadent hotels. The leader of the group was a manager with access to designs, diagrams, and the interior spaces of the buildings and rides. He knew where best to hide explosives to do the most damage, and he oversaw the clandestine activities of the twenty sleepers embedded throughout the four parks. While Norman prayed ecstatically, this man reviewed logistics.

Norman would be the last of the cell to arrive at Disney World just three weeks before the event. The group leader would give him access to the communications center, and Norman would disable the system to wreak additional havoc when the event took place.

The others were teams that trained together in the Saudi desert. They would be armed with massive firepower. Split up and assigned to specific parks, they would appear after the explosions were detonated. They would come seemingly out of nowhere, armed and willing to give their lives for the cause. Their task was to kill as many infidels in as short a time as possible, and then to keep opposing forces at bay as long as they could until they themselves were killed. They brought disassembled weapons into the parks with food deliveries. They would assemble and hide the guns in predetermined spots, and retrieve them just after the explosions.

The explosives were another matter. The food delivery man had been bringing in small amounts of explosives for a year, which were then hidden in obscure places throughout the four parks. Nightshift employees gathered the component parts and carefully assembled the bombs. Sanderson, the group leader, supervised their strategic placement for doing the most damage to the crowds.

During the evening parade was chosen as the best time to kill and injure the most people amid the chaos and confusion. The appearance of the gunmen would incite more fear and panic. They set as a goal to kill three times the number destroyed on 9/11.

Even as the excitement mounted, the group leader constantly reminded Norman that patience was the key to their success. Final bomb assembly would be completed just days before the attack. Detonation would be achieved using an ultra sophisticated ignition system. He also explained that huge sums had been paid to a foreign supplier for the equipment involved. Everything must be done correctly the first time. There would be no second chances. "Planning for this mission evolved through many stages. Every aspect must be executed flawlessly," he'd said. One of the top orchestrators of the scheme, he had been placed in the amusement park to ensure things came off without a hitch.

Norman understood why the amusement parks had been chosen for the mission. Americans would not expect an attack in such a place, believing it would be too obvious as a potential target. The presence of security at park entrances made it seem unlikely that explosives and weapons could be brought into the complex undetected. And, maybe most importantly, enough time had elapsed since 9/11 for Americans to grow lazy and less vigilant.

Norman Blesco continued to pray in spiritual ecstasy. The thought of the destruction he would help to cause filled him with elation. There were no words for what he was about to accomplish. He could hardly wait. To slaughter and maim the infidels by the thousands would be wonderful beyond words! His dream would come true!

The phone rang, startling him. He picked it up. His boss, Mr. Rumfolo's voice squwaked in his ear. Could he come in early today?

"Yes. No problem." He hung up the phone.

He wished he could cut the man's head off. *One day...*

CHAPTER 28

L ife for the Stonebreakers would never be normal again. Now that Joan, Susan, and their mother knew the truth, Michael and Henry could speak openly when they were together. That would still not be often because they still had to continue their lives and careers as though there were nothing extraordinary afoot.

The children would not be told about what was going on until it was time to move everyone into the underground city. Including the children would have made it more difficult to keep knowledge of The Movement and TR2.0 from the wrong people.

Two weeks after they returned home, Michael was ordered to attend an intelligence briefing with the president at the White House. He would accompany Brigadier General Avery Thompson, his section chief, to the seat of power to discuss activity detected in the mountains of Afghanistan near the Pakistan border. There was something going on; the Taliban's electronic chatter had increased. The nation's threat level moved up a notch, heightening security around the country.

July 4th, the nation's birthday, was at hand. The usual cast of US enemies was suspected of planning another terrorist attack. Their favorite target still seemed to be the Big Apple, but the president wanted to know if Thompson and his people thought there was anything worthy of concern.

As he surveyed the Oval Office, the thoughts raging inside Michael's head were anything but peaceful. The idea that he might someday sit behind that desk unnerved him. He looked away. How could he, Michael Stonebreaker, lead the nation? Managing his own life was enough to do, and his affairs were relatively simple.

What was coming wasn't clear in his mind. He knew that The Movement's elaborate plan to restore the nation to Constitutional order would be carried out swiftly at a particular time, but logistical details of TR2.0 had not yet been revealed to him. Eric said that a handful of people knew the who, what, where, when and how of the plan's execution.

Just being in the room now felt surreal. He focused on his boss, appearing to listen intently as the general briefed the president on potential terrorist activity connected with Independence Day. He kept his eyes fixed on Thompson.

He was a very good man, a West Point grad who knew his stuff. Michael was proud to serve under him. It entered his mind that someday his boss might be answering to him, a thought that struck him as beyond bizarre. He stifled the impulse to leave the room before he jumped out of his skin.

Michael quietly took a deep breath and held it. He let it out slowly. He did it a second time. Fortunately, he sat on a sofa behind Thompson and to his left. He was window dressing today, wearing all his ribbons and medals. He'd carried materials into the room, and he would be carrying them out when they left. No one was paying any attention to him.

He let his eyes wander over the details of the room. This was the focal point of the United States of America. This was where Harry Truman said the buck stopped. Sadly, old "Give 'em hell" would be very disappointed at just how many bucks passed through here on their way to oblivion. The nation was broke. That thought made Michael angry. Politicians had been spending the future to party in the present for far too many decades. There was plenty of blame to go around. Leaders from both major parties and a multitude of political factions were all at fault. Freedom demanded respect for the office and responsibility to the people, two elements that had been missing from Washington for long years.

Michael couldn't bring himself to believe politicians were all inherently bad people, but he did believe that the heady elixir of power tainted the thinking inside the Beltway for so many years that too many believed they were the aristocracy of the nation. If they won more than one term they began to believe that the office was theirs for the keeping. Three elections and the position was theirs by divine right. Such untethered power led to arrogance, and the resulting mix of condescension, superiority and false pride led to deception, misdirection and manipulation. The process of corruption was as old as man and always ended in destruction. A new day was coming sooner than anyone expected, and Michael would be part of it.

He looked forward to leaving the building and getting back to his office. When the meeting ended, they said their goodbyes, exited the White House and got into a waiting SUV.

"So, Michael, what do you think of the President? Thompson asked him.

"He's taller than I expected him to be, sir."

"That's not what I asked you. What do you think of him?

"I'm not sure what you mean, sir."

"Oh, I know you too well to accept that as an answer. How do you feel about his politics? Do you agree with him?"

"He's the commander in chief, sir." Michael responded.

"Always the diplomat! You never have a bad word for anyone. I think that's a very good thing in this town. That's how the game is played here, through the art of deflection."

"Sir?"

"You know what I mean. You've mastered the art of being politely evasive. That's how all these people act, though they're not nearly as polite. They never answer anything with a solid yea or nay. You never know what they believe, what their core values are, if they mean a word they say, or if they're simply playing a never-ending game of C. Y. A. If it wasn't so damn important to the nation it would be a comedy. Except no one ever laughs."

"Yes, sir."

"You're a good soldier, Major Stonebreaker. However, it's not necessary for you to fall on your sword."

"I'm not sure I understand what you mean, sir."

"I'll pretend I didn't hear that. You're the best intelligence officer on my staff. I know your record at the Point. You're smarter than I am. There's a good chance that someday I'll be answering to you."

Michael was startled by the comment, but he clenched his jaw and hid his reaction. *Did the man know something?*

"No comment? All right, have it your way. I'm simply trying to make conversation to clear my head. Every time I visit that place I need two days to recover. Give me men and women who look me in the eye, say what they mean, and mean what they say. That's why I wear the uniform, Major. When I leave that building I feel like I need to take a shower."

"I understand, sir."

"Good. I knew you did. Now, what do you think about that little problem in Afghanistan? Would a drone resolve it?"

Michael smiled. "Sir, I'd recommend a drone today if you felt it was the right thing to do."

"In the words of my favorite Star Trek captain, 'Make it so!'"

When Michael got back to his office he called in the order for the drone. An hour later one more terrorist leader and four of his colleagues left the earth, no longer to do its inhabitants harm.

He spent the afternoon reviewing highly classified intelligence reports. When he checked the regulator clock on his wall, it was a few minutes passed six. He dialed home from his cell phone.

"Hey, Joanie."

"Who is this? Oh, wait, I remember you. Didn't you live here at one time? How have you been?"

He let himself smile for the first time since he'd left home that morning. "You don't have to get smart with me."

"Should I make an appointment to see you?"

"Point made, point taken. I'll be home by 7:30 if the traffic allows. Love you."

"I made meatloaf."

"Meatloaf? I'll be home by 7:00!"

"You get more excited over meatloaf than you do me. What is it about meatloaf?"

"It's a cultural thing."

"Meatloaf is a cultural thing? Where? In the Pennsylvania hill country? You people need to get out more," Joan said, laughing.

"Listen sweetheart, it's your home, too. My mother's meatloaf is the best, but your meatloaf is even better."

"Now you're trying to placate me."

"See you in an hour. I'll bring the ketchup."

When Michael got to his car a folded piece of paper was tucked under the driver's side windshield wiper. He removed it, unlocked his car and got in. Inside the paper, a hand-written message read, "The party is about to begin." There was no signature. Michael recognized the handwriting. It was Eric's.

CHAPTER 29

The man who loved the Gulf let his gaze wander from a lawn so green it made his eyes hurt, to the cool blue waters of an Olympic-sized pool, on to the brooding hulk of the sea wall and over the white-hot sand beyond, finally allowing it to rest on the azure waters of the Gulf sparkling under the early morning sun. The white sails of a boat floated far out in the distance. Gulls screeched, soaring in the blue of the sky overhead.

His thoughts wandered with his eyes. Something happened to the contract man in Omaha. He had not come back from his assignment. The vibe was all wrong. *Did Robert Hoopes discover he was being followed? Was he capable of killing someone?* He thought not. Considering everything he'd learned about the man thus far, he pegged Hoopes for a coward incapable of that level of physical violence.

Where, then, was Sal? A less guarded man might be content to write off Sal's disappearance as a short-lived aberration. He may have taken a wrong turn, had car trouble, or been temporarily delayed by some other distraction. Experience convinced him otherwise. This smelled funny.

The man who loved the Gulf was tall and athletically built, with black hair that was graying at the temples. He resembled Hollywood's leading men of a generation ago, in the tradition of Cary Grant or Clark Gable. His features were distinguished, and his eyes were dark and deep set. Many women came close to driving off the road at the sight of him in his red Ferrari on the rare occasions when he ventured from his compound.

He prided himself on being loyal to his current wife. They were married last year. She was twenty-five years his junior, and she continued to pique his interest. He married two other wives prior to this one. Both lived well, thanks to generous divorce settlements. He fathered no children.

The man who loved the Gulf did not visit others; they came to call on him, and only at his invitation. He'd long ago lost count of how many businesses he owned. He left such things to his managers and accountants.

A particular senator had done him the biggest favor of his life twenty years ago. He disliked being in anyone's debt. It threw life out of balance, and he believed in balanced living. The opportunity to repay the senator after so many years was gratifying, but now that a man had disappeared he needed to find out what was going on. He picked up a "burner." Like the phone the senator used to call him, this phone was recently purchased to be used one time and then destroyed. He dialed a number.

When a voice answered he said, "7:00 pm."

The voice responded, "It is lovely, indeed."

He hung up.

The afternoon slipped by. The man who loved the Gulf left his compound at 6:30, and strolled over the sand to the water's edge. He stood, drinking in the beauty of the scene. After about fifteen minutes he made his way to a jetty that ran out into the water. He walked its length and stood at the end. A powerful, sleek silver speedboat glided over the water and pulled up to the jetty. Two men in the boat made a strange pair, one a darkly handsome Latino whose teeth flashed white when he smiled, and the other brown-haired, blue-eyed bruiser the size of an NFL lineman. His muscles rippled as he grasped an iron ring set into the jetty deck.

The man who loved the Gulf got into the speedboat. The big man released his grip and the speedboat headed out to sea. They made good time. Their destination was a magnificent yacht anchored a mile offshore. *Gulf Maiden* was emblazoned proudly on her hull. The hundred-foot ocean-going palace with a crew of twelve was owned by one of the man's companies.

When they boarded the yacht the man made his way to a huge enclosed lounge at the bow of the ship. Three identical men waited there for him, and they stood as he entered the room. He sat down and motioned for the triplets to sit in comfortable white leather chairs. "Report."

Tall, well-built, and with clear blue eyes, each of the men possessed one distinguishing physical characteristic. The man in the middle chair sported a black crew cut, while the brother to his left was perfectly bald, and the brother to his right wore his hair all the way to his shoulders. It was the man in the middle who spoke. "Our man followed the subject for two hours. He was cut off by two vehicles. He used his cell to call our Omaha contact before whoever drove him off the road broke his car window and took him. We recommend follow up."

The man who loved the Gulf looked steadily at Derek, Duke, and Damien Dupree. The brothers had been born out of wedlock to a nurse in Sydney, Australia. She had died of complications arising from their birth. Their father had been a career military man. He wanted nothing to do with them.

Their mother's older sister Helen, who was unable to have children of her own, took the boys in. Her husband, August Berenson, was a brutal man who was suitably employed as a butcher. From their earliest days in the Berenson household the little boys learned to be silent, careful, and to not speak unless they were spoken to. At seventeen they went off and joined the Australian Regular Army, but by their twenty-first birthday they were working as mercenaries in Africa. A coup went bad and they fled for their lives, taking a circuitous route to England where they worked for a time as bodyguards for wealthy English celebrities. The brothers came to America as part of the protective entourage for an English singer.

Over the course of a year they experienced New York, Hollywood, and Miami, where they came to the attention of the man who loved the Gulf. The Gulf Maiden was docked for a long weekend. The English singer, who drank too much, often acted outrageously. He made the mistake of saying something offensive to the man and his second wife, who were dining at an exclusive restaurant in the city. The man did not like public conflict. It attracted too much attention. He left the restaurant and entered his limo. He ordered a car to take his wife home and waited. Over the years he had learned patience.

When the singer came stumbling to the parking lot supported by his entourage, the man's bodyguards confronted the singer's bodyguards and demanded an apology.

Duke Dupree recognized professional muscle when he saw it, and sensed that these were people one did not want to antagonize. The diplomat of the three brothers, Duke managed to persuade the singer to apologize. Impressed with the way the young bodyguard handled the situation, the man who loved the Gulf gave Duke his card and invited him to pay him a call. That was seven years ago. The man who loved the Gulf mentored the young men, sent them to college, saw to their education in finance, economics, business, weaponry, and self-defense. He paid them very well, and in exchange they served as his personal bodyguards. With their considerable training even professional military personnel, would have difficulty standing a chance in a fight against them. Over the years the brothers came to respect the man who loved the Gulf as a father. They would give their lives for him.

"I believe we need to go to Omaha," Duke said to the man. "We can't do this by phone. Our man in Omaha is as upset as we are. He lost a good soldier. We need to find out what happened to him. If you approve I'll go alone. Derek and Damien can handle things here."

"I don't like this. My instincts tell me there's something very wrong out there. I trust my instincts," the man said.

"Then, two of us will go."

"No, I'm not ready to send you in. Put together a team. Make it the best we have outside of the three of you. Send at least five players. Make sure our man in Omaha sets them up with everything they need. I believe in firepower. Have them go slow and careful. There's something lurking out there and we don't know what it is. Find it. And kill it."

"I'll have Rico run the team," Duke said.

"Good."

"We'll send six men outfitted with whatever tech they'll need. We'll have them go in low on the ground with the best surveillance detection available. Whatever is out there we'll find it."

"Did the man have a family?"

"A wife. He just got married two months ago."

"See that she's taken care of immediately."

"Consider it done."

"I'm having a dinner party Saturday. Big affair. Lots of VIP's. Wear a tux. Bring a date." The man laughed.

The brothers Dupree never brought dates to anything. They were always too busy protecting the man who loved the Gulf. He paid them handsomely, and took exceptionally good care of them. They always returned the favor.

CHAPTER   30

Robert Hoopes wasn't feeling like the Special Assistant to the President today. He woke up with an awful hangover. Thank God it was Saturday. When he sat up, his head was pounding, his mouth tasted really bad, and for a moment he felt like he was going to throw up.

What a way to start a weekend, he thought. He didn't feel like going to the gym. He didn't feel like running. The thought of eating breakfast was nauseating. He decided to take a shower.

He'd been in the shower for less than a minute when the phone rang. *Why did the phone have to ring now?* His position required him to be available around-the-clock, every day of the week; he had to take the call. He lurched out of the shower, and nearly fell trying to grab a towel. Cursing, he raced into the bedroom and picked up the phone.

He recognized the voice on the line, and responded appropriately. "Yes, Mr. President?" He listened for the next five minutes. The president finished delivering his instructions. "Understood, sir," Hoopes replied. "I'll take care of it."

He ended the call and swayed slightly on his feet. His stomach did a queasy roll. *The damn senator was playing hard ball again.* He wasn't cooperating, despite the pressure. The president needed his vote, and his influence. *The man needed to get with the program.* The question was, *how was he going to intimidate him this time? The senator had the nerve to threaten him at their last meeting!*

He made a telephone call. *Time for more dirty tricks.* He'd find out what the old boy had been up to lately and nail him with it. *Why was it that people in power thought they couldn't be pushed around?* When he got done with him the man would never try to intimidate him again. Even old dogs needed retraining from time to time.

As the head of what he thought of as the *Department of Dirty Tricks,* Robert Hoopes could do things even one of the President's czars couldn't get away with. He was at once openly visible in his circle of colleagues, yet he was also the go-to guy for getting nasty things done behind the scenes.

He'd been kind the last time he looked into the senator. This time he'd dig all the way back to the man's grade school years if necessary to put together a dossier thick enough to choke the old curmudgeon. *No more Mr. Nice Guy.* The senior senator from Illinois was trying to play hardball with the wrong people. He would hang him out to dry on the White House clothesline, that is, if the White House had a clothesline.

That was a funny thought. He wondered if anyone who had lived in the White House had ever used a clothesline to hang out the wash during its long history? He let another thought drift through his mind. *If you give a man enough rope he'll hang himself.* He chuckled. His headache felt better already.

He padded to the kitchen in his towel and made himself a Bloody Mary. Sometimes it was best to start the day with the hair of the dog that bit you. He returned to his shower with the drink.

Outside, two men in a gray van parked across the street from his apartment recorded his phone conversations. Surveillance equipment had been installed throughout his apartment, and his phone had been tapped soon after his initial encounter with the senator.

Robert Hoopes would have been shocked by the power of the man who loved the Gulf to reach into his life, turn over every rock in his past, and expose what dirt lay underneath. He would have been utterly dumbfounded by the extent to which the man could employ such information to destroy him. The dossier of nasty secrets Hoopes was compiling on the senator paled in comparison to the one being put together on him. The self-proclaimed Master of *Dirty Tricks* was a piker in comparison to the man who loved the Gulf.

"That was straight out of Comedy Central!" The men in the van laughed as Hoopes stumbled from his shower. They recorded every sound in the apartment and on Hoopes' phones with state-of-the-art equipment.

The call from the President of the United States upped the ante significantly. Robert Hoopes was one thing, but the president himself? "This is getting very interesting,"

Just then, Hoopes broke into song in his shower. The men monitoring him laughed at his very bad attempt at a Broadway show tune. His voice cracked in all the wrong places.

"This guy should definitely keep his day job," one of the men said.

"Definitely," said the other, nodding. "He's got no future in show business."

In truth, Hoopes had no future at all.

✱✱✱✱✱✱

The man who loved the Gulf enjoyed receiving the information from the morning's surveillance session. He understood power and its influence in ways lesser men couldn't even dream about.

CHAPTER 31

Michael asked General Thompson to be excused for two days. His boss voiced his concern. "Is everything all right, Major Stonebreaker?"

"Yes, sir. I need to take care of some family business, and if I could have Thursday and Friday, plus the weekend, I should be able to see to the problem."

"Anything you need to tell me?"

"No, sir. It has to do with my mother—"

"Is she all right?" The General was obviously worried. He lost his mother the previous year.

"No, sir. My mother is fine. She needs my help with some financial matters."

"I understand. A man must always help his mother. People don't seem to understand duty to family anymore. Please give her my regards."

"Thank you, sir."

At home Michael let Joan know he would be making another visit to The Movement headquarters. "Would you like to go with me?"

"That place makes me nervous. It's underground. You know how I feel about that."

As a girl, Joan and three of her friends had gone exploring in an abandoned mine. The experience frightened her. Years later Michael had taken her for a drive, and they ended up at Penn's Cave. It took him an hour to talk her into taking a boat ride through the cave. She was so upset at the end of it that he never asked her to do anything like that again.

"Eric says everything is about to begin."

"Michael, this is so upsetting!" She turned toward him from where she stood at the kitchen sink, wringing a dish towel in her hands. "I just don't know how I should feel about it. Are you sure you're doing the right thing? What happens if something goes wrong? How will we survive? Where will we go?"

"Joan, sweetheart..." Michael took her in his arms. "This has been planned for almost sixty years. My whole professional life is spent protecting this country from outside threats, but the greatest harm is coming from inside. It's threatening to destroy our people and way of life."

"Michael, you're talking about what will be the most dramatic event in the history of this country—"

"Yes, and nothing has been left to chance. This is a nationwide movement. There are facilities like the one you saw all across this country. There are literally tens of thousands of people involved who have one goal—restore the republic."

"I'm trying to get my head around it as much as I can, Michael." She looked up into his face. "Nevertheless, I think I'll pass on going back to the compound for now."

"I understand." He kissed the top of her head. "I've been called for a strategy and planning meeting. I'll be meeting Henry Wednesday night and coming home Sunday afternoon. Since you don't want to go with me, would you want to stay with Mom and visit with Susan?"

Joan pushed away from him. "I have things to do right here. There are papers to correct and tests to score. I have more than enough to do. Supper is ready. It's time to set the table."

Michael stood in the middle of the kitchen staring after her. He was torn. He did not want to hurt her, but he also knew that what was about to happen would change everything in their lives forever, whether he was involved or not.

They ate in an uncomfortable silence When the dishes had been cleared and the kitchen cleaned she went to the study to work on her students' papers. She was angry, hurt and scared. Michael knew that trying to reason with her would not make anything better. He learned when to speak and when to remain silent.

He turned on the TV in the living room and watched a cable show about the oceans, but his thoughts bounced back and forth between his wife's misgivings and what the nation was facing.

In bed she turned away from him. He lay in the dark for a long time thinking he would not be able to fall asleep. He was wrong.

Sometime during the night he awakened. She wasn't next to him. He sat up. She was sitting in the dark in a high backed chair crying softly.

Michael went to her and took her in his arms. "Michael, I'm so scared..."

"I know sweetheart. I know you are. I am, too."

"You are? But, how can you say that?"

Michael held her for a long moment, and gently rocked her in his arms. He had never said that anything scared him in all their years together, but this time he said what she needed to hear.

"The man who is not scared by things that are frightening is either an idiot or without a soul. On the battlefield you stay alive by practicing what your teachers have taught you. I was taught well, and I was scared every minute I was at war. A young man died in my arms crying for his mother. I saw others lose limbs and eyes, and be horribly maimed. I knew fear that almost overwhelmed me, but I kept on.

"There is no explanation for why one man lives and another is blown to bits. The randomness of battle is the ultimate insanity. You learn to take nothing for granted. When the battle ends you are surprised to find yourself still alive.

"The flip side is your training—and yes—your anger and

determination to find the enemy and kill him before he kills you. We are trained to kill. You are married to a trained killer. The military's purpose is to destroy others before we are destroyed. A police officer tries to keep the peace. A soldier tries to preserve the conditions that allow the policeman to do his job when the battles are all over. The coming battle will be nationwide, but bloodshed will be held to a minimum.

"I can't tell you what's going to happen, because I do not know all the details of the plan. That is deliberate. The Movement protects its plan—even from its members—until the need to know supersedes the need to be silent. I will know everything I need to, when it's necessary."

He took her hands in his own. "I love you, Joanie, with all my heart. I will protect you, our girls, Mom, Susan, Henry, Dylan, and Grover, too."

Their dog had awakened from his bed in the corner, and shuffled over to them in the dark. Hearing his name, he pushed his wet nose against Joan's leg, and she laughed. They heard the swish of his tail wagging, though they couldn't see him clearly in the dim light.

"I know you will, Michael. It's just that, well, I never imagined anything like this would ever happen."

"I didn't either, but it is happening. I'll have a role to play in this plan, and you will, too. You have my word that if it's possible for you to continue to teach, I'll see that you do. If not, you'll still have meaningful work to do."

They got back in bed. He held her in his arms until they fell asleep.

He went to work the next day, and at day's end he got on his way to Pennsylvania. Joan still elected to stay at home, but they had mended their argument. Michael was glad to be at peace with his wife as he drove north.

He picked Henry up from his house, and the brothers drove to The Movement headquarters. When they entered the conference room Eric was waiting for them.

The next three days were spent in strategy sessions with a host of people inside the Truman building. Michael learned much more about the details of TR2.0, and gained a greater understanding of its enormity. Grave circumstances would launch the plan into action. The assets in place and the precision with which TR2.0 would be executed increased Michael's respect for The Movement's commitment a thousandfold.

A key emphasis of the plan was that it should be executed without harming anyone. Perfect execution might be impossible, but TR2.0 would come as close as was humanly possible. Fail-safes had been embedded with four levels of redundancy at every juncture, which was paramount where computers and other equipment were concerned.

On Sunday Eric, Henry and Michael gathered in the conference room. "So, you believe the administration's framework is in place? They'll be making a move pretty soon?" Michael asked.

"Yes. It will be before the election."

"Do you know exactly when?" Henry asked.

"That hasn't been shared with me. It's need to know."

Michael said, "I thought you knew everything?"

Eric smiled. "You give me too much credit and importance. I'm not in the inner circle. Frankly, I don't want to be. The people who know all that is to happen are unknown to me. I have no wish to identify them. What is going to happen is so immense that we must protect the plan until the very moment it's executed."

"What if they're wrong? What if they've misread the signs?" Michael asked. "What if the administration isn't planning anything at all?" Michael asked.

"We know differently, Michael." Eric's voice was confident. "We know the truth."

"How? Ah, I see it now. You have a man inside. They've been compromised!

That's brilliant! That's it, isn't it? You have a mole in the White House!"

"I didn't say that."

"You don't have to say it. You know exactly what is going on, don't you?"

"I'd appreciate it if you kept that to yourselves." Eric said.

"I underestimated the deviousness of this place, Eric. I must apologize. Forgive me for not thinking clearly. Of course you have to have someone inside. How else would you know what they're planning? It's brilliant. It bothers me, but it's brilliant."

"Why does it bother you?"

"It somehow seems unfair to me. We've stooped to their level and are playing by their rules."

Eric's face hardened. "Look, Michael, I'm the one who works in black ops here. I'm not a nice guy. You were chosen for your role because of your character. You are the strongest, most moral man I've ever met. You are a genuinely good and decent man who believes in God, family and country.

"But our enemy has no soul, or what's left of it is so twisted that they will do anything, including killing millions of people, to stay in power. They are evil personified! If you are going to fight fire with fire and win, you have two choices - get burned or get a bigger flame thrower! When I tell you we leave nothing to chance that's the truth!"

Michael's face reddened. "I'm sorry, Eric. I didn't mean—"

Eric softened his tone. "Michael, I'm sorry, too. I don't want to hurt your feelings, and I don't want you angry at me, but these are not nice people. There's nothing redeeming about any of them. They hate America and everything it represents. They despise ordinary people. They intend to take control of this nation before the election."

"But they're already in power." Michael said. "What more do they want?"

"They want it permanently, and they intend to keep it by force if necessary."

"They can't expect the military to help them take over the country. That's madness," Henry said.

"You have to remember how subtle they are. They have no intention of attacking the people without first deceiving them into believing that it's necessary.

"How can they pull that off?" Michael leaned in.

"They plan on instituting martial law."

"Why? For what possible reason?" Henry was incredulous.

"They've planned a national crisis...another 9/11."

Henry gasped, and Michael's face turned white, "Dear God, you can't mean it!"

"I do." Eric's face was deadly serious. "They have planned an event so devastating that it will persuade people to accept martial law for their own good. They're counting on people to be so shocked that they will do two things." He held up his fingers as he continued. "One, accept the imposition of the military in every visible area of life, and two, vote to halt term limits and allow the current administration to remain in power in gratitude for its perceived leadership and protection in the face of an unprecedented national crisis."

"However, there's a fly on the wall, so to speak. They don't know that we 're clued in on their plan. They have no idea that The Movement even exists, and they have no inkling about what we are going to do." Eric said. The three friends sat staring at each other, the implications of what they were facing settling them into silence.

Michael spoke first. "I've got to get on the road."

"Indeed. The party is beginning." Eric said.

"Should I bring the hotdogs?" Henry asked.

Michael put his hand on his brother's shoulder. "Henry, you bring the hotdogs, Eric can bring the buns, and I'll bring the ketchup."

"Sounds like fun to me." Henry added. "But there's just one thing..."

"Yes?"

"When the party is over how are we going to put out the fire?"

"Easy, my friends," Eric said. "We're going to use a very big extinguisher."

CHAPTER   32

Pierce Armstrong was too anxious to enjoy his breakfast of scrambled eggs, wheat toast, orange juice, and coffee. Ollie disposed of the intruder's body, but he gained little knowledge from his victim. He tortured the man for four days before putting an end to it. He then burned the remains in the gas furnace off the underground chamber built for that purpose.

In all the years his grandfather, father, and he had been in the game, no one had ever come anywhere near The Farm. He employed a team of armed men to guard the perimeter of his domain, but no one had come close enough to engage them. *Who had the power to order surveillance of the Special Assistant to the President? And for what purpose?*

He fancied himself a spider spinning a web of the powerful and wealthy elite. Those he summoned were allowed limited knowledge of him. Even the leaders in the Progressive hierarchy came to him blindfolded and permitted no clue to his exact location.

The appearance of the man posed a maddening distraction to the task at hand. The stage was set for the attack to take place before the next presidential election. *The ignorant masses in America must be brought to their knees to pay homage to their masters.* Nothing must hinder his plan.

Armstrong trusted no one completely. The giant oaf who served as his bodyguard and butler was the closest thing he had to a friend. Unfortunately, Ollie's murderous rage rendered him little more than a mindless animal. He was hardly anyone with whom one could have a rational conversation. Ollie did as he was told, as it should be. *Inferiors must know their place.*

Armstrong spent the morning and the early afternoon contemplating what to do. He couldn't afford a knee-jerk reaction. One intruder came; the odds were that others would follow. A nameless enemy lurked somewhere out there—one with the power to breach the cloak of anonymity he had maintained all the years of his adult life.

Armstrong picked up a cell phone. He made a call and engaged in a long conversation with the person on the other end. Money talked. He ordered a discreet investigation into the origins of the man who had been reduced to ashes in his furnace.

He put down the phone with a satisfied smile and picked at a bowl of grapes on the table. Relishing their juicy sweetness, he mulled over preparations for another possible invasion. He touched a button beneath his desk. The head of his perimeter detail responded. "Yes, sir?"

"We need to talk. I expect others may be coming."

"I understand. Is there anything we should consider in particular, sir?"

Armstrong thought for a moment. "We need to be prepared for anything. I've learned to never underestimate an enemy. That means you must use every means at your disposal for detection, capture or destruction. Do you understand me?"

"Yes, sir."

"I'll be in your office at three o'clock this afternoon."

Armstrong swung around in his chair and took in the exquisite view through the window. He doubted those in his employ were capable of fully appreciating the idyllic beauty of this place. They were too far down the food chain. Besides, dreary lives of toil devoted to his well-being left them little time to enjoy the world around them.

He smiled. One day he would write a book about the great disparity, indeed, the insurmountable gulf that separated the true elite from the masses. Life was so enjoyable when one possessed the intelligence to live it well. He said a silent thank you to his dead father, though he was certain the old tyrant no longer existed to hear it. He did not believe in an afterlife. *When you were dead you were gone forever.*

An evolutionist of the first rank, he believed mankind evolved from the primordial slime, and that he represented the pinnacle of human growth and intelligence.

He reached for another grape and chuckled as he bit into its tart flesh. *Wheels within wheels,* he thought. *How stupid the masses are.* No one even knew that Pierce Armstrong was not his real name. He chose it because he liked its sound. It had class. His far too ordinary family name was shrouded in the mists of time.

Armstrong would have bolted in terror had he known that The Movement knew his real name, who he was, and exactly where he was.

CHAPTER 33

Rico "Rick" Rodriguez was movie star handsome. He stood six-foot-one, weighed in at a solid one hundred-ninety-five pounds, and had served in Special Forces. In his current position he served as Security Chief under the direction of the Dupree triplets.

Whenever the man who loved the Gulf needed to be picked up in the speed boat, it was Rick who piloted it. He never allowed anyone else to take the wheel when the man was aboard.

Wherever Rick went, John Smith, his second in command was never far behind. The guy who looked like an NFL lineman had actually been one in a previous life. Smith's career was cut short after his second year because of an undisclosed drug problem. "Big John" drifted into the Tampa area, where he met Rick in a bar one night. The pair hit it off after the two of them cleaned the place out in a brawl. When it was over, they were the only two standing, so they shook hands and had a beer. Rick took Big John to meet the man who loved the Gulf. John promised to leave the drugs alone and had been working for the man beside Rick ever since.

Duke Dupree explained the plan to Rick. He, in turn, chose four men to fill out the remaining spots on the team. Their contact in Omaha would supply the necessary weapons and gear needed for their surveillance and possible assault.

The team traveled on three different flights in groups of two. Dressed in suits and ties, they appeared to be ordinary businessmen. The fact that their business would be mayhem and destruction was unknown to their fellow passengers.

They arrived over several hours in Omaha, changed into jeans, plaid and chambray shirts and work boots, and made their way to their contact, a local who ran a commercial farm a few miles from the target. They assembled in a big red barn on the property and began choosing their gear.

Rick and Big John saw to it that the team was equipped to take on a small army if necessary. They were each equipped with a REC7 assault rifle with a shortened PDW 12-inch barrel and five 30-round detachable box magazines. Rick and Big John also packed a 100-round C-Mag drum magazine. They also chose Glock 21 side arms with five magazine clips each, and a San Mai Gurkha Kukri machete.

Each man traded his farm clothes for a set of camo fatigues, boots, helmets, and an item Rick did not immediately recognize. He stared at what looked like a black t-shirt, but when he picked it up he was surprised by the weight of it. "What's this?"

"It's experimental. Military grade." Their contact explained. "It's made of boron carbide."

"What the heck is that?"

"B4C body armor. In fact, they're T-shirts that have been turned into body armor. Their flexibility and lighter weight allows you to move better, but they're almost as hard as a diamond."

"Oughtta stop a bullet." Rick tossed one to Big John.

Each man was given two concussion grenades, a hand-held GPS, and a pocket knife, before being fitted with a state-of-the-art communication system. When they were done, they were led to a room inside the barn where a large table and chairs were waiting.   T w o men were already sitting with a map of the area spread out between them.

"Please have a seat, gentlemen." A blond man, clearly muscle for the organization, motioned toward the chairs.

When everyone was seated, the other man, whose black hair stood spiked atop his head picked up a pointer and indicated an area on the map.

"This is where our man called from. Nothing has been found. There's no trace of him or his car. We combed as much of the area as we could before dark. We came back here and that's when you were contacted."

The blond muscle spoke again. "Outside the barn you'll find a gray Lincoln SUV. Your equipment will be hidden in compartments beneath and inside the car. You'll be shown how to retrieve them. The car is equipped with a powerful computer and GPS system, as well as tracking and signal jamming gear. The engine, drive train, and other components have been waterproofed."

Spike continued, "We recommend you approach the area from the opposite direction that our man took. We also recommend you activate the signal jamming equipment five miles out from where he disappeared. Do a wide sweep around the area and come in slowly and carefully. We'll have a car five miles behind you in case you need to make contact."

"If anyone stops you you're simply buddies on a hunting trip. Questions?" The blond muscle looked around the room. There were no questions.

The men exited the barn and stowed their equipment at various points throughout the big SUV. The specially designed cabin was set up so that the more esoteric equipment was not visible until it was activated.

As they prepared to set out their host approached and stood beside the driver's side window where Big John was behind the wheel. Rick rode shotgun next to him.

"I want you to find out what happened to him," he said. His voice took on an eerily quiet tone, but his face betrayed his emotion.

"I know he's dead. He was too good to be taken easily."

Rick looked at him. "It hurts to lose a soldier."

"He was a hell of a lot more than a soldier!" Rick and Big John waited silently for the man to elaborate. "He was my son!" the man said. He turned and walked away from the car.

The members of the teamed looked at each other. No one said a word. Big John turned the key in the ignition. The Lincoln's souped up engine roared to life.

CHAPTER 34

Colonel Eric Dryden drove into East Potomac Park and made his way to the golf course and driving range. He parked his car, got out, and opened the trunk. Eric picked up his golf bag and walked to the pro shop.

He was early for their 10:30 a.m. tee time, but the contact was there waiting for him. He loaded his bags onto the cart and the contact drove them out to the first tee.

After they hit their drives the man, looked at Eric. "They're moving everything into place. It's hard to believe that they've planned this on American soil, but I guess we shouldn't be surprised at anything they do."

"Why be surprised? You're the one on the inside. You know what they're capable of because they believe you're just as ruthless as they are." Eric said. The man smiled but there was no humor in his eyes. "True, but these people are without mercy. When I contacted you I didn't tell you where the attack would take place. I draw the line at children."

"They're going to attack children? Where will they do it?"

"You're the black ops man. Where do you think it will be?"

Eric's eyes grew wide. "You can't mean—"

"Precisely. It's the happiest place on earth."

"My God. Don't they value anything?"

"People like them destroyed over a hundred million men, women and children in the last century. Do you think the Nazis felt any remorse when they marched children into the gas chambers?" the man asked.

"I think we should move on them now!" Rage radiated from Eric. "They need to be destroyed before they take one innocent life!"

"This isn't the time to be angry. You'll deal with them." The man handed a package to Eric. "The details are inside. I suggest SEALs. We have time to plan and coordinate everything down to the last decimal. Miscalculation will mean disaster. This must be executed with precision. The good thing is that the dupes who are to carry out their mission don't have a clue that anyone knows anything about what they're planning. They're sleepers. They've been here a long time and they think they understand America."

"How long have you been a sleeper in their ranks?" Eric asked.

The man got a far away look in his eyes. "All my life. They killed my grandfather a long time ago. It drove my father outside the law. My grandfather immigrated to this country. He tried to build a decent life. A friend talked him into attending a meeting in New York. When he heard what was being said he walked out. They were afraid he would talk. He was dead a month later. They made it look like an accident.

"My father and uncle grew up vowing they would never allow anyone to do to them what had been done to their father."

Eric grunted, nodding his understanding.

The man went on. "Each of them fathered a son. I decided to go into government work. My cousin went in a different direction. After I got out of the Marines, I went to college and took a degree in political science. I helped a man get elected to Congress. One thing led to another and I became known as someone who can fix things.

"Twenty years ago I was introduced to some people at a private home outside Chicago. If I gave you the names of those who were there you'd understand how I became an insider. They're not very trusting people. It took a long time to convince them that I'm one of them."

"Do they trust you now?" Eric asked.

"They trust me as much as they can trust anyone. It has taken a great deal of effort on my part to listen to the stuff they spout off every day. The fact that they believe the crap they talk about all the time is frightening.

"I may not look like it, but I'm a reader. I read everything. Years ago Whitaker Chambers wrote a book called Witness. In it he claimed that no one was more dedicated to a cause than a committed Communist. He was wrong. I don't think he ever met people like the ones I work for, and it's obvious he never ran into an Islamic jihadist."

"Agreed," Eric said. "Let's call it quits at nine holes. I want to get back and see what you have in the package." He tapped the envelope. "You mentioned your cousin. Where is he in all this?"

"He has his own interests. He loves the Gulf so he spends most of his time at his home. I'm not sure he'd even care about what you and I are discussing. He's a very powerful man, a billionaire." The man stopped talking and Eric didn't ask for more information.

They played nine holes and then went to the club house. When they parted Eric headed for his car, the package safely hidden inside his golf bag.

Eric had never seen his contact before, although he had known of him for years. He would not have recognized him on the street.

Special Assistant Robert Hoopes would have instantly recognized him as the man he'd seen in the president's office the day he'd been sent to Omaha.

CHAPTER 35

Michael sat with Henry and the men and women he met on his first visit to The Movement headquarters. Angry silence charged the air around the conference table. Eric finished his presentation.

"I know how you feel." Eric said to the group. "When I first read through this I wanted to find one of these people, stand him up against a wall and shoot him on the spot. However, this isn't the time to lose our tempers. It's a time for careful planning and cool heads."

A general seated at the table spoke for everyone present. "This is the most damnably outrageous thing I've ever heard! They want to turn the Magic Kingdom into an abattoir. These...*these*...people need to be removed from this country and never allowed to return! It's absolutely monstrous!"

For several minutes, many of the others vented their outrage and anger as well. Eric let anyone speak who wanted to say something. When the room quieted he looked at Michael. "Mr Brown, what do you conclude from this intel?"

"You said your contact mentioned SEAL Team. I believe they're perfect for the job. We need to get them in place and training right away," Michael said.

"It's already in the works."

"Good. I believe everyone here now understands the gravity of what we're facing.

"Anyone who would authorize such a heinous act specifically targeting innocent children deserves no place on American soil. They must be removed—or destroyed."

An attractive middle-aged woman on Michael's right spoke next. "Mr. Brown is correct. They've forfeited any right to remain here. As to killing them, I would give my vote to it in a heartbeat, but I understand that the moment The Movement has been working towards all these years is now mere weeks away. We can't let personal anger get in the way of what we have to do."

"The SEALs will arrive at the target before the week is out. They will come in undercover as new cast members and be assimilated into the complex. We've identified most of the sleepers in the workforce there thus far, and we expect to ID the other players shortly. Their so-called communications expert won't arrive on site for sometime yet. "We intend to let the crisis occur and—"

A man on Michael's left blurted out, "You can't mean that! The loss of life would be horrific—"

"You misunderstand me, sir." Eric said softly. "What I mean is that the crisis will be thwarted by the SEAL team, but it is we who will control the information coming out of the complex. It will be reported to the mainstream media that the crisis has indeed taken place, and martial law will be imposed on the nation. It is precisely at that moment that TR2.0 will be executed. It's essential that our enemy believes that they are in control of the situation."

Michael nodded. "Yes, and TR2.0 will unfold simultaneously all over the country. The full nature of the plan has been kept from all of us to protect its implementation. Shortly before it happens everyone in this room will be told in detail what is being done. At that point it will be too late for anyone to stop it. Execution of the plan will be swift and irrevocable. I have been told that we are using the enemy's own plan against them, but I have not been told how that will be done."

Eric resumed speaking. "Obviously, I'm unable to reveal the person's identity, but I've been assured recently by one of the authors of TR2.0 that all is well. It's wise to proceed with caution in the face of such a vast undertaking, but the person who spoke to me convinced me that nothing has been left to chance. We will succeed. When it's over, the planners of this heinous act will no longer be able to spew their venom and hatred on the people of this nation."

It was at that moment that Henry spoke, to Michael's surprise. He may have lacked the educational and occupational status of the others at the table, but his words rang out like a clarion call to everyone in the room.

"I'm an ordinary man who has been gifted with a wonderful family. I work with my hands. I served in the Marines. I understand the value of hard work. I believe in God. I love my country. Our country. You see folks, it's our country. It belongs to us because my grandfather drove a tank over a hill and the Germans blew it all to hell, but he lived to come home, thank God. It's our country because my dad served in Vietnam, and though he too escaped death in battle, Agent Orange ensured he made the ultimate sacrifice in our country's defense. It's our country because each of you was given the opportunity to sit at this table with me, and I believe you love it as much as I do. I don't make speeches. I don't think deep thoughts. I'm not much for hot air and running my mouth. I live in a small town, an American town, and I love its quiet streets, my home, my wife and son, our family...and I love you, too."

One woman near the other end of the table stifled a sob. There were tears glistening in the eyes of several people.

"I know God brought us to this place and time. Some may argue otherwise, but the Good Book says there's a time, place, and season for everything. This is our time and place. Am I scared? Yes. But, do I believe in what we are about to do? Yes, again. We can't get through this without each other. It's all hands on deck. As we say in the Corps, *Semper Fi!* Always Faithful! I've got your back, and I believe you have mine. We're in this together, until it's over. We're doing the right thing. That's all I have to say."

The room erupted with cheers and emotion. Michael shouted above the din. "That's my brother...the greatest brother in the world! When he tells you something is true, you'd better believe it! We're in it together, and we will succeed!"

Henry turned, surprised at the tears on Michael's face. In that moment his heart felt ten sizes too large for his chest. He was not alone.

CHAPTER   36

As instructed, Rick turned on the jamming device when their SUV was five miles from where their man disappeared. They followed a circuitous network of roads far to the east of where they suspected he had been taken. They made their way south and set their GPS on the only small town in the area. Ten miles out from town they drove off the road into a cornfield and stopped.

Rick pinged an encryption of their exact location to the car following them. Then it was time to move out. Big John drove the Lincoln to within seven miles of the town, and they scouted out a place to hide the vehicle. Vast fields of cornstalks and an occasional copse of trees promised to provide easy cover, and dirt tracks that led nowhere would make their own tire tracks less noticeable.

They settled on a location well off the road and partially into a stand of trees on the edge of a salt marsh. They quickly disembarked, removed their gear from the SUV, covered the car with camouflage, and prepared to move out.

The team had gone to radio silence some miles back, and now they ceased speaking, communicating instead using hand signals. There was to be no talking unless absolutely necessary. Rick led them silently on a track that took them towards the town. Each of them carried weight because their ammo and gear was heavy but they benefited from extensive military training, and were up to the task.

Moving steadily across country over fields, dirt roads, and irrigation ditches, the only sounds were made by birds, the wind, and the noise of their nearly undetectable passage through the vegetation.

They'd traveled about three miles when they spotted a building in the distance ahead of them. It was a one-story, wooden affair painted white, with a dark shingled roof. Two barred windows in the front bracketed a single door. Rick signaled to the man on his right flank, who melted into a corn field and made his way to the small clearing where the building sat.

The setting struck Rick as highly unusual. The building was about fifty feet square and surrounded by corn fields that were planted to within a few yards of its walls. A dirt lane led from the rear of the structure into the field. If someone wanted to hide a building this was the perfect place to do it. Rick waited with the rest of the team while his man moved around the building, under cover of the corn. There were no windows on the sides or the rear of the building. A second door was centered on the rear wall of the wooden structure.

The man returned to the team hidden in the corn. He signaled silently to the others. They spread out and approached the rear of the building.

Big John and Rick came out of the corn and went to the rear door of the building.

The others secured the perimeter and kept watch on the road. The big man tried the door. It wasn't locked, but he didn't open it. He and Rick looked at each other, silently counted and on three opened the door and moved rapidly into a hallway on the other side with their weapons drawn. The hallway ran straight through the building to the front entrance. The walls were painted a nondescript white. There were no pictures or other decorations on the walls.

Three doors lined the walls of the hallway on both sides, for a total of six. The doors stood open. They carefully approached the first set of doors. Rick took the right door and Big John the left. They entered the rooms swiftly and found no one. Both appeared to be ordinary offices with two desks and some chairs.

Rick's room also held a four-drawer file cabinet against the wall. He inspected the room more closely as he stepped to the file. He checked for trip wires and other devices. He didn't see anything. He carefully tried the top drawer. It was unlocked and empty. He checked the other drawers. They were also empty.

The hair stood up on the back of his neck. Something wasn't right. *What was it?* He examined the room with an even more critical eye. What was it that was bothering him? Then, it hit him. There were no telephones on the desks, no computer keyboards, no paperclip holders. The desktops were bare. He looked closer. There was no dust. Someone was keeping the room clean and neat.

Big John's room was almost a mirror image of Rick's room, minus the file cabinet. Both men checked for video and listening devices and found none.

They met in the hallway and continued using sign language. They moved down the hall. This time Big John went right and Rick took the room on the left. The room on the right was empty. There was nothing to be seen. The room on the left was also empty, except for what appeared to be a holding cell that occupied the rear half of the room. Rick found that odd. *Why would someone need a holding cell in a building in the middle of a corn field?*

The two men moved again into the hallway, signaling and slowly advancing on the remaining two rooms at the front of the building. They switched positions again. Big John went left, and Rick went right.

When the big man stepped into the room he heard what sounded like a release of air. Something bit into his throat. He reached up to see what it was and he felt a needle lodged in his throat. The room was booby-trapped. He staggered and started to fall. It was fast-acting. He went down on his knees with a bang that shook the wooden floorboards. "Got to warn Rick—" He tried to crawl toward the door. Everything went black.

Rick heard the sound of Big John falling. He raced into the

room and found his friend lying face down. He reached down to check for a pulse and heard the sound of the back door slamming shut. Outside he heard what sounded like small arms fire.

Instinctively, he stepped out of the room into the hall and turned toward the front door. It wasn't a door at all. Someone had painted a picture of what looked like a door on the wall, but it was not an entrance. He returned to the room where John lay and looked through the heavy bars on the window. At that moment he heard a hissing sound.

Light gray smoke poured from a vent in the floor beneath the window. *Gas!* He raised his REC7 and fired a burst at the window. In the next second he was on the floor. His rounds bounced off the window and into the room. One of them slammed into his body armor and the impact knocked him down. *What the hell kind of glass was in the window?*

The room was filling with gas. He coughed. He was passing out. He activated his radio and called for help. "Man down. Man down. Need assistance." There was no response from the team.

He was blacking out. Then he was gone.

There were no dreams in the blackness that enveloped Rick. When he began to awaken he felt nauseated. He was strapped to some sort of table. He turned his head and looked around a large room. He fought to focus his eyes, and then wished he hadn't as things came into view around the room that reminded him of scary movies he'd seen as a kid. They looked like torture devices.

He felt his skin go slick with cold sweat. He closed his eyes and when he opened them again, a huge, doughy white face topped with pale blond hair loomed over him. To Rick, he resembled a human caricature of the Pillsbury Doughboy, but that was where the similarity ended. The creature smiled evilly at him.

Rick tried to speak. "Where…where's my friend?" His throat hurt from the gas he had inhaled.

"Oh, dear me. I'm afraid he's dead. In fact, they're all dead. Sad but true. There is but one who remains, and that one is you. Yes, yes, just you." The man's voice was ludicrous. It did not match his appearance.

Rick exploded with rage, straining to break free of the bonds that held him to the table. "You killed my friends? You have no ideas who you're playing with! When we get through with you you'll wish to God you'd never been born!"

"But, my dear man, that's precisely what we intend to find out. Oh yes, we must find out who sent you, and you will tell me. Yes, I'm afraid you will. But first, we must have fun. First, the fun." A jolt of electricity hit Rick and he screamed, his back arching off the table.

When the flow of electricity stopped the giant reached down with his massive left hand and gripped Rick by the throat. "Now, tell me. Who sent you? Why are you here? We must know. We will know."

The hand closed like a vise on his throat and just when Rick thought he would black out the hand released him. Before he could take a breath the electricity into him again.

The man's voice reached him, even through his pain. "We have time, all the time in the world, and we will have fun together, you and I. Yes, so much fun."

CHAPTER 37

The three men in the car that followed Rick and the team received his encrypted message and got a fix on their location. They took up a position along a dirt road under a swamp white oak and waited.

When Rick's call for help came they started the car and sped along the dirt track back toward the paved road.

Two cars were parked where the dirt joined the asphalt. Men with weapons at the ready were waiting to ambush them, but that was not to be. The sun roof was open on their sedan, and the man in the backseat rose up through the roof. The driver stopped just short of the waiting cars, and the man fired a hand-held missile into their midst. A tremendous explosion sent the cars arcing into the air, and gravity slammed them back down onto the roadbed.

The man quickly lowered himself through the roof into the backseat and the driver jammed the gas pedal to the floor. The car lurched forward and they slid around the carnage under a hail of body parts until the tires dug into the pavement, sending them racing down the road. The sound of sirens blared in the distance, but the driver kept his foot on the floor, taking advantage of the hard flat Nebraska dirt roads to quickly put distance between them and the sound of the sirens. Within minutes they hit paved road where maintaining a high rate of speed was easier. They were heading for Omaha. The mission failed, but they would live to report in.

The man who loved the Gulf was very still when he heard the report. He sat in the lounge of the and listened as Duke described what they knew or suspected. Anger mingled with sorrow on the man's face said it all.

When Duke finished speaking the man looked out the window in silence. No one spoke. The triplets knew when to remain silent.

After a long time the man sighed. "It's my fault. Rick and Big John knew the risks. They were well equipped. Our Omaha contact gave them everything they needed. We're dealing with someone with the resources and experience to anticipate our first move. Now this enemy knows we're something to be reckoned with, as well. My instincts tell me our team did not survive. It's very upsetting. I had great affection for Rick and Big John. I'm going to miss them very much."

The brothers remained silent. "However," the man who loved the Gulf continued, "their deaths mean that this enemy must be destroyed. You have my permission to do whatever is necessary. I place but one restriction on you." His tone softened. "Come back alive. I will not be able to bear it if I should lose even one of you."

He made a tent of his fingers and brought them slowly to his lips. When he spoke again his voice was deadly calm. "Think long and hard about how you'll resolve the problem in Nebraska, and then act swiftly, surely and without mercy. Whatever evil is there must be eradicated. What Hoopes is part of must be discovered, and he must be removed, as well. I made a man a promise that Hoopes would be terrified, suffer, and then be gone. I rarely make promises, but I keep the ones I make.

"Whatever waits for you in Nebraska is to be obliterated. If it is possible for you to bring me the one responsible for Rick, Big John and the others, I will deal with that person, or persons, on my own terms." He sighed and sat back in the white leather chair. "May I have your thoughts?"

Duke, normally the spokesman for the trio, said nothing. It was long haired Damien, usually the quietest of the brothers who broke the silence. "Rick and Big John are—were—friends of ours. Whoever set them up is smart. We need to be smarter. This time we go in force. They went as a team. We will go as an army. When we're done there will be nothing left of whatever is there."

Derek, the bald brother, said, "Damien is right. When we go in we go fast, hard and furiously. You've surrounded yourself with the best soldiers the world has to offer, and Rick and Big John were the best among them. There will be no mercy. You also have my word that we'll come back from this mission. The brothers Dupree never give our word unless we're prepared to back it up."

The man's eyes rested on Duke. "What say you?"

"I feel the same about Rick and Big John. Rick was full of life. I don't know anyone who enjoyed life more than he did. He was funny, dedicated to his work, a brave soldier, and a true friend. Big John was all of those things, as well." Duke looked steadily at the man who loved the Gulf. "No one here could possibly know what we were getting Rick and the team into. The price we've paid is too high. Each one of those men was a friend of mine and utterly loyal to you, sir. We will make whoever did this pay beyond anything they could ever imagine. You have our word on it."

The man who loved the Gulf said, "I know the three of you will take care of it. It is…it was Rick's job to take me home. Would one of you take me? I'm feeling very sad, and I need to arrange for the care of their families."

Duke nodded. "We'll take you home and I'll bring the beer. The last time I had too much to drink Rick brought me home and made sure that I was okay. I feel like getting very drunk."

"You'll have to wait until we get back to the house. The law doesn't permit operating a boat while inebriated," the man said.

Duke looked at his mentor. He smiled, but there was no humor in it. "You're the law in these parts, sir, and you're the only law we recognize."

The man stood up. "Let's go. We've got planning to do."

CHAPTER 38

José Alvarez was Rick Rodriguez's closest friend on the team. Rick recruited José, and they'd grown up together in the old neighborhood. They joined the Marines together, and when basic training was over they'd shipped out to different assignments and locations.

A few years later they'd run into each other in a Tampa bar. Alvarez was down on his luck. He'd been laid off from his work as a bricklayer. His wife and young son waited at home while he sat alone feeling sorry for himself and drinking away the pain.

He was well on the way to drunk one afternoon when Rick put his arm around his shoulders.

"José, you S. O. B., how come you never wrote me? Man, I've been wondering for years what the hell happened to you!"

Tears sprang to José's eyes. "I lost my job, Ricky. I can't make my mortgage payment. My wife and kid are gonna be on the street by the end of the month. I'm a good man. I work hard, just like my old man. I need a job. This unemployment doesn't cut it, man."

Rick recruited José on the spot. He was tough as nails and

utterly loyal. The man who loved the Gulf paid him three times what he'd made as a bricklayer. He moved his family into a better neighborhood, and his wife, Talia gave birth to a little girl. Life was good.

Now, José lay deep in a cornfield in Nebraska. He had been farthest from the building at about a hundred and fifty yards out. A skilled lookout, he lay deep in the corn near a dirt road that cut through the vast fields. Rick, Big John, and the other three surrounded the building, then Rick and the big man entered it.

Rick always liked to have a man on the perimeter so that if things went south someone would have a chance to get away and report what happened. José was supposed to be that man.

All hell broke loose. Four-wheeled vehicles loaded with men came roaring in from every direction. A black SUV nearly ran over him where he lay still in the field, his fatigues blending in with the colors of the corn and dirt. He didn't dare move.

He was hopelessly outgunned. Forty or more men rushed through the corn and surrounded the building. He heard his friends open up with their firepower. Someone yelled who'd been hit. The sound of breaking glass came from the direction of where the SUVs encircled the building. The team fought furiously, but they were sorely outnumbered. The other men also had the advantage of the vehicles to hide behind. Trapped in the corn, his friends had no place to run, nor could they make it across the open space to the protection of the building.

It was over quickly. José didn't move. He had been ordered to stay still and to get back home at all costs. But Ricky and Big John were still in there. He owed his life to Ricky and the man who loved the Gulf.

The men who attacked them were not uniformed. They wore jeans, boots, work shirts and jackets. They moved quickly to the building and came out a couple of minutes later carrying the bodies of Big John and Ricky. One of the men outside examined them. He must have determined that Big John was dead. The others put Ricky in the back of an SUV and sped off.

José knew there was no way for the attackers to determine the identities of his dead comrades, but they captured Ricky. He had to follow them and find out where they were taking him.

He lay in the cornfield while the other men carried the bodies of his friends to the back of a pick-up and threw them into its bed. He wanted to stand up and mow the bastards down, but he lay where Ricky ordered.

Some thirty minutes passed before the men left the scene, but to José it seemed like hours. His face itched from the corn. Again and again he stifled the impulse to sneeze. He watched as the SUVs had gone down the dirt lane that stretched away across the cornfields from the back of the building. After the men left he lay there for another half hour.

He got up and worked his way through the corn, keeping well away from the building. He moved slowly and carefully, his Marine training in full effect. He intended to find out what the hell was going on in this place.

He followed an extremely convoluted track through the vast fields. The dirt road switched back and forth every couple hundred feet or so. He hoped he was going in the right direction. He had gone about five miles on his trek when he saw the edge of the cornfield and a line of trees ahead of him. They were evergreens about sixty feet high and planted close together. The lower limbs were trimmed to twenty feet above ground. The trees provided a dense green canopy overhead, and the trimming appeared to have been carefully done to create the desired cover above the ground. It would be difficult, if not impossible to see what was on the ground from the air.

José remained low in the corn. He was torn between finding his friend and reporting in. He wanted more than anything in the world to get to Rick and get him the hell out of this place, but he understood the odds against him.

He'd trained in Marine Recon, and he relied on those skills now. He had enough firepower to go out in a blaze of glory, but this wasn't the time to play John Wayne. He decided to spend an hour trying to find out what was ahead of him beyond the trees and then get back home.

An inexperienced man might have plunged into the woods at this point, but José correctly surmised that listening devices, cameras, tripwires, and more awaited anyone foolish enough to approach that way. He also concluded correctly that the dirt road running through the woods a hundred yards to his left was too obvious a route in to offer safe passage. He moved another hundred yards away from the road.

Tom Simpson was one of the friends who died in the attack. He loved to talk about growing up in the Pennsylvania woods, and José recalled a conversation in which Tom talked about "tree walking" when he was a kid. He told José that he and his friends would climb up into the trees and walk within the canopy by stepping carefully from one branch to another. He'd said it was like walking on an evergreen carpet when the foliage was really thick. José hid his rifle and climbed a tree until he got above the lowest limbs.

It took the better part of two hours for José to approach the area where the enemy's headquarters lay beneath the trees. He'd almost fallen several times, but he'd managed to catch himself, avoiding disaster and probably certain death.

The main building was large and showy. It was in the English Tudor style, with two massive wings extending left and right from the main house. Several barns and out buildings dotted the property, and he saw what looked like a military-style barracks off to his left. It looked big enough to house a hundred men. The buildings had been painted in such a way as to blend in with the woods. It would be very difficult for someone in a spotter plane to make out what was on the ground amidst the trees.

José got a fix on the sun and looked at his watch. He took out his compass and made several notations in a small notebook.

It took just as long to get back to where he'd started high up in the trees. When he got there he started to climb down the tree, when his instincts kicked in and he froze. There were men on the ground directly beneath where he clung motionless to the side of a tree. He held his breath. The men were talking in low voices. One of them must have said something funny because the others laughed.

José carefully climbed higher up the tree. He would have to wait to climb down. Dusk was coming on, and the wind had picked up. He was getting cold. It was after nine when the men left and he could finally come down from the tree. He found the spot where he'd hidden his rifle and retrieved it.

Wherever he was going it would be a damn long walk. He struck out across country. He was a tough man, a Marine. He walked through fields that seemed like they'd never end. His compass was his guide, that and the stars above him.

He crossed several paved roads but chose not to take any of them. He was still too close to the hell that waited behind him. He needed to get back to tell the man and the Dupree brothers about this place. He would be coming back here. It would be too late for Ricky, he was sure of that, but not too late for payback.

Twenty-four hours later he arrived in Omaha thanks to a long-haul trucker who'd felt sorry for him. He made the phone call.

★★★★★★★

Duke put down the phone and smiled at the man who loved the Gulf. "One is coming home, after all, sir. He knows where we're going, and what we need to do."

"Who is it?"

"José. He got out. Rick must have had him out on the perimeter."

The man smiled at him. "We go to war, Duke. As my father used to say—*Don't get mad, get even.*"

CHAPTER 39

The date was set. And it was a wonderfully significant one. Norman Blesco was happier than he'd ever been. The attack was to take place October 2, a month before the American election, on his birthday. It was a gift from Allah.

Word came for him to prepare. His vacation was coming, and it would be a time like no other in his life. He was so happy, his usual frown turned into what was for him, a grin. His co-workers thought perhaps he was having an attack of painful gas or something, though he was not his usual taciturn self.

He was nearly dizzy with anticipation. The very thought of slaughtering the infidels was like ambrosia to his mind. He pictured himself dancing down the street covered in blood and singing aloud.

Big Donald Callahan chose that exact moment to put a meaty arm around Norman's neck. He was about to playfully run his huge hand through Norman's hair like a scrub brush, when Norman overreacted.

The sight of Callahan flying through the air and crashing into a file cabinet stopped the entire office in its tracks. *Norman Blesco had done this? Mild mannered Norman? Who would have ever thought Norman capable of throwing a man the size of Callahan across a room?*

Norman's blood-curdling scream made them all jump. Even the biggest men in the room were frightened by the sound. The maniacal look on his face caused everyone to take a step back. He looked like a man ready to commit murder.

Suddenly, Norman seemed to regain his sanity. He closed his mouth. The look of hellish anger left his face. His eyes glazed over. He'd lost control in front of infidels. He had blown his cover. Surely he was found out. The color drained from his face. He stormed from the room and ran outside.

Men went to Callahan and picked him up. He was moaning about his back. They gently placed him in a nearby office chair. Everyone was talking at once. Someone suggested taking Callahan to the hospital.

Joe Rumfolo had been standing about fifteen feet away from Norman when the man snapped. As crew boss it was his job to keep everyone in line. He helped get Callahan settled in the chair and stepped back, instructing two of the crew to take him to be examined. Then he headed for the door.

Rumfolo found Norman standing in the parking lot with his head in his hands mumbling something that sounded foreign. When he called out to him, approaching from behind Norman whipped around to face him.

"Whoa, Norman. Don't hit me. Man, what the heck got into you? Are you okay?"

Joe was sure that Norman, usually the most courteous and mild-mannered of his workers, was having a melt-down. He was struggling visibly to get control of himself. He face was flushed, his eyes were bulging, and he was clenching and unclenching his fists.

"I—I'm sorry Mr. Rumfolo. I didn't know why Callahan was grabbing me and I reacted very badly."

"I'd say he had it coming, Norman. After all, you never get mad about anything, and everybody here is always ragging on you for one reason or another. You don't hang out with anyone, you never go out for a beer after work, and some people here think you may be some kind of religious nut."

At these words Norman's face grew even more flushed.

"Hey, I'm just the messenger here!" Joe stepped back a pace. "Whatever you believe is okay with me. If you want to read the Bible at work I don't care, as long as it's at lunch time and not on the job. To each his own."

"Yes, sir. Of course." Norman didn't look any better.

"Look, stay out here and cool off for a while. I don't think anybody on the crew is going to bother you from now on. I sure won't. I know how good a worker you are and I can vouch for your work ethic to anybody, but if you ever go off like that again I might have to write you up. I don't want to do that. Do we understand each other?"

"Yes, I'm truly sorry. I won't let my temper show again," Norman said.

"Super! I'm gonna go check on Callahan and make sure he's all right. Don't need a lawsuit on our hands, do we? Hey, that vacation of yours can't come soon enough, can it? You gotta blow off some steam and mellow out. This kind of stress will kill you."

Norman looked at the back of the man as he walked away from him. You haven't seen killing yet, he thought, but I'll enjoy every moment of it.

CHAPTER 40

The date was set, and The Movement was preparing. Michael, Henry, and Eric had been invited to a very special meeting. A dozen people joined them at the conference table.

A video played on the monitors at the front of the room in honor of the historic moment. The Founders of The Movement appeared on screen in the first few minutes of the video. Now that they knew who these mythic people were, they felt humbled. What followed was a documentary of The Movement's history, relating how it had begun and evolved into its present form. When it was over the room remained silent for several moments before anyone spoke.

A distinguished-looking man in a dark Armani suit and red silk tie sat opposite Michael. "It's a go, then," he said. "October 2 will mark the end of the nightmare, and the beginning of the new Republic of the United States of America. How does that make you feel, Mr. Brown?"

"Elated and terrified, Mr. Chrome," Michael replied. "Elated, because it is finally going to happen, and terrified for all of us if we should fail."

An impeccably attired woman of middle years sitting next to

Mr. Chrome voiced her opinion. "There will be no failure, Mr. Brown. Sixty years of preparation will culminate in success. What is planned is of such a monumental nature as to be compared with few things that men and women have ever attempted in human history. Perhaps D-Day in 1944 would compare in size and scope, but Eisenhower and his colleagues didn't have six decades to put things in place. We have, and we're ready."

Henry spoke up. "Did you ever hear of the 'Theory of Gum,' Ms. Yellow?" he asked.

She said, "No, I can't say that I have. Would you explain it to us?"

"Well, it's equivalent to that old line about the best laid schemes of mice and men." A small ripple of laughter made its way around the table. "It's also on a par with Murphy's Law," Henry continued, "and the one that says, If three things can go wrong, the one that will go wrong will be the one that will do the most damage."

There was no laughter at the table. "The Theory of Gum was developed by my grandfather. We called him the Old Man, not because he was old, but because his wisdom was bottomless. He ran a dragline not many miles from here. If you've never seen a dragline, it sits on tracks, like a bulldozer or a tank, that are almost six feet high. The cabin is about the size of a small ranch house, and there's a hundred-and-twenty foot boom extending into the air that allows the operator to move above the earth in a circle, or to hover over where the digging will take place. Steel cables as thick as a man's arm are attached to a drag bucket that holds eight cubic yards of dirt—about the volume of an automobile. The bucket goes out from the boom and is dragged back towards the machine, cutting into the earth as it comes, hence the term 'dragline.' The operator can then pick up the earth and swing right or left and dump it into a pile. The machine can dig to a depth of a hundred feet, opening a trench so the coal seams can be revealed.

"Anyway, there are two men on a dragline—the operator and the oiler. Petroleum based lubricants are the lifeblood of these machines. The grease is absolutely essential to reduce friction.

"One day there was a breakdown. The Old Man was an

operator, and a first class mechanic to boot. He had to tear things apart and put them back together, and he had to do it right the first time out in the coal fields where, like most places, time is money. Well, he and his oiler found a huge mass of gook in the oil. When they cleaned some of it up it appeared to be pink in color.

"Apparently, someone either accidentally or intentionally put something in the oil when they changed it. Whatever it was really gummed up the works. The Old Man's *Theory of Gum* was born that day. It says, gum is the most dangerous substance on earth when it is in the wrong place. It lurks on the street waiting for your shoe, under chair seats waiting for your hands, and in your mouth waiting to get lodged in your throat, a lung, or somewhere else it should not be. In our plan we have to ask, *Where's the gum?*" Henry said.

Colonel Eric Dryden, soon to be vice president of the United States, chuckled and said, "And that, ladies and gentlemen, is why this man is at this table. We can have all the theories we want about how TR2.0 is supposed to work, but on the day that is coming we cannot afford to have gum in the wrong place. Our task is to find the gum that can muck up the works. Thanks for keeping us straight, Mr. Jones."

Of the fifteen people in the room, four were the hidden insiders, called Directors, who knew every aspect of TR2.0. Only one of them was known to Eric, and the redundancy of having four was another of the fail-safe mechanisms in place to keep any unforeseen problems from affecting the teams at the critical moment of execution.

Two people were needed to open either of two vaults that would begin implementation of the plan. One was in the hidden city in Pennsylvania, and the second was in a similar facility under a mountain in northern California. One team would be at each location during the twenty-four hours leading up to the plan's execution. Either vault could be opened to access the ignition keys required to start the process.

Michael looked around the room. "We have our date. We know where the epicenter is located. We have SEAL team in place. All aspects of the TR2.0 stand ready. We'll be using the enemies of freedom's own devious scheme against them. As someone who works in intelligence, I find it difficult not to be aware of all the variables—the gum as Mr. Jones put it—that might mess up what we are about to do. That makes me nervous.

"For that reason, I would like to have some idea what I should expect to happen when it begins. I believe the ultimate decision makers are at this table. If not, then I'm sure they're monitoring this meeting. Can anyone tell me what I need to do when things get underway?"

"No, Mr. Brown, I'm afraid we can't share that information just yet." The response came from a Navy Captain sitting three seats to Michael's left. "I am not, by the way, one of the people who will make the decision, but I am someone who can tell you that before the plan is executed we will be moving our people, their families, and friends into our facilities all over this country. This will be done quickly and without fanfare. Each of our people will be informed of that operation one week prior to its execution. We do not want people to be vulnerable when the plan starts. We expect all of our people to be protected when the world shifts on its axis. You'll understand why I use that term when the time comes. I'm telling you this because you will need to instruct your immediate family and friends to be at home on that date and ready to move."

Michael saluted the Captain, who returned his salute. "Thank you. We'll be ready to move out when we receive the word."

Eric surveyed the room. "If there's nothing else, we need to get to work. There is still much to do. May I add, in the words of Tiny Tim, *God bless us every one.*"

Their voices rose in a unified chorus of "*Amen.*"

CHAPTER 41

Robert Hoopes was almost beside himself with glee. His meeting with the senator had gone well. Naming the girl the senator got pregnant as a senior in high school didn't faze him in the least. The birth certificate of the child who'd been born out of wedlock and a recent photo of that child, now an adult who'd never known his father, well, at that the great man crumbled.

There was no need to threaten. The senator understood exactly what was expected of him. He appeared to be quite contrite, and agreed to do whatever the administration demanded without giving Hoopes or the president any trouble in the future.

The *Department of Dirty Tricks* won the day once again. Hoopes practically skipped down the hall of the Senate office building. Power was such a heady thing. He breathed power in and breathed it out. He was the go-to man for the Big Man himself.

Don't mess with me! Hoopes laughed and pumped his arms shadow boxing like a prize fighter.

The senator sat at his desk and smiled. He signaled for his secretary to come into the room.

"Yes, sir?"

"Please hold my calls. I have something I have to work on. It will take about twenty minutes. I'll let you know when I can resume the afternoon schedule."

The door closed softly behind his secretary. The senator unlocked a bottom drawer in his desk and took out a new cell phone. He dialed and waited.

The call was answered with the usual code and he responded in kind. "I've reached the end of this. If you have the data I've requested, I'd like to see it right away. When I've reviewed it, you have my permission to act in keeping with our agreement."

"You'll have the data tomorrow morning."

"Thank you. It's deeply appreciated," the senator said.

"This makes us even."

"I understand."

"We will not speak again."

"I find that to be sad."

"It's necessary. The subject will be terminated a month from today. That should allow you enough time to make life interesting."

The senator shivered, even though it was warm in his office. The way the man said "terminated" so matter-of-factly. It chilled him to the bone. There was no compassion in the voice. It was simply something to be taken care of…like ordering eggs or cereal for breakfast.

"Goodbye," the voice said.

The senator turned off the cell phone and placed it on his desk. He stared at it for a long time.

He'd accomplished many things in his long career. Some had been good, and others bad. He'd never ordered the death of anyone before. He did not know how he should feel about it. He hated the despicable excuse for a human being who was the object of his investigation. He was certain whatever had been found out about the man would fill a thick file. Now, he would have to decide how to confront Hoopes with it. He must handle the situation delicately. Timing was everything. The election was bearing down hard on everyone inside the Beltway.

Regardless of how the election turned out, he was sure of one thing. Young Mr. Hoopes would not be in the White House for a second term. He would never again assault the senior senator from Illinois with dirt from his past. He would toy with him, and then others would come for him a month from today. However it ended, things would end very badly for the Special Assistant to the President.

There was something to be said for networking. And indebtedness paid.

He'd saved the man on the other end of the phone a world of grief, and a long prison term. Now they were even.

He knew that the man was a semi-reclusive billionaire. The man preferred to be left alone. I don't blame him, he thought. I wish I could be left alone some days. But then I'd miss all the fun I have in this place. His lips twisted in a wry smirk.

The senator looked at his watch. He signaled his secretary. "Please send in my first appointment."

"Yes, sir," came the reply.

CHAPTER 42

The brothers Dupree, the man who loved the Gulf, and José Alvarez met in the lounge of the Gulf Maiden. State-of-the-art surveillance tech and a proprietary electronic cloaking system ensured her invisibility out on the open seas.

"Speak your mind, José. Tell us what happened and what you saw." Duke said.

For the next hour José relayed the tale of the attack, the slaughter of the team, and his trek to the estate hidden in a forest surrounded by vast cornfields in Nebraska.

"Aside from Big John, are you sure the were dead?" the man asked.

"Yes, sir. Rick was the only one they took right away. I'm sure they must have interrogated him by now."

"You believe he's dead, don't you?"

José dropped his eyes to the floor and his face sagged with emotion. He wiped a hand across his forehead. "That's what I believe, sir. They weren't concerned about the others…they just threw them in the back of a pick-up and drove off. Probably to dispose of the bodies. But Ricky they put in the backseat of an SUV."

"How big is the main house?" Duke asked him.

"It's difficult to say, Mr. Dupree."

"Call me Duke, José. You'll be taking on Rick's job for now. If he's still alive and we find him in time, you'll be his second-in-command."

"I hope he's okay, sir…Duke."

"Me, too. So, if you could make a guess as to the size of the place that will help us gauge what we're dealing with here."

"With the wings on either side I'd guess the main place is about two hundred feet long. The barn a little more than a third of that, and the barracks building can probably hold a hundred men."

"Do you have any idea how they were tipped off that the team was there?"

"There's got to be surveillance all over the place. We walked in, but hell, when you're walking through corn that high there could be a million bugs all around. You'd never see one of them." José said.

"The building Rick and Big John went into…something or someone had to be waiting for them inside right?"

"Must have been. After they wiped out the guys outside they went in and just carried them out of there. Big John had to be dead. I…I wished that Rick had been dead, too. There's no telling what they're doing to him."

Derek Dupree spoke up. "Rick isn't a man who'll be easily broken. In the worst case scenario they'll find out where he came from, and they'll know we'll be back."

"Agreed," said the man who loved the Gulf.

"However, something tells me these people are outside the law. They can't turn to someone else for help anymore than we can. We settle it once and for all. We find the one behind it and we bring him here."

"What about tactical advantage? Is there anything José has said which you think we could exploit? " The man who loved the Gulf waited for Derek to reply.

"Seclusion might be a potential weak spot. José says the forest is designed to hide the place from the air. I think that may be a vulnerable point we could use to our advantage. They've got to know, based on our team's gear, that we can do a lot of damage. But, I'm sure they're stirred up like a hornet's nest right now. We've rattled their cage. They'll be looking in every direction for the next attack, but what we lose in the area of surprise we can make up for with force. We overwhelm them." Derek said.

"How many men?'"

"We come in fast from the air and drop down right on top of them. This is going to be a big operation. I'd say we need a hundred men." Derek rubbed his chin. "The question is how the hell do we get that many men out there, let alone on the ground safely? We either parachute in, or use choppers, but I don't know how we get that many choppers over Nebraska without stirring up the Air Force, the National Guard, and the Marines."

Everyone sat silently looking at the man.

"And we'll definitely need a way around their surveillance," Derek added.

The man who loved the Gulf sat, lost in thought for a long time. Finally, he looked at his men. "I own a trucking company with a fleet of privately labeled rigs for transporting cargo by the tons. We'll ship our men and equipment to Nebraska."

"Sounds good," Derek said. "I recommend we travel at night."

"Agreed. Like I told you, gentlemen, we're going to war. I don't intend to lose again."

"Sir," Duke said, "You said we. Do you intend to go along on this?"

"Our man in Omaha lost a son to these bastards. I talked to him last night. I wouldn't miss it for the world. We'll use one of the jets and fly the five of us to Omaha. We'll get to our man's farm and do our staging there."

"And the choppers? How do we get enough choppers big enough to take in the army?" Derek asked. "Choppers make too much noise. They'd be ready for us before we hit the ground. There's another way to do this but it's going to require some training. I think I may have a way to get that handled, but it'll have to be set up today." He sighed.

"The time slips away. The longer we wait, the more fortified our enemy becomes. We've already seen that going there in anything less than a tank is suicide. Duke, can you get me a safe phone?"

"Yes, sir."

Duke went to the rear of the lounge and touched a switch hidden by a beautiful photograph of the Gulf on the wall behind the bar. Silently, the picture swung aside, revealing a wall safe. He dialed the combination, opened the safe and took out a cell phone. He returned to the group and handed the phone over to the man.

The man pulled a small address book from his pocket, looked up a number and dialed.

A voice answered. "Hello?"

"Long time no speak, cousin. How are you?"

"It's been ten years, but who's counting?"

"Don't you ever get tired of that town? I'd think you would have had enough of Washington by this time," the man who loved the Gulf said.

"You do what you have to. So, to what do I owe the pleasure?"

"How are your military contacts these days?"

"Better than yours, I'm sure."

"I need to get some night jump training for some people."

"How many men?"

"A hundred."

"Good Lord, man are you invading Colombia?"

"No, Nebraska. I got out of Colombia years ago."

The man on the other end of the phone laughed. "Nebraska? What's worth anything in Nebraska besides all that food they raise?"

"It doesn't concern you. Can you help me?"

"Yes, but it'll cost you."

"You know I'm good for it."

"How many 'chutes?"

"Enough to train, and then for the drop."

"Delivered where?"

"Here. We'll truck them to our destination. I have a facility we can use when we get there, and I have the trainers on staff." The man looked at the Dupree brothers and winked.

"You'll have them by this Thursday."

There's one more thing. Do you know anybody in intelligence with access to satellite imagery?

"Now you're pushing it. Why?"

"I have the coordinates of the place we're visiting but it's heavily forested. I need a better idea of where things are beneath the trees. Can you get that data for me if I give you the specs?"

"Yes, there's a man I can talk to. What shall I say in the way of explanation for needing such information?"

"Tell him you owe someone in your family a favor."

"Sure. I think he'll accept that as an excuse." He sighed. "What are the coordinates?"

The man relayed the coordinates José recorded in his notebook. "I'll make the call when we say goodbye."

"You're the can-do guy. I miss you. When are you going to come and see me?"

"I didn't know I was invited."

"You just were."

"How's Thanksgiving? I miss the old days."

"No you don't, and neither do I."

"Yeah, well I miss seeing you. We're family. The only ones left. Are you still hanging around those crazies in Washington?"

"Yeah, and they're crazier than any bedbug in any one-star motel you'll ever stay in. However, there's big doings going on. Things are about to change."

"Really. How?"

"Not on the phone."

"If you can't tell me then why did you say so in the first place?"

"You know that yacht of yours?"

"How do you know about that?"

"It's my job to know. Anyway, at the end of September I suggest cruising somewhere out of the country. Take everyone along…the ones you care about. Go somewhere that's nice. If you have to dock, try an island paradise somewhere out of the way, and stay there until

November. Kapish?"

His cousin's words sobered the man who loved the Gulf. "You're not kidding me, are you?"

"Do I kid around? I've got to hang up now. You'll get what you need, and I will see you at Thanksgiving. It's been too long. Be well, take care." The phone went dead.

The man looked at his team. "Don't make any plans for the end of September or the month of October. We're taking a cruise."

CHAPTER 43

Pierce Armstrong had a bad case of indigestion. Who were these people? One had been bad enough, but six! His stomach was rolling.

His underlings had taken care of the bodies. One had been nearly as big as Ollie. It took four men, plus Ollie, to get them all into the furnace to dispose of them.

Ollie told him the man who just barely remained alive was Hispanic. Armstrong hated Hispanics, Blacks, Jews, Christians, Muslims, Europeans, Africans, the Slavs—*Hell, I hate every race and ethnic group on the face of the earth.*

His stomach rumbled. He swallowed against the salty taste in his mouth and fought the urge to be sick. He was beside himself with worry. What the hell had that Hoopes gotten into? On whose radar was he being tracked? It was maddening.

There were fifty-six men in Armstrong's private security force. "Captain," Arnold Jacoby, reported that the intruders carried powerful and sophisticated weaponry and tactical gear. The vehicle they came in had yet to be found.

During his grandfather and father's rule no one ever detected their family's safe haven. Now, two assaults in less than a month! It was intolerable! His mind roiled. Who would dare launch such an unprecedented attack on the *Master of the Master Race!*

But Armstrong could not enlist more men. The population in this area of Nebraska was sparse. Their were fewer than five hundred people within a fifty mile radius of The Farm, including those in the town where he bought his supplies. There were probably only about three hundred people living in Schickley, almost a hundred miles away. The possibility of drawing unwanted attention was too great.

Employee loyalty was non-existent beyond the pay and benefits. Armstrong paid better than anyone in the area, and perks included meals, housing, and medical care. A saloon on the property that was open nights and weekends with access to the services of "ladies of the evening" on a regular basis completed the package.

Ironically, and despite the presence of the bar, there was a zero-tolerance policy for drinking on the job. Anyone discovered in such a state was turned over to Ollie for "re-education." The trouble with that solution was that re-education at the hands of Ollie was permanent. No one survived it. Ollie enjoyed it, but it had been two years since the last man had fallen into his hands. The men who remained had no desire to ever face him.

The barracks once held close to a hundred men during his father's prime, but with the decline in the rural population during the farm crisis in the 80's there were fewer young men around to recruit. Most young people migrated to the cities, and the seclusion and secrecy required to remain in Armstrong's employ at The Farm ultimately outweighed the perks.

The men in Armstrong's private army never saw him, except for Jacoby. Armstrong refused to allow his image to grace the mind of any one of them. As far as he was concerned, they were a necessary evil. He spent a lot of money maintaining them, but he wanted nothing whatever to do with them. He preferred it that way.

****

The *Master of the Manor,* as Jacoby called Armstrong behind his back, was a royal pain-in-the-backside. The man treated him like some low-life creature whose only role was to do his bidding without question. Jacoby hated Armstrong, but he was no fool. He kept his mouth shut and did his job, which on most days were boring beyond belief.

The recent flurry of activity had the whole compound astir. After seeing the weapons the intruders carried, Jacoby made himself a solemn promise to move on in the relatively near future. Whoever was behind the recent incursions was no one to mess with. Big trouble would soon follow. He was certain of it. Though, in his opinion, bad things happening to Pierce Armstrong would benefit the world. If the invaders were also capable of taking down the butler from hell, well, that would be icing on the cake.

Ollie Larson was the sickest freak he'd ever met. Jacoby only saw the torture chamber when ordered to deposit someone there. He felt sorry for the poor S. O. B. they had out there now, but not sorry enough to run and tell anyone.

****

Ollie Larson was enjoying his latest assignment immensely. Armstrong ordered him to keep the captive kept alive long enough to reveal who sent him. So far he'd left the man's handsome face untouched, anticipating the day he would carve it up with his scalpels. Instead, he inflicted hellish torture on nearly every other part of the man's body.

The man lay unconscious in a cell off the torture room. Blood seeped from his tormented flesh. He moaned in dark dreams, but no one but Ollie heard his agonized cries.

Armstrong was determined to have the man broken, but Ollie lacked subtlety. Admittedly, he had no finesse. He was so brutal in his methods that he usually ended up killing his victims before they could tell what they knew.

✳✳✳✳✳✳✳

Rick had not broken. How he'd borne so much was beyond comprehension. His loyalty to the man who loved the Gulf was something to behold, but he was hanging on by a thread. It would be over soon. The creature from hell that tormented him was eager to kill him. Rick knew it. If he could muster his strength one final time he would goad his captor into killing him. He would do it somehow. His mind and body hurt so bad that he wanted to die. Not to feel any more pain would be the greatest blessing.

Unbeknownst to him, friends were gathering mere miles from where he lived out his worst nightmares.

✳✳✳✳✳✳✳

Armstrong's stomach rumbled again. How dare anyone come to his haven uninvited! It was a blasphemy against the sanctity of his life. He could not help it; he threw up all over his lovely granite-topped kitchen island, the foul mess soaking into his neatly pressed trousers and splattering the sparkling clean ceramic tile of his kitchen floor.

The sight and stench of what he'd done nearly caused him to pass out. He hadn't vomited since he was a child. His father had beaten him for messing up the bathroom on that occasion. He had been so mortified that it never happened again. *Until now.*

He staggered toward the doorway to the living room, but was again seized by the uncontrollable urge to vomit. His stomach convulsed violently, and a great gusher of half-digested food spewed from his mouth, covering the front of his stainless steel refrigerator. It was too much. Pierce Armstrong, smartest man in the world by his own admission, swooned and passed out on the floor.

He was discovered moments later by his housekeeper. She stared down at him in disgust. What a sight! If he weren't such a nasty mess she might have kicked him. *And the smell!* She pushed a button.

Almost immediately, Ollie came lumbering from his room in the basement. At the sight of Armstrong lying on the floor covered in puke, he suddenly wished he could take him to his special room. Over the years he grew to dislike the man more and more. His father had beaten him physically, but under Pierce Armstrong he'd come to know even worse mental abuse. Ollie fantasized about doing bad things to him.

He stood staring down at him for a long moment, then picked Armstrong up like a rag doll and carried him to his suite of rooms. He sat him on the floor in the enclosed shower stall with his back against the wall and turned on the water. He adjusted it for comfort.

Pierce Armstrong came sputtering to awareness. He swore loudly and looked through the glass at Ollie. The giant stared back at him. For the first time ever, Armstrong looked away. Shame burned his face, and he felt hot tears in his eyes.

****

In the cell beneath the barn Rick moaned in pain. He wished he could see the Gulf one more time.

CHAPTER 44

E ric wasn't in the conference room deep beneath the earth when
Michael arrived for his meeting. Henry remained at their
mother's home in Clear Haven with Joan and Susan. Michael
had driven to the meeting alone.

Two men and two women sat in the room. They stood as he
entered. He recognized them as having been at previous gatherings, but
this talk would be quite different. They were the two teams of directors,
one of which would set the plan in motion. They would activate the
mechanisms that would set an irrevocable course for the nation.

A distinguished looking man in a dark grey suit and red silk tie
with carefully styled white hair and a deeply lined face was the first to
speak. "With your permission," he began cautiously, "we will address
you as *Mr. President* from now until you sit in that office. You have
committed to the plan, and we are at your disposal to answer questions
regarding its execution."

"First off, if you must call me by that title then I would like
to ask you why I was chosen for the job. I understand your vetting
process, but I cannot, for the life of me, understand why someone

else wasn't chosen. I'm a military man. There are countless others who are far more politically qualified than me. Why choose me?" Michael asked.

A handsome, well-dressed woman sitting to the right of the man who'd first spoken said, "You may find this hard to believe, Mr. President, but we've been watching you since you first entered West Point. We have made it our focus to monitor all of the people in all the service academies, both men and women, for decades. We knew this day would come, and that we'd need a leader we were confident would be equal to this monumental task."

"I didn't even finish first in my class."

"Academics are not the only factor we considered in our search. You finished first in our selection process for many reasons. Character matters. So does your patriotism and dedication to this nation and all it represents in this world. You served bravely in battle. We know your record, Mr. President, and your record with regard to the most important issues is second to none."

Michael was humbled by their assessment. He remained silent for a moment.

The second man in the group appeared to Michael to be the academic type, comfortable in dark rimmed glasses and patches on the elbows of his corduroy sport coat. He looked slightly over the tops of his glasses as he addressed Michael. "We got to know the souls of the people we examined for this incredibly important role. We spoke to myriads of people regarding each of our finalists with the goal of determining who each person truly was during the most stressful moments of their lives." He paused before going on, gesturing with a hand as he spoke. "My colleague said that character matters. Indeed, your character matters to the extent that there was no one else we could have possibly chosen. This wasn't a horse race. It wasn't based on popularity or slick-tongued political rhetoric.

"You're so well thought of that if I told you the comments made about you by others your head might swell up to the size of the Goodyear Blimp." He laughed. "However, we all know you're not an egotist. You have a reputation for putting the needs of others before your own. You may be the most selfless man who has ever walked the earth, with the exception of the man born in Bethlehem." He smiled.

The distinguished gentleman addressed Michael again, the lines in his face deepening as he spoke. "You should know that we've also spoken to the men you led in combat. They would lay down their lives for you in a heartbeat because they knew that you would do the same for them without hesitation. You are an American patriot...an honorable man who believes in this nation and all it once stood for. You come from a family of like-minded men."

"What lies before us is frightening for all of us, but we know that you will do your best for the people of this nation. You have the intellect, values and fortitude needed to lead in this hour. I will be proud to salute you as our president. We all will. We've needed someone of your calibre in the Office for a long time."

The second woman in the group, who appeared to be in her seventies spoke for the first time, "My grandmother was one of the founders of The Movement. My mother would have been her successor had she not died very young. Grandmother finished the task of raising me, and in turn, her passion and dedication to this county became part of my life. You are being called upon to help unite a nation that is deeply divided. It is, as has been stated, a monumental undertaking. Rest assured, you have the support of generations of men and women who have dedicated their lives and fortunes to preserving this great nation. We will be beside you every step of the way."

"I appreciate that, ma'am," Michael replied.

"The shock of what lies ahead will hammer this nation from coast to coast, but our enemies' plan to takeover every aspect of American life will be wrested from their hands; their own scheme will be used to remove them from every position of influence in this nation, Mr. President."

Michael said quietly, "You're talking about a coup...and coups can turn very bloody—"

"Not if they are executed in such a way that Americans are unaware of what is happening until it's over," the distinguished-looking gentleman said. "That is precisely what our enemies plan. Their evil plans are made in the darkness. They do not do their work in the light. They never have. They cleverly play one group against another. They believe themselves to be the true masters of guile and manipulation." He paused, looking steadily at Michael. "They would be that, indeed, if not for the existence of The Movement."

"Are you saying that we are more devious than they are?" Michael asked, eyebrows raised.

"No. I know your commitment to truthfulness and fair play. Trust me when I say that we feel about such things as you do. But, in order to escape the horror that our enemies would visit upon us we must know their thoughts, plans and players. To that end, it has taken decades to infiltrate their ranks and become trusted members of their army of Progressives."

The handsome woman spoke. "There is nothing they will not do to control us. They completely lack morality. They do not believe in God. They believe in expediency, apparent compromise. I say apparent compromise because they are content to appear conciliatory, when in fact they are biding their time, all the while scheming to seize power. They would rule you, your wife, your children, your brother and his family, your mother, and everyone in Clear Haven. They would rule all of us. They are, in their minds, the Master Race."

Michael's face was grim. "Will we have to kill them to rid ourselves of them?

"No, but they will never again be in a position to affect our lives or rule this country."

"But how is that possible?" Michael asked. "There are obviously thousands of these people all over this nation, let alone their fellow travelers who go along to get along with them. Do you have a magic wand to wave and make them disappear?"

"There is no magic wand. There will be unrest when they are gone from our midst. Americans will be confused as to what has happened. Government will cease to function as a giant cookie jar for a time. The day of taking from the haves and giving to the have-nots will end. It will be a painful time for millions of people as they adjust to the new reality. Those who are capable of working will be able to work…but no longer for the government."

"Even the days of career politicians are coming to an end. The example, will of course come from the top. Contrary to the Progressives intent to eliminate term limits, even the president may only serve one term in the office. If you wish to remain in the Office you will have to be elected to a second term."

"What if we fall into temptation and decide we want to rule as an oligarchy? What if we become like them? How do we keep ourselves from becoming what we have come to hate?" A long silence followed Michael's question.

Finally, the founder's granddaughter replied, "In every human enterprise there are dangers, Mr. President, but it is precisely because you asked such a question that we've chosen you to lead this nation in what will, at first, appear to be its darkest hour. You will not allow such a thing to happen. As the men in that sacred hall of liberty pledged so long ago in the city of Philadelphia, we have also pledged all that we have to its success.

"Ultimately this confrontation was inevitable. The Progressives have been planning this for a hundred years, patiently waiting for the perfect storm of circumstances, natural or engineered, to completely usurp the people's God-given freedoms and constrict the masses to their narcissistic will. It is their dream, their utopian ideal, and they will not go quietly into the night."

"This country is about to experience a course correction," the academic spoke again. "The ship of state has been steered in the wrong direction for a long time. It's time to get back to basics. If a tooth goes bad you go to the dentist to have it removed. We are the dentist. The tooth will be removed.

"We cannot co-exist with Progressives any longer because they cannot tolerate any viewpoint but their own. The American ideal is based on the freedom of the individual. Progressives find freedom abhorrent. They love power and control. They see themselves as a hair's breadth away from achieving their dream, and their success will reduce this country to a living hell."

"I would rather be dead than live another day under their

domination," the founder's granddaughter said.

Michael read the strength of her convictions and the determination in her eyes. "You told me when we began this meeting that you would answer my questions fully and without reservation."

The men and women at the table nodded their agreement.

"Then let's get to it. It's time I knew everything. If I am to lead then I must know where I am leading the people...and how the journey begins."

The group did as he asked. Over the next four hours they carefully explained every detail of TR2.0 and its execution. Computer monitors came to life with images of the mechanisms, sites, equipment, and people in place. All were ready to move. They explained how the imminent crisis engineered by their enemy would be turned against that enemy.

When they finished they quietly got up from their chairs and left the room, closing the door behind them.

Michael sat alone, lost in thought. His viewed the people who'd just left him with immeasurable respect, and he was amazed by all they told him. The nation stood on the brink of change, and for all intents and purposes, he would be at the helm when the dust settled.

Michael Stonebreaker felt small and humble, yet somewhere deep inside he knew it was going to work. He had no doubt.

CHAPTER 45

Robert Hoopes sat bolt upright in terror. Somehow the blaring ring of his cell phone dovetailed with the nightmare he was having. He was running through the halls of his boyhood home. His father was chasing him, swinging an ax that clanged against the metal light fixtures as he lurched along. Except his father's face was that of the esteemed senator from Illinois.

The image burning in his mind refused to give way before his unfocused eyes. He fumbled for his cell phone on the bedside table. It was 3:17 a.m. "Hello?"

"Robert Hoopes?"

"Yes, dammit! Do you know what time it is?"

"The time doesn't matter, but indeed, the hour is late. Look for the first gift outside your door." The call ended. Some A-hole was playing games. He lay back down, and rolled on his side, the cell phone still in his hand. He was tired. He closed his eyes. The phone rang again.

"The gift is outside your door. It is strongly recommended that you retrieve it before your neighbors find it. It would be devastating if they did." Again, the call ended.

This time Hoopes swung his legs out of bed and stood up. He padded slowly from his bedroom and down the hall to the door of his apartment. He cautiously opened the door.

A package lay just outside in the hall. It was about the size of a Washington, DC phone book, and wrapped in light brown paper. There was no name or address on the package. He was afraid to pick it up. *What if it was a bomb!*

Screwing up his courage he reached down, picked it up, and softly closed the door. He took the package to the living room and placed it gently on the coffee table.

He turned on a table lamp, sat on the couch and stared at it.

It was sealed with Scotch tape. He picked it up again and gently waved it up and down. There seemed to be a box inside the paper, and whatever was in it was as heavy as a ream of copy paper.

He was the *Special Assistant to the President.* Perhaps he should call the police? His curiosity won out. He opened the wrapping paper to reveal a white box. Hoopes gingerly pulled off the top of the box and looked inside. Inside lay a large manila folder with a single white sheet of paper on top. On the paper someone had typed the words, *…and so we begin…*

He picked up the folder and opened it. When he saw what was inside his face flamed with shame.

When Hoopes was fifteen he and two of his friends raped a girl on an August afternoon in the woods not far from his home. His parents and those of the other boys exerted a great deal of their wealth and influence to cover the whole thing up. The girl was from the wrong side of town, and she and her family could do little to persuade anyone of what actually happened. She became pregnant in the attack. Three months later she threw herself off a bridge.

The horror of what Hoopes and the other two had done was never revealed to the public. A large sum of money was paid to the girl's family. The mother had been in and out of institutions, and the father was out of work, so he agreed to accept the money and keep his mouth shut. The mother never understood what happened. The girl had been an only child.

The truth never came out. Hoopes turned the page. The top of next sheet of paper also read, *...and so it continues...*

He could not believe his eyes. Before him, typed neatly in black and white lay a detailed account of an incident from his college fraternity days. There had been a party—a drunken, dope-smoking party—one Saturday night in November. Hoopes tried to talk a girl into sleeping with him. He had been chasing the girl without success, and again she refused his advances. An attempt at rape followed, but he was too drunk to succeed in the attack and she got away.

The girl had been too embarrassed to report the incident. Hoopes dodged another bullet. He stared at pictures of himself and the girl at the party. There was a written report the girl had made, about which he'd never learned. Apparently, the report was never submitted to anyone at the school.

He turned the page. He read, *...and so it goes, on and on...*

Hoopes sat for an hour and read through every dirty, nasty thing he'd ever done in his life, up to and including his work in the administration. All of it was there in print.

He was most frightened by the transcripts of his recent telephone conversations with the president. The record of his own deeds was more thorough than anything his investigative source ever compiled for him to use in bringing heat to someone.

Someone bugged his apartment. His eyes darted around the room in fear. *Where the hell were the bugs?* He broke into a cold sweat. Was he on camera?

He forced himself to read the last page, and almost wet his pants.

Greetings Mr. Hoopes,

> *The deeds of men are always noticed. You cannot escape your past. Your next gift will arrive at a time when you least expect it. This is only the beginning, but the end will come in due time. We want you to think about the end, to ponder what it might be, to examine it again and again in your mind.*
> *As you know, fear is a great motivator. You have used fear time and time again as a whip for others. Now, fear has come to you. Taste it, savor it, drink deeply of it. More*

*fear is coming...and there are good reasons to be afraid.
Until we meet face-to-face...*

*Yours truly,
Fear*

Hoopes was beside himself. *What the hell am I going to do? How can I tell the president about this? Do I dare tell him?*

He was not so much afraid of the president as he was the people who surrounded the man. Some terribly frightening henchmen occupied the shadows behind the throne.

Sweat was pouring from his body. His heart raced. He was approaching a panic attack. He stood up abruptly and bolted for the bedroom. He searched frantically for bugs and cameras, but he could not find them. They were too well hidden or unrecognizable.

He needed to get the hell out of his apartment. He took a two minute shower, dried himself and threw on his clothes. He shoved the odious package into his briefcase. Within ten minutes he was out the door and hailing a taxi.

The men in the van parked on the street laughed hysterically. The guy had really been spooked. His was scared off the charts. The driver slid into traffic a couple of cars behind, discreetly following Hoopes' cab.

"Take me to the Washington Mall." Hoopes snapped. At the end of the ride, he swiped a credit card for the fare and nearly stumbled from the cab.

"You okay, buddy?"

Hoopes slammed the door, ignoring the driver's concern. He began walking toward the Washington monument. He found a row of benches and choosing one, sat down. His thoughts were a furious jumble. He needed to clear his head. *What should he do?*

Given his personality, Hoopes had a hell of a lot of acquaintances, but damn few friends. In fact, he had no close friends. He was on speaking terms with a host of people. The sheer volume of numbers in his contacts would make one think he was a popular guy. Nothing could have been further from the truth. Most of his contacts only tolerated him because his position provided them access to The Man. Privately, no one liked him. He was an arrogant pain-in-the-backside.

Hoopes discovered a life-changing revelation sitting on the bench. He suddenly knew what it felt like to be on the receiving end of what he normally dished out. Exposing and using other peoples' shadowy past was his forte, but his whole damn life was documented on just about a full ream of copy paper. Hell, every mean and sordid thing he'd ever done, from his boyhood to the present moment was neatly spelled out for the world to read.

He chewed his lip and nervously ran a hand through his hair over and over again. He wanted to stand up and run screaming in fear. The note said to fear. He was afraid. What was he going to do?

Robert Hoopes had a sudden thought. *Was it the damned senator from Illinois? Was this payback time?* If it was, the wayward deeds of the senator paled in comparison to the record of his own sins. The dossier revealed Hoopes to be only slightly less monstrous than Hannibal Lecter. He shuddered and clutched the briefcase even more tightly to his chest with his other hand.

He must do something. He couldn't return to the apartment. His cell phone rang and he nearly leaped from the bench. He held it in his hand, looking at it as though it were a poisonous snake. His hand was trembling. The screen read, *Restricted.* He did not answer it. He did not want to hear it, but at the telltale ping he tapped the phone and voicemail icons. He entered his password.

The now familiar voice spoke evenly in his ear. "Mr. Hoopes, you move quickly, but we'll credit that to your youth. However, you cannot move fast enough to avoid your next gift. It's waiting for you on the bench to your right. You are strongly advised to retrieve it at once before someone else finds it. That would certainly prove to be an embarrassment to you.

"Remember, fear is gaining on you with each passing moment. This next gift is unique in its meaning. You will certainly recognize it. Enjoy it while you can. Time slips away.

"Please give my regards to the president. On second thought, that would not be wise. He is surrounded by men who might be capable of terrifying you as much as we intend to. I say "might," because you have yet to experience true terror at our hands. Wait for it. As they say at your bank, "Have a nice day!" The call ended.

Hoopes sat open-mouthed listening to the voice. At the mention of the location of the next package, he leaped to his feet and ran to the next bench. He could see the plain wrapped parcel, but he hadn't noticed anyone placing it there. He picked it up and strode toward the street. He did not want to open it in public. He walked to the White House at a frantic pace, went though the gate, entered the building and went to his office.

Hoopes closed and locked the door behind him. He dropped the briefcase in a chair, afraid to let it go, but even more afraid to ignore the new package. He placed the box on his desk and sat staring at it. How could what was inside possibly be worse that what he'd already been sent?

Carefully, aware that his fingers were trembling, he opened the tape, removed the wrapping, and saw that it was another copy paper sized box. He removed the top and looked in. A piece of typing paper on top contained another message.

> *"All things come to him who waits. We've been waiting for the right moment to give this to you. You'll soon discover that there are people in the world who are so powerful that one would never dare incur their wrath. You have angered such a person. The penalty for doing so we will leave to your imagination. Are you afraid, Mr. Hoopes? Read on. Fear is coming."*

Hoopes lifted the page and found what looked like a bound manuscript with a blank cover. He flipped it open, and began reading. His chest constricted, tightening so much he could hardly breathe. The air was sucked out of him like he'd been punched in the gut. He felt light-headed, as though he were going to faint.

He dropped the manuscript and stood up on quavering legs, struggling to catch his breath. As a boy he suffered from asthma. He hadn't had an attack in years, but right now he was gasping for air like he had as a kid on the playground.

The story of his father's life spilled out over the neatly typewritten pages; sordid details crawled like black maggots across pristine sheets of bright white stationery.

He picked up the manuscript and began reading again. A string of Judge Randall A. Hoopes' extra-marital affairs, criminal financial dealings, bribes in exchange for favorable rulings from the bench, and worse were chronicled in detail.

Hoopes moaned aloud as he read of the night his drunken father hit a child on a bicycle, loaded the body and bike into his car, then drove them to a swamp and sunk them where no one would ever find them.

On the last page of the horrible account he read,

The apple does not fall far from the tree, Mr. Hoopes. When we have finished with you, your father is next. Are you afraid? You should be.

Yours truly,
Fear

Robert Hoopes both hated and loved his father. He always sought his approval as a child, and rarely got it. These people threatened his father's ruin. They'd uncovered and intended to make public every sordid detail of his past. His father would surely go to prison.

Despite his mixed feelings, he wondered if he could ultimately come out the hero, saving his own skin as well as his father's. The man would never love him, but he could be indebted to him for his freedom. Given the choice, Robert preferred obligation to love. *But what could he do? How could he fix this?*

A piece of paper at the bottom of the box caught his eye.

Like a ghost worthy of the wonderful Dickens tale, your third gift will arrive when you least expect it. It will be delightfully terrifying. Be very afraid.

Yours truly,
Fear

It took him five full minutes to calm his breathing. He shoved the manuscript in the box alongside the other and left his office. Out on the street, he hailed a cab and directed the driver to take him home.

When Hoopes got to his apartment he stood in the doorway, so spooked that he wasn't certain if he should enter. He was afraid of what might be waiting for him. Finally, he opened the door and flipped the switch in the short hallway that led deeper into his apartment. Nothing moved; the hallway was empty. He inched along the hall to where it opened onto the combination living room/kitchen. Nothing appeared to be out of order.

He crossed the room, and stopped just outside his bedroom door. In the dim light from the hallway he could make out a huge dark shape on his bed.

He gasped and pulled back, crashing into a small end table. He froze, waiting for whatever he'd seen to come looking for the source of the sound. *What the hell was that on the bed?*

He stood motionless for what seemed like an eternity. When nothing appeared in the bedroom doorway, he crept forward an inch, and then a few more, until he could see into the room again. The shape was still there. It had not moved.

Hoopes steeled his nerves, reached around inside the doorway, and flipped on the light switch. What he saw scared him so badly that he wet his pants and cried out in terror.

A lion crouched on his bed. Panicked, he fled across the room and down the short hallway to his front door. He jerked it open and ran into the corridor of his apartment building, his breath coming in ragged gasps. If either of the other two tenants on the floor heard him, they didn't come to his aid. *No matter,* he thought. He was sure the lion would be upon him, tearing the flesh from his bones before anyone opened a door.

Nothing in the world terrified Hoopes more than lions. When he was five years old his father had taken his brother and him to the Bronx Zoo. Robert's active imagination was working overtime with anticipation. Never in his wildest nightmares could he have anticipated what was about to happen. The three of them stood looking at the lions in a natural enclosure several feet below them. His father picked up young Robert by the shoulders, and holding him in front of him, asked, "Bobby, do you know what I do with boys who don't do their chores?"

Robert's eyes grew big. He didn't know what his father intended to do. He hung, frozen in his grip, feet level with the top of the short railing. His father turned him around and held him aloft above the enclosure. "I feed them to the lions!"

As his father began to lower Robert over the railing, one of the big cats came over to the wall, and looked up at the boy. Robert twisted in his father's grip, screaming, "No! No, please don't let it get me!"

The lion threw back its massive head and roared, baring its teeth. His father lowered him more.

The lion stood on its rear legs, and pawed at the steep wall of the enclosure. Then it dropped on all fours, circled, and withdrew some distance from the wall. In the next instant it charged, roaring and leaping as high as it could.

At the last second, his father pulled him up, swung him around, and placed him on his feet. Robert slumped to the ground. He had wet his pants.

His father and brother stood laughing together as he sat, sobbing uncontrollably. He had never known such terror in his young life.

A small sob escaped his throat. Now, there was a lion in his bedroom. He'd made it halfway down the hall and toward the stairwell before he realized the lion wasn't following him. And there was no sound coming from his bedroom. He stood still, listening for a long time. When he still didn't see or hear anything, he screwed up his courage and walked cautiously back to his apartment.

Once inside, he tiptoed through the living room / kitchen and angled up to the side of his bedroom door. He peeked around the doorjamb to have a look at what had frightened him. The lion on his bed was a life-sized stuffed plush toy. His mind had convinced him it was real.

A sign in front of the lion read,

Isn't this fun, Mr. Hoopes? We hope you enjoyed gift number three. Do you wonder what will be next?

Robert Hoopes made up his mind. He got a suitcase out of

a closet and began throwing his clothes into it. He changed his wet pants. *Time to get the hell out of Washington, and find somewhere to hide!*

He couldn't tell the president without revealing the horrible truth of the documents that threatened to destroy his life. When he got to where he was going, he would call the president and tell him he had come down with the flu and would be staying home for a few days.

His father had disowned him for all practical purposes, so there was no telling him.

He lugged the suitcase to the hall, did a quick check of his apartment to make sure he wasn't leaving anything he'd want with him, and left, locking the door behind him.

He hailed a cab and instructed the cabbie to take him to the nearest car rental outlet. He rented a Honda Civic, put his bag in the trunk, and headed for the Maryland countryside.

As a young man he spent a wild weekend at a hunting lodge that belonged to the family of a friend, James Wendham. They threw an outrageous party at the place while the boy's parents were away on a cruise.

It took the better part of two days to clean up the mess afterward. The upshot was that James' parents found out about the party when they came home, and grounded him for three months.

Hoopes thought he remembered how to get to the lodge. He stopped at a service station, and bought a Maryland map. He puzzled over the route numbers and roads before finally settling on the location. He filled the tank in the Honda, purchased a case of water and enough food for a week, and set off.

Two hours later he found the access road marked by a wooden sign that read, *Wendham Camp,* and turned onto it. No one would be here at this time of year. He drove down a dirt lane for a half mile before pulling into a small parking area in front of the two-story camp. The place looked closed up for the off-season.

Hoopes got out of the car and approached the building, picturing the spot where James had shown him the family kept a key hidden. On the back porch, he felt above the top of the doorframe until his fingers found a small plastic bag. He walked back around to the front, put the key in the lock, and opened the door.

He returned to the car to get his bag and the food and carried them into the lodge. Instead of turning on the lights, he found some candles and lit them in the kitchen. After he ate some food and drank a bottle of water he felt tired enough to try to get some sleep. The adrenaline pumping through his system had tapered off, leaving him exhausted.

He went into the first floor bedroom that belonged to James' parents and lay down on the bed. He fell asleep.

A noise awakened him in the middle of the night. He lay frozen in the bed, and waited. The low rumbling sound came again from within the room. A familiar, powerful odor filled his nostrils and struck terror in his heart. Robert Hoopes reached for the bedside lamp and turned it on. The hair on the back of his neck sprang up, and he screamed.

A lion crouched inches from the bed. It was not a toy.

CHAPTER 46

The Dupree brothers were very pleased with how well the training exercises went. The Boeing C-17 Globemaster III was the delivery plane of choice for the night drop, and she'd be nicely accommodated on the commercial farm's big landing strip.

True to his word, the man who loved the Gulf landed in Omaha with full satellite imagery of their target, procured through his cousin's resource in Washington. However, he was not content to remain in the staging area for the balance of the mission. The brothers argued against his going with them to engage the enemy for a full two days. "You are too valuable!" Duke Dupree said. "This is a nasty business. We have the best men available trained for this mission. Every one of them has volunteered to be here. We've already lost six good men to whatever is waiting for us out there. When we go in it's going to be a bloody night. People are going to die. Sir, we can't have you on this part of the mission. My bothers and I are trained for this. We know what we're doing!"

"I want to be there…for Rick and the others. I'm paying for this. It's my deal and I say, I go."

Derek spoke up. "You know how we feel about you. You're a

father to us. You gave us a life we never dreamed we'd have. I won't speak for anyone but myself, but if you're going then I will find a car and leave. I'm not staying around to watch you get hurt or perhaps even killed. Dammit, we love you and respect you. There is no one who can replace you!" The war of words and emotions raged on.

Finally, the man from Omaha whose son was killed following Hoopes took the man who loved the Gulf aside. "We've known each other a long time," he said.

"I know."

"You've already lost damn good men to these bastards. They killed my son. These boys are like sons to you. You might even lose them in this."

"Duke's right, they know what they're doing," the man who loved the Gulf replied.

"I see what they know, and they know the military way. They're good. Very, very good. Let them lead their men. If you're along the others will be conflicted about who to obey. Don't do that to them. They'll be so worried about you that it'll screw them up. Do you want that?" He paused, and then went on. "I don't think you do."

That was the tipping point. The man who loved the Gulf relented. The man who loved the Gulf and the man from Omaha would head up a land force stationed a few miles out from the target in Humvees. They'd stand ready to go in on Duke's signal that the situation was under control and stabilized.

✳✳✳✳✳✳✳

In three days there would be no moon. The weather forecast was favorable, with light winds. The men were ready. Because of the heavy tree cover at the drop site, the Duprees made the decision to ring the target in the corn fields surrounding the farm. They would be over the target at 2:00 a.m. They would be carrying enough firepower with enough men to do tremendous damage to whomever or whatever awaited them.

✱✱✱✱✱✱✱

Pierce Armstrong made a decision. He told Ollie that he must have whatever information their captive possessed immediately.

The butler from hell had been toying with his victim every day, but he had yet to damage his handsome face. He'd been saving that joyful activity for the end.

"You haven't marked his face?" Armstrong looked annoyed. "That's good, Ollie, but time is slipping away. We must know who he's working for and who sent him. How can we get it out of him?"

"I will cut his face to ribbons with my scalpels," the giant declared with savage glee.

"No, no, you must not do that." Armstrong waved away his enthusiasm. "Torture is a psychological game, Ollie. It must be well played. It is a game of the mind, even beyond the tactics employed to inflict pain on a human body. I've studied these things at length."

Ollie looked bored.

"Torture is an art," Armstrong continued. "Brutalizing someone is easy. It is far more difficult to be subtle. The hint and the terror of what is to come is the force needed to loosen the victim's lips. What device in your collection evokes the greatest fear in your victims?"

Ollie didn't know what half the words his employer said meant, but Armstrong was asking about something that brought him endless delight. He knew well the instrument that most intensified his victims' fear as they faced death in hellish pain. He answered quickly. "The guillotine!"

"Ah, yes indeed, a marvelous instrument. It is doubly diabolical because the victim faces downward and knows not when the blade will fall. Tomorrow I want you to put him into the machine and threaten to drop the blade. Let him lie there all day. Take him out of it tomorrow night, and tell him that your employer will have him placed in it the next day. Spend the day with him describing the excruciating pain he will feel when the blade is dropped, dull and rusty from the frame." Ollie resented having his every move dictated in this way. Did Armstrong have to control even his fun? He listened, the initial gleam of excitement gone from his eyes.

"Remove him from the machine that night, and tell him that we cannot wait any longer. He must reveal his employer's name the next day or we will cut off his head, but only after you've mutilated his face. As you have told me, he is a handsome devil, and I'm sure his vanity will rage unabated when you threaten to disfigure him," Armstrong went on, oblivious to Ollie's disinterest. "Let him sweat the night away, and then do with your scalpels as you will. Be sure to have the recorder turned on so we can save his remarks."

The giant did as he was told. Rick decided that death would be preferable to torture, but when the huge man carried him to the French beheading device, cold fingers of fear crawled up his spine, settling in a spot on the back of his neck where he was certain the blade would land. He tried not to dwell on his helpless position, but the thought of the blade hanging above terrified him.

He sat, tense and immobile in the restraints for what must have been hours; he could no longer estimate the passage of time. Ollie returned and put him back in the cell. On Ollie's next visit Rick was again placed in the device. More time passed. He assumed each time Ollie returned another day had passed. Finally the monster told him he would be beheaded the next day, but not before his face was shredded.

Ollie produced a set of scalpels, and then held them up for Rick to see from where he lay in the cell. He arranged them neatly on a table beside the gurney where he restrained his victims. "I will have fun in the morning. My tools cut deep." Light glinted off the edge of a blade as he held it up and examined it. "I will carve out your eyes and cut off your tongue. It will be hilarious!"

The outer door slammed, and Rick lay alone in the darkness, shackled to the cot. Even if he were not handcuffed, excruciating pain all over his body made it better not to move. Thoughts of the coming morning filled him with black despair.

****

One hundred men floated silently into the cornfields. Led by the Dupree brothers, they were armed to the teeth and ready for battle. Most of them knew the men who were killed. "Let's ride, troops," Duke Dupree ordered. "It's payback time."

The teams moved into the trees, carefully avoiding the traps José warned them would be waiting. As careful as they were, someone snagged a tripwire, and the wail of a siren sounded at the barracks building.

Just fifteen of the more than fifty men hired to guard Pierce Armstrong's sanctuary were awake and on duty when the alarm went off. They all fell dead where they stood, overwhelmed by a hail of automatic gunfire.

The others raced from the barracks, but were cut down immediately. Armstrong's army was unprepared to counter the onslaught of men armed with automatic weapons overrunning the compound.

The Duprees led a force of twenty men to the mansion. Storming into the house, they were greeted by the most bizarre sight they'd ever seen. A huge figure stood in the living room, wearing pajamas with pink bunny rabbits printed all over the pants and top. The man looked like the Pillsbury Doughboy on steroids. A smallish older man dressed in a plush burgundy robe worn over white pajamas peeked around the Doughboy's girth.

"Kill them, Ollie! Kill them!" the man screamed. "They've seen me! They must all die! No one can see me and live!"

The giant moved with amazing swiftness, grabbing one of the men nearest him and lifting him over his head. He threw the man headlong into the other soldiers. "Spread out, secure the rest of the house!" Derek ordered as the men regained their feet. "We got this!"

Ollie reached for another soldier, but was sent reeling backward as Duke Dupree launched himself toward the giant, landing a kick to his face and smashing his nose. The huge man fell on the robed man behind him, squashing him with a "Yelp!"

The giant was on his feet immediately with blood streaming over his mouth, down his chin and all over the front of his pajamas. Ollie lacked military training, but he made up for it in bulk and surprising quickness for a big man. The Dupree brothers were well trained and accustomed to fighting together. They executed their close-combat skills in tandem. Ollie squealed like a pig, and lunged at Duke. This time Derek landed a kick to the side of Ollie's head that sent him sprawling, smashing a glass coffee table flat.

Again, he was on his feet in a split second. He picked up an ornate high-backed armchair with blue cushions as though it were made of balsa wood and was about to throw it at Derek,when Derek landed a third kick to his head that knocked him on his rear.

An all out brawl ensued. The giant would not go down, waging the most brutal physical battle the trio ever fought. Circling, the three brothers drove Ollie's massive bulk back and forth all over the room. "No guns!" Duke yelled. "Don't kill him! We need to know what he knows. We need to find Rick!"

Ollie was more than a match for a single man, even without military training. He was unbelievably strong. However, three Duprees were more than equal to one Ollie. He staggered into a towering armoire, and lumbered over tables, smashing priceless *objets d'art*. More than one blow sent him reeling over sofas and splintering tables into kindling. Everything he landed on was destroyed.

Pierce Armstrong, the self-proclaimed greatest mind of the twenty-first century, watched the scene from a corner while being held at gunpoint by two soldiers. He clenched and unclenched his fists, seething at the destruction of his possessions by these mindless brutes.

Back and forth, up and down, around and around they went. Ollie Larson was afraid. These men were hurting him the way his late father hurt him before he killed him. He tried to hurt them but he couldn't get a hold of them. They were too slippery and quick.

He was beginning to tire. He stumbled, flipping backward over a chair that had long before been knocked on its side. Before he could recover, they were on him like a fox on a hen. His legs were bent awkwardly beneath him, and he could not get up. Two of them stood on his arms, pinning them to the floor. The third man whipped out a wicked-looking knife and held it to Ollie's throat.

"What's your name?"

Ollie tried to twist away from the point of the knife, but the man pushed it closer, pressing the blade into the fleshy skin of his jowl. He winced at the pain. "O-O-Ollie!" he blubbered.

"If you want to die, Ollie, that's all right with me," the man said. "I'm not very happy about what you and your friends did to my friends. I'll open you up like a can of sardines if you don't shut it down right now. Do you understand me? Enough! We'll quit beating on you if you stop fighting. We need information and we need it right now." Duke said.

"I'll be good." Ollie said. "Please don't hurt me anymore."

"You'll get no information from him." Armstrong's smooth voice emanated from the corner of the room. "He's not bright enough to tell you anything. He's an employee. He's not worthy to speak for me."

The words were said with such utter disdain that the Dupree brothers turned to look in disbelief at Pierce Armstrong. It was hard to comprehend that such condescension and scorn had come from a man imprisoned at gunpoint in a corner of what remained of his living room, which lay in shambles.

It took all three of them to pull Ollie to his feet. Derek and Damien then put Ollie's hands behind his back and cuffed him.

Duke turned to the man with the smooth voice. "Who are you?"

"None of your business! But if you knew who I am you'd run into the woods shivering in terror."

"I see you have a very high opinion of yourself." Duke smiled. "It appears you need an attitude adjustment." Swifter than the eye could follow, Duke slapped the man across the face. His hand left a bright red mark where it struck, snapping the man's head left with the force of the blow. He howled.

"Now, once again, who are you?"

"How dare you!" the man shrieked.

A hand flew again, and Pierce's head snapped in the other direction.

"I can do this all night." Duke said. "Again, give me your name."

Pierce's mouth was bleeding where a tooth cut into his lip. "I will not give you my name!" A third blow, from the right hand this time.

"Please…please don't hit me."

"Your name! Are you so stupid that you don't understand what I'm asking you?"

This remark infuriated Pierce most of all. "Stupid! You call me stupid?" he sputtered. "I am the most intelligent man who has ever lived. I—"

The left hand flew again. "Enough! Give me your name! Now, or I'll start hitting you where it really hurts!"

"Pierce—"

"Pierce? Is that your last name? What's your first name?"

"Pierce Armstrong."

"And so, Mr. Armstrong, what do you call this place?"

"The Farm. I call it The Farm."

"And what do you do, Mr. Armstrong?"

"Do?"

"Yes, what do you do for money? Drugs? Firearms? Smuggling? How do you make a living?"

"I don't do any of those things."

"How do you get the money to run this place?" Duke waved a hand, and Armstrong flinched, anticipating another blow. "And just what the hell kind of place is it?"

"I'm independent. I do not work. Work is beneath me." This last was said as Armstrong struggled to gather the tattered remains of his smug attitude.

"Okay, Mr. Armstrong, if you say so, but I need to know what kind of place this is, and you're going to tell me."

"I will tell you nothing. You do not order me! It is I who will order you. When the New World Order comes you will grovel—"

The hand whipped again, and in a flash Duke had drawn his knife. He held it to Pierce's stomach.

"Mr. Armstrong, you and your people killed six very, very good men. Unfortunately for you, one of my men got away and made it

THE REVOLUTIONISTS

home, but not before he visited this place and saw what you have here. There is one man missing, a very good friend of ours. I need to know where he is, and you're going to tell me right now. I will ask you one more time, what is this place?"

The color drained from Pierce's face when he heard that a man had slipped away. The thought of the condition of the man being tortured beneath the barn caused him to stammer in fear, "I-I-I didn't hurt him! Ollie did! I had nothing to do with it!"

"What is this place and where is my man? Tell me now, or I swear I'll carve you like a turkey."

"You cannot do that! You wouldn't dare!"

"Why wouldn't I?" Duke pressed the blade into Armstrong's stomach through his pajamas. A small dot of red appeared, wicking slowly into the fabric.

Armstrong looked down, wincing at the pain and gasping at the sight of his own blood. "You're dressed in military uniforms!" He looked around for confirmation from the others, and found none. "Even you uneducated bastards have regulations regarding prisoners of war."

Duke and his men started laughing. "I'm sorry, Mr. Armstrong, but we aren't military. We have no regulations, except those we impose upon ourselves. Now, once again, where is my man and what is this place?"

"But your uniforms—"

"Oh, I see. You've made an assumption that turns out not to be true. I guess you're not the smartest man in the world, after all. We do have an employer. He'll be along at any moment. Believe me when I say that you'd best tell me where my friend is before he gets here. He's not as gentle as I am."

"He's in the barn—in the basement—and—and this place is the International Headquarters of the Progressive Movement."

"Well, that sounds like a big deal, Mr. Armstrong. And I did go to college. I have a degree in finance and world monetary systems." Duke lifted the knife. "But my first love is this knife in my hands." In a flash, he flipped the blade forward sending it swishing past Pierce's face, the blade embedding itself in the wall behind him.

Armstrong screamed, and the men laughed at him.

"Bring him and the big one," Duke said. "We go to the barn. Mr. Armstrong, our friend better be all right. If he isn't, there's a world of hurt coming your way."

Other members of Armstrong's staff had been rounded up and were being held by the men who'd gone to secure the rest of the house. "Keep them under guard. We'll be asking them a lot of questions very soon," Duke said.

Just outside the front door two more of their men stood guard over a prisoner. They'd found Arnold Jacoby, the so-called captain of Armstrong's army, hiding in a crawl space under the barracks.

Duke addressed him. "And who might you be?"

"Don't you dare say a word!" Pierce said, before the man could reply.

Jacoby glared back at him. "You ain't in charge anymore *Mr. High and Mighty!* Besides, I was gettin' the hell outta here anyway!"

He spoke to Duke. "My name's Jacoby—Arnold Jacoby. I ran the outfit—the men here, to protect the place. I ran everything, except the freak." Jacoby jerked his head toward Ollie.

"Why is he a freak, Mr. Jacoby?" Duke's voice was quiet.

"You'll know when you see the room below the barn."

When they got to the barn, Jacoby pointed out the spot where the trap door lay hidden, covered with straw. They opened it and carefully descended the stairs. Armstrong was made to go first in case there were any traps. Duke followed close behind. Jacoby went next, with Derek and Damien bringing up the rear. Damien kept his eye on Ollie and held his gun aloft, ready to put a bullet in him should he try to cause any trouble down below.

The men gasped in surprise and disbelief upon opening the door to the torture room. It was one thing to kill a man in battle; the torture devices in this place spoke of unutterable evil.

Duke raised a fist to smash Ollie in the face, but Derek grabbed and held his arm. "Don't. We need him to find Rick. Maybe he's alive."

Damien was the first to notice the small door at the far end of the room. He opened it. Rick lay inside on a narrow metal cot, bound and covered in blood. "Is it morning? Oh, God…" He struggled weakly against handcuffs that held him, shackled to the cot.

Duke and Derek gently removed him from the tiny cell and lay him on the gurney. He was crying. The brothers and their men cried with him. His bloodied and broken body bore witness to the suffering he'd endured.

José gently embraced Rick, with tears running down his face. "Todo está bien." He murmured comforting words to his dear friend. "Se acabó. Vámonos al hogar."

Two more soldiers came into the room. "We found something you should see, Duke. It's not good." The men led them to the furnace. Bone fragments littered the floor of the chamber. Duke's face flushed white hot with anger.

The man who loved the Gulf and the man from Omaha entered the torture room at that moment. Silently they took in the horrific scene as they made their way to where Rick lay on the gurney.

"You're going home, Ricky." The man who loved the Gulf spoke gently. "Until now, I had three sons in Duke, Derek and Damien. But you are my fourth son, with all the rights and privileges thereof. You did not break. Welcome home, son!" He embraced the sorely wounded man gently and kissed him on the cheek. "Rest now, son. We'll be out of this godforsaken place soon."

Medics tended to Rick, transferring him to a stretcher and carefully carrying him up the stairs, out of the barn and onto a waiting helicopter. José went with them.

"Where are the bastards who did this?" the man who loved the Gulf asked.

Duke indicated the cell where Rick had been bound. Damien and Derek had shoved Armstrong, Ollie, and Jacoby inside, and now stood guard over them. They pulled them out and lined them up against a wall. "The big one is called Ollie," Derek said. "He's the one who used this room, the one who hurt Rick."

The man from Omaha spoke directly to Ollie, a murderous glint in his eyes. "You son-of-a-bitch! You killed my son in here, didn't you?

You tortured him, too, and then burned him in that furnace!"

The man from Omaha was a big man, easily weighing in muscle what Ollie did in fat. He swung with all his might, smashing Ollie in the mouth. The blow broke bone and sent teeth splattering in all directions.

The man swung a second time, burying his fist up to his forearm in the flesh of Ollie's stomach. The giant sagged to the floor in a pile of sobbing, quivering blubber.

"Enough," the man who loved the Gulf said. "This creature does its master's bidding," he turned to look at Pierce Armstrong. "And that would be you, sir, would it not?"

Pierce Armstrong stood frozen, caught in the man's deadly and unrelenting glare. His bladder let go, soaking his pajamas in a stream of urine that ran down his legs to puddle on the floor around his feet. No one laughed.

The smell of his own urine and the wetness on his legs and feet snapped Armstrong out of his fearful trance. "I-I never hurt them," he stammered. "Ollie did. Ollie—"

Duke's hand flashed out, and Pierce's head snapped to the left.

"But you are master here, are you not? This man is your instrument." The man who loved the Gulf waved in the direction of Ollie, whose own bunny covered pajamas were soaking up Armstrong's urine. "You've been weighed in the balance, and found guilty. The punishment should fit the crime, don't you think? From the look of this place you've been at this business of hurting and killing people for a long, long time."

He let his gaze wander around the room, and finally allowed it to settle once more on Armstrong. "I too, have killed men in my lifetime. The difference between us is this: I take no pleasure in killing a man. I do so out of necessity, and those I have killed deserved it. You, sir, are the worst kind of creature, even worse than this instrument of yours. You're like the Nazi who insisted the trains run on time to the concentration camps. You divorce yourself from the pain and suffering of others by pretending that you're above it all. If you cannot hear their screams, then you are not responsible.

"I've met your kind before. Compared to you, I am a simple man because I understand the value of men. You think yourself superior to everyone, but I know that every man is my equal. However, I am very good at making money…in good and bad times."

Pierce Armstrong looked at the man who faced him. A single word slipped from his mouth, "Mafia—"

Duke's hand again whipped swiftly through the air, but the man who loved the Gulf halted it in mid-flight. "No, my son," he said gently. "I said the punishment must fit the crime."

He signaled for men to bring Ollie to his feet. The huge hulk stood, swaying on his feet, his face smashed, with what remained of his teeth protruding between his lips.

He spoke gently. "Ollie, I understand that until now you've had a good time in this place. You've tried many things. Some have succeeded, and some haven't. Your master here might say something like this, Ollie, you need to be a little more creative next time. Make it last a little longer. Get more enjoyment out of it. So, I'm going to allow you to practice your craft one more time. You're going to take this man here," he pointed to Pierce Armstrong, "and do your best to enjoy yourself. Take as long as you need. Make it long and hard for him. Draw it out. You know what I mean, don't you son?"

Ollie's eyes grew wide with wonder, despite his pain. Pierce was screaming.

"No! *God, no!* Please, no, anything, I—"

Duke and Derek picked up the world's smartest man by the arms and carried him to the gurney. Armstrong struggled, kicking and screaming until the Dupree brothers strapped him securely to the gurney.

"Use your imagination this time," the man who loved the Gulf said to Ollie. "Be very creative, but don't kill him. I have something else in mind."

He and the team exited the room. One of the soldiers moved Jacoby along in handcuffs. Damien shut the door behind them, cutting off the sound of Armstrong's screams.

"What now, sir?" Duke asked.

"Now, we take this place apart. We find out everything there is to know about Armstrong and whatever he's running here. We leave no stone unturned. Top to bottom, I want to know what this is all about."

"What about Ollie and Armstrong?"

"Let them have the day. Bullets don't cost that much. The world will be a better place."

"What about Jacoby?"

"He and his men killed our men, did they not?"

"Yes, sir."

"We don't take prisoners, Duke. Prisoners talk. We were never here."

"I understand, sir, but there are women in the house who may not know anything."

"Question everyone. If they're clean see that they're given a sum of Armstrong's money and sent somewhere far away to live. You're the banking and finance expert in the family. I know you'll take care of it."

"Yes, sir."

"One more thing, Duke."

"Yes?"

"When we get home we're taking Rick on a long, relaxing cruise. He needs some R&R."

Duke smiled at the man. "Yes, sir. I'm looking forward to it."

"Me, too."

CHAPTER 47

It took two days to go over The Farm with a fine-tooth comb. A secret apartment was discovered under the main house. It was apparently designed as a hiding place of last resort for Pierce Armstrong. The panic area was accessed through an elevator, which was hidden in the wall of a game room in the huge finished basement. Basically an underground bunker, the apartment consisted of a bedroom, a massive kitchen outfitted with state-of-the-art appliances and stocked with enough food and water to last two years, and a living room/ communications center fully equipped with radios, TV's, computers, and other office equipment. Armstrong had spared no expense in furnishing the house above, and this was true of his subterranean hideaway, as well.

A fourth room was a garage where a Range Rover packed with food, water, medical supplies, an assault rifle, a Glock handgun, and enough ammunition to wage a small war was stored. A gated tunnel at one end of the garage led to an elevator at the edge of the property, which would lift the Range Rover to the surface. The exit above ground was hidden inside one of the out buildings on the property.

****

Ollie, Armstrong and Jacoby were no more. The man from Omaha had seen to their demise behind the barn.

Back at the main house, The Man Who Loved the Gulf selected a crystal decanter of Macallan from Armstrong's bar and poured it neat into two Glencairn whisky glasses. "Shooting them was too quick...too merciful." The man from Omaha expressed his regrets.

"I agree, my friend," said the man who loved the Gulf. "But we are men of higher standards." He patted his friend's shoulder. "We kill only when it cannot be avoided. These scum killed for enjoyment, and because they felt themselves superior to other men."

He raised his glass. "To the treasured memory of your beloved son." The two men drank together in silence.

****

The brothers Dupree and their men did not leave an inch of The Farm unexamined. They took the house and grounds apart, methodically searching every inch of the place. In addition to the secret apartment beneath the basement, they also discovered a large vault concealed behind a false wall in Armstrong's master bedroom. Apparently he'd opened it when the assault began two days ago, but hadn't time to re-seal it before the men reached the main house.

Records of Armstrong's financial holdings, bank accounts, properties and investments on hard drives and paper files were thoroughly examined. A vast library of information on the Progressive movement in the US and around the world, including names and contact information was also catalogued. First editions of Armstrong's many publications under various aliases, forty million dollars in cash, and an estimated five million in gold rounded out the cache.

The man who loved the Gulf and the man from Omaha surveyed the contents of Armstrong's empire. They smiled as Duke showed them the cash and gold. While no amount of money could ever pay for the loss of a son and the deaths of good men, the unexpected windfall more than covered the expenses incurred in underwriting the assault on the compound.

The only members of Armstrong's staff who remained alive consisted of three housekeepers who lived on the property, who Armstrong hired because they had no families of their own. Interviews revealed they knew nothing of their former employer's activities, but they were in complete agreement about his personality.

"He was an obsessive-compulsive, royal pain in the backside!" one of the housekeepers volunteered.

The second chimed in, "And the most condescending person you'd ever want to deal with!"

"I'm glad to be rid of them both," the third housekeeper said, nodding. "Good riddance to that wacko, Pierce Armstrong and Ollie Larson, the butler from hell!"

The housekeepers were given the option to be relocated, provided they complied with certain stipulations. They were to never discuss what happened with anyone, nor were they to ever speak to one another again. If they dared speak of what happened at The Farm, they were assured the same fate as Pierce Armstrong and Ollie Larson.

One woman chose southern Florida, and a second southern California.

"I'm not very imaginative," the third woman said. "I'd like to stay here in Nebraska."

"That's not an option we can permit, ma'am." Duke's response left no room for argument.

She thought for a moment. "I've always wanted to see Saint Thomas in the Virgin Islands. Would that be all right?"

Duke laughed. "That means you could go snorkeling every day! But they do get the occasional hurricane there. Is that your final answer?"

His remark about hurricanes spoiled it for her. "Ireland," she said after a moment. "How about Ireland in County Mayo? Could I go there?"

"Done, and a wonderful choice I might add. It's settled then. Armstrong's fortune will take care of you for the rest of your lives. And then some."

Duke Dupree traced Armstrong's financial records through to various off-shore banks. At the man who loved the gulf's instruction, he distributed all of the funds, a tidy sum of $147 million, equally among three brand new accounts off-shore. The women were ecstatic at their good fortune.

****

Further investigation of Armstrong's papers revealed something Duke found very strange. "Sir," he said to the man who loved the Gulf, "this place, The Farm, as Armstrong called it, well, for all intents and purposes, does not exist. It's not on any map, nor are there any official records of it—no deeds, no tax records, nothing."

The initial plan was to destroy the compound, leaving no trace of its existence. After a lengthy discussion, and at the suggestion of the man who loved the Gulf, it was decided that the man from Omaha would take over The Farm. It would be renamed Warrior's Retreat, in honor of his son and the others who had given their lives trying to learn its secrets. Its location would remain hidden, and it would serve as a private retreat, a secret safe haven, and a training center for trusted members of the organization.

****

The man who loved the Gulf made a call on the afternoon of the third day.

"Thank you for your generous help."

"It went well, then?"

"Yes. Have you ever heard of a man named Pierce Armstrong?"

There was a sharp intake of breath at the other end of the phone. "My God, you mean that's who you were after? Is he—?"

"He departed the planet along with the rest of his people. Gone, and I hope, forgotten forever. I don't believe anyone will miss him. We found documents detailing his organization. They've been at this a long time."

"I'd like to see those documents, cousin."

"Why? What good would they be to you?"

"We've known about him for decades. His real name isn't Pierce Armstrong. That's a name he gave himself. He was born Timothy T. Tweedle."

The man who loved the Gulf laughed. "Are you serious? No wonder he changed his name!"

"Laugh long and well. In our opinion he is…well,was, the most dangerous man alive in this country."

"I don't get it. The guy was despicable, I'll grant you that, but he didn't look all that dangerous to me. And, you keep saying we and our. Who are you talking about?"

"That's not a topic for a telephone conversation. Secure the documents and leave them where they are. When it's doable I'd like to see them. There will be others who will want to as well. Now, I've got to get back to work. Are you taking that cruise I advised?"

"Yes, we leave in a few days."

"Good. I will be in touch. I'll come to you in November for Thanksgiving. There will be much to discuss at that time. Godspeed."

"I haven't been on good terms with Him for far too many years," the man who loved the Gulf said.

"You have done a great service to this nation and the world, my cousin. Don't be too hard on yourself. Forgiveness often hides in strange places."

"I don't understand."

"Armstrong's camp is folding, at least in this country. I cannot speak for the rest of the world. Get on your beautiful ship and sail away. You'll hear all about it. When we see each other we'll both have much to be thankful for. That is a promise I can keep. Be well."

The phone went dead. The man who loved the Gulf sat silently in what had been Pierce Armstrong's spotless kitchen for a long time. After half an hour he decided it would be a good idea for him to read Armstrong's documents more carefully. He intended to find out as much information as he could, to fully appreciate what his cousin said.

The world was changing. He would be ready for whatever those changes would bring.

CHAPTER 48

Michael spent every moment of his leave in his office at The Truman Building studying and being prepped by members of The Movement's staff. The underground city was a pleasant enough place to work, with numerous office buildings, libraries, archives, and gardens. He had also begun reviewing those parts of TR2.0 that were available to him in advance of its final execution. Sixty years of planning was a lot to cover.

He didn't try to cover every idea that was suggested and then scrapped over the years, instead he set about gaining an understanding of how their thinking had evolved into its present form.

He had never studied so hard in his life. He was that rare combination of gifted athlete with a mind to match. He devoured countless articles, plans, and white papers; he took copious notes during lectures from learned members of The Movement who came to instruct and advise him.

He discovered three flaws in TR2.0 that had been revised. True, they were minor oversights, but his careful scrutiny had revealed them, and the others were grateful for his attention to detail.

The fact that Joan was visiting with his mother and Susan in

Clear Haven eased his mind. They had returned for an extended visit to The Movement's headquarters at Eric's insistence. Over two days the women got a chance to ask questions and spend time with some of the members. They understood more of what their husbands faced as they prepared for what lay ahead. Michael talked with them for a few moments in the car before they left.

"We all have a better grasp of how hard you're working," Joan said. "Better to invest the time now. There will be just one chance to get it right."

"Definitely," Susan added. "Even after sixty years of planning, there are so many things to check and double check."

Michael's mother said what Michael needed to hear best. "Dad and Granddad would be proud of you."

More than anyone, Michael appreciated the need to be better prepared than anyone who had ever served in the Oval Office. The nation was about to undergo an event that had never happened in its entire history. A complete takeover would happen in one day. Michael's demeanor, his confidence, and his faith needed to be at their highest levels when he stepped before the cameras for the first time as president to declare that the situation was under control. Nothing could be left to chance. There could be no loose ends. He had to exude strength, and convey a sense of purpose that the people of America would trust and embrace.

The takeover would impart a psychological blow as well as a physical change in the government. He would be giving the most important speech anyone had ever given in the nation's history. He needed to deliver The Movement's message clearly and with unequivocal confidence.

Speech writers who had worked for several presidents collaborated on the speech over the years. Over the past few months a team worked with him to fine tune it for delivery to the present generation of Americans. They agonized over every word. The speech did not have to be lengthy, but it did have to be powerful.

Michael was reviewing the latest draft of the message when there was a slight rapping on his office door.

"Come in."

Henry stepped into the room and smiled. "I brought you some coffee. I thought you might want to take a break."

Michael stood up. "Let's go outside." They stepped through French doors that opened onto a rooftop garden. Henry led them to a small wrought iron table and two chairs. He set the tray he was carrying on the table. The brothers sat for a few moments looking out over the underground city. The artificial sky overhead displayed white, puffy clouds moving against a vivid blue background. An artificial sun appeared to rise above the horizon.

"Isn't science wonderful?" Michael said, and laughed.

"I'll say. It looks real, doesn't it?"

"It looks like something from a movie set. The best I can say is that it makes me feel less claustrophobic."

"How's the speech coming?"

"Hard. Not easy. We've got to do this right or there will be heck to pay."

"Hell to pay. It's okay to say hell, Michael."

"Heck will turn into hell if we don't get it right." Michael said, frowning.

"Why don't you do a Lincoln?"

"What do you mean?"

"When Lincoln spoke at Gettysburg he spoke from his heart. He wrote his remarks on an envelope, if I remember the story correctly, and he didn't go on for a couple hours like the other guy. We don't remember the other guy's speech, but we sure do remember his Gettysburg address. It's one of the greatest speeches in human history."

"So, I should—?"

"Get to the point, make the point, say just enough, don't say too much, and know when to shut up."

"But I—"

"There is no 'but' in this speech. Tell them who you are, why you're on camera, what happened, and how it's being fixed. Give them that old Michael Stonebreaker stare that we know and love, and then be quiet. People will get it. Give people the benefit of the doubt. It's not necessary to be pedantic. You don't need to tell them, and then tell them what you told them, and then summarize what you said. Leave that to the talking heads and the yada-yada-yada that will follow. People are going to be afraid. You are going to tell them that it's going to be all right. They'll want to believe you. Make them believe you."

"How do I do that, Henry?"

"The same way you've been doing it your whole life. The same way the Old Man did it. The same way Dad did it. Look, you believe in this, don't you?"

"Yes, but—"

"Again, there are no 'buts' in this. It is or it isn't. Tell the truth, Michael. Tell it like it is. The adults will get it, and they'll explain it to those who have yet to grow up and grasp reality. This isn't rocket science. America and Americans will go on. We'll survive." He took a sip of hot coffee. "It won't be a cakewalk, but it'll get done. These people haven't spent six decades preparing for this to blow it in the end. You don't need high-sounding, lofty words. You need down-to-earth American English and concepts a sixth grader can comprehend and act on. Tell them what happened, explain who you are and what you represent, and tell them what's expected of them, as well. They won't buy into it if they're not part of it. The people need to take ownership of this new country. Be who they want you to be. You already are. It's time to trust them, too. The problem is that the elites who are running the show don't trust the people and it shows. Be real, Michael. Be yourself."

Michael took a sip of his coffee and looked at his brother.

"Henry, you always come through for me. When I try to make things harder than they ought to be you come along and say, Keep it short and sweet. Me and a team have been literally slaving over this thing, and you drop by and put it into perspective in a few seconds. Will you help me write it?"

"Sure. All you have to do is ask."

"Let's get back to work. Thanks for the coffee and advice. Would you consider being Secretary of State?"

"Thanks, but I'd rather fix 'dozers."

"We need a bulldozer at the UN."

"I thought it needed an enema?"

Michael laughed. He looked at Henry. "Have you ever heard of Will Rogers?"

"No, but I've seen Will Smith in the movies. Maybe you could get him to be Secretary of State?"

"He'd be a good choice."

"When you start this job, why don't you ask him?"

"I just might do that. And who would you recommend for Secretary of Defense?"

"I thought The Movement already had people lined up for these positions?" Henry asked.

"They do, but I always like to hear your thoughts on these things."

"Why?"

"Because, brother, you make more sense than most of the people I know."

Henry smiled. "I've got your back, Michael."

"That's why I can sleep at night, Henry. I've got yours, too."

"Let's go write the Gettysburg address."

"Can't."

"Why not?"

"It's been done."

"Maybe we adopt some parts of it."

"You mean like, Eleven score and some odd years ago?"

"Henry, that's too hard to figure out!"

"Well, what do you have in mind?"

CHAPTER 49

Norman Blesco landed in Orlando, got off the plane and looked around the waiting area at the arrival gate. Someone named Sanderson was supposed to meet him, but no one seemed to be looking for him. He hung around for a while. No one approached him. He brought a single carry-on, but he wondered if he should head to baggage claim in the main terminal. He decided to wait.

No one came to him. He finally boarded a train that took him to the main terminal. Half an hour had gone by, and he was beginning to feel nervous. He was reluctant to approach the customer service desk to ask if anyone had come forward looking for him. Instead, once inside the terminal he made his way to the baggage claim area. He walked around for a few minutes before deciding to step outside. On the sidewalk, people were loading their bags onto busses and vans, and still no one approached him.

He stood there waiting, trying to look inconspicuous. Every few minutes he would pretend to talk to someone on his cell phone, or look up the street as though he were expecting a ride. Another thirty minutes dragged by. Finally a man walked up behind him and whispered as he passed, "Get on the next bus." The man walked away.

Norman got on the next bus that pulled to the curb. The sign on the front of the bus flashed the name of a Disney resort. It meant nothing to him. He rode the bus with other tourists and stared out the window at palm trees, traffic, and hotels along the road. Fluffy white clouds dotted the bright blue sky overhead. He barely noticed. The scene was benign, but the feelings raging inside Norman were anything but peaceful. He was here! He'd made it. The years he'd waited for this moment were coming to an end. He was Allah's warrior in the midst of the infidels. He would make history.

The bus turned off the main road and into the resort entrance. A recorded announcement said there would be four stops inside. He felt panic. Which one should he take? The bus made its first stop, and he sat rigid in his seat. Fortunately, there was no one sitting next to him or he might have snapped from the tension.

The doors closed and the bus continued on to its second stop. Again, he sat riveted to his seat. How would he know where to get off the bus?

The bus continued to its third stop and still he remained fixed in his seat. What was he to do? Beads of sweat sprung up on his scalp, despite the air-conditioned bus. He had to get off. When the bus pulled to the curb he jerked his bag behind him and got off the bus in front of an elderly couple and their grandchildren.

"Hey, be careful. You almost knocked me down!" the man said.

"Sorry...I'm sorry," Norman said without turning around to look at the man. He walked to the end of the kiosk where the bus stopped. He stood there looking around as the other passengers got off the bus and walked away to their respective lodgings.

Norman stood at the kiosk trying to gather his thoughts and decide what to do. He had been given the name Sanderson and told that someone would meet him at the airport. His next instructions came from the man at the airport who'd whispered, "Get on the next bus," but he was long gone.

Norman looked up at the sound of a tram approaching. The operator looked to be about his age. He had sandy blond hair, a mustache, and a narrow face. His eyes were deep set. Norman couldn't tell if they were black or brown.

"Get in," the man said.

"Where are we going?"

The man didn't answer. He drove the tram down the road, and turned onto a paved side road marked, "Cast Members Only."

He drove on in silence until they reached an area that was not visible to tourists. The man parked the tram and they got out. Norman extended the handle of his carry-on and dragged it behind him. The man stopped. He turned around and said, "I'm Adam Sanderson. I'll be your contact here. We're going to go get you into your costume. I'll take care of your bag. At the end of the day I'll see you again and get you set for where you'll be staying."

"Costume?"

"They didn't tell you?"

"Nobody said anything about a costume."

"Look, this is the land of make believe. The best way to hide you is in plain sight. You'll spend your days dressed as Mickey Mouse."

Norman's eyebrows rose above wide eyes.

"You don't have to speak, but you have to be friendly to children and adults." Sanderson waved away Norman's surprise and continued, "Pose with them for their pictures. Walk around the park. That's all you have to do."

"The costume can get uncomfortable after awhile, so I'll show you where to go to cool off out of sight. Rule number one, don't break character when you're in public. Be friendly at all times. Rule two, never take off the head in view of people. Never! Rule three, don't break rules one and two. Understood?"

"I know nothing about this…this Mickey Mouse. How can I—"

"You'll see a film explaining how you are to act when you wear the costume. You're a bright man. You'll figure it out. This isn't hard. Use it to good advantage. You'll need the costume to get away when the deed is done. Don't screw this up. Be brave. You're going to be entertaining children. How difficult can that be?"

Norman had not come to Florida to play an American animated icon. He came to kill and slaughter the infidels and their children! His face flushed with anger.

"Why do I have to do such a thing? I have not been prepared—"

"Listen to me. During the day you'll be wearing the costume, but at night you'll be learning how to control the communications in this place. This is a huge complex, far bigger than you can imagine. We're all assigned specific tasks and have jobs in the parks as cover."

He stuck a finger in Norman's face. "You're a very important part of this operation. It cannot succeed without you. You'll be wearing the costume during the day and going from park to park over the next few weeks. You must be familiar with the layout of the four theme parks. You need to know where everything is and how it fits together. This isn't a game. It's for real. We've planned many years for this. Don't complain. Do as you are told."

Norman kept quiet. He sensed that if he complained it would not go well with the people above him. He was here to serve.

Sanderson turned and led Norman through a doorway and into a building. They walked down a hallway to a small room set up as a theater, complete with perhaps thirty theater seats in rows. It was not a big room, and no one else was present. The man told Norman to take a seat. He sat in the back row.

"You're going to have to be more confident if you're going to play this role. Why did you choose the back row?" He spread his arms wide. "The whole room is empty. What's the matter with you? Are you afraid?"

No one had ever asked Norman such a question. He felt his anger rising. He steeled his self-control.

"I sat here because I choose not to make others aware that I am there. It is my custom—"

"Look, you're about to go out in public in the costume of a much loved American symbol. I'll let the irony of that sink in." Sanderson pointed a finger at Norman. "You have to play your part here. You must be an actor pretending to care about these people. They must want to be near you, be around you, to have their picture taken with you. Can you do this? If not, let's end this now. I'll take you to the airport and put you back on a plane. Choose."

Had the man slapped him across the face, Norman could not have been more stunned. He started to rise out of his seat, his face flushed with rage, and then he stopped. Sanderson was smiling at him.

"I...I am sorry. I have been hidden so long from this society that it never occurred to me that I would have to do anything like this. Please, show me what you have to show me. I will do as you say."

"That is what a good soldier of Allah should say. Take a seat at the front of the room. The time will come soon enough when we will sit in the seats of power in this nation. Until then, we must all play our roles. Some of us will die; some will live. It is our service and loyalty that matter. Watch the movie. Learn about this character, and play it well. You're a very bright man. You can do this."

Norman moved to the front row and sat down. The man disappeared through a doorway at the rear of the room. The lights dimmed and the film began. It was about twenty minutes long.

Norman was introduced to Walt Disney and the creation of Mickey Mouse. Norman dutifully sat through a recounting of Disney's history from the earliest cartoons to the first theme park, the TV show, the Mickey Mouse Club, and finally the founding of Disney World.

The last seven minutes of the film showed the costume and how it was to be worn. An actor, or Cast Member, as they were called, donned the costume and walked through the park interacting with guests. Norman was lost in a reverie of his own. A true introvert from his childhood, he did not normally make eye contact with people. It was not his nature to be assertive.

He understood that he would need to pretend to be this character. He would gain the trust of the infidels through this game of make-believe. It wasn't very different from the way he did his job among his peers in New Jersey. He was glad that he did not have to speak.

The film ended. A voice out of speakers hidden in the room startled Norman. "Do you want to see it again?"

"Yes, please. I need to see the last part. It will help me play the role."

The film began again.

Norman Blesco again studied the images on the screen. His own childhood had been a nightmare. What he was looking at was a display of fantasy. America was weak if its people believed in such things. There was no room in his twisted soul for such weakness. It would be very hard, but he had already mastered the art of pretense. He would be this Mickey Mouse.

CHAPTER 50

The President of the United States was deeply concerned. Robert Hoopes was officially missing under suspicion of foul play. The Special Assistant knew far too much about things the president dare not risk others finding out.

Moments after Hoopes made a panicked exit from his apartment, a clean team swept in, clearing it of all the cameras and bugs, along with the stuffed lion and any evidence of what happened. When they left, closing and locking the door behind them, no one would suspect they had ever been there.

Clean up at the lodge in the Maryland countryside was another matter. Lions could be messy with their prey. This one had been extremely hungry. Coaching the beast out of the building was one thing; cleaning up the blood and gore was another. However, the team was exceptionally good at their work. Two days later there was no evidence that anyone had ever been there.

The lion magically reappeared at a zoo several states away. It had been missing for two weeks, and the zoo's staff was at a total loss as to how it had first disappeared, and then shown up again. They hadn't reported the missing cat because funds were tight and the bad publicity would have worsened the zoo's already precarious financial condition.

They hoped the lion would not attack anyone, and if someone sighted it, they planned to say it had gone missing that same day. As the days slipped by their worry increased. They were nearly overwhelmed with relief to find it suddenly back in its cage.

The lion appeared no worse for whatever it had experienced, and even seemed to exhibit a new vitality. It roared and leaped against the bars, causing the chief keeper to jump back in terror, nearly knocking over a veterinary intern.

"What the hell has gotten into Leo?"

"Maybe he met a lady friend while he was away," the intern said.

"Whatever happened to him, keep the bars between you and him from now on. No sense taking chances."

✻✻✻✻✻✻

The senior senator from Illinois received a package delivered by courier to his office at ten in the morning. A note said, "Open privately: Your eyes only."

The day dragged by. For once he was glad to come home to an empty house. His wife was visiting her mother, who was suffering from Alzheimer's and living in a nursing home near Washington.

The senator opened the package, which contained a DVD in a blank sleeve. He put the DVD in his player and turned it on. He watched an expertly edited documentary of Robert Hoopes's last fright-filled days on earth. He saw the terror the man suffered, and was satisfied. When the lion appeared on-screen in the lodge, he switched it off. He had no stomach for such gore, and he regretted that the man's life ended in such a grisly manner. He would have preferred a bullet, even a lethal injection, but it had not been his choice.

The senator shredded the DVD and burned the package it arrived in. He checked his watch. It was too late to make a call. He sighed, and headed for the kitchen. He microwaved himself dinner, and then fell asleep on the couch.

When he awoke in the morning he realized his wife must have covered him with a blanket when she returned. He felt old and stiff. He got up and went to his private bathroom to take a shower. Once he'd dressed, he returned to the kitchen where his wife was finishing breakfast. "I'll be at home in the office for awhile. I need to make an important call."

She barely acknowledged him. "Fine. I'll be going to a friend's house for lunch. I'll call you later." She knew he was having affairs. He did not know that she was returning the favor on a regular basis.

When she left he went to his office and sat staring at the phone for a few moments. He dialed the number. The voice on the other end of the phone was that of the leader of the free world, or at least it was somewhat free this morning. At the rate they were going, China would own them by year's end.

"Good morning."

"Good morning, Mr. President."

"It's a beautiful morning. I assume you're calling about Cap and Trade? How many votes can you deliver?"

"That's going to be a problem."

"We're not going to be having problems again, are we?" His tone was decidedly less cordial.

"I'm afraid so. You know I'm up for re-election. My people don't want to go near that thing. They believe it's a bad idea, so I won't be able to support it."

"I thought we had an understanding, Senator." The voice was blatantly angry.

"Yes, Mr. President, we had an understanding, but I've come into possession of some information that I believe should be handled with the utmost discretion. In fact, this information is so sensitive, I believe we need to sit down together to discuss it."

"Senator, that depends. Could you describe what you're talking about in greater detail?"

"Not on the phone. I know you are terribly busy, but would you have a few moments to share with me tomorrow? It won't take much of your time, and I know you'll appreciate my discretion in this matter."

"If the matter is substantive I could clear my schedule for a few moments tomorrow afternoon."

"Let's make it tomorrow morning, Mr. President. Say, ten o'clock." The senator was enjoying his moment of impertinence. But he dared not linger in the moment too long.

Before the president could respond, he continued. "By the way, how's that young lion, Robert Hoopes doing? He's a real pusher. He may have a great future in this town, or perhaps he won't. Funny how things happen, isn't it? One moment you're sure you've got the world by the tail, and the next moment your hopes are torn to pieces."

Dead silence hung between them on the phone. For the first time in his political career, the president felt a finger of fear run up his spine. Obviously, the senator knew Hoopes was missing. Was he involved in his disappearance? What the hell had the man done? The senator also possessed information that he could not afford to have made public. The phone conversation had begun with him being in charge. Now, the senior senator from Illinois had him in check.

"Tomorrow morning at ten will be fine."

"Good. I'll see you then, in my office."

"That may be difficult, Senator." The president spoke from between clenched teeth.

"I know you can make it happen, Mr. President. I respect your ability to make things happen. That's why I called you." The velvety tone of the older man's voice barely hid the malice that came through the phone.

The president didn't try to conceal his frustration. "Could we make it around eleven? I have some things I simply cannot move."

"Certainly. What we have to discuss will necessitate our taking a walk together. Your detail will need to remain at a distance sufficient for us to speak a privately." The senator couldn't resist a jab. "Given the lapses they've made, discretion is of the utmost importance. You do understand the need for discretion, don't you?"

"Yes, Senator, I do. I'll be there by eleven-thirty."

"That will be fine. May I suggest a photo-op lunch after our talk? It could help poll numbers."

✱✱✱✱✱✱✱

The president hung up the phone a little too forcefully. He felt both fear and rage. The senator obviously thought he could be played for a fool. He had underestimated him. Now, there would be hell to pay.

✱✱✱✱✱✱✱

The senator sat smiling at his desk. A consummate poker player, he always made sure to have an ace up his sleeve. In this particular case, he had a handful of them. The man in the White House had met his match.

CHAPTER   51

Michael and Eric sat in the conference room with the four directors selected to open the vaults that would launch TR2.0, and set The Movement on an irrevocable path to restore the United States of America as a constitutional republic.

The founder's granddaughter addressed them. "Until now, I've addressed you as Mr. Brown to protect your identity on the off chance our enemies breached our security to pick up our conversations. Anonymity protocol remains, but since you've accepted your new roles, I will now address you by your proper titles.

"Mr. President, Mr. Vice President, besides the four of us you are the only two people privy to what we are about to discuss. Your questions regarding TR2.0 will be answered to the extent we are free to reveal the information. Where that is not possible, we will tell you why it must remain hidden; mostly to keep our plans from being discovered prematurely."

"Has information ever been leaked in the past?" Michael asked.

"Surely our enemies would have tried to break down the doors to get at us if they knew we existed at all. I'm happy to say our security has never been compromised, as evidenced by their absence. " Her eyes twinkled with pride. "I don't say this to be smug; the Good Lord knows how grateful I am that we've kept our secrets these many years."

She brought the palm of her hand down on the table. "Now, it's your turn to ask questions."

Michael responded immediately. "Having reviewed the parts of TR2.0 presently available to me, am I correct in stating that the military plays a key role in its execution and success?"

"Yes, and with very good reason. Those who wear the uniform are sworn to protect the Constitution and the Republic. The Progressive leadership abhors the military, and sees it merely as a tool, a necessary evil that they will use to control and finally crush the people under the pretense of providing national security." She pressed a hand to her heart.

"What the Progressives do not understand is American patriotism. They cannot grasp that there are ideals and principles based on love, regard for our neighbors, duty, honor, and sacrifice that transcend any political ideology built on the intent to control people. They think that the great mass of our people are stupid and should be controlled in all aspects of their lives for the benefit of the so-called elite. The military is on our side, although most of the rank and file has no idea that we even exist."

Eric said, "You talk as though you control the military. Is that possible?"

"Mr. Vice President, without the cooperation of the military, what we've planned would not be possible."

Eric stared at her. "You can't be serious—"

"Yes, quite. Do you know who Progressives fear the most in a free society?"

"I suppose you're going to say the military?"

"Exactly, and do you know why?"

Eric shook his head. "No, I can't say that I do."

"The military has sworn an oath to protect and defend our nation and its people. On the whole, they are patriots, which makes Progressives nervous. They understand that if the military were to rise against them, their cause would be lost. They believe that controlling the man in the White House is tantamount to controlling the military. They have never controlled the Office of the Commander in Chief... until now."

Michael said, "That may be true, but you can't expect military personnel to turn on their commander in chief. How are you going to overcome that fact?"

"We are not orchestrating a mutiny. We respect the office of the president. But no man can be allowed to trample the checks and balances established by the Constitution to impose his personal ideological agenda. He certainly cannot be permitted to permanently establish dictatorial rule."

"That's absurd!" Michael exclaimed. "How can we bring down the government of the United States and ignore the man who leads us?"

"We have no intention of overthrowing the government, Mr. President. We are merely replacing it."

"That's equally absurd. I can't see—"

The founder's granddaughter held up her hand. "We have come to a place where your question cannot be answered at this time. Suffice it to say that the military will be carrying out the president's orders to the letter. He will be in agreement with what is happening—"

Eric looked flustered. "How is that possible? Is the president on our side?"

"No, of course he isn't on our side. He isn't aware that we exist. The military will obey the president's orders until the transition is complete, at which time he will no longer have the authority to give them. He will believe it is his agenda that is being implemented, or rather the ideological agenda dictated to him by a man hidden in the heartland of America." She paused. "At least, he lived there until recently."

Michael asked, "Where is that man now?"

"I'm afraid he came to a very bad end."

"Did The Movement have anything to do with his death?"

"Not directly."

Michael was half way out of his chair. "Are you saying you a man murdered?" he demanded. Eric grasped his arm and pulled him down.

The founder's granddaughter's tranquil face was transformed by anger. "Mr. President, The Movement has never murdered anyone! The man met his end because he ran afoul of someone he should have left alone. He was an egomaniac who murdered many over the years, as did his father and grandfather before him. He was a monster who commanded unspeakable acts of torture to extract information...and for the pleasure of his chief minion." She nodded, her lips pressed together in satisfaction. "I am thankful they are both no longer among the living."

"At great risk to his own life, one of our members has spent decades working his way into the inner circles of Progressive influence. The Movement's indirect link to the death of the monster was forged because our man acted to help avenge the deaths of six good men lost to protect his evil secrets. Before you judge us or our motives, it would be best to know the facts!"

Michael felt like a little boy who had just been reprimanded by his mother. "I'm terribly sorry. I apologize. I did not mean to offend you."

The woman smiled, the hard edges of her face softening. "You are a true leader, Mr. President. We understand your heart. That's why you were chosen for this monumental task." She dismissed his contrition with a wave of her hand. "No apology is necessary."

"We never harm anyone unless it cannot be avoided. We do not even wish to harm any Progressive. However, we will not serve them any longer. Their heyday is coming to a close."

"I still don't understand how you can help implement their agenda and expect to come out on top," Michael said.

"I'm not at liberty to say at this point, however, when TR2.0 is executed you will understand why I've been evasive. I can say that coming events will trigger national implementation of martial law."

"Are you preparing for bloodshed in the streets, then?" Eric asked.

"I cannot promise that there will be no bloodshed, but it will necessarily be kept to a minimum." She shrugged. "It's unrealistic to expect all Progressives to give up quietly. After all, they've been working their evil for a hundred years, and now that they believe they're going to finally control this country they will be insufferable in their arrogance."

"There are just a few things I can think of that would warrant the implementation of martial law across the entire country," Michael's voice was low and grave. "I wouldn't want to be kept in the dark if we're about to face any one of them."

"The moment the wheels are in motion you'll be told everything. Once the final pieces of the puzzle are in place and revealed, I'm certain of one thing, Mr. President."

"Yes?"

"You'll be glad to have played such an important role in the remaking of this great nation."

The woman smiled at him. It was a warm smile. Michael relied on his instincts as a good judge of character. He saw that she was sincere, and he knew he could trust her.

For now, the clock was ticking. There was no turning back. His one wish was that he knew what was about to happen. Michael Stonebreaker did not like uncertainty. Fortunately, he didn't have to wait long for answers.

CHAPTER 52

From the sleek lines of her aerodynamic hull, to the billowing furls of her crisp white sails, every aspect of the ship was beautiful. A foamy white wake trailed behind her as she glided across the Gulf and out onto the Caribbean. She sailed along at a leisurely ten knots toward her first stop.

Rick leaned on the rail, his eyes focused on the wake, but his thoughts a million miles away. It would be a couple of months before he was mended in body. The healing of his mind was another matter. The terror of the torture chamber and Ollie Larson's demented abuse were fixtures in his recurring nightmares. Sleeping or awake, he suffered the horrors of post traumatic stress disorder.

The man who loved the Gulf saw to it that Rick received the best medical care money could buy when he'd returned from Nebraska. A psychiatrist advised a long rest, and there was no better place to get it than aboard the Gulf Maiden.

His fellow travelers learned to make their presence known when approaching him. Their first day aboard, a steward made the mistake of slipping up quietly from behind to serve drinks. Rick whipped around so quickly that the poor man had no chance to get out of the way. The blow broke his nose. Thankfully there was always a doctor on board when the ship was at sea, and the astonished young man was treated in the ship's medical room.

Rick felt so badly about what happened, he cried. The steward, a Brazilian named Coco, forgave him for what happened, but Rick was having a hard time forgiving himself for hurting the guy.

"Hey, Rick. How are you?" Duke Dupree called out as he approached. When he reached where Rick stood, he gently put an arm around his friend's shoulders. "It doesn't get any better than this, does it? The sky, the sea, and thee…a little Shakespeare parody there."

Rick laughed, but it was a shaky sound. He was not like the old Rick.

"I won't disagree with you. It's good to be here. Fact is, it's good to be anywhere. I thought I was a dead man." He covered his eyes with his hand. "That Ollie was one sick S. O. B."

Duke squeezed his shoulders. "It's all right, amigo. He's in hell where he belongs. Get him out of your mind. I came to see if you want some lunch. The guys are getting into a little poker game after we eat. Are you up to it?"

"I don't know, Duke. It's hard to get my head straight. I keep having these flashbacks. This is bad. I need to get my mind together."

"Look, the doctor prescribed R&R, and part of that is just doing normal things. Come have some lunch, play a little poker, and take a snooze on the aft deck. When you're up to it we'll go to the gym and start some rehab. There's no hurry. This trip is for a couple months. It will take as long as it takes. Priority Number One is to get our Rick back to his old self again."

Rick looked out over the water and into the distance.

"Besides," Duke continued, "when we hit port we plan to party hard. You're the best looking guy on this boat, so you've got to lead the way to the ladies. We'll follow you."

Rick's smile was like the sun coming out. "I know you and the brothers have no trouble with the ladies." The smile retreated. "But if you don't mind I'll just stay here for a while. I've got to get that bastard out of my head. Just standing here upright and breathing is enough for right now. I'll get some lunch in a little bit."

Duke nodded and patted Rick on the back. "Okay, buddy." He turned around and headed back toward the lounge. He took a seat at the bar where the others waited.

"How is he?" the man who loved the Gulf asked.

"This is going to take some time. He's shaky. That giant freaked his mind. I can't say any one of us would be any different if we'd gone through what he did. It must have been like something out of a horror movie. Damn, I wish he never had to face that crap!"

"Maybe he'll listen to me?" José said hopefully.

"You can speak to him later on if you want. But I'd just give him some time and space for now," Damien said. "He knows we care about him, and he's one tough man. He'll sort it out, and we're here to see that he does. When we get to St. Thomas we'll see if he wants to go ashore. If not, maybe he'll join us at the next stop."

Derek added his thoughts. "Rick's a deep thinker, and a Marine. They don't come any tougher than him, but we all know it takes time to heal deep wounds. The change of scenery will help, too. There's enough beauty in this part of the world to heal a broken mind. Let the trip do what it is supposed to do. He'll come around."

The man who loved the Gulf nodded. "Derek's right. Rick needs time. We'll see that he gets it." He smiled. "At least his face is intact, and there's not a woman between here and Chile who doesn't love that face."

They all laughed heartily.

"So, you were advised to get out of the country for a while, sir? Is there a reason you'd like to share with us?" Derek asked.

"My cousin said something very big was going down in the states and suggested we take a long cruise, at least through Thanksgiving. I thought we'd make it a grand tour. We'll do as many islands as we can, and then sail to Rio." He drained the contents of his glass. "Rick is too important to rush through this trip. This is home for the next couple of months. If I have to go anywhere I'll take a chopper."

The man who loved the Gulf recited his favorite rules. "Rule Number One: Have fun. Rule Number Two: Don't break Rule Number

One. Pass the rum over here. Let's have lunch and play some cards."

Duke looked through the lounge window to where Rick stood by the rail. It would take time, but his number one soldier was going to mend. He was sure of it.

CHAPTER 53

The first time Norman put on the mouse suit he felt as though he was committing some sort of blasphemy. He stared at his image in a large mirror. The iconic American creature stared back at him. He practiced walking and making the movements he learned. He spent several hours getting into the character, and the employee training film provided plenty of help.

The late Walt Disney had been a genius, and his successors at Disney World brilliantly insisted on continuing his commitment to excellence. Mediocrity would never find a home in the Magic Kingdom, or any of the other parks. Each cast member was expected to *practice, practice, practice* until every performance was executed flawlessly. Norman had little ham in his personality, but he realized that if he failed he would be replaced.

Norman was certain the sleeper system was also redundant. Even if there were a backup for his position, he did not want to lose the chance to play his part in the attack. Failure was not an option. The park's security systems were excellent, but the sleeper cell's plan exploited the one thing against which Americans in general had little defense. They were wont to defend themselves against people who looked like them. Even worse for them, they would not even suspect danger from the beloved characters of their childhood fantasies. He and the other sleepers fit right in. Norman smiled at the thought.

He was ready to make his first public appearance at the Magic Kingdom as the beloved mouse. The September sun was hot. The suit was uncomfortable. Throughout the morning he posed with families and children. He danced, clapped his hands, and pretended to have a jolly time. If the innocent families had known what hatred Norman harbored for them within the suit, they would have run screaming.

He strictly adhered to the schedule he'd been given, periodically taking breaks and disappearing to assigned areas out of the sight of park guests to cool off before returning to work. Each day dragged by. He faced three weeks of this before the day of the event. Until then he was to practice getting around inside each of the four parks during the day. He would need to master the use of every passage, hidden and otherwise, for getting from one place to another.

When he took off the suit at night there was a different set of tasks to be mastered. He was amazed at how much information had been gathered about the task he'd been assigned. At 2:00 a.m. each night Norman was taken to the central communications center by another sleeper. He spent an hour studying the complex via the state-of-the-art surveillance system.

At 3:00 a.m. his guide escorted him through a hidden gate to a waiting car. He was driven back to the resort, where he studied diagrams and plans in his room until four. He was to report for Mickey duty at noon. Such would be his schedule for the next three weeks.

As the days slipped by, Norman found himself thinking about the people he was going to slaughter. In the abstract, he'd had no problem thinking about shooting or blowing to pieces nameless faceless individuals when the attack came. However, a sea of children's faces now surrounded him each day. Brown, black, blond , and red-haired children, some with blue eyes, some with brown, chubby ones, thin ones, tall and short children of every race, color and creed flocked around him, eager to spend a moment with the friendly giant mouse.

He was stunned when on his first day in costume, a Muslim family happily approached him and asked him to be in their photographs. He felt like shaking them and screaming, *"You don't know what's going to happen here! Run! Get away!"* Instead he got control of himself and posed for the picture. It had not occurred to him that Muslims lived happily in America, or that they also enjoyed visits to Disney World.

Now the nameless infidels wore faces. He could see their happiness, and he envied them. He had never been happy in his life. He envied the children having fun with their parents. He envied the love he saw between them. It was eating him alive. He was going to kill them.

Alone in his room, he couldn't get the faces of the children out of his mind. Some were rude and pushy, but many were so wide-eyed and innocent that he experienced something he never felt for anyone in his life. He felt compassion and empathy for them. His thoughts raced. *I mustn't allow myself to become weak!* He fell to his knees, beating his right hand on the floor of his room until the pain forced him to stop. He must not pity them. He recited the old mantras. *They were infidels! They must die!*

The sooner this task was over, the better things would be. He had taken five weeks vacation from his job in New Jersey, and intended to return to when his assignment here was over. He could not wait to go back to his old life. He would never come to this place again. It would be left a raging inferno and abattoir.

One evening after long hours of study, he fell asleep. During the night, he dreamed he stood in the midst of the attack, surrounded by explosions and flames. Gunfire erupted all around him. People were being blown to bits before his eyes. Bullets ripped into bodies, and people were being tossed around like disjointed puppets under a hail of machine-gun bursts.

A small hand grabbed his leg. He looked down. A little blonde haired girl reached up to him. She was screaming. He picked her up. He ran. He was running with all his might. His lungs felt like they would explode. She was crying for her mother. He ran. "I'll save you!" he yelled. He ran.

Suddenly, he was awake. Lying in his darkened room, he raised his hands to his face. He felt moisture there. He sat up and turned on the bedside lamp on the nightstand. He stood up and padded over to the sink in a little alcove across the room. He flipped on the light above the mirror and looked at his reflection. There were tears on his cheeks.

Norman choked back a cry and smashed his fist into the wall next to the light switch. The pain was excruciating, but he preferred it to the sorrowful aching that squeezed his chest like a vice. He must not feel. He must not care. He must not see them in their weakness. He must feel nothing. He was a warrior of Allah. He must do his deed. He must do what he had been trained to do.

Norman returned to his bed. The face of the little girl loomed in his mind. He had never felt so alone. There would be no more sleep this night.

CHAPTER   54

The president's appearance at the senator's office set the place in an uproar. Such a thing was unheard of, and the aides whispered among themselves, trying to figure out if it ever happened before. The senator's stock-in-trade shot up many points. The president made his way down the hallway in a frenzy of glad-handing as the news spread of his arrival. Everyone on the floor emerged from offices along the corridor, first to see if the rumor was true, and then to snap a photo and have a hand shaken or back slapped by POTUS. Had there been babies present, they would have been kissed. Secret Service agents kept the party moving, along with an entourage of aides dutifully in tow.

After a closed-door meeting the two men exited the building and went for a stroll. Everyone had been ordered to follow at a distance and out of earshot, which set the Secret Service agents completely on edge. So many snipers arrayed on roof tops were called on alert that a war would have broken out if anyone even thought to harm the man. Fortunately, no one did.

"I'm here, Senator. This won't happen again. What is it that you have?"

"Recorded telephone conversations."

"What conversations? I don't have time—"

"You'll make time for this, Mr. President. They are between you and your attack dog, Robert Hoopes." The senator tented his fingers, adopting his most thoughtful pose. "Mr. Hoopes, by the way, seems to have disappeared. I can't imagine where he is, but I'm hopeful he'll turn up."

"How do you know...?" The president's voice trailed off with the question.

"Mr. President, with all respect to you, sir, you've got to remember that this old war horse has been long in this place. Keeping a secret here is as impossible as standing under Niagara Falls with an umbrella. A mighty river of secrets, innuendo, hints, half-truths, and gossip flow through this place, and the river's name is not Potomac."

"Are you threatening me, Senator?"

"Good heavens! I would never do such a thing. We're on the same team, Mr. President."

"I wonder about that, Senator."

"Let me put it this way. The dossier I have collected contains enough information to bring down the present administration. That's simple truth. We are both men who understand power, leverage, and gravitas. We know when to bargain—and when to destroy. As a younger man I sought wisdom from those who'd broken trail before me, and it prevented me from making gross errors in judgment. May I give you the benefit of my experience?" He went on without waiting for an answer. "It's a wise man who recognizes when he's in a corner. I'd like to consider you such a man."

The president looked for a long moment at the Washington Monument. He spoke quietly from the corner of his mouth. "What do you want?"

"Everything."

"What does that mean?"

"Exactly what I just said: everything. When I ask for something from here on I expect to be given it. If I want something for my district I promise it will be within reason. I'm a wealthy man. I will become wealthier as time passes, but I will not be greedy."

"In return?"

"I will back you all the way. What you ask will be given to you, what you seek you will find," the senator said.

"That sounds biblical."

"My late uncle would have called it blasphemous. He was a clergyman."

"You're not a believer?"

"I believe in money, power and excess whenever possible, Mr. President. What do you believe in?"

"At the moment I believe I have to get back to the White House. There are people waiting. Do we have an agreement then?"

"Yes, sir, we do. I will vote for the amnesty you're seeking. I expect that little public works item in return. It's how well we grease the wheels that helps keep this train running."

"Good day, Senator. This will be the last time we meet like this."

"Is that a threat, Mr. President?"

"You're an impertinent man, Senator. But I'm sure you know that."

"I've been called far worse by your Mr. Hoopes, sir."

"Do you know where he is?"

"No, sir. However, if I were a religious man I would speculate as to where he just might be."

"Are you saying...?"

"The Christian faith suggests two possible destinations. I've only met Mr. Hoopes on two occasions, you know him far better than I. In which of those destinations do you think he would end up?"

A chill ran up the President's spine. "You can't mean—"

"All I mean, Mr. President, is that Mr. Hoopes could be anywhere. He might be on some island with a drink in his hand. He could be in New York at a Broadway show. Anywhere is a very big place. Wherever he is, I wish for him what I wish for all who play this game—"

"Meaning what?"

"Mr. President, we did not get where we are by being stupid. Stupid might describe some of the people who elected us, however,

I believe I have a better opinion of those folks than many so called public servants in this city. Our constituents are people who are merely trying to live their lives." He plucked an imaginary speck from his lapel. "What we do here is try to live their lives for them. Wouldn't you agree, sir?"

The look on the President's face was ambivalent. "Senator, wherever Mr. Hoopes is, I can only hope he's well and safe. Our time together is over. We're mutually assured of our positions. That's what we can expect from each other—nothing more. Good day to you."

The president turned and walked back to his entourage. They surrounded him, and led him to his waiting limo.

The senator found a nearby bench and sat down. He felt his age. Verbal jousting with the president had been enervating, but the adrenaline high had worn off. He was bone-tired. He studied the tourists strolling on the Mall. He envied the simplicity of their lives. They came to Washington to admire the monuments to America's past greatness. He was here to shape their future, even if it was against their will. He knew that if the people even suspected what was in the hearts of their masters, they would rise up and throw them down.

He had made a new and extremely powerful enemy in the president, but he wasn't afraid of what the man could do to him. He ordered copies of the recordings made. If he met an untimely death, there were instructions in safe hands that would bring the man in the White House down.

The weather was warm, even for September. He wiped his brow. It was time to go back to his office.

The senator was satisfied. He had drawn a line in the sand, and he did not think his new enemy would cross it.

He needed to make a call. His friends back home were going to be happy. It would put a lot of money in their pockets. It would buy him many votes. He was happy. He recalled the words that had alienated a former president. *Mission accomplished.*

CHAPTER 55

Commander Jonathan O. Chalice served as Squadron Commander of SEAL Team Six, under the auspices of the United States Naval Special Warfare Development Group (DEVGRU). Nicknamed, "Jock," he and ninety of the elite of the elite would be inserted into Disney World as part of special-mission unit *Operation Mousetrap*. Arguably the most deadly special warfare counter-terrorism group in the world, Commander Jock and his men had the pleasure of bringing about the much desired end of one of the world's most sought after terrorist leaders. The "head bearded wonder" as Jock had come to refer to him, was believed to have been hiding in a cave somewhere on the Afghan-Pakistan border. Intelligence gathered revealed he was actually living in a compound in a suburb in Pakistan, and the SEAL team went to work.

Chief Petty Officer Bill Jenks opened his intelligence report and began briefing Commander Jock and the lieutenant commanders of his three SEAL task units. "The mills of God grind slowly, gentlemen, but thanks to the SEALs a notoriously troublesome enemy met a much-deserved bad end." The room erupted in cheers and applause. "Having rid the planet of Osama bin Laden's presence, we raided his compound and gained full access to his activities during the years he evaded capture. In particular, we've uncovered plans to launch a second major terrorist attack against the United States." At this the room returned to deadly silence.

"With the announcement of his death, of course, much of his plan was scrapped or re-engineered." CPO Jenks continued, "However, key elements of his organization's deep infrastructure remained unchanged long enough for intelligence to get a bead on significant targets. We've infiltrated far enough to identify that threat, and we've ascertained that it is now imminent."

"Before OBL's death, he was deep in fleshing out the details of enacting a four-fold strategy to once again attack on our soil." CPO Jenks directed the team's attention to a slide on a flat screen at the front of the room. "His objectives were relatively straight-forward; He would (1) Exceed the kill level of 9/11 by thousands (2) Kill as many civilians as possible to instill the greatest levels of fear and despair (3) Show the rest of the world that resisting jihad is futile by once again bringing death and destruction to the hardest target anywhere on earth, i.e. the United States, and (4) Inflict the most psychological damage by destroying another icon of American happiness and prosperity.

"Initially the running argument had been whether to detonate four massive bombs in various locations across the country in their next attack, or to use a series of smaller bombs timed to kill as many people as possible. In the end smaller bombs were chosen because the logistics of transporting and concealing the bigger bombs proved to be too difficult to manage."

"From that point discussions progressed to choosing the most viable targets, and it was decided that theme parks presented the best opportunity to inflict the most casualties. Because of their iconic status, the Disney parks were chosen as the most psychologically damaging target. Not only would parade routes packed at dusk make it possible to slaughter many thousands at once, following the explosions gunmen would emerge to kill and maim hundreds more in the confusion and hysteria. As a sick bonus, Disney parks provide them with an opportunity to kill untold numbers of children in the attack, thus also fulfilling the goal of instilling fear and despair."

The temperature in the room rose perceptibly. A mixture of anger and resolve settled on the men's faces. Commander Jock addressed the men from his seat at the head of the table. "Your reaction is exactly why you're part of this team, and why I'm proud to serve as your commander. It's clear that dive-bombing airplanes into skyscrapers and the Pentagon was one thing; intentionally targeting children for slaughter takes this fight to an entirely new level."

CPO Jenks nodded. "These fanatics are carrying on a tactic espoused by their now dead leader. OBL argued vehemently that killing children was the only way to get America to back off from confronting jihad around the world. He believed the people of America would be so stunned by such an attack that they would embrace isolationist policies and completely pull out of the Middle East, allowing the jihadists to wreak havoc with impunity.

"There were those, even in his lunatic circle, who saw this as madness." A new slide appeared on the screen. It showed two middle eastern men walking toward a black SUV. "Taliban leader Yousef Al Ahmad questioned the approach, cautioning that Americans would be insane with rage and demand revenge at all costs if children were slaughtered. He predicted that America would be driven to exact a punishment on radical Islam the likes of which the world had never seen. Ahmad's warning and fears weren't ignored." Jenks pointed toward the slide. "That's Ahmad on the left. The day after this photo was taken the SUV was found abandoned outside Kabul. Two heads in the trunk. His and the bodyguard's. The bodies never turned up."

"Are we talking east or west coast on the targets, sir?" one of the officers asked.

"Florida was chosen as the target, it appears because moving assets from where they are up and down the East coast is the most expedient. They've got a telecom expert in from Newark. He's a radicalized mixed breed who was taunted and rejected because his mother was American. Father was killed when his homicide vest detonated prematurely. His mother left him with the father's family. She was killed in the 1991 failed coup attempt to oust Mikhail Gorbachev by hard-line

Communists. The organizers were opposed to his policies of Perestroika and Glasnost, which basically constituted a move toward free markets and more social and political rights for the people."

"An interesting historical note," Commander Jock added, "is that the coup failed largely because the military refused to fire on their fellow countrymen. Its organizers realized that without the support of the armed forces there was no way they could subdue the population of the entire country."

CPO Jenks returned to the slide outlining the terrorist's objectives. "Expedience also dictated that they target just the theme parks. They weren't able to figure out the logistics of moving bombs and weapons into the water parks...evidently there's nowhere to hide that kind of stuff in a bathing suit." He sighed and shook his head.

"With the strategy outlined and the Disney World theme parks set as the target, OBL started deploying sleepers, who've subsequently worked their way into key positions over the years. All of them look as American as if they'd stepped out of a Norman Rockwell painting." Jenks paused. "Permission to speak freely, sir?" he addressed Commander Jock.

"Granted. Speak your mind, major."

CPO Jenks' brown frame stood a full six-foot-four. "Rockwell painted black folks, too. *Negro in the Suburbs* is one of my favorites."

A wave of smiles made its way around the room. "The point is, we won't be able to pick these guys out of a crowd just by looking. We'll be relying tight on intelligence to ID the jihadists, but we'll need to keep our guard up. They'll be trying hard to blend into the crowds right until the last minute."

"Point well taken," Commander Jock nodded. "Don't be fooled by a pretty face."

"Exactly, sir."

"What other counter-terrorism units are we working with?" the commander asked.

"We're coordinating with Homeland Security here in the 'States, Commander. SEALs and Army Special Operations Group in Afghanistan are working that end. Marines stand at the ready off the

Florida coast, sir."

"And on site?"

"Our man is deep in as one of the sleepers, sir. His name is Adam Sanderson. He's heading up the cell and training their recruits. Dossier says he was a student in France, his parents were murdered by the Taliban in Afghanistan. He was on his way back to the Middle East, bent on avenging their deaths when he met and was recruited by a CIA operative in Jordan." Jenks flipped and scanned a page from the report. "Sanderson is a Muslim, sir, but he doesn't believe in the radicalism practiced by the jihadists. He hated what they did to his family, and he became a willing recruit to the hidden world of sleepers."

CPO Jenks fielded questions from around the table as the lieutenant commanders of each task unit dug into the intel and assessed the situation they'd be leading their men into.

"How long has Sanderson been undercover?"

"He infiltrated this particular group a dozen years ago in Saudi Arabia, sir. He's moved up in the ranks since OBL was taken out. He's been in on their high level planning and was chosen for the Disney op, presumably because he's been around, they trust him, and he's got the right look, sir."

"What are we looking at as far as their assets?"

"Sir, according to Sanderson, they've got a team of five sleepers in place in each of the four parks. Four of the teams have extensive experience constructing IED's in Iraq and Afghanistan. New bomb tech allows for creative design and camouflage. The explosives are hidden throughout the parks in fake rocks, trees, statues and other decorative features. By our guy's estimate, there are more than enough bombs to kill and maim thousands, sir."

"What about firepower?"

"On top of the explosives, assault rifles, ammunition, and grenades were broken down and transported into the parks in food deliveries. They were later gathered and reassembled over many months, so the shooters will be heavily armed, sir.

"We've also got high level intel by way of our friend in the Gulf. His cousin has been a fixture within the inner circles of the Progressive movement, and at great personal risk to his own life he learned of the plot and delivered the intel to his contact within The Movement. Their involvement has introduced a situation that presents us with a unique problem, sir."

"What are we looking at, Chief?" Commander Jock looked intently at the CPO.

"Sir, as devastating as the attack would be if the jihadists were to succeed in carrying it out," he paused, and then plowed ahead. "What if after we've stopped the operation, the media, the country, and the world is led to believe that the terror attack has actually taken place?"

"They want to pull off a simulated terrorist attack in the Magic Kingdom?" the commander asked, eyebrows raised.

CPO Jenks nodded. "Yes, sir. They've also presented a novel solution: make a movie. We'll go in and get the job done. Sir, once the targets are neutralized, it'll literally be show time."

✳✳✳✳✳✳✳

What began with Forrest Gump meeting George Wallace and John F. Kennedy had come a long way in sophistication and expertise.

Convincing the world that terrorists had attacked Disney World and thousands of people were dead and dying called for Hollywood special effects worthy of an Oscar. The Disney people knew how to stage special effects. They had the awards to prove it.

The movie was filmed in Disney World and the special effects were married into it in their California studios. A Disney executive, who was a member of The Movement oversaw the project.

The result was incredible. The movie conveyed an attack on Disney World with such reality that those who screened it at The Movement headquarters were overcome by the horror and terror it depicted. Through the magic of CGI and state-of-the-art makeup techniques, blood, horrible injuries and unspeakable chaos came to life on-screen. There were no recognizable faces; instead actors from small town theater groups were cast. They had done a remarkable job.

The budding thespians were told that they were participating in a pilot for a TV disaster movie, but that there was no guarantee that the pilot would be picked up by a network. They were paid union scale for their involvement and enjoyed free access and accommodations at the parks for the three-day filming. They happily signed non-disclosure agreements which prohibited them from talking to anyone about the movie unless it made its way to the small screen.

****

CPO Jenks finished the briefing. "If there are no more questions, the floor is yours, Commander."

"Thank you, Chief," Commander Jock said. He stood, facing his men. "For now, we'll deploy sixty men in platoons of fifteen each throughout the four theme parks. The thirty remaining SEALS will be directing the involvement of local law enforcement." He paused, looking each man in the eye before continuing.

"A terrorist mission has been green-lighted on US soil for the jihadists in question. Their assets are in place, and they've chosen a date. They are resolved to act." A small, deadly smile played about the corners of his mouth. "However, we have them in our sights, and they are totally unprepared for the heat we're bringing. Gentlemen, *Operation Mousetrap* is set to spring."

CHAPTER 56

The president was not a happy camper. The disappearance of Robert Hoopes could not be kept secret. In just three days the rumor mill that is Washington, DC was buzzing with what might have happened to the Special Assistant to the President.

No trace of him had been found. The police and others checked his apartment but they found no evidence of foul play. He was simply gone. No one had seen him, and calls to his family revealed nothing. He had no close personal friends, and his acquaintances at work had no clue as to where he might be. It was a mystery that kept talking heads on the cable networks and the local news anchors chattering away for the better part of two weeks. It would be a long time before interest began to wane, and what had been dubbed *The Hoopes Affair* was replaced by other stories.

Worried calls had come in from Progressive leaders, and he himself battled a constant barrage of doubtful questions swirling around in his own head. Could Hoopes be counted on not to spill the beans? Was he being held hostage? Would he reveal what he knew about the administration's more sensitive dealings?

The fear was real. The worst thing that could happen was that he would turn up and start running his mouth. If he was dead that was fine, except that it brought another worry if he'd been a victim of foul play. Who could have killed him, and what did they know?

Time was short. The attack must go on as planned. The imposition of martial law across the nation had to take place. He needed the military to control the population and make his stay in office permanent. Failure was not an option.

Where the hell was Robert Hoopes?

****

There were concerns of another kind at The Movement. October 2 was fast approaching, and every sector of the Pennsylvania mountain complex was literally abuzz with feverish activity as people prepared for what would be the most well coordinated event of the twenty-first century. Nothing could be left undone or unchecked. Even the most seemingly inconsequential elements of TR2.0 were scrutinized to insure that no mistakes were made.

Michael was closeted away with Eric, Henry, and the four Directors charged with throwing the switch on the plan. They spent endless hours in the Truman Building poring over details as the day of the attack approached. At the appointed time, they would open their vaults simultaneously, officially setting the final phase of TR2.0 in motion. Michael, Eric and Henry were seeing more and more of how the final pieces of the puzzle would come together.

****

During the day, Norman Blesco seemed to happily play the role of Mickey Mouse on the streets of the Magic Kingdom, but at night he was a man being torn apart by his nightmares. The day of slaughter was fast approaching. He had waited years for the time when he would become Allah's true warrior. Despite the bad dreams, he convinced himself he was prepared.

The laptop was hidden in his room at the resort. He had downloaded the DVD's and the program was ready. He would take over the Disney communication center moments after the explosions and gunfire began. He was to delay communication between the complex and the outside world for as long as possible. He would jam the lines long enough for his comrades to kill as many children and adults as they could before the authorities arrived.

The software program he'd copied onto the DVDs was pure genius. It took a year for programmers to design it, and another year of debugging and testing to make sure it would function properly when the time came.

He was to carry out his personal part in the attack right after the explosions. He would boot up the laptop and run the program. He was to kill anyone who was in the communications center when he arrived, or who entered before he completed his mission.

Once the program was running, he was to wait fifteen minutes and then leave the complex. Amidst the terror and confusion he was to take a secret route out of the park and then head for the airport. His flight was scheduled to depart at 10:15 p.m. Two hours later he would arrive at Newark, and with any kind of luck he would be back at his home in New Brunswick by 1:00 a.m.

Sanderson informed him that he was his back-up. In the event that Norman could not complete his assignment, he would step in and do what was necessary. Norman, despite his tormenting nightmares, had no intention of failing in his part of the mission.

****

The beautiful *Gulf Maiden* anchored at Virgin Gorda in the British Virgin Islands. The man who loved the Gulf was hosting a party at the upscale Bitter End Yacht Club, an exclusive five-star resort in the North Sound.

Rick was feeling better. The party was being held in a private room in his honor. The man who loved the Gulf raised his glass in a toast. "To Rick, my son, and to the future of our family. I am honored by his love and dedication to me, and I ask all of you to welcome him on this night. When you speak to him, you speak to me. When you take his hand in friendship, you take mine. When you have his back, you have mine. Now and forever!"

Everyone stood and raised their glasses. They whistled and cheered, genuinely shouting encouragement and welcome. There were tears on Rick's face as he looked around the table. He smiled and made a toast of his own. "To my father and my brothers, I pledge my life, my service, my honor, and my duty. I am blessed beyond words. I thank you with all my heart!"

There was a long way to go before he was whole again, but the changes in Rick were evident. He would once again be a man among men. His adoption by the man secured his life and future. His happiness resonated palpably in the room.

The man who loved the Gulf smiled at him. Nature had not given him sons, but adoption had, and what sons they were! His legacy was secure. They would see to it long after he was gone.

The thought of his cousin ran through his mind. He wondered how he was doing and hoped he was well. The man was as bright as anyone he'd ever known. They were family. Suddenly he found himself hoping fervently that his cousin would survive whatever was coming. He had taken his cousin's advice and planned to be at sea on October 2. He would not dock at any port on that day. They would be safer far from land when the world shifted.

He'd spent considerable time reading through the materials his men collected from The Farm. Pierce Armstrong had, indeed, been among the most evil men he had ever encountered. He was glad Armstrong was dead. He wished he could round up the rest of the Progressives and solve the problem once and for all. But even he did not have the resources to do such a thing.

Perhaps the people his cousin served would be able to do the job. He hoped so. If not, whatever was about to happen in America would be costly. It might mean he could not return to the Gulf and his home. That made him sad. But, he owned other homes in other countries. Life would go on…and he had his sons. Their education was just beginning.

He surveyed the faces around the table fondly. These men would die for him. He would do the same for them. He knew it in his soul.

His thoughts turned to the young wife he'd left behind. She did not like the ship. The rolling of the water upset her stomach. In truth, she had grown weary of him, and he knew that she needed younger men to make her laugh. He would grant her that privilege when he returned. If he could not return, he would see that she was well taken care of through his people. He harbored no animosity toward her in his heart. He was a realist. Times, seasons, and affections change. He smiled. In a past century the mandates of the church would have dictated that they remain together. He took a sip of his drink. But these were modern times and he was not a religious man.

He stood up from the table and put his arm around Rick. He said, "There's a woman I want you to meet after the party. She's spectacular." He patted Rick's shoulder. "You need a little companionship. Enjoy this night. You are my son, Rick. Always."

He stepped away and walked through open doors to the veranda beyond. The soft sound of the surf was soothing and the air was warm on his face.

Rick watched the man who loved the Gulf go. *My father!* He let the happiness of the thought fill his heart and his mind.

CHAPTER 57

Michael Stonebreaker sat alone at the card table in the garage behind his childhood home. The pivotal day was fast approaching. The life of his family and his country was about to change forever.

He was as prepared as he ever could be after months of study. Up until yesterday he'd taken in more reading, instruction, films, videos, lectures, and interactive learning modules than he ever imagined he would in a lifetime. He needed quiet time, and this was the one place he wanted to be.

His family gathered inside the house. On his word, they would all leave for the compound in three black SUVs parked at the curb. Drivers in fatigues waited patiently behind the wheels.

The sun was shining through the window. He sat in the chair that the Old Man had claimed as his own long years ago. He sat in his grandfather's chair, but his thoughts were of his father. He admired Dad's quiet spirit and was proud of his faithful service to his country in Vietnam. He had inherited his father's physical strength and tenacity.

Before his father died too soon from the cancerous effects of Agent Orange, he called Michael to his bedside. He chose to leave the world from his own home rather than from a hospital room. Hospice care had been arranged to keep him as comfortable as possible until the end.

His nurse was having a cup of coffee with Mom down in the kitchen. The Old Man, Henry, and the rest of the family talked softly in the dining room. Michael and his father shared a moment alone.

Michael sat on the side of the bed and took his father's hand. The wasted figure lying there tore at his heart. He felt tears squeeze involuntarily from his eyes. There was no strength in his grasp. The disease had taken away so much. He wanted to weep, but he fought back the tears. He did not want to add to his dad's pain.

In a frail voice his father said, "Take care of your mother."

"Always, Dad. You know we will."

"I've been a man of few words. I'm sorry. I didn't tell you enough how much I love you…"

Something broke in Michael. It was his quiet, steady reserve that always equipped him to deal with everything that confronted him. He sobbed, "Dad—Daddy, don't you know how much I love you?"

His father tried to smile. "Michael, when you come to this time you realize that there was so much more you needed to say. I know you love me, son. But I want you to know how much I love you back." He sighed. "I wasn't much of a man for church, but I know God is real. I've made my peace with him. I believe in the next world. I may end up in the back row, but I think I'll get in."

Michael wiped away his tears and laughed softly. "I know you'll get in, Dad. Bet you'll be in the front row."

"Hey, I'm trying to have a real moment with you here…and you're laughing at me."

Dad's typical dry humor almost overwhelmed him. He felt like crying. Instead, Michael smiled at him. "You're a very funny man when you want to be."

"What I want to be now is your dad. I want to give you some advice that will help you on life's way." He paused, looking intently into Michael's face. "Every man needs others. I know you're tough-minded, and you're very good at many things. But there are times when you need a friend. I know. I've been lucky to have had a friend in the Old Man. You simply can't do it alone."

"I've got you, Dad...and the family. There's Eric—"

"Eric? You can't talk about what you do for a living, and he wont talk at all! I asked him once what black ops was all about and he said, "If I tell you, I have to kill you!" You guys must be fun at parties. Michael, you need someone you can have a real conversation with when things get screwed up. I have just the person."

"Who are you taking about, Dad?"

"He's a man after my own heart. He's every bit as bright as you. He thinks you're okay, too. He's wise in ways the world doesn't understand. He's got more wisdom in his little finger than most of the people inside that city you serve every day."

The conversation seemed to energize his father. For a moment he sounded like his old self, but the effort was great. He sank back onto his pillow, and a great weariness overshadowed his face again.

Michael gently squeezed his hand. "Dad, take it easy."

"No, let me finish what I'm saying. It's too important—important not to say—"

"What, Dad? What is it?"

"Henry. Outside of Joan, he's the best friend you'll ever have. He loves you more than you'll ever know. You were his hero when he was little. In many ways you still are."

"I know that, Dad."

"Excuse me, Major Stonebreaker, but you know damn little about your brother, the man. It's time you got to know him. It's time to stop seeing him as the kid you protected from the bully at the Y. It's time you see him for who he's become. There is no finer man on this earth than Henry." He struggled with the effort to take a deep breath. "Henry loves you. More than that, he's got the wisdom of the Old Man in him. He may work with his hands, but don't you dare think less of him because of it. West Point gave you a hell of an education, but Henry has wisdom that can never be learned from books."

Michael was stung by his father's words. He didn't know how to react.

His father placed his hand gently on his wrist. "I didn't mean to hurt you. I love you, Michael. More than you'll ever know. Trust me. Trust your brother. He can help you in ways you never thought about."

Now, years later, Michael sat in the silence of the garage, surrounded by shadows from the past. He recalled his father's words.

Henry was unique. His father had been right. Two of the best writers in Washington labored for days over the speech he was give when the world shifted on its axis, but it was Henry who smoothed out the words, carved the sentences, and included the expressions that ordinary people would understand, embrace and remember.

Henry Stonebreaker might work with his hands, but they were the hands of a patriot. Besides, while the intellectuals argued, wrote impassioned prose for posterity, then went home at the end of the day, someone still needed to make sure the toilets flushed and the lights came on when a switch was thrown. Men like Henry saw to it that the underpinnings of civilization did not fall apart.

Henry shared Will Rogers' pioneering spirit. He saw through the gnarly, convoluted crap that made up so much of political rhetoric, and he laid it bare. Henry could routinely best the brightest in debate, but he would rather be, as he put it, fixin' dozers.

Michael sighed. His brother was extraordinary. He would find a role in the administration for him far more important than merely "First Friend." He needed Henry's insights, his strengths, and his love.

He looked around the room. There were no ghosts here. His father and grandfather were in a far better place. He was certain of it. He got down on his knees and prayed for wisdom and strength to face all that lay ahead. It was time to go.

Michael stood up and walked to the door. He looked around the room. I wonder when I'll ever be able to come back here, he thought. He turned off the light and closed the door behind him. Duty called. His family waited. He breathed deeply and steadied himself.

He entered the kitchen and his mother greeted him with a smile, but behind that smile he saw her fear for what lay ahead. Impulsively, he stepped to her and wrapped his arms around her. She leaned her head on his shoulder. "Did you learn anything out there?"

"Yes, Mom…I learned that I'm the luckiest man in the world."

"I hope your luck covers all of this. I don't want to leave our home."

Michael stepped back from her and looked into her eyes. "Mom, unless we do what we must, there will be no home worth returning to. Let's go change the world."

CHAPTER 58

The morning of October 2 dawned warm, with a balmy breeze in Orlando. Inside his hotel room, Norman Blesco had been up for hours pacing. He'd awakened from the nightmare about the little golden-haired girl at just after 4:00 a.m. He sat up in bed in the dark until the sun came up. He had wanted this day to come for so long. Now that it had arrived, he felt sick to his stomach. But, he needed to be strong. He must do his duty. *I am a servant of Allah,* he reminded himself. *I must not fail.*

The bombs would be detonated simultaneously in the four theme parks at precisely 8:50 p.m. One minute after the explosions the gunmen would emerge from their secret hiding places and sweep through the crowds, killing everyone within range. Wearing explosive vests and carrying a thousand rounds of ammunition, they would fire until they ran out of ammo or were killed by the authorities. If the ammo ran out first, they'd detonate the vests. They would not be captured alive.

Norman would enter the communications center dressed in his Mickey Mouse costume at exactly 8:45 p.m. He would neutralize any opposition with a silenced pistol. When he'd fulfilled his role, he would escape in costume via one of four pre-designated escape routes.

✳✳✳✳✳✳

Unbeknownst to Norman and the other sleepers, their cell had been compromised. Undercover CIA anti-terrorism operative Adam Sanderson had secretly transmitted the details of their plan to his unit. His report was relayed to Navy Chief Petty Officer Bill Jenks and shared with SEAL Team Six Commander Jonathan "Jock" Chalice and his squadron.

At 3:00 a.m., Commander Jock and the team assembled behind closed doors in the Hall of the Presidents theater for an *Operation Mousetrap* briefing. The Disney executive who was a member of The Movement updated them on the current operational status of the parks and the simulation.

Captain William Wisor, code named Prince, was a tough-as-nails Gulf Warrior who commanded a team of equally rugged and deadly SEALs. Wisor and CIA operative Adam Sanderson, both communications experts, would override the terrorist blackout program and establish a satellite link between the Truman Building and the Disney comm center.

Wisor had spent the past three weeks wearing a Goofy costume and roaming the park. His platoon was assigned to the Magic Kingdom, where his men also patrolled designated areas disguised as cast members and park staff. Platoon leaders and the men of teams Donald, Daisy, and Minnie were similarly occupied in the other theme parks.

Morning turned to afternoon. Afternoon slipped into evening, and people began to gather along the Disney parade routes. The air was warm and held the promise of another beautiful evening in Disney World, the happiest place on earth. The SEALs were determined to see that it stayed that way.

The jihadists slipped into their hiding places at 8:30 p.m.

At 8:35pm Commander Jock gave the signal for the men of Team Goofy and the others to advance on their assigned targets.

Captain Wisor stepped in front of the entrance to the Thunder Mountain roller coaster, as one of his men slipped into the ride operator's booth. Seconds later he returned, walking closely behind a man whose hands were tightly handcuffed behind his back. Hidden from view, he held a gun snugly against the small of his prisoner's back.

"Good job, Carson."

"Thank you, sir."

Throughout the Magic Kingdom, the SEALS dealt with each of the hidden terrorists in a similar manner. Five of the jihadists resisted and were dispatched to eternity within seconds; the rest were neutralized and captured. The scenario was also being played out by platoons in the other three parks.

The gunmen wearing explosive vests posed a different problem. If they got wind of the fate of their comrades they might emerge and detonate their bombs amid the crowds. Three of the four were dropped where they hid; one inside a pirate ship, another in the center of a carousel, and a third inside a walk-in refrigerator in the kitchen of one of the larger restaurants.

The fourth man was the youngest in the group, and his inexperience gave way to nervous energy. Before he could be taken out, he burst forth from his hiding place within the Haunted Mansion and into a crowd of children and their parents.

Dressed in black from head-to-foot and sweating profusely, he appeared to be a creepy zombie who'd escaped from the haunted house.

He raised his assault rifle to spray the crowd, but Navy SEAL Nathan Johnson shot him dead before he could pull the trigger.

The crowd thought it was all an act, since Albertson was dressed as Pluto. They laughed and cheered, applauding Pluto for taking out the scary zombie. SEALs, dressed as other characters, quickly surrounded the man's body and carried it off before it became evident that something very much out of the ordinary had occurred.

The SEALs and local law enforcement proceeded to lock down the parks. Guests were advised that they would need to remain inside for a couple of hours as part of a routine Homeland Security safety drill.

The clock ticked past 8:40 p.m.

******

Norman Blesco entered the communications center at precisely 8:45 p.m. dressed as Mickey Mouse. To his surprise, he found no one there. Adrenaline rushed through his body. Had someone yelled, "Boo!" he would have shot anything that moved. His breath was ragged beneath the Mickey head. *Where was everyone?*

Norman waited for the sound of bombs detonating. At 8:50 he heard and felt an explosion massive enough to vibrate the walls of the comm center. *The attack was on schedule!* He took off the Mickey head and pulled the laptop from a case hanging in a leather satchel slung over his shoulder. He took a seat in front of the main console, plugged into a USB port, and hit the power button to boot up the computer.

Eager to get on with the job, he waited impatiently for the program to load. Cold sweat broke out on his brow. He punched a key. An icon appeared on the screen. He hit another key.

A noise startled him. Freaked out, he whipped around and fired two shots. One bullet ripped the ear off the Goofy costume, and a second struck the giant dog in the shoulder. Norman wouldn't get to fire another shot. CIA operative Adam Sanderson stepped from behind Goofy and began firing. As recognition, and then confusion registered on his face, three bullets hit Norman in a close group in his heart. He dropped like a stone. His last vision was that of a little blond girl. She was smiling at him.

Captain William Wisor tore off the Goofy head and spoke into his com. "Rodent wasted. Situation controlled. Activating link."

He turned to Sanderson. "Thanks, buddy," he said.

"My pleasure." Adam Sanderson nodded and holstered his weapon.

Wisor pushed Norman Blesco's body aside with his foot and stepped in front of the main console.

The Directors of The Movement opened their vaults. Michael, Eric, and Henry sat in the communication center inside The Truman Building. They watched in awe as the final pieces of TR2.0 fell into place.

At 8:58 p.m. the call came in from Disney. Michael knew he'd made the right decision. "Twelve minutes to show time," he said.

****

Captain Wisor was expertly trained for the task in front of him. He shed the costume to access a leather backpack containing a piece of classified equipment that resembled an ordinary laptop. He and just one other operative had been cleared and instructed in its use. He plugged one end of a cable into the unit and the other end into a port on the console. The screen lit up, and his fingers flew over the device's keyboard. Several icons and a digital clock readout appeared on screen.

At the same time, CIA Operative Sanderson clicked several keys on the laptop Norman Blesco had connected to the Disney communications hub. He paused for several seconds, then nodded "We're synched. US Naval Observatory time, 09:10:00."

Wisor clicked one of the icons, and the unit up-linked to a satellite high above the earth.

****

Deep beneath the central Pennsylvania hills, an icon appeared on a computer screen in the communications center of the Truman Building. The clock was ticking. A great deception was about to be perpetrated upon the people of the United States of America.

Michael, Eric, and Henry, along with several other people clustered beneath flat screens and watched the clock. Twelve minutes dragged by.

The digital clock flipped to 09:10:00, and a technician sitting in front of the screen said, "The link is open."

Michael said, "Let's go to the movies."

The technician clicked a mouse. The feed began. No one in the room dared to even breathe.

After a long moment, Henry Stonebreaker said, "Hickory, dickory, dock. Three mice ran up the clock. The clock struck one... and the other two escaped with minor injuries."

The room exploded with laughter. The tension evaporated. Several people applauded and clapped Henry on the back.

Smiling, Michael turned to Eric. "The Marine has landed."

Eric laughed heartily. "Maybe Henry missed his calling. He should be doing stand up."

Henry turned to Eric and said, "Are you kidding? Stand up? I feel like lying down." The laughter contrasted sharply against the horrific scenes playing out on the monitors.

Jerky cell phone images of chaos and carnage filled the screens. A voice over the video was heard saying, "*Oh, dear God...the blood... there are body parts all over. We've got to get help!*" The person started to cry.

More feeds began streaming in from the other Disney World parks. The scenes were just as horrible. A reporter on assignment in the Magic Kingdom when the attacks occurred came on screen. "This is Maria Samuelson, WORL News Orlando, live from a horrific scene at the Magic Kingdom. At approximately 8:50 tonight a bomb exploded here in the park...the loss of life is horrific..." Tears streamed down her face, as Maria and her cameraman roamed Main Street covering the death and destruction.

Across the country, the nation watched in horror as channel after channel replaced its regular programming with scenes from the attack.

Communications experts in the Truman Building assisted in disseminating the story to the Associated Press, seamlessly routing news feeds from The Truman Building under a mountain, to the Disney comm center a thousand miles away, and then out to the world.

The Movement had begun the execution of a charade of monumental proportions.

✳✳✳✳✳✳✳

After the "duds" exploded overhead, the fireworks displays went off without a hitch throughout the Disney World theme parks. Some parents were upset by the lockdown, worried that it would be too long before they could get their sleepy little ones back to their hotel rooms and into bed. Cast members assured them that the test wouldn't last past the usual closing time. Until then, strolling entertainers performed throughout the parks, delighting the crowds while they waited for the Homeland Security drill to end.

✳✳✳✳✳✳✳

Thirty minutes into the lockdown, reports of a terrorist attack on the Disney complex were broadcast through the main communications center to news outlets around the world. The disaster movie streamed from The Truman Building via every form of broadcast media, while all other communication from within the parks was blacked out.

✳✳✳✳✳✳✳

The president learned of the attack via scenes televised from the parks. He and the National Security Advisor, along with members of his cabinet convened in the White House Situation Room. Several had received calls from credible sources indicating that more attacks would soon take place.

The decision was made to declare martial law across the nation. Thirty minutes after the first broadcast reached the White House, the president took to the airwaves to address the American people.

"As you are probably well aware, a despicable and heinous act has been perpetrated against the United States at the site of one of our most cherished and iconic national treasures. Our hearts go out to everyone who has suffered as a result of this horrific incident. Let me assure you, I am doing everything in my power to prevent further attacks on American soil. It's my job to protect this country, and it's one I take very seriously. Effective immediately, I am declaring that the United States is under a state of martial law. Do not be afraid of the armed troops that will soon appear on the streets of our cities and towns. Instead, know that every resource at my disposal is being brought to bear to find out who is responsible for this gruesome act."

✷✷✷✷✷✷✷

The helicopter waited on the South Lawn. Within minutes of concluding his speech, the president and his family boarded Marine One and were whisked away to Ronald Reagan National Airport. Senior cabinet members and their families waited for them to arrive, then followed them aboard Air Force One.

Members of the legislative and judicial branches and their families followed security protocols for reaching designated airports. They boarded military transport planes for immediate evacuation to an undisclosed secure location.

Around the country, SUVs pulled into driveways and union heads, college professors, media and entertainment executives and their families were taken to nearby airports. They were told that as the country's best and brightest, they were being airlifted to a secure location for their protection until the crisis passed.

The US military was up to the task, superbly coordinating the collection effort and flying planes and their cargo westward toward a pre-determined safe haven.

Aboard Air Force One, the president was kept informed about the crisis via up-to-the-minute reports delivered to his iPad. He watched as images from Disney World scrolled across numerous flat screens. Seated at the conference table with his cabinet and advisors, he struck a pensive pose for the photo that would be leaked to the public to bolster his image as a decisive leader during the crisis.

"Did you get my good side, Pete?"

"Yes sir, Mr. President."

"You always do!" The president flashed his trademark smile. His position as leader of the most powerful country in the world was secure. *All would be well.*

CHAPTER 59

I f the existence of The Movement was the best kept secret in the world, the island had to be the second best.

Discovered by a fighter pilot who strayed from his squadron on a World War II reconnaissance mission, the unnamed island was far from any shipping lane, and did not appear on any map.

The pilot managed to find his way back safely. He made a mental note of the island's coordinates, but was running low on fuel and chose to press on toward home rather than ditch on what appeared to be an uninhabited island in the vast blue of the Pacific.

The war ended. He survived, came home, and promptly forgot about the island for more than a decade.

During The Movement's early years, no thought was given as to just what should be done with the Progressives who intended to remake America in their utopian image. Eventually, the organization's conservative founders reasoned wisely that they, or their like-minded followers would be shot on sight if the Progressives achieved their dream of taking over the country. The Movement would resort to bloodshed only absent a reasonable alternative; its members' shared faith in a benevolent higher power dictated they act with forgiveness and tolerance. The Progressives' faith in themselves alone required no such restraint.

In 1961 the pilot, who was also the eldest son of one of The Movement's founders, remembered the island and led a covert mission to explore it more fully. It was found to be almost eighty square kilometers in size. By comparison, the island of Bermuda, at fifty-three square kilometers was home to sixty-five thousand residents, with more than enough room to host the thousands of tourists who arrived by cruise ship and airplane throughout the year. Initial exploration revealed a fragile fresh water supply. On a return trip, a desalination plant was constructed to provide copious amounts of fresh water for anyone who might end up living there. Over the decades, many similar improvements were made in order to make the place habitable.

★★★★★★★

As the planes landed and the passengers disembarked, they were ushered into a massive hanger not far from the runway. The flight was long enough to require refueling in midair. People were tired and impatient; tempers flared.

Not even the president knew where they were.

★★★★★★★

A temporary news blackout was put in place two hours after the attack. The networks and cable channels kept their coverage going by replaying scenes recorded from the earlier feeds. They speculated that the government and local law enforcement were in the midst of bringing the situation under control.

At 11:00 p.m. the gates were opened at the Disney parks, and people were permitted to leave. Reporters who ringed the perimeter set up by the SEALs and law enforcement were mystified; no one in the parks knew anything of a terrorist attack. They had seen no such thing. The parks were closed for the night. No one was being allowed in to survey the damage.

From outside the parks reporters continued to ask what happened. *Were there really thousands of people slaughtered? Where were the bodies?* Ambulances had been dispatched from throughout Orlando and nearby cities during the purported incident, but no one was being brought out to be transported to the hospitals. A rumor spread that Disney had produced some sort of disaster movie, and the whole thing was a publicity stunt to promote the film.

A network anchor posed questions to a reporter on site, "What exactly is going on? Was it some sort of hoax?"

"At this point, we're not sure," the reporter said. "If that's the case, it's like Orson Welles and *The War of the Worlds* Martian invasion back in 1938."

"Indeed," the anchor replied. "That particular fiasco frightened half the country out of its wits. To describe this—if it proves to be a hoax—as in bad taste would be a vast understatement!"

The furor raged in the media.

****

Armed military personnel directed the flow of people into the hangar, where thousands of folding chairs stood in rows. An army colonel personally led the president and his family, along with his private security detail to the center of the front row. After them, Progressive members of the mainstream media, academia, the scientific community, and every arena of public influence followed. For the better part of two hours people disembarked from the planes and streamed into the hangar. When all the seats were taken, they spilled into the aisles and spread across the rear of the building. The sound of complaining and speculation about what was happening filled the air while outside, the planes refueled and took off.

A uniformed Air Force general approached a raised platform at one end of the hangar. He climbed the steps onto it, then turned to face the crowd from behind a microphone. He stood at attention, but did not speak or raise his hand. Soon, people noticed, and after a few moments, the crowd settled down.

"Mr. President, members of the cabinet, Congress and the Supreme Court, ladies and gentlemen," the general said, "you are gathered here today because of the attack on America." His voice reverberated off the mic.

The president let out a sigh of relief. Obviously, the man was referring to the attack at Disney World.

"You've been brought to this place for your protection. We have gone green here, which should make many of you happy. The vehicles are electrically powered. All the homes and buildings are equipped with solar panels, and there is a wind farm. Enough food, drinking water, staples and other supplies have been stockpiled to last for many years. You'll find land for farming, a supply of seeds, and the necessary tools for growing your own food—"

The senior senator from Illinois raised his voice from within the crowd. "General what-ever-your-name-is, what's this about growing our own food and enough supplies for years? We've got to get back to Washington, immediately! We're in charge—the people need us to lead them in the aftermath of a monstrous terrorist attack. When the hell are we going home?"

Several people shouted, "Yes, when are we going home?"

Not to be outdone by the senator, the president leapt to his feet. "General, just what is your name? I don't know you. As your commander in chief, I demand to know what's going on here!"

"With all due respect, Mr. President, who I am is not important. What does matter, is that this is going to be home for you and the people with you. You see, sir, you have arrived at the Progressive utopia of your dreams. There is no wealth to redistribute. Each one of you has the opportunity to contribute your fair share to the success of this place. No house is better than another. The furniture is all the same. You'll find the library filled with histories written from the Progressive-socialist perspective. There isn't a conservative book in the place. Even the movies at the theater herald the virtues of socialism. You'll have a wonderful time—"

Several people jumped to their feet prepared to rush the platform, when the sound of locking and loading weapons echoed loudly around the room. Everyone froze. One by one they sat down.

The president said in a loud voice, "You wouldn't dare—"

The general politely dismissed the president's outrage. "While we have everyone's attention, sir, I would be happy to offer the explanation you demanded a moment ago."

"That's more like it!" The president nodded vehemently.

"Throughout our history the United States military has embraced the task of protecting our republic from foreign invasion," the general began. "We are good at what we do. However, confronted with an assault from within, we face quite another challenge," he paused. "I'm speaking of the Progressive takeover of America."

What the hell was the man saying? The president started to rise, but froze where he sat under the general's penetrating gaze.

"A plot by a sleeper cell of jihadists prepared to kill thousands of children and adults in the Disney World parks was thwarted by US military forces. What was televised via the news networks was a movie—a very realistic one—but, nevertheless, a movie."

A collective gasp arose from the crowd.

"Some people sitting here know that the actual terror attack was a plot orchestrated by the Progressives to take over the United States by declaring martial law—which has been done. Though the attack was stopped cold before anyone could be hurt, the real danger to the United States of America is the Progressive movement. And so, we've cut the head off the snake, so to speak. The American people were led to believe that the slaughter of innocents had taken place so that you believers in a socialist utopia could be safely removed to this place—without bloodshed."

The crowd went dead silent.

"In the coming days and weeks, Americans will be told what really happened. You have been brought here to protect you from potential violence in the aftermath of that disclosure. You have also been brought here to protect the people from your continued abuse of power."

The president lost his temper. "Just who the hell do you think you are?"

"I am a general in the United States Air Force. I've served America in many places and conflicts around the world. But this isn't about me. It's about the people of the United States of America—"

The senator was on his feet. "You're not the only one who has worn the uniform, General," he bellowed. "I was a Marine. I—"

Others were on their feet shouting similar protests.

The general remained silent, patiently waiting for the crowd to quiet. When it did, he addressed the senator directly. "Thank you for your service. Unfortunately, like your Progressive peers, your honor has given way to back-room deals, political favoritism, and a host of murderous schemes. You allowed self-serving ideology to trump principles of right-thinking and true patriotism."

At that moment soldiers rolled in stacks of documents and deposited them on tables around the perimeter of the hangar.

"Details of the thwarted terrorist attack and a plan to establish the current president as the first dictator of the United States have been compiled for you all to read. I wish the document were a work of fiction. On the contrary, it is irrefutable proof that Progressives entrusted to lead the nation, instead set out to enslave it under a scheme masterminded by a tyrant named Pierce Armstrong. "

The President's face contorted in horror. His mouth fell open, then closed without making a sound.

"Ladies and gentlemen," the general continued, "the slaughter of innocents at the Disney parks was just the beginning of the Progressives' hellish plot to reduce the United States of America to the status of a cash cow to be plundered at will."

A flurry of audible gasps and nervous choking sounds erupted throughout the hangar.

"There are no televisions, no radios and no phones here, so you will have ample time to read the document fully. The truth will burn you. Thankfully, there are doctors among you, as well as engineers, scientists, and other professionals. The one problem you may have is that so many of you are lawyers. What good that will do you here, I'm not sure." He smiled. "I must be going now. It's time you settled in to your new home."

"Wait, dammit! That can't be it! You can't just walk out of here and leave us!" The senator's voice and a thousand others rose in protest.

The general held up his hand, silencing the crowd.

"Too many of you believe you are superior to other people. In your elitist worldview you think you have the right to decide who is acceptable, and who is expendable. You callously dash people's hope. Learn to value the right of every man to life, liberty, and the pursuit of happiness while you're here." He shrugged. "Repatriation may be possible for some of you. Unfortunately so many of you are utterly incorrigible; it would never be safe for you to set foot on American soil again."

He looked steadily out over the crowd. "The world has shifted. Deal with it. If you are as bright and as gifted as you purport to be, you might survive and grow. We've given you the tools. What you do with them is up you. Goodbye…and God speed."

The crowd roared its disapproval as the general stepped off the rear of the platform and exited the hangar.

Guns leveled, the soldiers filed out slowly behind him. Heavy metal doors slammed shut as the last of the troops left the building.

Bedlam erupted inside the hangar, and the president found himself surrounded by screaming masses. His eyes darted about frantically searching for an exit, but there was no escaping the crowd.

He froze as the senator's enraged face loomed in front of him.

The terrorist attack may have been thwarted, but the sickening lurch in the president's stomach convinced him; there was bloodshed to come.

CHAPTER 60

The motorcade made its way down Pennsylvania Avenue. There were no crowds gathered on the sidewalks. The long line of black SUVs turned in at the White House gate; its passengers disembarked in front of the presidential estate. No mob of reporters awaited them.

Michael, Eric, and Henry, along with their wives and children stood looking about them at the entrance.

"Funny, I haven't spent more than ten minutes in this city since my high school senior trip," Henry said. "And I've never been inside the White House." He nodded toward Michael and Eric. "I imagine the two of you have visited the seat of power on many occasions."

"Yes," Michael said, "but never like this."

"Never in my wildest dreams..." Eric shook his head.

The door opened and a military honor guard escorted them to where Harold Cosby, White House Chief of Staff, met them. Cosby was a friend of Eric and Michael's from their days at West Point. After graduation, he had gone on to build three successful companies before selling everything and retiring to his Pennsylvania farm to raise polled cattle.

"Harold, you're a sight for sore eyes!" The two men shook hands and embraced.

"It's good to see you as well, Mr. President!"

Harold warmly greeted Henry and Eric next.

Michael then introduced Howard to Joan, Susan, and Yvette. "It's a pleasure to meet you, ladies." He smiled and shook each of their hands. "I'd be honored if you would allow the staff to show you around your new home, and then to your private quarters. My wife Helen will be along in a bit, then we can all get acquainted before President Stonebreaker gets ready for his big speech."

The families smiled their thanks before heading off to get settled in.

"So this is what it took to drag you away from those hornless Herefords!" Henry teased.

"You never know," Harold laughed, "I might be able to scare up enough space around here to raise a few."

"Yeah, Michael's a meat and potatoes man," Eric joked. "He'll definitely want some beef to go with all those vegetables in the White House kitchen garden."

Harold led the way to the Oval Office.

Michael recalled the last time he had been in this place. He walked in and looked around. The room had been decorated as he requested. Framed pictures of his father and grandfather as young men dressed in their Marine and Army uniforms adorned the alcoved shelves. Pictures of Joan and the girls awaited him atop the tooled antique leather and mahogany that was the massive desk of the President of the United States.

"This ornate masterpiece was carved from the timbers of *H.M.S. Resolute,* and presented as a gift from Queen Victoria in 1879 to then president, Rutherford B. Hayes," Harold explained. "It's been a fixture in the Oval Office of many presidents since then."

"That's ironic," Michael said. He pointed toward the desk and nodded toward Henry and Eric. "This desk was a gift to Rutherford B.

Hayes, a president elected in one of the craziest and most controversial elections in the history of the United States."

"Enlighten me," Henry said.

"Hayes lost the popular vote, but in exchange for a promise not to seek re-election and to keep federal troops out of Southern politics, Congress gave him twenty contested electoral votes...and a presidential victory against Democrat Samuel J. Tilden."

"Unfortunately withdrawing the troops and conservative political influence literally crushed civil rights for Blacks in the South until the 1960s," Eric added. "Jim Crow, violence, disenfranchisement—all those horrors and more thrived under the leadership of the Democratic South."

Harold nodded. "He tried to unite the nation in the aftermath of the Civil War and Reconstruction. Some of those efforts proved successful, others, not so much."

Michael took a deep breath, held it, then let it out slowly. "We've got the benefit of historical hindsight to help us rebuild this country as a land of opportunity for all Americans, regardless of race, religion, economic status, or any of the other things the Progressives use to pit us against each other."

"Amen, brother," Eric agreed.

"I can't think of a better reason to forge ahead with The Revolution 2.0," Henry nodded, agreeing as well.

Michael nodded. "Then it's time to get to work."

✳✳✳✳✳✳✳

President Michael Stonebreaker would deliver his inaugural speech from the Oval Office at nine o'clock. Until then, Henry, Eric and Harold coached him and helped him with the nuances of speaking before the nation.

They were interrupted by a tap on the door. "Come in," Michael said.

The TV anchor Michael met on his first visit to The Movement conference room had come to help him with the dynamics of speaking on camera.

"Mr. President, the eyes are the window of the soul. It's a cliché, but it is true. Television is a visual medium; you can't hide the truth." She smiled. "Look directly into the lens of the middle camera and say what you believe."

"Is it true that when people are live on the air they're one step away from hysteria?"

"Thanks for asking, Henry." Michael twisted his mouth in a wry expression.

"No problem, buddy."

The TV anchor laughed. "As a matter of fact, I did a live radio interview early in my career with an impeccably professional guest. About halfway through the interview, the woman started laughing and couldn't stop. She was unnerved by the thought of all the people listening to her. She just lost it."

"This is such an important speech—the country is in such an unsettled state—"

"You'd be surprised. Subjects that are not remotely funny can suddenly become rip-snorting hysterical when you're broadcasting live." She paused, looking directly into Michael's eyes. "The best advice I can give you is this: Deliver the speech to one person, not to the whole world. Think of the most important person in your life and speak to that person with all the strength, passion, and determination you possess. Forget the audience. Talk as if you're sharing with your best friend and it will succeed."

Late in the afternoon everyone got together as Harold mentioned. His wife Helen arrived, and he introduced her before they sat down to an early dinner. Afterward Michael went alone to the Oval Office to think and pray before the speech. The hours slipped by until finally, it was time to change his clothes and sit through the uncomfortable, but necessary application of television makeup.

He sat down in the chair at 8:55 p.m., and at 9:00 the broadcast began.

✳✳✳✳✳✳

"Good evening, my fellow Americans. My name is Michael Stonebreaker, and I am the acting President of the United States. First and foremost, let me assure you that the union is safe, our republic is secure, and the executive order imposing martial law has been rescinded.

"Last night a terrorist attack on American soil at Walt Disney World in Orlando, Florida was successfully thwarted thanks to the combined efforts of a coalition of the United States armed forces anti-terrorism units, including the Navy Seals and the Office of Homeland Security. Once again, we owe a debt of gratitude to the most elite fighting forces in the world.

"More than twenty jihadists were captured or killed before they could carry out a heinous plot to kill thousands of men, women, and children, and deal a devastating psychological blow to our collective American spirit. Those terrorists who survived are being transported to holding facilities at Guantanamo Bay, where they will be tried and sentenced to the harshest penalties we can levy against enemy combatants of the United States.

"What is more shocking is that the activities of the terrorist cell were funded and orchestrated with hard-earned American taxpayer dollars by members of the Progressive movement at the highest levels of political power and influence in this country. At the core of their insidious plot was a plan to use the carnage, fear, and heartbreak of an unspeakable act of terror to place the entire country under the dictates of martial law, and to suspend the election process indefinitely.

"Rest assured, the news footage you saw of a terrorist attack at the Disney parks was not real. It was a film created and broadcast throughout the world to convince the Progressives, and the jihadists that their evil plan had succeeded. You have heard them declare that a good crisis should never be wasted. They were willing to engineer such a crisis, and to use it as a pretext for enslaving the population under martial law by executive order. The moment they showed their hand, actions were taken to peacefully remove them from their positions of power.

"Reckless government spending, irresponsible policies, and rampant corruption has our country barreling down the road to destruction. It has taken decades to sink to the level we're at now. It will take time to fix what is broken and to make the crooked places straight, but effective immediately we will begin restoring accountability and the power to govern to the people. We will restore the right to privacy and personal property, eliminate government intrusion, over-regulation, and oppressive taxation, while taking steps to restore the United States to a rightful place of honor and respect in the world. In the weeks ahead I will be speaking to you on almost a daily basis about those plans. Some are of the opinion that America's best days have ended. I'm here to tell you that our best days are just beginning.

"I have been proud to serve this country, and to defend its freedoms for all Americans, regardless of race, religion or creed like my father and my grandfather before him. When our children can once again compete in all the academic disciplines at the highest levels, and our people are again free to use their creative genius and entrepreneurial spirit to create new opportunities for the betterment of mankind, we will be free, indeed.

"Our claims to freedom have not come easily. They have been purchased with the blood and sacrifice of those who've gone before us. It is for both them and ourselves that we must prevail against the Progressive ideologies that would enslave us to the whims of the self-proclaimed elite. They have been removed. The second American Revolution has been achieved. The executive, legislative, and judicial branches of the government of the United States are fully functional and are now occupied by persons committed to serving the needs of the people.

"My face and my name are new to you, but we will learn much about each other in the coming days. Together, we are going to re-build America into a place where freedom and personal responsibility walk hand-in-hand.

"Finally, I wish for you and your family the same things I wish for my own: peace, prosperity, faith and love.

"Sleep well tonight. A new day of great promise built on our God-given inalienable rights to life, liberty, and the pursuit of happiness is dawning in America. Once again, we've been given the gift of a republic. Let's do our best to keep it. Good night, and God bless you."

Michael continued to stare across the room and into Joan's eyes as the lights and cameras were turned off. He had delivered the speech to the person he loved the most.

EPILOGUE

The ship anchored in Rio. The man who loved the Gulf sat at the head of a table set for a sumptuous Thanksgiving holiday meal. Duke and Derek sat to his right; Damien and Rick were on his left. His cousin sat opposite him.

Their adopted father's cousin made quite an impression on the young men. The family resemblance was striking. The man who loved the Gulf and his cousin looked more like twins than cousins.

The man raised his glass. "To my cousin—it has been far too long since we broke bread together. Here's to health, wealth, and long life."

The men raised their glasses and their voices in agreement around the table.

The cousin raised his glass. "To you and your sons; I wish you all the best, and God's blessing."

"Thank you. God and I have not been on speaking terms for some time, and I'm not sure how my sons feel about the Lord," the man spoke his next words softly, "but I accept this from you because I know your heart. You were the good seed in the family. I was the black sheep."

"You forget. The Lord knows His sheep, and He uses them as He wills," his cousin said.

"So, how does it go in America? How is the new president doing?"

"There was a media firestorm in the beginning. The talking heads nearly exploded. It will be months before things settle down. No one knows where the Progressives are, or what happened to them." The cousin sighed and took another sip from his glass. "Not all of them are gone, unfortunately. The big players are gone, but the whole situation is driving liberals left in the media insane."

"Ah, but liberals are not necessarily Progressives, are they?" the man who loved the Gulf asked.

"True, and that's good. Many liberals are bright and well-meaning, and you probably wouldn't want to invite every conservative home to dinner. As to the president, Michael Stonebreaker is a West Point man, a genuine war hero. He's combat tough, beyond smart, and deadly serious about his mission."

Thus far the sons had listened attentively, out of respect for their father's cousin, but that didn't stop Duke from asking, "Yes, but is he the kind of guy you can enjoy a beer with, or is he some hotshot who thinks he's better than everyone else?"

The cousin looked long in Duke's eyes until the younger man looked down.

"You're from Australia, aren't you?"

"Yes."

"Military trained?"

"Yes, my brothers and I are all former military."

"Have you ever fought alongside someone you'd die for, Duke?"

"Yes, sir. I have."

"I suspect if you served with Michael Stonebreaker you'd die for him."

"Why is that sir?"

"In battle, he valued the lives of his men above his own. There isn't a soul among them who would not lay down his life for the man.

He's earned their trust, and their respect," the cousin said.

"That's good enough for me, sir," Duke said.

The man who loved the Gulf said, "Now, I must ask something of far less importance."

His cousin smiled. "Yes?"

"Would you please pass the cranberry sauce?"

Laughter filled the room.

The beautiful *Gulf Maiden* rocked gently on the crest of a passing wave.

There was much to be thankful for.

For More on Biff Price Visit:
www.BiffPrice.com

CPSIA information can be obtained at www.ICGtesting.com
Printed in the USA
BVOW04*2349231114

376445BV00001B/1/P

9 780983 842798